**It seems they're always looking for a good time …
and finding it!**

# BOYS ON THE PROWL
## A New Collection of Erotic
## Tales
### *Volume I*

## Edited By
## JOHN PATRICK

STARbooks Press
Herndon, VA

# Worldwide Praise For STARbooks Press

"If you're an avid reader of all-male erotica and haven't yet discovered editor John Patrick's series of torrid anthologies, you're in for a treat. ...These books will provide hours of cost-effective entertainment."
– *Lance Sterling, Beau magazine*

"John Patrick is a modern master of the genre! ...This writing is what being brave is all about. It brings up the kinds of things that are usually kept so private that you think you're the only one who experiences them."
– *Gay Times, London*

"'Barely Legal' is a great potpourri...and the coverboy is gorgeous!"
– *Ian Young, Torso magazine*

"A huge collection of highly erotic, short and steamy one-handed tales. Perfect bedtime reading, though you probably won't get much sleep! Prepare to be shocked! Highly recommended!"
– *Vulcan magazine*

"Tantalizing tales of porn stars, hustlers, and other lost boys...John Patrick set the pace with 'Angel'!"'
- *The Weekly News, Miami*

"...We guarantee you that this book will last you for many, many evenings to come as you relive your youth, or fulfill your fantasies with some of the horniest, hottest and most desirable young guys in fiction."
– *Blueboy*

"'Dreamboys' is so hot I had to put extra baby oil on my fingers, just to turn the pages! ...Those blue eyes on the cover are gonna reach out and touch you..."
– *Bookazine's Hot Flashes*

"I just got 'Intimate Strangers' and by the end of the week I had read it all. Great stories! Love it!"
– *L.C., Oregon*

"'Superstars' is a fast read...if you'd like a nice round of fireworks before the Fourth, read this aloud at your next church picnic..."
– *Welcomat, Philadelphia*

"Yes, it's another of those bumper collections of steamy tales from STARbooks. The rate at which John Patrick turns out these compilations you'd be forgiven for thinking it's not exactly quality prose. Wrong. These

stories are well-crafted, but not over-written, and have a profound effect in the pants department."
— *Vulcan Magazine, London*

"For those who share Mr. Patrick's appreciation for cute young men, 'Legends' is a delightfully readable book...I am a fan of John Patrick's...His writing is clear and straight-forward and should be better known in the gay community."
— *Ian Young, Torso Magazine*

"...Touching and gallant in its concern for the sexually addicted, 'Angel' becomes a wonderfully seductive investigation of the mysterious disparity between lust and passion, obsession and desire."
— *Lambda Book Report*

"John Patrick has one of the best jobs a gay male writer could have. In his fiction, he tells tales of rampant sexuality. His non-fiction involves first person explorations of adult male videostars. Talk about choice assignments!"
- *Southern Exposure*

"The title for 'Boys of Spring' is taken from a poem by Dylan Thomas, so you can count on high-caliber imagery throughout."
— *Walter Vatter, Editor, A Different Light Review*

Book of the Month Selections in Europe and the U.K. and Featured By A Different Light, Oscar Wilde Bookshop, Lambda Rising and GR, Australia and Available at Fine Booksellers Everywhere

# Books by John Patrick

*Non-Fiction*
A Charmed Life: Vince Cobretti
Lowe Down: Tim Lowe
The Best of the Superstars 1990
The Best of the Superstars 1991
The Best of the Superstars 1992
The Best of the Superstars 1993
The Best of the Superstars 1994
The Best of the Superstars 1995
The Best of the Superstars 1996
The Best of the Superstars 1997
The Best of the Superstars 1998
The Best of the Superstars 1999
The Best of the Superstars 2000
What Went Wrong?
When Boys Are Bad
& Sex Goes Wrong
Legends: The World's Sexiest
Men, Vols. 1 & 2
Legends (Third Edition)
Tarnished Angels (Ed.)

*Fiction*
Billy & David: A Deadly Minuet
The Bigger They Are...
The Younger They Are...
The Harder They Are...
Angel: The Complete Trilogy
Angel II: Stacy's Story
Angel: The Complete Quintet
A Natural Beauty (Editor)
The Kid (with Joe Leslie)
HUGE (Editor)
Strip: He Danced Alone
The Boys of Spring
Big Boys/Little Lies (Editor)
Boy Toy
Seduced (Editor)
Insatiable/Unforgettable (Editor)
Heartthrobs
Runaways/Kid Stuff (Editor)

Dangerous Boys/Rent Boys
(Editor)
Barely Legal (Editor)
Country Boys/City Boys (Editor)
My Three Boys (Editor)
Mad About the Boys (Editor)
Lover Boys (Editor)
In the BOY ZONE (Editor)
Boys of the Night (Editor)
Secret Passions (Editor)
Beautiful Boys (Editor)
Juniors (Editor)
Come Again (Editor)
Smooth 'N' Sassy (Editor)
Intimate Strangers (Editor)
Naughty By Nature (Editor)
Dreamboys (Editor)
Raw Recruits (Editor)
Play Hard, Score Big (Editor)
Sweet Temptations (Editor)
Pleasures of the Flesh (Editor)
Juniors 2 (Editor)
Fresh 'N' Frisky (Editor)
Boys on the Prowl (Editor)

Published in the United States
STARbooks Press
PO Box 711612
Herndon VA 20171
Printed in the United States

Many thanks to graphic artist John Nail for the cover design. Mr. Nail may
be reached at: tojonail@juno.com.

Book and text design by Milton Stern. Mr. Stern can be reached at
miltonstern@miltonstern.com.

First Edition Published in the U.S. in March, 2000
Second Edition Published in the U.S. in April, 2007
Library of Congress Card Catalogue No. 98-06882
ISBN No. 1-934187-05-4

# Contents

INTRODUCTION: SURROUNDED BY SEX John Patrick........................ 1

I LOVE SEX  John Patrick ............................................................. 9

HOME FOR THE SUMMER R.J. Masters................................. 17

C'MON, KID R.J. Masters.................................................... 23

BORN HARD Thomas C. Humphrey.......................................... 29

RINGS Kevin Bantan............................................................ 37

MYSTERIOUS WAYS K.I. Bard......................................... 41

TURKEY BOY BLUES Thom Nickels..................................... 53

THE CHARMER Rick Jackson ........................................... 63

JUST THE BROTHERS  (Second of Three Parts) Ronald James .............. 71

FREE DELIVERY H.A. Bender................................................ 77

SHAKEDOWN Corbin Chezner.............................................. 85

THE TAKING OF A BOY from "Orpheus to the Men of Thrace". ........... 95

PRETTY BOY Brother Grundy.............................................. 97

IRRESISTIBLE Antler ......................................................... 99

OH, THAT PLACE  Carl Miller Daniels................................ 101

SPECIAL SECTION: COWPOKE TALES......................... 103

MUSTANG AND SADDLEBRED Lewis Frederick .............. 105

SIDESHOW Corbin Chezner................................................ 119

ANY COWBOY CAN Jack Ricardo .................................. 129

BILLY THE KID  (West Hollywood Cowboy) Peter Eros........... 137

ALWAYS ON THE PROWL  Jason Carpenter...................... 149

RAMBLING WITH CALIFORNIA SWEETWATER Joe Sexton ........... 155

PROWLING FOR A LONGHORN Lance Rush...................... 177

A COWPOKE DOWN UNDER QM3 Rick Jackson, USN........... 185

A HUSTLER'S CONFESSIONS – In a Series of Erotic Tales
by Frank Gardner ............................................................. 199

SPECIAL PREVIEW....................................................... 247

THE CONTRIBUTORS ................................................... 255

ABOUT THE EDITOR..................................................... 259

# EDITOR'S NOTE

Most of the stories appearing in this book take place prior to the years of The Plague; the editor and each of the authors represented herein advocate the practice of safe sex at all times. And, because these stories trespass the boundaries of fiction and non-fiction, to respect the privacy of those involved, we've changed all of the names and other identifying details.

Are you a good boy?
Yes.
Why are you wasting my time then?
– *British playwright Joe Orton*

"My father would pull a ten or a twenty from his pocket and say, 'Lay low for a while,' and off I'd go: no plan in mind, necessarily, just a street kid's faith: what might the day shape itself to be? And where would the night find you, that creosote-scented Tucson darkness, warm and, if you got away from the spreading lights of town, gorgeous with stars? Anyplace at all and no place; everybody knows a kid like that, in no hurry to get home, always with one eye turned to the next: next meal, next friend, next place to sleep, next place to score." – *Mark Doty in Firebird*

Always on the prowl: Long-time sex star and escort Ted Matthews, mentioned herein as one of superbottom Tony Cummings' conquests (or vice versa, depending on your view), returned to porn recently with an incredible scene in "Nude Science," paired with the always hot Derek Cameron. The video is available from STARbooks Press. You may contact the producer, Dino Phillips, at Great Dane Productions' website: greatdaneprod.com, or phone 1-818-487-0719.

# INTRODUCTION:
# SURROUNDED BY SEX
## John Patrick

"Surrounded by sex, Gavin answers every come-on with a sneer ... this guy needs to get laid bad...."
— *Adult Video News, describing a boy on the prowl*

It has amused me over the years to discover that some porn stars I've met are so highly sexed that they simply can't get enough and are always "on the prowl." Sexy video star and dancer Rod ("A Lesson Learned") Barry has what I would call a "normal" sex drive, as normal as such a man could have, of course, but he has met some fellow stars who have been insatiable. He recalled the time he was doing a dance gig in New Orleans with the consummate bottom boy Tony Cummings and several other porn stars. All the dancers were staying in the lodgings the club provided. Barry was shocked late one night when Tony returned to the suite and, even after dancing for hours and having had a couple of client calls earlier in the day, Tony was still horny. "I'm going out and find some big dick," he told Rod, who really wanted nothing more than a good night's rest at that point! Knowing Tony as well as I do, I'd presume he found what he was seeking!

Another time in New Orleans, Tony realized a long-held dream of going to bed with fellow porn star Ted Matthews. Tony said that Ted was a consummate cocksman, fucking him the night they met and then again in morning. Later that day, Ted took Tony to a sex party. They had to show ID but Ted didn't have any, so Tony went in alone. The orgy just happened to have been broadcast live on the internet and then the tapes were made available later by mail order. After all the "staged" sex we'd seen Tony have, it was a real blast to see him as the "star" of this orgy, fucking, sucking and getting fucked by "normal" looking Joes.

For insatiable ones like Tony and Ted, a career in porn, with its unlimited social and escort potential, is an ideal career move. Charles Casillo, in Alex magazine, talks about the possibilities: "A young boy, physically beautiful, comes to Los Angeles in search of fame and a future, has a lot of sex, does drugs, gets involved with the

1

porn industry, becomes a prostitute, dallies with celebrities...." Gavin Geoffrey Dillard was one of these beauties. In his memoir, In The Flesh ($23.95; Barricade Books), he paints an interesting picture of a boy endlessly on the prowl. We were only disappointed near the end of the volume when Dillard began searching for spiritual fulfillment. Indeed, reviewing the book in Lambda Book Report, Jeffrey Beam invokes Norman Mailer, who, in an admiring piece about Madonna, once said: "To be meaningless in a meaningless time is to be the Buddha of the befuddled."

"Because of media obsession," Beam suggests, "and our conversion to it, everyone wants to be a celebrity. "We live vicariously through those who are. The celebrity's career, sex, body, even faults and failures, become grandiose; more desirable than our own. I read Dillard's memoir cheered by his formidable charm and wit; his storytelling style; and his impulsive instinctive physicality. I read it with difficulty, too, for although we have never met, we have corresponded, we grew up in the same state, are almost the same age, and are poets. I wanted this book to be better, to convince me that another gay memoir was worth reading.

"...Flesh is fun to read because it's theatrical; however, it ultimately fails as Andy Warhol failed – by the incompleteness of its vision. If Dillard had presented himself as bad boy incarnate, still enamored of sex, drugs, and rock 'n' roll, I would be more at ease. But I am nagged by the unresolved question, which he implies he has answered, as to whether he has learned anything profound from the seductions, fucking, falling in and out of love, career moves, and self re-definitions. He certainly has not compromised his desire to become legend.

"...Dillard describes his failures, unrequited loves, gurus, and love affairs, with narrative and journalistic forthrightness, and with an offhanded concern for attention rather than any real, ferocious pain or joy. A Siddhartha story without the last chapters, the ending careens as if attempting to get a lot more in than the book allows."

The book was originally commissioned by Penguin, but with threats of lawsuits from moguls Barry Diller and David Geffen primarily, it was cancelled. Dillard comments, "Ultimately it took only one phone call for my book to be cancelled. It is not just rich men and their boys who are in bed together." Finally, Dillard was able to get the book published by Barricade, a renegade house with limited distribution. Still, the book sold out. Dillard changed names to protect the "innocent," but you won't have any trouble telling who's who.

"My intention never was to out anyone," Dillard says. "My intention was to write my story as honestly as possible, without political compromise."

Dillard says he never felt exploited as a boy toy: "I'm way too controlling for that. I believe I saw those gentlemen as my daddy toys. There was something in even the most tawdry of early experiences," he says, "that kept touching my heart."

He readily admit that prostitution is an addiction, "like a drug or so many other behaviors that balance darkness and danger against occasional peaks and thrills. And like a drug, while you might be able to control the flow and the supply, you cannot always control the quality or predict the effect. Nevertheless, it never stopped my romancing, though it certainly impinged upon any serious interactions. I would stalk down the street most every night and either drag home a bimbo from Studio One or hit the baths and fuck a half-dozen men there. Perhaps this was just my way of shaking off the vibes from the afternoon's visitors, reaffirming my faith in honest lust, taking back something that had been taken from me, or merely giving myself a more pleasant visage with which to fall into slumber. It was a wonder I had the sperm. It was a wonder I could still walk."

Dillard says he has learned where insatiable boys on the prowl are coming from: "We as a gay society have made this push for sexuality because we've been so repressed, but. we get carried away into this whole miasma of sex and sex need and sex drive 'til all we can do is look between a person's legs. That's not what life is about either. Sex needs to simply be integrated into physical reality. To perceive it as anything evil or wrong is a complete misrepresentation of the truth."

Dillard didn't go into nearly enough detail in *In the Flesh* to suit us so, left to our imaginations, we need to return to the original crime (s), the videos "Track Meet" and "Stryker Force."

"Paralleling the story of 'The Idol,'" Bijou Video's reviewer commented about "Track Meet," "this Steve Scott feature (theatrically released in 1976) presents a young track star's (lean, long-legged, saucer-eyed Gavin Geoffrey) tension in coming out and accepting himself.

"Surrounded by sex, Gavin answers every come-on with a sneer ... this guy needs to get laid bad... " Adult Video News raved.

"'Track Meet's' calm realism, gentle humor and ultimate optimism are all Steve Scott at his best."

"Romance, forcefulness, affection and lovemaking are explored by Gavin as he discovers himself and the world of gay sex," Bijou Video's reviewer commented. "Highlights: Duff Paxton services Michael Davis in the locker room, a fetishistic solo by Paxton (sniffing his jockstrap and wrapping it around his cock and balls), married man Don Ranger blowing Gavin, Paxton fucking in the back of a bus, and a psychosexual segment in which Gavin is forced to have sex with a hung, black hotel steward."

As if a boy on the prowl is ever forced into having sex, especially with a hung black!

"Forcing" someone may be more of an illusion rather than fact. Consider what a military chaser named Maynard says in Steve Zeeland's book Military Trade: "Most of the time I got permission for what I did, and most of the time the servicemen were pleased with the result. And most seemed genuinely happy to have known me, even if our bond was fleeting. I was driven by desire and lust. But I think many of those kids needed me, at least on some level, whether they realized it or not. And I needed them." He said he didn't know if he could ever truly explain to himself why he felt no immorality when he gave young men sexual relief and temporary companionship: "There was (usually) no guilt on my part. I hope the same was true for them. Lonely servicemen have needed guys like me since the first troops gathered into regiments and marched or sailed away from home.

"Once during Fleet Week, I was taking a leak at a crowded urinal in a rest room near Fisherman's Wharf: A handsome blond sailor in dress blues was pissing just to my left. His dick was perfect and semihard. I was staring at it. When I looked up, he was looking at me and smiling. He knew I liked what I saw and he didn't mind. He seemed pleased to show it to me. Even with a crowd pressing all around us, he lingered a little before he put it away. His buddies were waiting outside." Oh, my, more boys on the prowl! Whatever can we do; wherever do we go?

A Dirty magazine correspondent, Hank, suggests a visit to D.C.'s Crew Club, which bills itself as "a nudist's health club." Hank says the space consists of a large, dim room with some smatterings of architecture to create a narrow passageway on the far side and an L-shape of lockers forming a discreet alcove.

Once familiar with his surroundings, Hank decided to "grab up" a boy and put it all to use. He comments, "The numbers were thin and I watched a few good choices hook up and use one of the rooms that locked. Finally, I got a tall, husky blond to follow me behind the locker alcove. We started simply with a brush of the back of the hand against the stomach and nipple, all the while tugging on our cocks through our towels. We grabbed biceps and pecs and pressed our bodies together, grunting with the desire to get down to business.

"I usually sense the style of my partner and try to match it. If he's more softly sensual, I play that up. But I can turn on the aggression if that's what I feel is allowed. Chance (his name, as I would later learn) was unfortunately wallowing a bit, so I was very accepting when a skinhead in a jockstrap and boots joined us and started the fire going. The towels quickly were thrown on top of the lockers and both of our cocks were in his mouth at the same time. His nipples were firm and large.

"As soon as he had his first fill of dick, he shot his tongue racing down my throat. I grabbed the back of his head and rubbed his stubble. Chance started working on my nipples and I felt Tim's hand on my prick. I moved our faces closer to Chance's so that we could do a three-way lip-locking. As simple as this is, it always embroils me.

"Two others stepped forward to get at least supporting actor roles. One had short blond hair with a well-toned frame. The other was a black body double. They were very into each other and I watched eagerly as they sucked each other and kissed feverishly. All of this distraction was too much for my original ménage and they grabbed their goods and headed off. I wasn't about to leave these two new entrants, especially since the dark one reached over and encircled my cock with his hand.

"Two healthy erect penises were more than my knees could handle, so I dropped down and tried to position them just right so that they could both slide in and out of my face. I could feel my hair being brushed at as their stomachs pressed against my head. I stood behind the pale one and squeezed his chest and flattened him onto me. His ass was firm and round and got its fair attention from my kneading hands. As delicious as they were, these boys were more into themselves and the audience didn't seem to have any good contestants ready to step up and fill their spots. So I tied my towel back on and forced my woody down and over a bit so that it wouldn't be too obvious.

"I was halfway to the other side of the room before I chanced into Chance again. I immediately yanked him to me and suctioned our lips to one another. We headed to one of the side rooms. ...Before we could close the door, our missing third scuttled in. My eyes lit with the anticipation of what he would be like, now that he was less inhibited.

"My ass found out first as he squatted behind me and commenced licking and probing my hole. Chance took the opportunity to lay claim to my face, using it for kissing and, shoving it down to his crotch, fucking it slow and steadily. He dropped to the floor beneath us and pulled Chance's hips towards his open mouth. I could see by the look in his eyes exactly when his new seat entered his asshole. His pupils rolled to the top and he couldn't keep from letting out a gasp. I stood and drove my cock into his throat, pressing my hand against the back of his head.

"Chance came first, shooting his load onto Tim's chest; Tim then forced a couple of fingers up my bum to get me ready. I looked straight into him trying to determine if he knew what he was in for. I generally shoot a huge load. He said 'Come on,' and I did. There wasn't much of his thorax that I didn't cover. Somewhere along the way, he had sneaked in his own ejaculation. We lay on the floor for awhile, talking and catching our breath before heading to the shower to clean the semen and sweat off of our bodies."

Samuel R. Delaney, in his book, Times Square Red, Times Square Blue, talks about the boys on the prowl that he met at the various, infamous theaters in the area over the years. One of his favorites was a one-legged fellow named Arly, who was "good-looking, with a hard body, and a solid ten inches, uncut; and while a few people were put off by the missing leg, he seldom lacked for takers. He demanded endurance. But he was attractive enough – and big enough – that he could afford to be choosy. As I slid in beside him, he grinned up at me and grabbed my arm to pull me down: 'Aw, this is good, now – I got the man here who really knows how to do it!' You'd have to be a habitué to understand just how fine a greeting like that can make you feel."

He recalled another lad, the hugely hung Joey, who had incredible sexual self-confidence. Delaney remembers, "I was the one, though, who, after a month or so, missed our assigned Thursday meeting. Hustlers are just not my particular thing. ...When I ran into Joey on the street, he was all professional concern: 'I was worried about you, man. I mean, I was hoping that nothing had happened to you or anything. The money I could always get from somebody.' ...Oh, we had a couple more encounters. The last, most pleasant, messiest (on my part) and loudest (on his) was in a doorway on Forty-eighth Street, one night when I'd had a couple too many. Afterwards Joey put me on an uptown bus, then tramped off over the icy street into the December dark. It was only five bucks that night."

Then, a bit later, at (the Eighth Avenue) Cats, a black drag queen with exquisite crimson nails and a red-blond wig frowned at Delaney over her drink, then asked, "Did you know a kid out here named Joey?" Delaney said he did. The queen said that Joey had dropped dead of a heart attack, then confessed: "Oh, that boy was just the sweetest! I used to let him stay with me all the time. On my couch. He was always so nice. ...I have never known anyone who could get into sex more than he could. I mean, that boy loved to come! ...I have a few little kinks, myself, and he was always the world's most obliging lay. ...That boy was so talented."

Somewhere South of Market,
You said you used to be so beautiful
that people would pay to suck you off
and you didn't even have to come to collect
but now you would let anyone have you
you have no choice, you said,
and I agreed and tried to make you
feel like a million bucks for $4.99.
– *Justin Chin*

# I LOVE SEX
# John Patrick

"I love sex. I just love letting go and having a good time. I love every aspect of it ... looking at the guy's body, licking every inch of him, eating his ass out, sucking his toes, his armpits, and everything else!"
*– Famed porn director/actor Gino Colbert*

The youth had curly blond hair, soft blue eyes and a pale complexion. He wore tight white jeans, a form-fitting black T-shirt and sandals. As everyone sat in rapt attention, the boy danced around a bit, teasing those in the front row, until, suddenly, the host, a muscular stud about twice his age, kissed the boy passionately. Their bodies pressed tightly together, while the host lewdly felt the boy's body. They parted and, as the host began undressing, the boy danced again, showing off the now noticeably prodigious bulge in his jeans. The host was quickly nude and began working on the youth's garments, pulling and tugging them with difficulty down over his shapely hips. The boy wiggled and writhed, and when the boy was finally free of his clothing, he returned to dancing, teasing the men up front. His cock was indeed hard, and quite nice, and his body was perfectly formed. Several men in front gasped as the cock passed close to their mouths. Meanwhile, the host was busily engaged in retrieving a rope from a small bag, and then he looped the end. He feigned frustration with the boy's antics and walked over to him and tied his hands together securely, making sure that he could not free himself. Then, throwing the rope up over the beam, he raised the youth so that he was suspended from the ceiling, his toes barely touching the floor.

Now the host called out, "Who would like to suck him?"

Among the many volunteers at the club that night, the host selected one anxious man who was in his thirties and balding, but in decent shape. He walked up to the youth and fondled the boy's cock until it became hard. The man knelt down and began sucking the erect prick while the audience oohed-and-ahhed at the sight of the display.

The host whipped his own cock until it became hard, then moved behind the youth's backside. "Does anyone want to get his asshole ready for me?" he asked, looking over the audience.

One short man with a goatee nervously climbed to his feet. "Okay!" he shouted, while the others giggled delightedly, pleased that someone was willing to do it in front of everyone.

Positioning himself behind the youth, the man eased himself down so his face was between the cheeks of the boy's ass. He began flicking his tongue into the crevice wildly. The youth immediately began to squirm. "Ooooh, yeah, suck that asshole!" were the first words to come from his mouth. Then he said, "And you, you just keep suckin' my cock! That feels so good!"

The man in front was making loud sucking noises, which began to arouse the passions of those of us permitted to watch this incredible tableau. As the youth squirmed, the man behind kept lapping at the asshole hungrily. The host stepped in now and eased the man away, for it was obvious that the lad was in complete readiness. His upturned cock was soon aimed at the lily-white body of the boy. He pulled the cheeks of the youth's ass apart and eased his cockhead into the crevice. When he found the opening, he rammed the entire cock violently forward, impaling the boy, while the youth shrieked in agonized pain. It was quite a show; his moans and cries were very convincing and some in the audience came before the real thrusting even began.

Before long, we could see the host was straining himself, easing his cock in and out of the boy's body, panting loudly, biting the youth's tender flesh, while the boy writhed and squirmed, trying to free himself of the host from behind while the other man worked more feverishly on his stiff prick.

Faster and faster the man worked his hips, the buttocks muscles tightening as he rammed the stiff prick home again and again. The youth moaned every time the cock was shoved deep into him. The man's body trembled violently, then he pushed forward again, biting the boy, clinging to his hot body as he shot his load into him. When he finished, he withdrew to the hearty applause of the audience.

Short of breath, the host managed to ask, "Who'd like to fuck this hot ass now?"

My companion, Paul, who frequently joined me on these nocturnal forays on the wild side, seemed interested, but another man moved forward before he had a chance. The new customer quickly moved toward the suspended figure. His cock was bigger than the host's. The host, smiling up at the man, stroked the cock and put some K-Y on it.

"All right, studs, he's good and ready. You can fuck this ass now," the host said with glee as he took the man's cock and guided it toward the waiting asshole.

The boy arched his hips, moaning as it was being forced into him.

"Oh, yeah, ram that big dick home," the host instructed him now. "He needs it bad!"

Hesitating at first, the man finally pushed his cock in with all the violence that his body possessed. He seemed surprised that the cock slid in so easily, and he buried it all the way to the hilt

"Oh shit, did you see that?" Paul asked.

I nodded, too stunned to speak.

"Now fuck it good!" the host called to the man.

Soon the man's hips began to move sensuously, back and forth, impaling the youth. The man behind clung to the boy's hips and rammed his cock, slamming it viciously against his body. The youth ejaculated quickly in the other man's mouth, while the startled man sucked hungrily at the swollen prick.

When they had finished, the host walked over to the man. "Give me the kid's cum ... give it to me ... in my mouth." He pressed his mouth against the man's lips and received the jizz into his own mouth. The man behind the youth was working desperately now, his body perspiring profusely, and he finally came. When he finished, he removed his softening prick and the boy waited for the next one. It appeared as though he might have passed out, unaware of the line that had formed to screw him.

Paul sat quietly, stroking his meat, watching as man after man fucked the lad. Occasionally, after he had fucked the boy, a man would suck on the boy's cock for a few moments. It was nearly an hour before the last one had removed his dripping cock from the boy's ass. Finally, the host walked over to the boy and kissed him fully on the mouth, then seated himself between the youth's legs, the boy's buttocks facing him, and he moved his face forward, spreading the cheeks of his ass, forcing his tongue into the boy's asshole, sucking him out, while what remained of the crowd watched intently.

Then the man took the large tube of K-Y and spread a generous portion all over his hand. When his whole hand was lubricated, he eased it in between the cheeks of the boy's ass and closed his fingers, so that they formed a large shaft. He pushed forward. "Oh, no," Paul cried out nervously.

The youth began to cry as he felt the man's fingers working into his asshole. The host forced his hand forward, burying his fingers into the boy's butt until they were buried to the second knuckle. The boy cried out in agony as the man forced the remainder of his hand into the opening.

"Oh, shit!" Paul moaned.

The host continued his movement, and when his hand was completely buried, he smiled, and then slowly twisted his hand. "Oh god, you're hurtin' me!" the youth screamed.

The host ignored him. He saw that everyone was aroused, and he eased the hand out of the tight enclosure. Perspiration formed over the foreheads of everyone watching upfront, for it was, indeed, an unusual performance. Several of the audience members moved forward to help the limp youth down from the suspended rope.

The host helped him out of the room while the audience remained behind, anxious to view the movies that were part of the ritual at this club.

"Shit, nothin' could get a rise out of me now!" Paul said, as he tucked his cock back into his trousers. A man seated behind us said, "If you told me about it I wouldn't have believed it."

"Neither would I," Paul murmured.

The room darkened and a big projector was wheeled out, a screen pulled down from the ceiling. The film began. I recognized hugely hung Roger and big, hairy Bruno, two of my favorites. Roger was delivering geraniums to Bruno, and Bruno, I knew, having seen it before, would soon be balling Roger.

I excused myself and headed for the john. A yellow light fell across me as I pushed open the door. "Aw, gimme a fuckin' break," protested the boy. The host had sequestered him in the john.

"They're friends ... of mine ...!" the host said, trying to cajole the boy into letting two men, a Latin and a black, fuck him. The men were gazing cynically at the boy and, without a word, they began to rip open their jeans and expose their enormous cocks. I stood leaning against the door to watch this new spectacle close up. I couldn't have imagined becoming more aroused than I was already, but the sight of the boy kneeling now to suck the guys' mounting hard-ons did it. My thighs were quaking with excitement and I began coming in a nonstop stream. The black very deliberately peered over at me and, sliding his dick out of the boy's greedy throat, he stepped over to me. "Okay, you got your show, now you suck it," he hissed. I tried to escape, but he held the door shut with one hand while he forced me to my knees with the other. He began to slap my face with his hard-on. Next to me, the blond rose in stately fashion to his feet and twisted around into a low bend over the toilet; his rump arched, two round white mounds, ready. He was "presenting" – there's no other word for it – to the Latin man. The black's cock was as thick as a cop's flashlight and stuck straight up. The Latin's uncut dick was long and veiny. The black's cock, which was huge and cut, was now being forced between my lips. I tried to push him away, but he wouldn't hear of it. With a half groan, I surrendered. At first I gagged on his delicious piece of meat, but slowly I was able to take the thrusting of his dick with little effort. He put his arms around my head to force me to take him all the way. In a blaze of bliss I found myself wanting the black's balls to burst and fill me up. Before long, he stopped hugging me tight to his body, and pulled back so that he could watch as he thrust his cock in and out of my mouth. I looked over to see the host was standing next to us and he was staring at me with cold contempt. I knew then that he would much rather have the black's dick in the blonde's ass than in my mouth. I had stumbled in on a rather private gathering and might well have to pay dearly for my blunder.

Soon the black's cock was being rammed in and out of my mouth and an "Aaaaaaaahhhhhhh!" was erupting out of his mouth. He started to come and I had all I could do to pull back in time. His cum splattered across my forehead and ran down my nose and chin.

"You liked that big black dick, didn't you?" the host asked after the black had left the john.

I wiped my face with my handkerchief and nodded. No sense denying the obvious. It was too late for me to sample the Latin's cock as it was already buried in the blonde's ass.

"Take that dick...arrrgg!" the host cried, his attention returning to the young blond and the Latin.

Suddenly the door opened and into the tiny cubicle stepped Paul. He stared for a few moments at the sight of the Latin banging the blond and then looked down to see me on my knees, watching the relentless fuck.

"I was beginning to wonder if you had fallen in," Paul said.

The host turned and smiled at Paul. "Hey, you're next, babe."

"Oh, no," Paul said, shaking his head. "I was just looking for my friend here...."

"Him? Hell, he's gotta wait. He needs time to recover."

"Recover?" Paul asked, looking over at me.

"Yeah, he's had a big shock to his system," he joked.

"I'll explain later," I told him. "Go on, get ready."

Paul stood there, unsure of himself as usual. We had been at this juncture many times over the years and Paul always backed off. I knew he was embarrassed by the puny size of his dick compared to the ones we usually saw, and he really preferred just to watch and relive the events later as he masturbated.

Tonight, however, there was no crowd. Just the host and me, and the blond, who was in no position to complain, although I had heard from some bottoms that a tiny cock was the worst kind of torture for them.

Paul must have decided that if he was ever going to fuck this boy, now was the time, because he opened his pants and yanked out his erection just as the Latin was finishing.

Paul moved quickly once the Latin was out of the way. The host beat him to the ass, however, rimming the boy. Then the host turned and licked Paul's cock. As the host moved back to watch, Paul placed his cockhead against the blonde's ass-lips and pushed slightly as the boy let out a groan. Paul rotated his cock and then pushed. The head of his cock slipped in. The host gave the blond a hit of poppers and soon the lad's asscheeks were rubbing against Paul's pubic hair. Now the boy gently rolled his hips. The host slid under Paul and started licking his balls. I could see Paul's whole body curl against the blonde's as he shot his load up into him. When I saw my normally cautious friend enjoy a fuck so immensely, my own dick became rigid again. Paul saw what had happened to me and when he pulled out, he nodded at me, as if to say, "Okay, I got mine, now it's your turn."

Not waiting to ask the host's permission, I rushed over and slid my cock into the blond. I began to pump and he purred. My moans joined his as the host's tongue now found my asshole. The ass muscles that were clamped around my cock made my legs weak. The blond began to buck wildly as he spewed his jizz onto the floor, and my cock slipped from the opening.

The host bent down and started licking my dick clean. Stretching his mouth to the limit, he took my cockhead into his mouth while gently squeezing and pulling on my aching nuts. The blond turned around now and we kissed deeply, just as my second orgasm was gagging the host. Soon, my cum seeping from his mouth, he stood and the three of us embraced and kissed. At that point I realized our gracious host hadn't come a second time, at least that I knew of, so I dropped to my knees in front of him. His cock was hard and throbbing so much that I knew he must be in pain. I gently licked the shaft of his dick, feeling the veins under my tongue. His groans were muffled by the deep kisses he continued to share with the blond. As I licked his balls, I prodded his tight asshole with a spit-slicked finger. I took his dick into my mouth and sucked him while my finger slid into his tight hole. My finger poked him. Before long, he let loose with a geyser of cum into my eager mouth

. When he finished, I stood up and we kissed. I turned around to leave and noticed that the door was being held open by Paul and we had caused a crowd of five or six guys to gather, watching what had become a continuation of the stage show.

My heart was pounding and my whole body glowed. I turned to look at the blond and he had a smile of pure bliss on his face when he heard the host ask, "Okay, who's next?"

# HOME FOR THE SUMMER
## R.J. Masters

I watched him mowing the lawn next door and recalled the many times I had longed to reach out and touch him. Joey and I had gone to high school together, played varsity football together, and lived next door to each other since we were kids. I had always been incredibly attracted to him. But I had never approached him for fear of rejection. Now we were both home for the summer, back in the old neighborhood where it seemed nothing had changed. But I had changed. I was no longer a timid little boy. I knew what I wanted and was going to do whatever was necessary to get it.

I opened the back door and went outside. I perched on the corner of the picnic table, where I could get a better view. His sandy blond hair was being brushed back by the light afternoon breeze, as he pushed the sputtering old lawn mower. The tanned flesh glistened in the sunlight, as the beads of perspiration formed on his bulging biceps and washboard belly.

He was wearing a pair of faded cutoffs with strategically placed holes that left little to the imagination. My gaze focused on the trunk-like thighs and the swelling mass of cockmeat struggling to escape its prison of denim. I smiled and waved, and he waved back. Seconds later the roaring of the motor gave way to silence and he strutted toward me. "Long time no see," he greeted, extending his hand.

I accepted his gesture of friendship, while staring into those familiar green eyes. "Would you like to come in for a drink?"

"Love to," he accepted eagerly.

I followed him into the house, not taking my eyes off those firm, round asscheeks. I wanted to wrap my arms around his waist and crush my body against his, but I struggled to regain control. He had only come in for a drink.

My dick stirred and began to harden in my jogging pants and I could almost feel his body against mine. I hoped he wouldn't notice. The last thing I wanted to do was scare him away.

I went to the fridge, retrieved a beer for each of us, and tossed one to him. We stood there in the kitchen making small talk about our summer plans while he sipped, then guzzled the refreshing liquid. I

17

finally got up the nerve to invite him to my basement room to check out my stereo system and was relieved when he did not hesitate.

"This place hasn't changed," he remarked, staring at the outdated pin-ups on my wall.

"Have a seat," I offered, gesturing toward my bed.

"I'm kind of sweaty. Would you mind if I took a quick shower and cooled off?"

My heart skipped a beat. The man of my dreams was asking to use my shower, to get naked in my room.

"Sure, no problem," I replied, trying to sound casual, while my imagination began to work overtime.

He stood up, put his beer down on the desk, and unbuttoned the fly of his cut-offs. I stared in disbelief as he peeled them off, slowly revealing his impressive beer-can cock. His thick stalk was solid and the wet, sticky head was peeking seductively from its soft flesh hood. He didn't seem to notice that my eyes were devouring his magnificent slab of manhood as he reached down and tugged the loose foreskin over the deep purple head. I wanted to drop to my knees and engulf the hooded monster deep in my throat, to feel it squirm as it launched its wad from his lemon-sized orbs. It took all the self-control I could muster to keep from acting out my long-time fantasy.

"I'll need a towel."

I could barely speak as he cut into my sexy daydream. "Yeah, umm, in the drawer. You'll find a washcloth there too."

He turned and walked toward the bathroom, as I stared hungrily at his naked flesh.

I heard the water running, then the shower door closed. I rubbed my crotch, fondling my solid cock and wishing it were plowing into his hot chute. I was so horny I was tempted to yank it out right there and whack off, but I wasn't sure I would have the time.

"Nick...." he called. "I can't find the shampoo."

I couldn't believe my luck. Now I had an invitation, the opportunity to make my move. I quickly shed my jogging pants and hurried into the bathroom, my cock bouncing from side to side as I moved. I grabbed the shampoo from under the counter, then turned toward the shower stall. He shut off the water and pushed the door open, exposing his fully erect cock in all its tumescent glory. His eyes widened as I stood naked before him, so mesmerized by the beauty of his statuesque form that I could not look away. I half expected him to strike out at me, shoving me away. Instead he wrapped his right arm around my neck and pulled me close. His lips pressed to mine with a hunger, a desperate need I had not expected.

I could not believe my fantasy was actually coming true. I let my arms slither around his smooth, damp body, so that I could cup those sexy buns. My hands crept slowly down over his creamy mounds as I waited for him to pull away. But he did not.

His lips locked onto mine, his tongue darting into my mouth and dancing around my own. When he finally released me, it was as if he were looking right through me.

"I want you," he whispered. "And I'm glad you finally made your move."

He smiled at my shocked expression, then let his fingers circle my throbbing stalk while his thumb caressed the sensitive head. Erotic shock waves shot through my body. I shuddered as he began to stroke my length, squeezing and massaging, the rhythmic pumping driving me wild.

His hot breath on my neck was pushing me closer and closer to the edge. I wanted him more than I had ever wanted anything. I began to thrust forward, ramming my aching boner against his thigh. He looked into my eyes and I could see his desire was just as strong as my own. I locked my lips onto his and let my tongue snake inside his moist, warm mouth. I could hardly wait for the moment when we would join into one. My lust had taken control.

I reached down, touching his eight-incher for the first time. My fist wrapped around his stiff cock, the heat of his arousal fueling my excitement further. I let my hand slide slowly from the furry base to the deep red tip, squeezing even more of his pre-cum juice from the gaping piss-slit.

I longed to drop to my knees and devour his tasty cream, but I knew I should play it safe. I could only stand there, my mouth watering, as the need to worship his magnificent tool overwhelmed me.

As if reading my thoughts, he reached into the pocket of his discarded shorts and retrieved a shiny foil wrapper. He tore it open and handed me its contents, which I immediately applied to his throbbing cock.

I let my lips blaze a trail down his neck, pausing to suck on his large, pink nipples. I nibbled on each of them, letting my teeth sink into his tender flesh, then moved downward until I contacted the tip of his cock.

I ran my tongue along the bulging vein, feeling it pulsating all along his length. I lapped at the cloaked head, probing his piss-slit as deep as was possible with the latex barrier standing guard over the sweet honey.

"Oh suck it," he pleaded. "Take it all."

But I ignored his desperate cries and continued to tease and torment his horny cock, flicking my tongue against it, then lightly kissing the sensitive head. He moaned and humped toward me, trying to drive his cock into my mouth. I parted my lips and allowed only the head to slide inside. My tongue rolled over and around it, while my arms wrapped around his waist and my hands slipped into his hairless crack, seeking out the entrance to his insides.

His hefty balls slapped against my chin as he rammed forward rougher than before. Just as he shoved his length into my throat, my fingertips located his hot puckerhole. I pushed gently against the unyielding muscle until it gave way and admitted my index finger into the heat of his body. He seemed not to notice that I was finger-fucking his tight channel, as he rammed his prick deep into my gullet.

I felt his hand resting on the back of my head, the fingers entwining in my dark hair as he thrust to and fro, madly seeking release of the pent-up load that weighed him down. I nearly gagged as he blocked my airway with his oversized cock, but I recovered when he momentarily retreated.

His breathing was heavy and his balls were contracting close to his body. I jammed a second, then a third digit into his body anticipating the explosion that was only moments away. Each time he pulled back, readying himself for an even deeper invasion of my esophagus, my fingers plunged farther into his hole.

"Oh yeah, Nicky, I'm gonna shoot," he groaned.

His cock began to jerk and twitch in my mouth and his body tensed, as his load coursed through his length and erupted into the second skin. The condom swelled with the huge wad of cream, but did not spill a drop.

"Fuck me," he pleaded, his still-solid cock buried in my throat. "I've always wanted you."

My fingers slipped from his stretched manhole and I eagerly got to my feet. I grabbed a box of condoms and a tube of K-Y from the medicine cabinet and hustled toward the bedroom with Joey following close behind. He had already shed the rubber and wiped up before leaving the bathroom, so he was ready for me.

I turned back the covers on my bed and he lay face down on the cool sheets. I quickly applied a condom and greased up my raging hard-on, anxious to mount and ride my old buddy. He reached back and spread his fleshy asscheeks, exposing his rosy hole to my heat-seeking missile. I pushed the slippery cock against the tiny opening and it easily gave way, allowing my length to sink deep into his body.

He moaned as I retreated and plunged into him once again. I knew I was close to an intense climax, but I wanted to be deep in his belly when I finally let loose. I made several quick jabs, then my body shook as I was overcome by a wave of excitement.

"Oh man, I can feel it coming," he moaned. "You're blowing up the balloon inside me."

The first burst of cum was followed by a couple of smaller wads, then I collapsed on top of him, crushing him against the mattress. I left my cock inside him, while I gasped for air. When I had finally composed myself, I began to move slowly, until I was rock solid and ready for another round. He didn't make a sound as I began to ride him again, this time with long, deliberate strokes.

I plunged in and out of him for nearly an hour, working myself up to a second explosion. When he began to hump against me each time I thrust forward, I knew he was getting close again too. We moved in unison until both our bodies began to tremble. I felt his chamber tighten around my cock as he came onto the sheet beneath us and I shot my love cream into the used condom.

I was exhausted and let my weight again crash down on him. He looked back at me and I softly brushed my lips against his.

"That was pretty incredible," he whispered.

"Yeah, it was. Too bad we wasted all that time in high school. We could have been having fun back then, instead of feeling like no one understood us."

"Well, it's never too late. We've got all summer to make up for lost time."

There was no doubt this was going to be a summer we would both remember for a long time to come. We were both working, but only part-time, so there would be plenty of time to get together.

# C'MON, KID
# R.J. Masters

I fumbled with my key, trying desperately to get it into the lock, but was not successful. I leaned back against Harris' muscular body as the booze began to make my head spin, wishing I was already inside tucked into my bed. Finally his hand rested on mine and guided the key into the lock. It clicked and the door creaked open.

I reached for the light switch and nearly fell down as I left his embrace.

"Come on, kid, let me help you get to bed," he offered, wrapping his strong arms around my waist and half carrying me to my room.

I had never noticed before how good he smelled, the masculine, musky scent that emanated from his body. I buried my face against his chest and inhaled deeply, drawing in the arousing aroma.

Harris was my partner, my training officer. He had been on the force for sixteen years and it was his job to teach me how to be a good cop. I felt frustrated and disappointed when those two robbery suspects had gotten away from us earlier, but Harris hadn't seemed bothered. He simply said, "We can't win them all, kid." But he knew I was upset and he had taken me to Neil's, the local cop hangout, to unwind after our shift was over.

We had talked and drunk. I'm not sure how many drinks I consumed, but Harris had been a good friend and brought me home.

I wrapped my arms around his neck and held on tight as he lowered me onto my bed. He pressed his lips against mine, gently at first, then thrust his tongue inside my mouth with a desperate hunger. I gladly answered him by slipping my tongue into his hot, wet opening.

He fumbled with my belt and yanked down my zipper. I felt my pants and jockey shorts being pulled from my body. I did not resist, could not resist, as the room began to spin.

I didn't see him remove his clothing and I was shocked when I realized that he was lying naked next to me. His cock was hard and it pressed against my thigh. Then he rolled over on top of me, grinding his body against mine. His fiery flesh slithered alongside my own, burrowing into my pubic bush, then retreating, arousing my senses though I was only semi-conscious.

"You're so hot, kid! You've got such a nice body," he whispered into my ear.

His hot breath on my neck sent shivers down my spine. I was so tired I couldn't concentrate on what was happening, but I knew I felt good. As drunk as I was, my cock had hardened and was now thrusting against him. I needed the closeness, the intimacy that I was now sharing with Harris and wished it would never end.

I'm not sure when he put on the black condom, but he was wearing it as he inched his menacing cock closer to my lips.

"Kiss it, kid. Come on, make me feel good," he pleaded.

He brushed the cloaked head against my partially opened mouth and across my cheek. I pursed my lips and planted a kiss on the super-sensitive tip. He moaned and forced my lips apart, so that his cock could slide into my mouth. I swirled my tongue around the rim, then sucked the head into my throat. I was frightened when he began to slam into me, harder and faster, until his balls slapped against my chin. I gasped for air and gagged on the thick intruder, but he retreated quickly giving me a chance to catch my breath. Then he began to plunge into me more roughly than before.

I was sure he would come any second as his length slid in and out of my mouth, savagely face-fucking me, but he halted the assault as quickly as he had begun. I felt his fingers circling my aching boner, stroking the shaft, massaging along the bulging vein. Then he cupped my crinkled balls in his palm and began to lap it with his tongue, drenching them in his saliva.

"Oh, that feels so good," I moaned.

I lifted my ass off the bed, forcing my groin upward and into his face, as he sucked first one, then the other of my tender orbs into his warm, wet mouth.

"Suck it, please," I pleaded.

But he ignored my impassioned pleas, instead letting his tongue slide across my tight manhole.

Goose bumps spread down my thighs as his tongue danced across the virgin opening, teasing and tormenting my sensitive flesh. I gasped when the warm invader pressed against my unwilling muscle until it sunk into the heat of my body.

I spread my legs wider, allowing him easy access to my tight chamber. The snake-like intruder wiggled and twisted inside me, causing unfamiliar sensations and fueling a desire I had never acknowledged.

I wanted Harris. I wanted his cock inside me filling the emptiness, the desperate hunger that I had never before encountered. But I was afraid to speak.

"I want you, kid. Let me fuck you," Harris growled into my ear.

I couldn't say anything, but eagerly nodded my consent, then watched while he lubed up his monstrous cock with liquid soap he had found in my bathroom. I was mesmerized as his fist slid along the length of the black latex sheath, slowly and carefully greasing up the wrist-thick shaft.

My heart pounded in my chest as he positioned himself between my thighs, the massive head aiming at my vulnerable manhole. Then I felt it pushing, forcing its way past the inflexible ass-ring, stretching me so wide that I thought I would be torn apart.

"Oh yeah," he groaned. "Take it all, kid. Come on, do it for me."

Pain shot through me as he continued to violate my body. But little by little, the oversized stalk was swallowed up by the snug chamber until I was overcome by an incredible sense of fullness – a satisfaction I had never known, as the sensitive nerve endings were massaged by his length.

Once his entire cock had been buried inside me, he paused to allow me to become accustomed to this new experience. Then his enormous cock began to retreat, pulling nearly all the way out, before roughly reinvading my body. The pulsating manmeat was slammed harder and faster into my ravaged flesh as Harris' passion built up within him.

My cock began to jerk and twitch between us as my wad coursed through me, preparing for launch. I had never been so completely, so intensely aroused – and I was certain I would explode if the pressure was not relieved.

His thrust became more and more urgent, banging into my violated manhole with reckless abandon. I looked up at him, at his eyes squeezed shut, the desperate need locked in his expression. He wanted it – needed release so badly that he appeared to be in pain as he rammed into my body.

I moaned and squirmed beneath him, the pleasure nearly more than I could bear. Then my entire body convulsed, wracked with

25

spasms of ecstasy and my load burst free, the sticky white cream spattering my hairless chest.

Harris was not far behind me. I watched, fascinated, as his excitement peaked. His muscles tensed as the horny snake within me began to throb and his body shuddered. The condom swelled with his heavy cream and he collapsed on top of me – exhausted and obviously satisfied – smearing my juices between us.

"I knew you'd be hot, kid," he said, grinning.

There were so many questions I wanted to ask him, things I needed to say, but I said nothing. He pressed his lips to mine one last time, then I felt his softening cock slide from my stretched manhole.

Moments later he was gone and I fell asleep.

I awoke with a start from a sound sleep, my heart pounding in my chest. I had dreamed I was being fucked by another man! Or was it a dream?

I reached back to feel my throbbing hole. It hadn't been a dream. I had actually experienced hot, horny mansex with Harris. My gaping hole was still tender to the touch where he had plucked my cherry.

I knew I had to see him, to talk with him right away. What we had shared was new and different, truly more exciting than any sexual encounter I had ever experienced and I knew I had to recapture that feeling, had to have his stiff cock plowing into me once again.

I rolled over and looked at the clock. It was only three o'clock in the morning, but I had to see him. This just couldn't wait. I crawled out of bed, covering my nakedness with only a pair of gray gym shorts, and left my apartment.

The cool breeze of the autumn night was a shock to my system as I stepped out into the darkness. Harris' apartment was only a couple of blocks from mine, so I decided to walk rather than drive.

The walk was relaxing and gave me time to compose myself. I had to decide what I would say to him before we stood face to face.

I rang his doorbell, not sure how he would react to seeing me on his front steps at such an ungodly hour of the morning, but I knew I couldn't wait any longer to tell him how I felt.

Harris was still groggy from sleep as he answered the door, wearing only a robe.

"Scott, what are you doing here?"

"We need to talk. About what happened," I added nervously.

"Come in and sit down," he offered, finding his way to the recliner.

My cock hardened, poking straight out in front of me as his robe fell open exposing his manly physique and semi-erect cock.

"Look, Scott, if you're upset, I'm sorry. I took advantage of you and I shouldn't have."

"I'm not upset. That's just it. It was better than anything I've ever experienced. I'm here, I guess, because I want more. Teach me more, Harris. You've already taken me to places I have never been. Don't stop," I pleaded.

He was now fully awake, his complete attention focused on me. A smile crossed his lips, then he slipped off his robe.

"Follow me," he directed.

I did not hesitate to follow him into his bedroom, knowing that was where I would experience even more of the pleasure of hot, horny mansex.

I removed my shorts, letting my cock bounce against my abdomen, and stood in the middle of the floor, not quite sure what to do next.

He approached me, letting his fingers curl around my throbbing cock, then roughly yanked back the foreskin, revealing the deep purple head. His thumb circled the rim, smearing my pre-cum juices and sending shivers down my spine. He reached into the nightstand and retrieved a condom, which he expertly applied to my throbbing cock. Without saying a word, he dropped to his knees in front of me and began to run his tongue the length of my stalk, igniting tiny fires on the sensitive flesh.

He licked the head with slow, deliberate strokes, nearly sending me over the edge. He knew how to torment my body, how to tease it to the brink of orgasm but not allow it release.

While his mouth kissed and caressed my hard prick, his fingers traced a path across my chest, pausing at my already- erect nipples. I groaned as he began to pinch and pull on the tender nubs, causing an intense pleasure-pain to sweep through my body. I was so hot, I wanted him more than I had ever wanted anything in my life.

I entangled my fingers in his dark hair and forced his face into my groin.

"Suck it, please," I begged, unashamed of my body's desperate need.

He allowed the head of my cock to slide into his mouth, so that it banged against the back of his throat. I moaned as the pleasure – the pure excitement – swept through me. He tortured my vulnerable flesh, letting my swollen dickhead slither into his gullet and then swallowing it up. I had never experienced such ecstasy – and it made my heart thump in my chest.

He teased and tormented my horny cock – pushing me closer and closer to orgasm. His tongue rolled over and around the tender glans each time I pulled back, retreating ever so slightly from his ass.

I gasped, frightened by the sensation of his fingertips worming into the heat of my body, pushing against the already tortured ass-ring, kindling erotic fires within me. First one, then two, then three digits stretched me wide as he deep-throated my throbbing cock.

"Oh, man, that feels so good," I moaned, as his fist was shoved deeper into my gut.

My knees felt weak and I thought I would collapse as the unimaginable excitement, the most intense arousal of my life, took control of my body. His hand twisted and turned inside me while his fingers extended, sending waves of pleasure-pain through my tortured flesh. He grasped my prostate and rolled it expertly between his thumb and finger, pushing me past the point of no return.

My balls contracted against my body as spasm after spasm rocked my entire being. The wad of hot, white cream was captured in the tip of the latex sheath and I collapsed onto his bed, feeling more satisfied and exhausted than ever before.

He lay down next to me, neither of us saying a word, and drifted off into a restful sleep.

The last thought I had before surrendering to sleep was how good I felt about all that had happened and how much I wished this feeling would never end.

# BORN HARD
## Thomas C. Humphrey

Rocky reached for a beer as soon as I laid the food on the little table at the door of my cramped efficiency apartment.

"Hey, you old enough to drink?" I asked with a smile.

"You don't believe me, man?" He dug for his wallet and flashed me his driver's license, which showed he was telling the truth – by ten days. But the name caught my eye as much as the birth date.

"Rocky's your real name?" I asked. "How'd that come about?"

"'Cause I was born with my dick hard," he said, raising an eyebrow knowingly.

"And it's never been soft since, huh?"

"Not for very long. Not if I can help it."

"Yeah, I'll bet," I agreed. "You probably help it any time you can get your hand on it. But seriously, how'd you get named Rocky?"

"My old man used to do some boxing. He was hoping I'd be the next Rocky Marciano or something. But I'm a lover, not a fighter." He gave me a big shit-eating grin that just dared me to test him out. "So, can I have that brew?"

- - -

I had just met Rocky that morning. He had stuck out his thumb as I started through an intersection heading downtown. I've always had quick eyes, so I made a snap judgment that he was sexy enough at least to occupy my attention for a few blocks. I braked my Silverado to a stop just beyond the cross street and turned to watch him jog up and climb in the cab.

"Thanks. Nice truck," he said as he slammed the door.

Nice body, I thought, as I eased back into traffic. "Where're you headed?" I asked, wishing he'd say something like, "To bed with you," and then reminded myself that it was only eight o'clock on a Saturday morning, for Christ's sake, and the kid was probably on his way to work.

"Anywhere downtown'll be fine," he said. "I've got to try to find somebody with cables. My frigging truck won't start."

"I've got cables, but my backbone's threatening to puncture my stomach," I said. "You hungry? If you're not in too big a hurry, I'll buy you breakfast and then give you a jump."

"Sounds great," he said, rolling down the sleeve of his tee shirt to free a pack of Marlboros. I glimpsed a tiny homemade tattoo high up on his arm, the kind that more likely than not means a heavy drug scene or dead time in juvenile detention. Seeing it caused a slight ripple of excitement; I'm a sucker for bad boys I don't have to feel guilty about corrupting.

Over cheese omelets with sausage and home fries at the Southgate, I found out his name was Rocky and he claimed to be twenty-one, though I would just as well have bought seventeen or eighteen. He was an easy talker, and I soon learned that he had dropped out of school after ninth grade and had knocked about as a construction laborer. He was out of work at the moment.

Sitting across from him, I also got a good look at him. He was only about five-seven, five-eight, but his broad chest and toned biceps showed he had done some work, either in construction or with weights. He was wearing scuffed black work boots, faded Levi's with no belt, a tight, plain white T-shirt that showed the outline of his pecs with tiny nipples, and a Chicago Bulls cap, turned backwards. A shock of straight reddish hair covered most of his ears and stopped just short of his collar. He had a thin nose bridged by tiny freckles, full, sensuous lips, and the palest watery blue eyes I'd ever seen.

After breakfast, I drove him back north side and pulled in front of a beat-up Ford pickup parked at the curb in a staid old-folks neighborhood. As he popped his hood and I dug out cables, a pudgy, pink-faced old guy came out to join us, carrying a windbreaker. "Here, Rocky, you forgot your jacket," he simpered. I could have sworn Rocky blushed a little. I decided right away that I had this scene figured. I'd have bet my last dollar Rocky had spent the night hustling the old guy.

Try as we might, we couldn't get the truck going. After tinkering with it for nearly an hour, I knew Rocky had more of a problem than a dead battery. "Your starter's shot," I told him.

"Son of a bitch," he said, slamming the hood. "I can't afford a frigging starter."

"How much you got?" I asked. "You could pull one at the junk yard, and I'll help you put it in."

He shoved his hand down in his tight jeans pocket and pulled out a crumpled bill. "Twenty bucks, and I'm running on fumes besides," he said.

"Tell you what: It's my day to be a Good Samaritan," I said. "I'll front you the starter and you can buy gas."

He partially suppressed a knowing smile that said he had me figured, too. "I couldn't let you do that," he said.

"Why not? You got an honest face. You tell me you'll pay me back, I'll believe you."

"Yeah, but not working, I don't know when I could come up with that much cash. And I'd want to pay you back right away — somehow."

"Don't worry about it. You can pay me back whenever." I almost said however.

"Well, if you're sure...." he hesitated. "Well, I guess we could work something out."

"I'm sure we can," I said. I didn't mention I was banking on him being good for more than a used starter, or that my favorite pastime is trying to out-hustle young street kids. I've never liked to hurry things by outright propositioning them right away. I don't want to give them the advantage by seeming too eager; I like them to come to me. I was confident that I would be in this kid's jeans before mid-afternoon.

We spent the morning driving around to junk yards until we found one that let us pull the starter we needed and then tinkered with his old truck until we got it running. By then, we both were greasy and soaked with sweat.

"How about lunch?" I suggested.

"If you're buying, I'm eating," he grinned.

He followed me over to Baker's, where I bought barbecue and fixings and a twelve-pack of Bud, and then on to the shabby motel room that was home until this job petered out and I moved on.

That's been my life for the past dozen years, since my old lady and I split up and I took to the road. Town after town, construction job after job, bar after bar. It's been an all right life on the whole, except for the wear and tear of boozing it up every weekend with guys from the job and usually winding up in bed with some woman whose first name I would be lucky to remember next morning, both of us too drunk most of the time to do much besides pass out. It took a while for me to realize I never was too drunk if it was some boy in bed with me.

I guess I'm a slow learner, but I had had a hard time accepting a big truth about myself: Boys turn me on more than girls. They had even in high school, and getting married at eighteen hadn't changed that.

I had hired on at this job planning to make some major changes, like not going out drinking with guys from work, and concentrating on boys instead of girls. In the three weeks I'd been in town, I hadn't had any luck. I was never one for gay bars; the pretty-boy types who always seem to be hanging around are too willowy and delicate for me. My real turn-on has always been tough working-class kids who go for a whole lot of action and not much talk. After five minutes in his company, I was sure Rocky fit the bill all the way.

- - -

While we washed down our barbecue with beer, we talked about construction work and country music, about the only things we'd discovered we had in common so far. Into his third beer, Rocky spied my VCR. "Got any dirty movies?" he asked.

"What makes you think that?" I smirked.

"I just figured a guy like you, traveling around and living by yourself, you must get pretty lonely sometimes. Why else would you haul around a VCR?"

"You old enough to watch porn flicks?" I teased, moving to the table where I just happened to have a real hot bisexual tape waiting for kids just like Rocky.

Before the credits even rolled, a hunky guy with a dick that should be illegal and a very vocal blonde with hooters like basketballs screwed doggy style on the carpet while another pouty, baby faced kid spied through a patio door and jacked off. Rocky propped against the headboard of the twin bed and sprawled with one foot on the floor. As he watched the flick, he idly fingered his crotch with one hand and slowly rotated the beer can in the other as if he were teasing a big cock.

"Damn this is hot!" he said, raising his ass off the mattress and pinching at his jeans to rearrange an obvious growing bulge.

"Yeah," I agreed, adjusting my own pants. "Think you could be forced into humping that babe?"

"Nobody'd have to hold a gun to my head," he said. "I could suck on them knockers all night." By now he was openly rubbing his boner, which ran down his thigh, practically jacking off through his jeans. "I ain't managed to score with a chick lately. This flick's getting me so horny I'd fuck the crack of dawn."

"I know what you mean," I said. "The five sisters is all I've been able to make it with in this town."

"You as horny as me?" he asked. He moved over to my bed and crouched beside me on his knees. "Maybe we could help each other out." He dropped his hand into my crotch and squeezed my hard-on, which bucked under his touch. I spread my legs to give him free access and eased my hand up under his tee shirt, across his baby-soft, hairless chest, and rolled a nipple between thumb and forefinger.

Rocky popped the snap of my jeans and yanked the zipper down. I raised my ass to let him slide jeans and briefs down and hook them under my balls. My pole stood straight up my belly. Rocky ran his open hand up the length of it, one finger pressing down on the thick piss-tube.

"Damn, that's one big dick!" he said in a near-whisper. He shoved the heel of his palm beneath my nuts and wrapped his thumb and forefinger around the base of my pulsing shaft. He pulled my rod away from my belly and took it in his mouth.

I lay back across the bed and wrapped my legs around his waist. I grabbed his head with both hands and moved his mouth up and down on my cock. He almost brought me off with some experienced tongue action.

When I was about ready to explode, I shoved him off my joint and sat up. "Stand up," I said, tugging him to his feet.

With him in close between my legs, I bent down and played his cock like a harmonica, blowing my hot breath through his jeans. His rod strained against the worn fabric and fought to climb skyward across his leg. I unfastened his jeans and slipped them and his boxers down to his knees. His long, thin peter jumped out at me and stood quivering at forty-five degrees from his belly, poking through a sparse, bright red thatch. A typical redhead, his fair complexion gave his prick a pinkish-white cast of alabaster. One tiny pale blue vein ran its length a full seven inches up one side. He was uncut, and what part ᴄ. nis bullet-shaped cockhead that already peeked out of its protective shroud was reddish-pink. His nearly hairless, wrinkled nutsac nestled so tight under the base of his cock I could hardly see his little balls.

I swallowed about half of his pecker and then eased off and slid his foreskin back with my lips so I could get at his sensitive glans with my tongue. I cupped his firm, rounded cheeks in my palms and gradually worked a finger up his tight hole. "Ooh!" he moaned as I went deeper and deeper.

Every time I moved my finger in and out, he thrust his pelvis forward, trying to bury his cock in my throat. It throbbed insistently against my tight lips. A steady tremor ran through his thighs and into my forearms, which were pressed tight against him. When he started moaning and thrusting frantically with approaching orgasm, I shoved him away.

"Let's get shed of some clothes," I said, my voice so husky with lust I could hardly speak.

With us both naked, I tumbled him into bed and explored his smooth body. He was hard, lean and muscular everywhere, not a hair on his body, except for a trace of almost copper fuzz in his armpits and the small thatch around his dick. Even his face was baby-smooth, and I doubted if he had even started shaving. The tiny nubs of his dime-size pink nipples lay flat against his chest. My groping fingers fondled his balls and moved on back to circle his tight pucker. As I explored, he lay trembling and sighing, occasionally running his fingers through my hair.

I worked my body between his legs and went down on his cock again. As he got caught up in the pleasure, I rimmed his ass with a damp finger and gradually eased it in. Every time I moved it, his ass contracted and relaxed rhythmically. When I had him ready, I sat up and reached in the bedside table for lubricant.

"Uh-uh, I don't know if I can handle it," he protested as I crammed a glob of lube up his chute. "I don't get screwed much, and that's a damn big cock."

"Old men like that one this morning can't get it up to screw you, but I'm about to give you the fuck of your life, son." I lifted his legs and balanced his heels on my shoulders. With one hand I guided myself into him.

"Oh, god damn, that's the thickest one I've ever had. You're gonna split me open!" he said as the broad head of my cock parted his sphincter. He tried to shrink into the mattress.

Taking my time, I slid deep inside him, engulfed by clutching moistness and heat. I slowly rotated my cock against his inner walls, letting him get used to the unaccustomed stretch of my thick shaft. When I started moving in and out, his ass followed me, lifting off the bed each time I pulled back. Before long he was whispering and then calling out loud, "Oh, yeah! That's it, let me have it all! Fuck me! Hard!"

As I became more and more impassioned, I stretched out full length against him. In no time, he was humping for all he was worth, clawing and scratching at my back and sucking on a nipple. He went rigid, his ass clamped tight around my pole, and he spewed his cream all the way up to his chin, coating us both. After a bit, he resumed his ass movements in synch with my thrusts. I held out for a while longer before I buried my ramrod in him and flooded his pliant passage with what felt like a pint of hot come.

He went to the bathroom to clean up and pranced back in with his dick pointing to his navel. "My turn now?" he asked, a big shit-eating grin spread across his face.

"Climb on," I invited, lifting my legs. I usually don't get fucked, but after the treat I had just gotten, I was feeling generous. Besides, I figured he'd fuck like a rabbit and it'd be over before it got started.

Man, was I ever wrong! Rocky was as gentle and unhurried as could be. His movements inside me were almost imperceptible, and as he fucked me, he massaged my chest and neck and nibbled and kissed at my nipples. For what seemed like forty-five minutes, we honey-fucked real slow and easy, taking our time. Finally, his movements lengthened and strengthened until he was jabbing into me with all the force he could muster. He lunged into me once, twice, three times and then lay still, his buttocks clenched tight as steel. His cock pulsed and throbbed deep inside me and wave after wave of come blasted into me. When he was finished, he collapsed on me like a discarded rag doll.

Hours later, after a couple more rounds, we showered together, poking and teasing as we lathered up each other's body.

"What's for dinner?" he asked, shaking droplets from his hair onto my chest.

"Dinner?" I said. "Hell, I haven't even had dessert from lunch yet." I moved him back until the jet of water sprayed against the nape of his neck and cascaded down his chest. I ran my hands down his sides and cradled his taut, round buttocks as I kneeled in front of him.

Predictably, his cock was hard as a rock before I touched it.

# RINGS
## Kevin Bantan

I noticed the bulge first. It managed to proclaim itself despite the fact that his long shorts were also baggy. Man, I thought, the kid could be arrested for carrying a concealed weapon. Then I looked up to see a handsome face topped by a fuzz of brown hair, which would have been in bad need of fertilizer, if it were grass.

Because his attention was focused on something in the distance, I was able to study him openly. His lips were so full, they were past pouty to almost snarling, and they overwhelmed his modest nose. Huge silver hoops hung from round swept-back ears. I was surprised not to see a ring dangling from the pug proboscis, given that he struck me as being a punk. In light of that, his tanned skin was unexpected. Most of them affected the pastiness of spoiled white youth.

Besides his calf-length shorts, black combat boots reached up his legs in fervent hopes of union with the black cotton. A Y-shaped black suspender hugged his lean, muscled torso. A silver chain-link necklace and bracelet completed his rebellious sartorial statement. Even if he had been ugly, he was hot enough looking to be desirable. As it was, he was irresistible.

He was standing outside the park restrooms, one booted foot planted against the wall, hands carelessly shoved into the pockets of the shorts. Was it a come-hither pose? It was to me. So, going against common sense and my usual reserve in public places, I decided to approach him. Why else would he be standing there, striking a provocative pose?

My movements caught his attention, and his eyes, which looked greener by the second, focused on me as I approached. What could have been the tease of a smile played on those overly ripe lips.

"What's up?" he asked, as I came close. His blatant posture said he already knew.

"Not much." I smiled. "Cool earrings."

"Uh, huh. A guy needs his rings, you know?" His comment was as enigmatic as his sexy slouch wasn't.

"Especially when they look cool on a dude."

"Way cool, if they're in the right places." That comment only added to his mystery. "You come to the park for action or just to look?" Just like that. Kids these days. And I wasn't that much older than he was.

"Action sounds good."

"Uh, huh. You dig rings?"

"Uh, sure."

"Cool. Come on."

With that he pushed off the wall and headed off toward the woods behind the restrooms. I followed, incredulous that our brief exchange was going to result in an assignation, and in public, no less. I looked behind me and hurriedly scanned for people watching us. There were none. Still, I was anxious about the prospect of outdoor sex. But he was more beautiful than I was nervous. And I had a hard time, pun intended, watching his high ass cheeks undulate in front of me.

He stopped at a tree deep into the urban forest. The underbrush of native bushes created a convenient screen to hide the forbidden activity about to take place. Because there was no doubt in either of our minds which sex act was about to be played out.

His right foot planted itself on the tree, as if that were its natural position. He drew my head to his and covered my lips with his own genetic blessing. I let his tongue claim me as his temporary possession. I was swelling in my jeans from the caresses of his big lips. He felt me up, pleased with his oral talent.

"Something else liked the kiss, too. Cool," he breathed into my ear, as he continued to stimulate me.

My hand went to his crotch, and my brain nearly short circuited from the contact. Not only was he as hung as he had appeared, there was something strange to my touch down there. That was all the encouragement I needed to sink to my knees. I undid the button and pulled down the zipper. I shrugged the shorts over the shelves of his buttocks and my mouth opened at the sight. His long, thick cock sprang toward me, but it wasn't his length which made me react with wonder. It was how he was adorned.

A heavy silver ring was nestled behind his mushroom-shaped glans. Another girdled the base of his shaft. And, lo and behold, his suspender was attached to a third one encircling his cock and balls. My own organ twitched at the highly-erotic sight.

"Rad, huh?"

"Awesome," I said, trying to ape his lingo.

His cock was on the dusky side, from lying naked in the sun or a tanning bed, because there was no tan line. That made the contrast with the glinting silver even sexier. "Take it, man," he said in quiet command. "Suck it into you."

I did, caressing the plump crown with my mouth. I savored the unusual combination of metal and soft, taut skin. "Now do the other ring, man," he said, holding my head firmly on him. I moved it forward, sliding the long shaft into me. That would have been reward enough, but the embellishments on his cock made me all the hotter. The second ring tasted as sweet as the first, although my throat had difficulty managing to get air around his rigid sex. I would die happy, though, if I strangled on this magnificent maleness, my brain told me.

I began to worship him greedily, needing desperately to pleasure the beringed cock. My right hand played over his smooth torso, eventually focusing on the elastic suspender, which was anchored to his genital band. My own cock strained at my jeans, desperate to celebrate my coupling with him. His moans and increasing mewling sex sounds drove my mouth into a frenzy of sucking.

When I felt him begin the telltale throbbing of preorgasm, I came off the shaft to leave him in desperate need. I tongued the tight pouch and licked around the constricting bracelet girding him. His moans continued as I lavished the shaft ring with saliva. Then the one causing his beautiful head to bloat and purple. For a few moments I just admired the striking, ornamented example of male potency sticking straight up from his body.

He opened his eyes to see me staring at it and said, "Finish me with your hand, man. Jerk that ringed beauty." I did, beginning slowly and letting my hand enjoy the contact with the rock-hard member. The moans and noises returned as I gripped the shaft in desire, moving the skin faster as it twitched in urgent need of release. My other hand stroked my own needy cock in a vain attempt to effect the same result on myself. I stopped my self love, sensing that he was close. "Oh, shit, make me fucking come all over your face!"

A few more strokes brought him off, and I positioned myself to take the cum that began shooting from his wide slit. Jolt after jolt splashed hard onto my waiting face, no doubt a result of the rings forcing his come to explode from him. It seemed as if his balls were bottomless, but just as suddenly he stopped decorating my face with his essence. He remained stiff but spent.

He pulled me to my feet and kissed me hard. Then he licked himself from me, as if he were performing a lewd burlesque act. My facial nerves loved it, and my hard prick delighted in the sensation. So much so that I groaned in happiness and wet myself. "Rad," he whispered as he continued to clean me.

Once done, he kissed me lightly and wrapped his hand around his semi-tumescent organ. "Awesome, huh?"

"Yeah, it is."

"You give great head, man. Come back here in about a month. My birthday's coming up soon, and I'm gonna have my cock head pierced. Picture having one sticking out from there in your throat."

I did and liked what my imagination saw. I would be back to sample his new enhancement.

And I would never think of rings in the same way ever again.

# MYSTERIOUS WAYS
## K.I. Bard

"...The youth felt a lump grow in his throat. He knew how blessed and lucky he was to have found real friends and a true father who defended his freedom instead of wanting to limit it.

...God works in mysterious ways."

There was no missing it. Dan was angry.

At thirty one, he was a smoothly handsome man, but when angry managed all the ruffled grace of a kid. No, there was no mistaking his mood, because his feet told the story. The more annoyance, the louder Dan's footfalls

"All right." Frank frowned. "What's wrong?"

"Nothin'." Dan snapped.

Frank took a breath. He had enough experience to know the value of patient reply. Very calmly and without a barbed edge, he repeated, "What's wrong?"

"You know very well."

"I can guess, if that's what you mean, but I'd rather you told me."

"Why on earth did you call THEM?"

That's what I thought, Frank thought to himself. To Dan he said, "You don't like them."

Dan's answer came as a haughty sniff.

The THEM in question were members of a religious group (Dan referred to them as a "God damn religious cult") who lived in an obviously closed community that avoided contact with outsiders EXCEPT (and it was a large exception, indeed) when it came to earning money.

While most retirement and summer home owners on the shore were initially cautious, word spread that members of the group were reliable workers available at reasonable wages.

In that context, the religious group was entirely acceptable, whatever their personal convictions might be.

"Not hiring them to clean while we're gone won't make them go away, will it?" Frank asked, stating his position.

"Of course not." Dan fussed.

"I'm not in favor of control-groups like that, either, and you'll remember I avoided contact with them until now, until your back injury."

"Don't blame me!" Dan flared in neon anger.

"I'm not blaming you. I'm stating a fact. I don't want to aggravate your injury by having you climb to dust the overhead beams, and I'm in no condition to do so, either."

"Well, it's not that dirty. Couldn't it just wait until I'm recovered?" Dan's voice had a note of begging.

"I thought it would be nice to have it done while we were away. I'd no idea it would disturb you so much. It's not worth upsetting you, but can't you let it slide this time if I assure you now I won't call them next year?"

Dan's silence was a form of uneasy truce.

This disagreement was hardly a few degrees cooler when it took a sudden and unexpected swing prompted by a telephone call, dutifully answered by Dan. Frank, often occupied otherwise, left many on-the-spot details to Dan. After replacing the receiver he went quietly to the door of Frank's home office, where he tapped politely before stepping in. Looking up, Frank caught no more than a hint of what might come, its arrival foreshadowed by a hint of careful smugness in Dan's smile.

"The call was from them." Dan stated, reducing his usual tone regarding them to a minimum.

"OH?"

"Seems," Dan began with a pause, "I'm not the only one with misgivings. They would prefer not to have their young women clean for us."

Frank's jaw dropped visibly and a touch of angry color invaded his normally calm face. "Just like that?" He sputtered. "Going to leave us in the lurch, are they?"

"Not exactly." Dan smiled. "They offered to have some of their young men do the work. It was the patriarch of the cult himself, I gather, who called. You know how they are about money. Well, rather than lose the income they are willing to send some of their incorruptible males." Dan gave his twist time to settle in. "Seems their young women were uncomfortable with some of our art."

"Our art?" Frank blustered. "What on...!!!"

"It has to be the nudes. Two sculptures in the garden and the odd piece here and there in the house."

"The nudes?"

"What else?"

"You were right. Calling them was a mistake. I'd cancel the agreement now if there would be time to make other arrangements."

"I told them it was probably all right, but I can call them back and say NO if you'd like."

Frank thought a moment. "No." He sighed. "We'll let it go. Having the cleaning done while we're gone makes sense, and despite this show of stupid prudery they are reportedly honest."

Dan nodded. Even though he didn't fully approve he felt better having been proved correct in his assessment.

"You know," Frank began, using in a different tone. "I hate it when we quarrel."

"Quarrel? I thought it was more of a disagreement."

Frank applied one of his "give me patience" looks. "Either way, I don't like it. I could hardly concentrate on my work."

"I couldn't help it. I had a bad feeling about them from the start. The image of that leader of theirs running the lives of so many people makes me ill."

"I don't like THAT either. I thought to ignore it in favor of getting the work done. Now I know better. I hope this settles things between us."

"Well..." Dan's voice suggested.

"In the middle of the day?" Frank teased in a taken-aback way.

"You know travel will throw off our routine, so..."

"I'm twenty years your senior, you know. Perpetual horniness doesn't come so easily."

"We'll see about that." Dan smiled, moving close to begin enjoying the elemental pleasure he derived from the role he sometimes played of youthful temptation.

Travel is both broadening and reviving. Three weeks in Europe proved a wonderful treat, one that didn't require visiting the prime flesh pots of Amsterdam or Berlin to prove satisfying. Having sold the successful business he had built from scratch, Frank relished his just reward. As for Dan, well, he knew the contribution he made went beyond sexual convenience. In any workable pair the participants fill complementary roles, and Dan filled his with exemplary zeal. He wasted no time untangling snarled details of the

43

sort that frustrated Frank and he relished their intimacies because Frank was unfailingly gentle and considerate. With Frank covering and enfolding him Dan felt totally secure and happy.

Their return to America went exactly according to plan except for the very end. Frank planned a two-night stay in Chicago before heading north. Frank was a former Chicago boy who enjoyed occasional contact with the city of his youth. Unfortunately, the hotel booked a noisy convention group. Frank and Dan made a speedy decision to leave a day early and to inquire next time beforehand if the hotel would have a convention during their stay.

The pair returned home after dark a day ahead of time. As was typical, their entry was one of hushed gratitude. Being back home was especially welcome to Frank, who'd designed and built his second home more than a decade earlier. His mood of pleasure, however, came to an agonizing halt when he spotted a small pile of dishes in the sink of the otherwise spotless kitchen.

I needn't tell you how people react or move differently when trouble is sensed. Caution and silence descend in an instant as those made suddenly aware of possible danger go into search mode. There is a search for signs of forced entry one hopes not to find. The worst possibility would be to encounter an intruder who felt cornered and could turn dangerous. Carefully, room by room, the pair searched, quietly opening and shutting doors. All their searching, however, uncovered nothing out of the ordinary except for those dishes in the sink. Frank's office was undisturbed, as was the master bedroom. Each room was found in order until all but the tiny spare bedroom was left.

Thinking the spare room would prove equally innocent and that the dishes in the sink were an oversight left by the cleaning crew, Frank quietly opened the door and snapped on the light. Immediately, he knew he'd found trouble. There were assorted books scattered on the floor near the bed, which held the unmistakable form of a human body.

"I've got a gun!" Frank bellowed loudly. "I'll use it if I have to."

The contents of the bed moved. A startled face emerged. "I! I! Don't!" A young voice stuttered in abject fear. "Don't shoot! Don't kill me, please!"

"Don't move!" Frank hollered before adding, "Raise your hands!"

The bed's occupant obeyed. Doing so revealed enough to allay some of Frank's fear because the body revealed, bare armed and bare chested, looked to be that of little more than a boy.

"Who are you? What are you doing here?" Frank demanded, still pretending in a tone that said he was armed and dangerous.

"I'm ... I'm...." The youth's voice staggered with such fear Frank wondered if the bed wasn't being wet as he watched.

"Well?" Frank demanded.

"I'm ... I'm from the Family. I ... I didn't have anywhere else..."

"The family?" Frank said quietly, mostly for his own benefit.

"I think," Dan suddenly recover his faculties, went on, "he means the group who cleaned."

Frank nodded. "That true? You part of the commune?"

The youth nodded. "Don't kill me, please." His entire body shook.

"Should I call the sheriff?" Dan asked under his breath after having been utterly speechless and unaccustomedly devoid of action at the start of the crisis, which caught him entirely unprepared.

Frank shook his head. "I don't think there's need," he said softly to Dan before turning back to his trembling intruder. "Why are you here."

"The ... the schedule said you'd be back tomorrow. I ... I didn't have anyplace else to go. I didn't mean any harm. I'll clean everything up. Honest. I'm sorry. Please don't hurt me."

"You can put your hands down. I don't have a gun."

The youth dropped his hands and as soon as they fell to his lap he began to sob.

Crying comes in different forms, and this sobbing was clearly genuine, blending deep-felt sorrow with relief. The youth was entirely in the grip of awesome emotion of a sort more familiar to Frank than Dan. His tears signaled both surrender and a plea for mercy. He was someone in need of help.

Frank moved to the bedside, his feet accidentally scattering books. Trying to provide comfort, he dropped a hand to the boy's shoulder. It was a gesture Dan understood and feared, feared because it wasn't his shoulder being touched.

"You'll be okay," Frank said. "Maybe you'd like something to drink?"

For the time, the boy was unable to raise his head, which he shook in a way that said "I don't want to be any trouble."

Looking up at Dan, Frank said quietly. "Cocoa."

Dan nodded and departed.

In that fashion began the slow unraveling of what had transpired during their absence, beginning with learning the name of their uninvited guest, who accepted his mug of cocoa with a trembling hand.

"Now," began Frank, "tell me who you are."

"Hans," the youth spoke, quickly ducking behind his mug after taking a sip.

"And why are you in my house, Hans?" Frank asked, wondering if the lad's torso was nude under the sheets. (It wasn't.)

Dan, likewise, had similar thoughts, which included doubting his former judgment about the cult, especially if it had more treasures like young Hans. It was with considerable disappointment he spotted a hint of waistband at the boy's waist when he moved.

In any real life situation there are really, as you know, two dialogues. There is what people say aloud but there is also what they say to themselves. You will have to fill in much of the later on your own while I provide a presentable version of the disconnected tale Hans revealed. For the sake of brevity and convenience I've eliminated all the questioning and coaxing Frank had to do in order to learn the truth. In his own words, the crux of Hans' being in the house is as follows:

Father Walder put me in charge of Ben and Sam. At twenty, I was elder. Ben's eighteen and Sam's at least a year younger than that. Father Walder used to tell me I'd be the one to follow after him when he was called away, so I felt good about being allowed to lead others on a work party away from home. It wasn't until we got here that I felt things change. At first I thought it was the Devil tempting me, but after a few hours I knew it wasn't that. I felt (Hans steadied himself before continuing) free. Free. (His shoulders shook slightly at the memory.) There was something about being here that opened a door leading to something I'd kept hidden. I thought even God wouldn't know, but once it broke the surface there was no way for me to pretend. I felt good, but also happy and excited, along with being scared.

The funny thing was how I didn't want the job to end, so I kept adding things for us to do. I had Sam rake outdoors (Dan raised his eyes wondering what damage the boy might have caused his wildflower garden) while Ben washed the walls. That's what gave me time to dust the books and look at some of them. (It was Frank's turn to react, knowing his relatively tame interest in erotic content must have been potent for a youth who grew up in what amounted to a cloister.) There were things (Hans wet his lips) I'd tried not to think about. I'd been told over and over how my body belonged to God and I was not to use it except at his bidding. But your books showed people doing forbidden things and not being blown to pieces by His wrath. I made the job last, and every night back at home I thought about what I'd seen. I hardly remember those days except as a fire growing and growing inside me.

Finally, about a week ago, I sent Sam to weed ("My poor wild flowers!" Dan thought in a panic.) so I could be alone with Ben. Ben's been my only real friend, but we're not much alike. He likes to talk about the time he'll have his own wife and children and how they'll have to obey him. I told him I'd read the instructions for how to clean your tub ("My poor Jacuzzi!" Frank thought in fear of Hans having run it when dry) so we might as well use it at the same time. I told him we'd take turns, because I could see he didn't like the idea of getting in with me. ("Waste of a good Jacuzzi meant for two, if you ask me." Dan made a wry face.)

(Hans lowered his head.) I knew what I wanted. Back when I was twelve or thirteen Ben and I, only once because we were never alone otherwise, went for a swim ... and (Hans shook visibly.) I promised I'd never again. ("Damn religious repression!" Frank and Dan thought in duo.) But, but, I knew Ben remembered, and I knew if I touched him again he'd let me, even if he thought it was wrong. (Hans head hung lower than ever.) But, it didn't feel wrong. I liked seeing Ben excited and I liked it even better when I could see him pleased.

We didn't do much, not nearly what they do in your books, but it was great. I felt alive, I really did, even though Ben wanted to forget about it right away. I knew I couldn't forget. Never.

Even if I wanted to (Hans' tone changed) I couldn't. Sam,,, Sam spied on us. He saw. ("The view into the garden from the tub is one of its nicer features," Frank mused.)

Back home, he waited a day before I knew. We were supposed to be getting firewood when he told me. He said he wouldn't tell if I did it to him, too. I said I wouldn't, but he didn't get half way to the house before I called him back. Sam's father isn't with the family any more, so he visits. That's where Sam learned about what he called "cocksuckin'." He made me do it to him, telling me I had to do it whenever he wanted it. I was scared, so I did, but it was wrong. I knew it was wrong doing it for that reason. I knew it was wrong, too, because we'd get caught. There are too many people around.

Then, sure enough, someone saw us in the woodshed. They told Father Walder. Sam said I forced him to submit. I think Sam wants to be the future leader. Getting me out of the way opened the way because Ben's no leader. But before anything more could happen I ran. I knew where your spare key was because I found it while I swept cobwebs off the outside walls. I hid here. I knew the Family was looking for me. I was going to be gone before you got back. I'm sorry. I'm sorry.

Frank, more than Dan, realized the turmoil raging through young Hans' life. His repressed sexual feelings caused him to have the emotional reactions of a mere boy inside an adult body. On top of all that, which was formidable, rose the issue of losing the only life he knew. No longer among the "saved" he, no doubt, felt himself as having fallen amid the "damned." Frank knew that a youth cut loose from his past needed special reassurances and by virtue of his own experience understood the role he needed to play as elder.

"Dan." Frank spoke softly using a motion of his head to indicate Dan should leave him alone with Hans.

Dan nodded, though not without reluctant obedience. There was, in fact, a strong feeling of angry suspicion when he shut the door on the pair. Outside, Dan paced. A minute passed, then another. Dan neared the closed door, straining to hear but unable to make out anything but the softest sound of passing syllables. More time passed and Dan felt himself unable to stand any more suspense. He had to know whether their uninvited guest was on his way to becoming Frank's new lover. After all, the boy had ambition. Hadn't he considered himself Walder's chosen successor?

When the door suddenly opened Dan had no time to hide or pretend he'd been doing anything but standing there in suspicious agony. Frank quietly shut the door behind him before stepping to Dan and hugging him.

"He's gone through a lot these past few days. I hope you'll be patient with him. He's going to need time and people to help him. He's going to need you as much as me."

"Oh, God," Dan gasped, "I kept thinking...."

"I know. I'd think it, too. He's a gorgeous temptation, but he's both young and naive. It will take time and effort on our part to help him through all this. Can you imagine yourself growing up having gay feelings and homosexual sensibilities in an environment that daily murders your emotional life?"

"You really think he's gay?" Dan asked, gratefully returning Frank's hug because Frank was one of the few genuinely loving people he ever knew and felt privileged to be with.

"Very likely. Look how he opened up at the first opportunity, and think how confused he must be having to face at twenty what had to be kept hidden since he was a boy."

"We've all been forced to do that."

"Not to that extreme, we haven't." Frank countered.

"Frank." Dan kissed his lover's cheeks. "Emotional repression is a horror whether it's accomplished in a cult setting, on a farm, in a city, or a suburb. Having to lie about how you feel is never good."

Frank nodded. "You're right. Now let's get ready for bed. This is one night when I want to feel especially grateful having the freedom we've managed to gain."

"Me too." Dan smiled, punctuating his words with an impetuous kiss.

"I hope you won't be jealous of him." Frank didn't exactly warn.

"He's gorgeous, though, isn't he?"

"That's what I mean. He's a fine looking youth, but who knows which way he'll turn? There are all those years of modeling and repression to consider."

"I don't know," Dan began dragging Frank by the hand, "I might take up photography again."

"Making the best of a challenging situation, are you?" Frank asked in wry humor while thinking, Seeing himself as an erotic being might be a good thing for the boy, if he's ready. Maybe Dan should return to photography.

"Well, I had more than a little curiosity to see what was below the waist."

"Oh, he's...." Frank played a deliberate joke which he declared with a broad laugh upon seeing Dan's expression. "Got you!"

"You'll pay for that one." Dan said with relief.

"Oh, poor me." Frank sniggered, enjoying foreplay that hadn't gone out of control.

More than a week later Frank stood in his kitchen when quite suddenly the tall, almost nude figure of Hans flew past in the dazzling red Speedos he'd picked for himself.

There was no mistaking his destination, the spare room which he continued to inhabit by choice. It's door banged shut with definite purpose. "I should talk to him about slamming doors." Frank told himself, just as another sound got his attention. There was someone at the door.

"Yes?" Frank answered, opening the door.

"I'm here for Hans." A bearded, grave-faced older man intoned with seeming authority.

"Hans?"

"My son. My lost child. I'm here to take him home."

"Well, I don't know. In the first place," Frank spoke with deliberate care, "he is not your biological son, now, is he? In the second place, he has made it very clear to me he does not wish to return. My advice to you is to go away and leave him alone. He is free to return if he wishes, but that is definitely not what he wants to do."

"I want to talk to him."

Frank shook his head.

"I must see him."

Frank supplied another negative.

"He needs the word of God to save him from eternal damnation."

"I said no, and I mean no. It's time you understood that and left these premises."

"I'll ... I'll talk to the law and we'll see what they say about your corrupt life. You're kidnapping an innocent child. You're holding him against his will to use for your own evil ends."

"So that's it? You'll call in the law, will you?"

"I will. I will make a complaint unless you return my son to me immediately."

"I think," Frank said with a deceptive smile, "we can finally agree on something. I think you should call the law and report me."

The man was surprised. "That's what I'll do," he said, rather weakly.

"I should think they would like to hear what your "son" has to say about how he was treated as a child in your care. I wonder what a prosecutor would make of locking children in cold, damp, unlighted cellar holes for extended periods of punishment. I think a jury would be interested in knowing boys were put into cell-like beds after having had their hands tied behind their backs. And don't you think a judge would appreciate learning the special pains you took regarding some aspects of the private education of your charges? Perhaps you'd like to use my phone to make the call?"

A change came over the religious leader's face, which bore ashen fear alongside neon embarrassment and deathly vengeful anger.

Holding his ground, Frank spoke, though not without some tremble in his voice. "Hans is free to make his own decisions and I am free to leave matters as they now stand unless you force me to do otherwise."

"You're an evil, evil man." The elder turned, storming, away.

Watching the departing figure, Frank thought to himself, Coming from you, old man, that's high praise, indeed.

It was Dan, unseen, holding himself in reserve if needed, who later told Hans of Frank's defense.

Listening, the youth felt a lump grow in his throat. He knew how blessed and lucky he was to have found real friends and a true father who defended his freedom instead of wanting to limit it.

God works in mysterious ways, the youth reminded himself while taking Dan by the hand to lead him to Frank, and then conveying them as a trio to the Jacuzzi. Here, Hans shed his dazzling red Speedos and danced steps of improvised joy, like a Hindu God multi limbed and imbued with fluid motion. The youth danced the story of his own happiness which is also the tale of the joys of others.

# TURKEY BOY BLUES
## Thom Nickels

There's nothing that stirs up memories like rummaging through an old address book.

Going through one old book, I saw Christopher's name scrawled on the page as if I'd been given the number while on the run. Beside it was another number, the inevitable beeper number which had since been crossed out with the words – in my own hand – "transferred to Mary," written over it. "Mary," of course, was the person who got the number after Christopher dropped it. I remembered speaking with Mary twice. She was young, maybe in her twenties. "Did you call my beeper?" she asked, ringing me back three hours after I plugged in what I thought was Christopher's number.

"No," I said, "I dialed a friend's beeper number, a guy named Christopher." Then I held my breath. Christopher had warned me about his girlfriend. She was the ownership type. Christopher was her baby. For a second it annoyed me to think that maybe she'd gotten a hold of Christopher's beeper, but then she told me that she'd just gotten the number a week ago. This explained Christopher's change in attitude, a switch I pretended not to notice when he started to say that his work schedule was so crammed he couldn't find time to see me. After that he lowered the axe and spelled what was really bothering him.

"Well, I don't feel like I want to be sucked off these days. Something happened to change that but I don't know what. I used to want it all the time. But now I don't even want my girlfriend to do it...."

"Sounds like a science fiction story," I said, trying to sound casual. "I mean, what healthy American guy in his right mind doesn't liked to be licked, worshipped and adored? You know, no woman would ever do to you what I did every time we saw one another. Women want to be worshipped. They don't want to be the one doing the worshipping...."

I knew Christopher was getting the message: No woman would ever unlace his sneakers and place his feet on her knees as she stroked each foot and put her lips to his socks. Feet, to most women – and many men for that matter – were disgusting. But Christopher knew the oceans of sensuality unleashed during a good foot session: how the working of certain nerve endings in the feet, whether by hand or tongue, sent erotic shivers through the body and then straight up the shaft of the penis.

"I don't know," he said, fading off into what I knew was probably a shrug. "If I felt the urge in me, I'd be over there."

Then I said what I promised myself I'd never say: "What did I do? Is it something I said? Maybe you're just feeling guilty. Guilt can do horrible things. Look, I really miss you. It's been months. I'll even consider giving you, you know, a few extra dollars for your trouble – as a bonus. I miss your big feet, man."

And I also missed his long, lean body, the smell of his pubic hair, the deep recesses of his armpits, his large nipples which looked like moon craters with a small church spire in the center of each. Then, of course, there was his cock. Not mammoth or "porn historic" but a fine working machine that performed every time. Standing up or lying down; sitting in a chair with his legs spread as I knelt on the floor before him, or lying on his side on my living room sofa, Christopher dug any position, his cum always shooting straight across his stomach and far beyond his face, hitting the wall or pillows or sometimes ricocheting and hitting me in the eye. A marksman of sex!

Christopher in any way, shape, or form, was just fabulous.

After my monologue about missing him, the only thing he could do was laugh. It was a laugh of appreciation and embarrassment. Then he got very quiet. The quiet interested me; I knew he was having second thoughts. I was beginning to knock away his resistance. I pictured him at home lounging on his mother's sofa, shoes off, his big feet on the coffee table or propped on an end stool. I imagined I was his little dog, Sputnik, the miniature Terrier, sniffing the sensual aroma of his socks. Then I wondered if his girlfriend appreciated what she had or if she operated on sexual auto-pilot (a devotee of the "hands-off, passive, do everything to me" school of sex).

I didn't know what else to say. Offering him money was really a last resort. For me it was the last straw, a desperate pitch. At a certain point you just have to shut up. Christopher would have to miss me all by himself. I was also fairly pissed at this point: the truth is, I missed him; I wanted him. But there was nothing to do but let him go. It would be a long time, I knew, before I found a substitute for Chris. Boys with big feet just don't come that good.

Long before this happened, however, I had a few long months of bliss in which Christopher came to my apartment at all hours of the day or night. After work in the middle of the afternoon; late at night when he would wake me up with a phone call; at the crack of dawn after he left Bassett's Original Turkey and was working at RPS. I never knew when he'd be needing me. I only knew that he seemed to be thoroughly addicted to the way I gave pleasure. My unique style had him under my spell.

"Oh man," he told me on numerous occasions, "you should put out a fuckin' sign."

Then he broke his ankle at RPS loading trucks, and all hell broke loose. Months and months of solitary recovery in his mother's house set him on a different course. He had too much time to think; he got his girlfriend pregnant. The coming baby transformed him into Big Daddy. Conventional images took quaint little house in the suburbs, white picket fence, responsible family man. These screwed things up. Male-male sex had to go. No more undercover city blowjobs; no more wiggly-wiggly toe-sucking. Just in-and-out pussy thrusts and diapers to buy at K-Mart. And then death and a respectable funeral.

I wanted the "old" Christopher to return. The "old" Christopher of yesteryear who was adventurous and free.

- - -

I first spotted Christopher at Bassett's Original Turkey, where I used to go for dinner at least three nights a week with my best friend, Rizzoli. Rizzoli and I liked Bassett's because it was fast and nutritious. The service was also efficient, what with an army of black girls and serious young executives-in-training (EITs) behind the counter to take orders. We especially liked it when the black girls piled on the food in generous heaps, so much so that we'd always complain whenever the by-the-book EITs measured the portions out carefully. Rizzoli and I called these guys the anal-retentives of the culinary arts.

"This is not an old age home, and I do not have a bird's appetite!" I used to complain to Rizzoli when the EITs gave us little bits.

Christopher was standing behind the counter when I first saw him. He was dressed in a white Nehru cook's hat, white pants, shirt and apron. I didn't see him until I slid my tray past the muffin display; by that time Rizzoli was at the end of the tray track paying for his meal. I was still waiting for my platter – there'd been a mix-up so I had to wait for the server to return from the kitchen. I remember how I stepped aside in order to say something to Rizzoli, when I saw the most extraordinary youth: a tall, lean twenty something who studied the black girls as they removed the roasted turkeys from the ovens. A Bassett's understudy! I said to myself, Jesus, what a boy! And I meant it, too.

I must have looked long and hard because the intensity of my stare brought a response: Christopher looked at me and kept his eyes there for several seconds till I broke the lock. I broke the lock because I was not expecting my look to be returned in so ardent a fashion. And the look was ardent, that I was sure of.

My conversation with Rizzoli was distracted that night to say the least. Between mouthfuls of beans and potatoes I'd look up to see what the new server was doing. A few times we made eye contact again, but this ended when the place became too busy. When Christopher finally came out from behind the counter, I got to see his full form in motion, his graceful, slender self, over six feet tall, opening the supply closet not far from our seat in the restaurant. Rizzoli caught me giving him the once-over: my personal x-ray included an intense focusing in on Christopher's huge, tan Doc Martens.

"He must have enormous sweaty feet," I said to myself then. "A size 13, at least. This boy is to die for!"

As I chewed down on a mouthful of stuffing, I promised myself that, come what may, I was going to do everything I could to meet this boy. Even if it meant making a fool of myself.

Days passed. As usually happens when one lives in the city, where the pace is fast and where the abundance of good looking boys is plentiful, I put the boy at Bassett's on hold. I did, however, walk by the restaurant one night while on my way home from work. It was somewhere between nine-thirty and ten o'clock at night, the time when I usually find myself in the area of the restaurant. I stood on a street corner near a coffee shop directly across from Bassett's in order to spy on the workers inside the restaurant as they cleaned up. The restaurant was closed, of course, but it took at least an hour each night to complete the cleaning ritual.

Naturally, I was trying to see if I could spot Christopher. Then I saw him turning chairs upside down on table tops, his shirtsleeves rolled up above his elbows. He looked like a sexy revolutionary anarchist from history, a young man with big balls. From a distance, his Doc Martens looked like giant clodhoppers; inside the boots I imagined his sweaty, tender feet nesting in socks that had soaked up lots of his perspiration. That smell was his essence. "Essence of the boy from Old Bassett's Original Turkey." My mouth watered.

Since it was too early in the game to wait till he left the restaurant so I could introduce myself (though I did entertain the thought), I knew that something had to be done but I didn't know what.

I didn't tell Rizzoli about the new object of my affection because I was afraid that I'd jinx things.

My second encounter with Christopher had a noteworthy component. During the ordering of food, there was a tray mix-up of sorts and my order was botched. I had already paid Christopher at the check-out line, even nodded my head in a friendly sort of way when I noticed that something was wrong. When I mentioned this to Christopher he was more than conciliatory and saw to it that I received twice as much food as I would have gotten had the order been correct. His generosity made me think that he was an easy-going type and that he liked me enough in a general sense so that my introducing myself after work might work after all. In the meantime, I came up with another plan: write a message of sorts on the Bassett's bathroom wall.

Call this the last resort of the desperate; point a finger and label it sleazy or the easy way out. And while it's true that writing your phone number on a public bathroom wall exposes you to all sorts of men, from the terminally boring and unsexy to the criminally insane (not to mention the homeless), my plan worked. My simple "Center City Foot Massage for lean dudes, 545-9060," worked its magic four days after I wrote it on the wall.

It was late in the day, maybe 5 p.m., and I was dressing for my telemarketing job near the Liberty Bell when the call came through. As soon as I said hello I knew that whoever was calling was using a pay phone. The background noise was filled with the hum of passing traffic.

"Um, I'm calling because I saw an...ad about a...foot massage," came the tentative inquiry.

"Okay," I said, "you've reached the right number. What's your name?"

"Chris," said the now self-assured male voice.

"Where was this ad?" I wanted to know.

"Well," Chris said, "I saw it where I work...."

"If that's a secret, I understand," I offered.

Chris quickly added, "It's not a secret. It was at Bassett's Turkey."

My heart skipped a beat.

"You work there? That's good. I just put it there not too long ago. My name is Billy. I eat there all the time with my best friend. I've probably seen you. What do you look like?"

Naturally, part of me was afraid the voice might belong to a fat boy who worked another shift at Bassett's or to one of the pudgy EIT guys who were not very interesting. "I'm tall... I guess... kind of skinny with light brown hair. And I just turned 21," Chris said.

I knew right away it was my boy.

"I'm glad you called. You're the guy who works in the evening; you wear the white Nehru hat, you wear tan Doc Martens...?"

"Yes," he said. I told him about Rizzoli's fascination for Bassett's and reminded him of the food mix-up when he came to my aid. I mentioned that I wrote on the bathroom wall because I couldn't think of any other way to meet him. There's no privacy there, I added; you talk to one employee and everybody within earshot thinks they have a right to the conversation. "What are you doing right now or later tonight?" I asked, a fire raging inside my crotch.

"I'm off at nine ... but I have to pick my girlfriend up on the way home. Tomorrow night is better. I get off at six and I can come over then if you want."

Of course I said yes. After I gave him my address and we made arrangements for him to call me and confirm when he got off at work, I went back to dressing for my telemarketing job. "Christopher," I said out loud as I watched myself tie my tie in front of the bathroom mirror. "Sweet, sweet Christopher in the huge black boots!"

The next day, I called work and told them I had a scratchy throat and that, not only was it hard to swallow, it felt as if something awful was lodged inside (a moment after I said this I saw the symbolism and imagined Christopher's erect cock in my mouth). At 5 p.m. I paced my apartment nervously. What if he stood me up? When Rizzoli called and asked if I wanted to go to Bassett's I jokingly said, "Well, Bassett's is coming to me tonight." Then I told him I was staying home from work because I did not feel well.

At five minutes to six Christopher telephoned. "I'm on my way. Can you meet me outside your house. I guess it will take me fifteen minutes to walk over."

I said okay and went downstairs and stood on the front steps five minutes after we hung up. Standing on the steps and pondering passing traffic, I felt sorry for all the poor slob drivers who were not going to meet Christopher. It was also all I could do to keep from looking down the street in the direction Christopher said he'd be walking from. When I did eventually spot a slim figure in basketball shorts, sneakers and a red jersey with a white T-shirt underneath, I became conscious of the pose I was striking on the steps and went through a dance of changing postures.

When the figure gradually came into focus, I could see that it truly was Christopher with the engaging smile. When he walked up to me he held his hand out and said hello.

"This is better than Bassett's," I quipped. "Come on up – our orders are in."

In the apartment, Chris sat on the sofa, stretching his long legs in front of him while I took the side love seat, which enabled me to look at him head on. He wanted neither food nor drink but was content just to sit and talk.

He said he lived with his divorced mother in the suburbs, and that his girlfriend lived down the street. He grew up playing street hockey, baseball and basketball. He said he loved his girlfriend but that he needed something else. He mentioned answering a pay phone on the street a while back. A man called from a high rise apartment and said he could see him on the street and that he thought he looked good, and would he like a blowjob? Chris said he took the bait; he happened to be horny. He'd seen the man once more after that, but since he lived on the other side of the city, it was too far to travel.

"So what's this foot massage all about?" he asked.

It was at this point that I asked him to put his left foot on my lap and I'd show him. I told him to leave his sneaker on.

Having his size 13 sneaker on my lap, where I could caress and knead it with probing fingers, was more than a slice of heaven. As soon as I touched his foot, Chris' eyes froze. I noticed an eye glaze – the veil of pleasure – and then I felt him zone out. When I took the sneaker off his left foot and felt the slightly damp foot in the white sock, which showed each toe indentation in delineated lines, I inhaled deeply. Flowing into me was the special aroma of athletic boy feet, a true Christopher smell that had me taking off his sock. The bare foot was as magnificent as they come: soft undersides, elegant long toes. I tried not to seem too much under his spell but that proved futile. Putting my tongue between his toes, I tasted the salty creaminess of this very special guy.

The maneuver sent the neighborhood hockey player into quiet spasms. He slouched back on the sofa, his eyes closed and his body on the edge of rapture. He managed a quiet ''Wow'' as he relinquished the other foot, which I quickly unlaced and de-socked until I had both feet in front of my face – icons of the turkey god for sure!

Then his beeper went off.

It was his girlfriend, looking for him. Chris, to his credit, switched the beeper off and resumed his pose, saying only that he had just spoken to his girlfriend and that she was overdoing things by calling him too much.

"Yes, private time is holy," I said with a smile, recalling the wisdom of poet Allen Ginsberg. I no sooner said this than my mouth was once again over his toes, my tongue running roughshod along his foot bottoms. Soon I was kissing his ankles and heels and noticing how he was groping himself on the sofa, his hard-on making a wet mound under his basketball shorts.

In the bedroom, Chris stretched out on his back, his hands nestled behind his head. His cock, while not monumental, was comfortable enough in size to warrant a second look. It felt like a solid piece of bark or a large spike capable of being hammered into the earth. Dewy webs criss-crossed his cockhead and covered his navel.

I got up on the bed and leaned over him, lowering my face to his slim hips and letting my tongue run along the soft flesh, kissing veins as I went and then sniffing his abdominal muscles, my tongue tracing line curves and then concentrating on his nipples: there I planted succulent kisses on his quarter-sized nipples. His armpits, which seemed like fleshy hockey pucks, received my tongue's soothing administrations. Then in one fell swoop I was laying on top of him, squeezing, wiggling, pressing, my cock colliding with his, my face buried in his neck as I inhaled his various smells, a feint musk cologne, smoke from the turkey ovens, and something sour and sexy like a jockstrap.

As Chris shut his eyes and drew his head back on the pillow, I had an ample view of a trail left by clumsy Susie: a cluster of faded purple passion marks that looked like sparrow's feet. I imagined her as dead weight under his own "live wire" body – the passive princess not worshipping him like me but lying comatose – a total sexual bore!

I covered the sparrow's feet imprint with my tongue and then planted my own long suction-kiss over the mark till I made a sort of tattoo over his girlfriend's trail.

Pondering his body – especially at his huge feet hanging over the bed – I vowed to do anything to keep Christopher in my life. I sealed the thought with a blowjob, sucking him with the aid of my right hand, a slurping fast and then slow paced process that brought about the sticky shower I'd been waiting for.

Later, as we were cleaning up and handing one another towels, Christopher checked his beeper and saw that his girlfriend had beeped him two more times since he turned the beeper off.

"God, she just loves me too much. She can't help it," he explained, yet I could see strains of worry in his face. There was in his eyes the look of someone on a leash who has to account for every move. "I'll give you my beeper number but try not to call me at home," he said. And that was because he had another woman on perpetual watch, his mother, the divorced waitress who kept watch over him like a human lighthouse.

Of course, I wasn't to discover this until later, when I started calling Christopher at home for small, afternoon chats. I considered myself lucky when he answered directly; unlucky if his mother picked up.

"Who is this? Are you a friend of Christopher's?" was her usual refrain. The feeling was like you'd broken through enemy lines. At any moment you expected her to tell you to stop calling. And sometimes she sounded angry or suspicious.

"Oh, I'm just a friend at work."

"Is there anything wrong? Do you want him to come in early?"

"No, ma'am. There's nothing wrong. We're just buddies. There's no message. I'll just talk to him when I see him. It's okay, really."

Whenever Chris visited me, we usually followed the same procedure: I'd wait for him on my steps. We'd go inside. I'd offer him something to drink, which he'd refuse. We'd talk for a few minutes. Then he'd move into the slouch position: touch me, feel me. He'd stretch his legs towards me, his sneakers almost touching my shoes. Sometimes I'd swoop down and place one of his feet on my lap and begin the massage. I enjoyed unlacing his shoes myself and then slipping them off. Knowing what was about to occur, Chris' eyes glazed over as soon as my fingers began kneading his toes.

But that was last year. Today, "Mary" has his beeper number and Chris is off buying – as I stated – diapers at K-Mart.

# THE CHARMER
## Rick Jackson

I liked Charlie Donovan from the start. It was hard not to like the kid. He was perky and friendly, hard-working and competent, and cute as an leprechaun's behind. He was tall, well-built; a red-headed, green-eyed, freckle-faced, toothy-grinned boy whose charm makes a man want to tousle his hair just for the fun of it.

I liked having Charlie around. As a resident, I tried not to play favorites with my med students, but Charlie was always so friendly and puppy-like that deep down I always liked him better than the rest of the gloomy drones who bitched and moaned their way through our year together as though my sole purpose in life were to make their lives a living hell. That was one purpose, of course; but I had others.

Charlie was bright and quick on the up-take. What's more, he had the rare gift of being able to follow instructions, yet use his own initiative when necessary. In short, I was so sure Charlie had his act together, that when he came to me with his problem late one night when business was slack and we were in the on-call room, the little bastard surprised the hell out of me.

The minute he opened his mouth, he was blushing and stuttering around so much you'd have thought I'd asked him to catheterize the archbishop. He finally lurched around to the point that he'd heard from the nurses that I was – that there was a rumor that – he wondered whether it was true – that I was – that is to say – was I gay?

You see what I mean. The kid was cute as a colt in clover. Charlie was only about five years younger than I, but he seemed of another generation. I grinned at his discomfiture even as I wondered where he was heading and said that I sure was – and asked whether he needed his prostate probed. That really set him off, but by the time he had blushed and stuttered his story out, it was my turn to be at a loss for words.

The kid wanted me to fuck him up the ass. I knew it. He had apparently had a few unfulfilling experiences with women, had lurid dreams about sweaty naked men with big dicks and bad attitudes, and wanted somebody reliable to ream him out so that he would have enough data to formulate a reasonable hypothesis about his sexual preference.

I've had a lot of men approach me over the years in a lot of ways, but Charlie was the first to use the lab-rat data approach. Still, he was obviously worried. Doing him would be like reaming out Beaver Cleaver, but I had to confess that the idea made my dick twitch in a wicked, twisted sort of way. I patted the kid on the shoulder and told him that with sex, he should follow his instincts rather than his intellect C but that if he wanted what I had, he could come over to my apartment the next night and I would be happy to poke his cute little virgin butt until his ears bled.

I was still in bed – naked and very much alone – trying to recover from my duty rotation when Charlie pounded on my door about 6:30 the next evening. I stumbled to the door to see whether I needed to gird my loins in defense of public morals before I opened up. When I saw Charlie's bright-eyed face beaming at me and remembered our conversation, I decided to save the trouble and go with the ungirded option.

The kid was obviously surprised, though whether it was my bleary-eyed, unshaven face or my nine thick inches of resident dangle that did the trick, I can't say. He started babbling again about was he too early and how he'd thought somethingorother. The combination of his witless charm and a day passed in uneasy dreams soon had my dick standing tall and proud and Charlie's eyes locked on tight.

I gave a yawn and went wordlessly back to bed. Charlie was obviously confused, but when he wandered in, I told him to get naked and I'd do him if that was what he wanted. He was obviously hoping for romance rather than a clinical procedure, but I didn't want him to confuse sex and love just yet. Besides, I didn't need anyone falling in love with me.

Then I saw the body he was hiding under his clothes and reconsidered. The kid was what some like to call a stud muffin. Huge shoulders, biceps and pecs that tapered down to a flat, hard belly and hips that almost weren't there at all. Bright red curls swept across his chest and down in a thick band all the way to his crotch, almost as though pointing the way to the thickest eight-inch uncut marvel of modern urology it had ever been my pleasure to see. His ass was full and hard and high, just begging to be abused. His skin was Irish white and freckled but stretched so tightly across his muscles that, except

John Patrick

for the color of his swollen nipples and all that fur, he looked more like a Praxiteles Apollo than anything human.

My dick was throbbing and swollen almost to the point of pain as I motioned him onto the bed and took my time examining him. My fingers started out, tracing rings around his nipples and sliding down his flanks as my teeth tore into his tits to teach him his first lesson in the dangers of bearding the beast in his den. Charlie's hard young body shivered with every flick of my tongue and positively shuddered with wicked delight as the sharp edge of my teeth nibbled at his nipples' composure.

When I licked my way down to his furry nuts, the kid moaned once, slow and long, and then set to whimpering like some rabid chipmunk. At first I was content just to lick the taste of man sweat from his musky nuts, but I soon had to suck and chew his hard-packed sperm pods just because they were there. Charlie squirmed with girlish delight as my face ate his `nads' and I ground my beard stubble across the tender milky skin covering his powerful thighs. When I pulled backwards to stretch his cords to the breaking point and grind his balls against the back of my teeth, the poor bastard didn't know whether to moan or whimper, so he starting screaming out to every member of the Holy Family he could think of.

My mouth was so busy chewing his nuts that I didn't notice my hand had wrapped tight around his thick crank, jacking it as Charlie's hips writhed about grinding his crotch into my face. I must have lain there slurping at his balls for ten minutes before I eased up and gave his dick the attention it deserved – and it deserved a lot. My only problem was where to start – at the huge dorsal vein bobbling down his length, with the oversized foreskin sliding across his vast purple head, in the thick streams of slick pre-cum dripping from his pulsing knob to weave shimmering webs of sweet, crystalline dreams in the red belly fur below, or with the impossibly wide eight inches of meat that throbbed and bucked in my hand like a creature possessed? Where, oh where, to start!

I felt almost as though I were the virgin. I hadn't been so excited by a body in years. Everything about him was a delicious contradiction: his boyish face and gorilla-sized dick, the innocent sparkle in his eye and the worldly way his pelvis hammered upwards against my face, his brain's clueless indecision and the driving certainty of his loins. body. I jacked his dick, watching his foreskin slide up and down his shaft until the scent of mansex and the hot thrill of that dick in my hand had me half crazed.

At the very last moment, I managed somehow to stop myself before I flung my face down his dick and sucked his sap dry. There would be time for that later – if I could find a rubber that would fit him, though a glove or Hefty bag might be more on point. Meanwhile, it was time for me to cure my acute little friend of his chronic virginity. I flipped him over and spread those huge hard glutes to reveal a puckered mouth that ached to be kissed. Thick tufts of red hair guarded the approach, but the hole itself was the dictionary illustration of vulnerable desperation.

I aimed a jet of air against his shithole and set off a symphony of shudders and raptured palpitations that begged for my hand and dick and soul. I was gloved and lubed in an instant, pretending for the moment that Charlie's prostate really did need attention. My virgin sacrifice watched the show reflected in the mirrors at the head of the bed as I stroked my way across his shithole, lightly at first and then with a building insistence that left no doubt where our relationship would end up.

By the time I was rougher, poking slightly into his pucker with two fingers and my thumb and then darting back before his hole could eat me whole, Charlie was back waffling between coprolalia and prayer, his butt humping upwards against my hand as his dick plowed a sloppy furrow in my sheets. When I finally slid my fuckfinger through his hole, Charlie's whole body arched upwards and a groan of epic satisfaction rumbled its way from the very center of his virginal being. As I slipped across his prostate and got all rough and butch, Charlie went back to apostrophic screaming and blaming the Holy Family for his most grievous faults.

I gave him a break for a time as I used my second finger and thumb to loosen his hole, twisting and probing and stretching my way up his ass so that my nine inches of man-maker wouldn't rip loose anything I would have to stop and suture up. Then I went back to his prostate and rubbed him the right way – up his ass with one hand and along his spine and flanks and down his hard thighs with the other. His butt skidded way out of control, grinding and squeezing and lurching about like an electrocuted catfish; but I was so deep and happy up his ass, there was no way he was going to buck me free.

His hard, young body flailing around off the end of my hand was such a rush to watch that I let time and technique get the better of me. Charlie yelled something about needing to stop for a piss, but I was too busy to catch a clue. Then, suddenly, his butt seized up tight for an instant and then rammed forward as a fresh, hysterical "Jesus" ripped its way out of his mouth and his balls sprayed the last load of his boyhood in great spastic gushers of cream all over my sheets and up onto his furry belly and chest.

Ever the helpful healer, I ground harder at his butt-nut and reached low to squeeze his balls, too, as Charlie fucked my bed sodden and tried his damnedest to snap off my fingers. I let him have his fun until he was dry but for the dribbles, then I pulled my hand out, flipped his ass over, rubbered up, spread his stocky legs wide, and rammed my way through his shithole before he was even finished oozing out the last sweet threads of his Irish cream.

I reamed my way deep in one fast, cruel stroke until my soft pubes were molesting the shreds of his shithole and my swollen knob had found a new friend in his liver. Charlie's body had clenched tight against the pain of parting with his boyhood so I lurked deep and quiet within him for a time as his body paid the price for its education in the ways of men.

As my swollen dick purred away in the contentment of absolute possession up Charlie's ass, I took a slow, salacious stock of the ruin I had wrought. His eyes were still clenched shut against the pain, but his mouth gaped wide in panting Lamaze breaths as he gave birth to the realization of who and what he had become. I eased my eyes down across his rippled torso to find knots of outraged muscles half hidden below a sea of rust-colored curls and vast tides of pearly spooge.

The spectacle of young Charlie lying stunned and beautiful below me as his guts tried for the first time to find room for a man up his ass was too precious to rush. I hung there, suspended in the magic of the moment, for half an eternity. Then his gorgeous green eyes opened onto his new world and I couldn't resist leaning low to kiss his nose and lower lip. I reached down and twisted the last threads of his load from his still-swollen knob.

As I gave his butt a few jabs of warning, he licked my palm and fingers and was about to say something callow and cocky when I unleashed the full ferocity of my lizard up his ass.

His eyes clenched shut again, but I knew he could take everything I had to slam his way.

67

The next many moments were a terrible, tangled orgy of bodies hurled together, tongues lashed across cheeks and deep into ears, swollen nipples dragged beyond the brink of grief, and the ruthless ravages of my brutal man-maker slashing forever farther up Charlie's once-virgin ass.

His beauty and sweet virginity, both of body and spirit, conspired to make me forget myself. No longer was I a pal doing him the civilized favor of busting his cherry, I had become a brute beast, tearing from him his most tender secrets as my blood-gorged pizzle tore away the innocence of his flesh and reveled in every relentless, gut-wrenching thrust of bestial triumph.

My teeth held fast to his neck as my pounding hips powered the brutal instrument of his transformation and of my own rejoicing. Our bodies smacked together; our mingled grunts and moans and shrieks of pain-bred pleasure tore about my apartment like the tortured cries of Dante's most damned.

The sweet, sublime scent of jism and sweat and man-musk choked the air until we seemed to be gasping in great scalding lungfuls of golden honey that at once dazzled the senses and muffled the mind.

Sweat streamed and splattered from my body as I used Charlie's ass and his eyes finally opened again to offer absolution and encouragement and devoted gratitude. His lips kept pace with our love by mutely mouthing another "Jesus" each time my surgical tool slashed asunder yet another strand of that veil of boyish misconceptions which had so long hidden away his ultimate truth.

The harder I pounded his ass, the more he needed until we were trapped together through time in a place where nothing existed but our two hard, male bodies, each selfishly sharing the other until we ceased separately to exist and merged into a single, sublime, terrible whole of twisting flesh and rutting bone.

I might be there still if Charlie's body had not erupted again in another frenzied spectacle of excess, at once tasteless and savory beyond description. Jism flew up past his head, into my face, onto both of our sweaty hard-humping bodies in globular gushers that dripped and splattered and splashed like a terrorist bombing in a custard boutique.

I looked down between our surging bodies to watch Charlie's jism gape wider with every salvo, his tortured nuts huddled tight against my belly, and I surrendered unconditionally. Wave after searing wave of demoniacal rapture ripped my guts to shattered atoms and sprayed the plasma deep into Charlie's secret sanctum to glow there with a bright and penetrating radiance, binding us together, forever.

Even as I bucked and tore and blasted my way up his ass, I suddenly realized that however life leads us apart, however many men Charlie happens across or into, he will always remember the man who made him one. Every thrust and lick and sound and smell will burn bright in his memory until his final hour, linking us together in ways no medical training or rubber filled with jism ever could.

I slammed and spurted and tore up his ass until neither of us had anything left to give before I collapsed into his arms and wallowed about his sublimely gooey young body. We kissed and held each other, murmuring in the soft whispers of new love and accomplished lust, until both our dicks somehow found new strength and began slipping between our messy bellies, pulsing the promise of yet more passion to come.

After what seemed like an age, Charlie's hand drifted down my spine and slipped a wicked finger between my glutes, and I knew he wasn't finished with me yet – or I, him.

I also knew that our duty rotations would be a world more fun from then on. When we had patients, I would make him a doctor.

When times were slack, I would just take my time making him. A resident often has to ride his med students hard, but young Charlie's medical training was bound to be pure pleasure even if duty forced me to be an occasional pain in the ass.

# JUST THE BROTHERS
## (Second of Three Parts)
## Ronald James

It was two days after the sexual encounter with my brother Frank and his friend Ty, whom I'd caught playing with each other, before Frank spoke or even looked at me very much.

Of course that didn't stop me jacking off. I'd been doing that for about a year; I just wasn't hiding in the bathroom anymore or doing it quietly under my blanket at night.

We'd just gotten home from school that day. It was a Wednesday, and we were in the kitchen. Mom and Dad were still at work.

I pulled my dick out.

"You know if you keep doin' that you'll go blind," said Frank. "Then you do it for me. C'mon, Frank, look."

I practically ripped open my jeans, pushing them down around my knees. I stroked it a few times. "It's so hard, look! Come on Frankie, you know you like young stuff."

I moved close in front of him, hands on his shoulders gently pushing him down.

He sank to his knees and swallowed my cock.

I had my hands on his head now. All day long in school I'd planned to talk to him the way Ty had, tough, calling him dirty names, but as soon as he started sucking I forgot everything but the warm, wet, tingly feeling and just pulled his head into my crotch.

"I'm gonna come!" is all I said as I shot off in his mouth, then, "Thanks, Frank, it was good."

He stood as I pulled up my pants.

"Got a hard-on don't you?"

"No."

"I can see it."

"So what... leave me alone."

My brother had tears in his eyes.

"What are ya cryin' for?"

"I'm not."

"Ty's right, you are a fag."

"Leave me alone, just fucking leave me alone." He ran up to our room.

I did my homework in the kitchen and was finished by the time Mom got home to fix dinner. Dad got home a little later. W had dinner, then watched TV until ten.

"Okay, guys, time for bed."

"Goodnight," said Frank.

"Goodnight honey," said Mom.

" 'Night guys," I said.

"Goodnight, sweetheart."

"Night sport."

Mom, then Dad.

Frank was already in bed by the time I'd brushed my teeth and stripped to my shorts.

"Frank, hey Frank, Frank look at this." I was standing next to his bed. I'd hooked my thumb into my shorts and pulled them down just enough to expose my dick.

"Go to bed, Jamie."

Instead, I sat on his bed.

"How come you were cryin' before?"

"I wasn't."

"I'm sorry I called you a fag... okay?"

"Okay."

"Just blow me once... you can even jack off while you do it, then I'll go to bed. Really, it's okay, I don't mind if you beat it... I'll even watch if you want me to."

"No... come on... we're gonna get caught."

"No we won't, we'll be real quiet. Come on, just do me or I'll tell."

"Tell who?"

"Mom and Dad."

"What are you gonna tell 'em?"

"That you suck dick, that everybody at school knows, and.... Hey! That last time Ty said you should blow me so he could watch 'cause he likes to watch you. Who else do you blow?"

"Nobody."

"Yes you do, he said so... who else?"

"I said nobody," his voice began to tremble.

"Okay, okay don't start cryin' again, Jesus! Anyway I promise I won't tell, just tell me."

"His cousin Pat."

"Pat? Pat Lerner? Really? Pat Lerner on the football team?"

"Yeah, okay?"

"Jesus, he's like a star or something. Does he have a big one?"

"I don't want to talk about it."

"But you'll tell me another time, right? Right?"

"Okay."

"Promise?"

"I promise."

"Suck me off now."

I'd slipped off my underwear and was sitting naked, cross-legged on his bed.

"Look Frank, look at this," I pulled my dick down and let it snap up just as Ty had done a few days before.

Frank was sitting up now. "I love your dick, Jamie."

"I don't have any hair yet."

"I don't like hair."

"Man, Ty was right, you really do dig young stuff."

"I guess."

"You do anybody else beside Ty and Pat and me?"

"No."

"Never?"

"Never."

"Is yours hard?"

"Yeah."

"Let me see."

Frank folded back the covers. Somehow he'd slipped off his shorts while we were talking or maybe he'd been naked all the time. His dick was up, I could just make out the little hair around it in the semi-darkness.

"You can touch it if you want to," he said.

I leaned forward and touched the head then ran my fingers down the shaft to his hair, then down to his balls.

As I did this he reached out cupping my balls, stroking my cock.

"I like doin' this," he said. "You like playing with mine?"

"It's okay. But I don't suck."

"You don't have to, I'll suck you and you can just play with mine, okay?"

"Suck me now."

"Then you'll play with mine, okay?"

"Yeah, okay. C'mon, suck me! Suck me off."

"Lie back ... on your back."

As I did he crawled between my legs.

"You're beautiful, Jamie. I mean it, you're really beautiful. Your cock's so beautiful, it's really the only one I want."

All the while he spoke he was rubbing his dick head against my nuts.

"All day long I think about you, about blowing you. In gym class I see all the guys, some of 'em hung really big and some of 'em hung small like I like but the only dick I want is yours."

"I'm not small," I said. "Suck me!"

"You're my kid brother and all I want to do is eat your dick."

"I said, mine's not small, now suck me!"

"No, no that's... what I mean is you don't have any hair yet... that's all. I mean your dick is so beautiful I jack off in the boys room after almost every other class just thinking about it." "Eat me off now, Frank. C'mon, do it now."

"Tell me what to do."

"Eat me."

"No man, more. Tell me exactly what to do... you can call me names. Please Jamie, I like that, just the way Ty did."

I knew what he wanted, I didn't understand, but I knew what my brother wanted, needed.

"You're a fag," I whispered. "Aren't you?"

"Yes."

"You eat guy's dicks, don't you?"

Softly, "Yes."

"Say it."

"I eat dick, I'm a fag."

"You like young dick don't you, faggot?"

"Yeah, I do."

"Hairless dick?"

"Oh, fuck yeah. I love hairless cock. I think about hairless cock all the time, jacking it, sucking it, taking it up the ass. I'll be your slave, Jamie. Just tell me what to do, I don't care what it is, I'll do it, just tell me."

"Lick me, Frankie, lick my fucking dick."

He licked my dick from the head down to my balls.

"Now suck my cock, faggot."

He went down on me, taking the whole thing in his mouth: It felt so good lying there naked getting sucked.

I rose up on one elbow so I could watch him, pushing his head down over me with my free hand.

"Eat me, Frankie," I whispered, "eat me off, girl, little bitch girl, little dick lover, eat ... oh ... now, Frank, now, do it now." I creamed in his mouth. "Okay, okay, stop ... stop."

He let my dick slip from his mouth and began nuzzling my balls with his nose and tongue.

"You can jack off now," I said.

"Will you do it for me? You said you would."

"What do I hafta do?"

"Just play with it. Just like you do to yourself. Here, I'll lie back and you can do it easier."

He lay back and I leaned forward and started to jack it for him.

"Oh, oh yeah, it feels good! It feels so good getting my dick jacked off. I love getting a hand job. Do it, please do it. Oh, Jamie, I'm gonna shoot... don't stop, don't stop 'til I say to."

The jiz arced out of his dick twice, then dribbled down onto my fingers but I kept pumping like he said.

"Okay stop, Jamie. Stop. Wait, don't wipe off your hand. Straddle my chest... just come up here, come on, just come up here."

I straddled his chest and without being told what to do rubbed my cum slicked hand over his mouth. He licked and sucked my fingers, sucked his own jiz off my fingers.

"Did you like it, Jamie? Did I do a good job for you, licking your balls and giving you head just like you told me, and swallowing your cum just like you told me?"

"Yeah."

"Tell me how good I was; I was a good boy, wasn't I?"

"You were good, Frank."

"Frankie!"

"Yeah, you were good, Frankie. You suck dick real good, Frankie. You're a real good cocksucker."

"You want to fuck me, Jamie? You can if you want. You can fuck me up the ass if you want."

"Now?"

"We really can't do it now, but Saturday night when Mom and Dad are out we can do it then. You'll like it; it feels really good. When we do it, Ty tells me I'm better than a girl 'cause my asshole's tighter than pussy."

"I don't know.... "

"It's okay, you think about it, but it'll be great. Ty says it's miles better 'n a blowjob. You just think about it, okay?"

"I guess."

I went to my bed without putting my shorts back on. Naked under the covers I played with myself but I wasn't ready to come again.

"Jamie?"

"Yeah."

"Think about Saturday, okay?"

"Okay."

"'Night, Jamie."

"'Night, Frank ... Frankie!"

(The first installment appeared in Fresh 'N' Frisky; the final installment appeared in the STARbooks anthology *Taboo!*)

# FREE DELIVERY
## H.A. Bender

I had put off finishing my thesis for too long. Now here I was 32 and still without my doctorate, which I'd sworn I'd complete by the age of 30. Finding myself unexpectedly unemployed due to a corporate downsizing maneuver, I decided I'd get the damn thesis done before looking for another job.

Fortunately, money wasn't a problem. I lived cheaply, had earned well, and had a nice nest egg put by. But my friends were a problem. They thought the fact that I was unemployed meant I had lots of time on my hands – plenty of time to party, time to listen to their romantic woes and sexual frustrations, time to just sit and talk over a few beers or white zinfandels. In desperation I decided to finish my research as quickly as possible and then get out of town while I did the actual writing.

The cabin was simple but not primitive. There was one large room that served as living room with dining area and cooking area, and then a small but adequate bedroom. The plumbing was indoors, I was relieved to see. The overall appearance of the place was rough-hewn, but the woodstove kept away the chill of the September nights, the bed was firm and welcoming, and the round maple dining table served as a decent enough desk for my laptop computer.

The owner, who lived in town and mostly just rented the place out for summers, was grateful to get a renter out of season and gave me a break on the price. "It gets kinda lonely up by the lake, this time of year," he warned me. "Nobody much around."

"Great! That's just what I'm looking for!" I enthused.

But by the third day, I was hungry for a little human companionship. In addition, although I'd brought a supply of groceries with me, I was beginning to run low on a few items. I knew there was a cafe in town, where I hoped I might get a decent cup of coffee and some conversation. I also knew there was a small grocery store, where I might get the food supplies I needed without having to drive to the nearest big town and its supermarket.

Thinking I didn't need that much, I put two canvas bags in the basket of my bike and pedaled my way into town instead of driving. With a bagful of groceries in the basket and a canvas bag hanging from each side of the handlebars, I figured I'd be in good shape. But I bought more than I'd planned to and soon realized I'd have to make two trips to get it all home. Stuffed with the stack of pancakes I'd consumed in the cafe, I didn't really feel like doing all that pedaling.

"I could run it out for you, if you want."

I looked up. I'd been talking to the proprietor, who was behind the counter, and hadn't even realized there was anyone else present. In the doorway that led to the back of the store stood a young fellow. He was so young; he couldn't have been more than 19, and 18 seemed more likely – with a soft, babyish face, a trace of baby fat on his frame, long lashes, green eyes, reddish-brown hair, and big feet. I immediately found myself wondering if big feet really meant a big dick.

"You're the fellow renting Logan's cabin, right?" the soft voice asked. I nodded my head. "We don't get many strangers here this time of year. Summers, yes, but not now. I'm Curt. Bob's son." He strode out with his hand outstretched, and I turned away from Bob, behind the counter, to shake Curt's soft, pale hand. When I squeezed, he squeezed back and seemed to linger. I wondered if I dared read anything into that.

Though I don't swish, I've never hidden my gayness. I have a pink triangle on my bumper, and news travels fast in small towns. If anyone knew the significance of the symbol, by now the whole town probably knew my orientation.

"I was going to bring everything home on my bike," I explained apologetically to Curt, "but I'm afraid I got carried away and bought too much."

"You run your perishables home," Curt said, "and anything else you're going to need before this evening, and I'll be out later with the rest. It's no trouble. Just leave them here. But I won't get there till after supper."

"Would you like to have dinner with me?"

"Oh, no. Mom's cooking supper. But I'll be out after that, say around seven?"

True to his word, Curt showed up in an old but cared-for truck. He was all spiffed-up, with his hair slicked into place, his clothes changed, his face looking freshly washed. He had every appearance of a young guy out on a date. Hmmmm....

He didn't beat around the bush. After bringing in my groceries, he stood there as if he had something on his mind. I thought it was money and offered him something for bringing out the groceries. "Oh no, the delivery's free!" he protested. "But I would like to ask you something." He hesitated a second, then took the plunge. "Is it true you're ... uh ... I mean ... they say around the village, that you're ... uh ... gay?" His own eyes went wide as soon as he had said it.

I stared back at him.

"I hope I haven't offended you!" he blurted out.

I smiled. "You can't offend me with the truth – and I am gay."

"Well, then, I am too!" For the first time, his eyes met mine straight-on and looked deeply into them. "And it's so tough around here. There's nobody else that's gay in this town. I have to go so far away to ... well, you know ... to find someone to have fun with. Would you want to ... well, you know ... fool around?"

He had all the eagerness of a puppy who wants to play. He had the stick in his mouth and was offering it to me, if only I would toss it.

I looked him over again and liked what I saw. The youthful eagerness, the soft body, the fresh face, the hopeful eyes, and now I saw an interesting bulge discreetly hidden in his corduroys. Hmmm ... he might have been small, but his basket sure wasn't. Maybe it was true about big feet and a big dick. "Sure," I said, grinning. "Let's have some fun."

Curt's body absolutely quivered as he lay there on the bed. Even the hairs of his pubic bush seemed to shake with eager anticipation. His yearning eyes followed me around the room as I undressed, gathered up rubbers, made ready. When I returned to the bed and began grazing his thighs with my teeth, he tensed and started so strongly that I didn't know whether to think he was about to jump up and run off or about to come there and then. Fortunately neither was the case.

I nibbled at his thigh, working my way to his pubes, then grasped a few of his hairs in my teeth and tugged, pulling at them, till he was moaning loudly and tossing back and forth on the bed, begging me, "Quit teasing! I need it too bad!"

Fair enough ... but I wasn't really ready to start sucking him yet. I wanted a go at his balls first, so I took that wrinkled sac into my mouth and began to suck at his stones. While Curt beat the bed with his fists, groaning as if I were inflicting the worst kind of tortures on him, I traced the surface of his scrotal sac with my tongue, investigating the wrinkled furrows. I sucked the sac deeply into my mouth, respectful of his precious jewels but hungry for the salty-musky flavor. It's not safe to suck uncovered dick anymore, but fortunately it's still open season on the musk-rich flavor of a guy's ball bag.

As I sucked on his nutsac, the funky odors of a crotch rich with the day's sweat assailed my nostrils and went right to my brain. Those scents went straight to my cock; as the acrid sweat-smell went up my nose it seemed to travel straight down to my crotch. Soon I had a hand on my own wood, jacking lightly as I sucked Curt's stones.

"Suck me, please!" he groaned, begging. "Put a rubber on me and suck this load outta me." So I dressed him and sucked him, my lips encircling his corona and then slipping downward. I clenched the base of his prick in my hand as I sucked downward, jacking and sucking simultaneously, while his ass bounced on that bed as if someone had touched an electric cattle prod to it.

He had the bumpiest shaft I've ever sucked. Every guy's got veins and protrusions that keep his rod from being smooth, but I had never met a dick before that had as contoured a surface as Curt's did. Every jutting protrusion titillated my lips as the cylinder slid in and out of my mouth. Soon I began imagining what it would feel like sliding in and out of my ass. I'm usually a top, but there are exceptions to every rule, and just the imagined feel of this dick sliding in and out of my butt-hole sent thrills through my pulsating cock.

But for the moment I went on sucking. Curt wasn't lying there passively letting me suck, though. His ass was busy on that bed, lifting up, propelling his dick down my throat, stuffing my mouth full of hot meat. He crammed me full of dick and did his best to gag me, but I relaxed my throat while keeping my lips tight, and I kept up with him. As his meaty shaft prodded in and out of my mouth, my tongue flipped up and down the underside of it, tantalizing all the nerves that lived there.

But my mouth was having all the fun-and my hands wanted in on the action. One hand had been at the base of his dick but had long since let go to allow my mouth to take in the entirety of his shaft. That hand now went to work on his balls, squeezing the cum-laden containers rhythmically. The other hand squirmed beneath Curt's butt till one finger was planted right at the opening to his rectum.

Despite the fact that the finger was dry, it slid in without any fuss. Curt must have had the hungriest asshole in the East – his bunghole simply gobbled up my finger, so I inserted another and another, till I was fucking in and out of him with three fingers, driving them deep and tickling nerves that lined his asswalls. Curt was emitting a series of whimpers that sounded like an eager puppy.

His explosion came almost without warning. One minute I was driving three fingers deep up his humid rectum, feeling the clench of his anal sphincter as it grabbed my hand. The next minute, he had made a particularly powerful lunge, and his asshole was clenching my fingers so tightly it felt like he was trying to break them right off.

At the same time, his dick lunged deeper than ever down my gullet, and then he held the pose while his manmeat pulsated wildly in my throat, and I knew he was disgorging a massive cumload into the rubber. I squeezed his balls and swallowed a few times so my throat muscles would stroke his pounding prick as it spewed.

When he pulled out of my mouth, he had barely lost his hard-on; he was still more than halfway erect. I dressed his dick in fresh latex. Curt seemed confused; he apparently expected to suck me off next and didn't know why he needed a rubber for that. When I explained that I had a different plan in mind, his eyes lit up. Apparently, though he'd been fucked before, he'd never topped anyone.

Working the cool lube onto two fingers, Curt thrust the fingers roughly up my bunghole. In his eagerness, he was none too gentle, but his enthusiasm and excitement were contagious. Soon his fingers were sliding easily in and out of my willing asshole, which was itching to feel something bigger up there. "Fuck me," I urged him. I didn't have to ask twice.

Curt slathered generous dollops of lube all over the fresh rubber on his dick, then took his dick in hand and aimed it at my asshole. I felt the nose of his dick begin to poke its way within the grip of my sphincter, and then the whole head popped through and his dick was burrowing along my ass and zipping right up toward my belly.

When his balls were banging up against me, and he had no more inches to feed me, he pulled out again till only his dickhead remained lodged within me, then slammed his way back in again, driving his dick deep within me. I felt full; it had been a long time since I had been filled like this, and I found he was scratching itches I didn't even know I had, fulfilling needs I'd been oblivious to, and setting off sensations I'd forgotten about. I clenched my asshole as tight as I could and squeezed the guy's cock in a relentless clench.

"Play with my tits!" I seethed at him, and Curt gladly grasped my nipples and squeezed tight on the protrusive nubbins. Reaching up, I squeezed his tits as well. We molested each other like that as he went on driving his dick as far up my asshole as he could. It felt as if he were aiming so deep that I'd feel his dickhead poke up from my throat any minute now.

Thumping my ass up and down, I rode his pole while he drove it relentlessly in and out of me. Powering his dick up into my guts over and over, he broke out into a sweat and grew red in the face. I looked at that cute face and tried to remember what it was like to be 18, inexperienced, and on a voyage of discovery. It was hard to remember. But it was good to be sharing it with Curt.

My load was boiling in my balls. But I couldn't quite get it off without a little more help. "Jack my dick," I urged my young fucker. "Get me off."

So Curt let go of one of my nipples and wrapped his soft hand around my cock. With a practiced motion – if he was under-experienced at fucking, he surely had plenty of opportunities to jerk himself off – he slid his hand back and forth on my woody, urging my cum to erupt.

As he tugged demandingly at my cock, he continued fucking my asshole with his own rod, dicking me deep. Now he was urging me on: "Go. Come for me. Do it. Shoot, man, shoot your load!" He sounded like the soundtrack to a bad porn flick, but I was too hot to laugh. His words inflamed my balls, and I felt my whole body tensing as my balls tried to deliver my load.

He was about to deliver too. He wasn't waiting for me. He was too hot. Well, that was okay; I was about to spurt myself, about to ... about to ... ohhhhh! We came in unison, unplanned but happily, his throbber spurting a massive load deep in my bowels just as I shot my own load.

When we disentangled, I pushed young Curt down onto the bed and peeled my rubber off, sprinkling the contents onto his smooth, hairless chest, and then licked him clean of any hint of jizz.

This struck him as kinky to the max, but in the nicest possible way, so he traded places with me, peeled his own rubber off, doused me with his cum-cargo, and licked me equally clean.

By then, of course, we had both sprouted fresh hard-ons.

"I could arrange to...."

"Yes?"

"Well, I could deliver your groceries once a week ... or so," he said just before he gobbled up my freshly rubbered cock. "How long are you stayin'?"

"I may just have to stay longer than I'd planned," I answered. "And I like these deliveries the best," I added, squeezing his newly engorged dick. "You can deliver all the cream you'd like, as often as you'd like."

Then both our mouths were full as we worked our way into a heated sixty-nine, and neither of us said anything more for a while. But that's okay. We understood each other's needs perfectly well.

# SHAKEDOWN
## Corbin Chezner

"...He prowled the streets for cock, but he would never be satisfied again. Not until he had more dick from that damn blond...."

Wakefield appeared in the middle of the night - unexpectedly, as always. Harding, who would take the Chief's big cock any way he could get it, finally gave Wakefield a key to come and go as he pleased. Tonight, a full moon filtered through Harding's bedroom windows, illuminating Wakefield's magnificent body as he stood at the foot of the bed and undressed. Rubbing sleep from his tan-colored eyes, Harding, 28, watched transfixed, his self-control weakening- again. As desire surged through Harding's loins, his heart hammered against his chest. With clammy hands, he grasped his throbbing seven-inch cock. Already, the tool was so hard, pain shot through the engorged shaft. Moonlight danced off Wakefield's sexy shaved head as he dropped his shirt to the floor. Harding salivated, his mouth hungry for the Chief's powerful pecs. The Chief's pecs were damn near perfect -- symmetrical and muscular and covered by a carpet of black hair. Below the chest, the dark hair converged to a line that plunged to Wakefield's muscular stomach. Harding had never seen such a body on a 45-year-old. As Wakefield reached to unbuckle his belt, Harding's rock-hard cock pulsed in anticipation. Sometimes, when he arrived like this in the middle of the night, Wakefield maintained virtual silence. Other times his curses spewed like venom as he plowed whichever of Harding's orifices he favored that evening. Harding was no pansy. No one had ever controlled him. No one, that is, until Wakefield.

Wakefield stepped out of his underwear and his swollen meat sprang free. "Lube up." He directed a laser glance toward Harding. "Tonight, I want your butt."

Harding always followed Wakefield's orders. Always. Reaching into the nightstand next to the bed, he located the lube. He squeezed some of the lube onto his finger, lifted his legs off the bed, and massaged it into his quivering fuck hole. Wakefield threw back his head and laughed. When he met Harding's gaze again, the mirth had drained from his eyes. "How bad do you want this big cock?"

85

Gyrating his pelvis, he set his tool into motion. Harding stared at the swinging cock, his tan eyes unblinking, spit dribbling from the corners of his mouth. "Fuck me," Harding finally managed. "Please - fuck me now."

Laughing again, Wakefield climbed onto the bed, flipped Harding on his stomach, and before the younger man knew what had occurred, slipped his long cock halfway up Harding's hot ass. Wakefield's 8-inch cock was a good fit. Tight but good. That's what Wakefield liked - a tight fit.

The first time Wakefield tried to plug his butt Harding protested. "You're too big." But Wakefield just laughed and fucked him anyway. Moments later, Harding was begging Wakefield NOT to stop. It had been that way ever since - tonight included.

The day the Criminal Justice Authority awarded the jail contract to a private firm, Sheriff's Department personnel braced for the worst. Although the contract required United Corrections Corp. to offer current Sheriff's Department workers first shot at jobs at the new jail, word quickly circulated that major changes were imminent. Particularly miffed were the Guards. Under the sheriff, guards had functioned as deputies. In contrast, at UCC they would be demoted to the role of caretakers. Guards would lose not only their guns but also the power to arrest. Even though pay scales would increase slightly, guards generally considered the new positions an insult to their manly image. Particularly galling was the fact that at UCC they would be renamed corrections officers. Simmering with anger, some within the brotherhood, as they called themselves, vowed sabotage. If they could prove to the public that the Criminal Justice Authority had erred, the Sheriff might eventually resume jail operations, as God intended.

Jake Stemmons, 32, a five-year veteran of the Sheriff's Department, hired on at UCC, but only, he told himself, until something better came along. He longed to kick ass, the way they had at the old jail. But, no, the pansy-asses at UCC wanted him to treat inmates with "respect." Ha! Most of the mother fuckers deserved a hot poker up the butt, if anything. The brotherhood who hired on at the new lock-up had to be careful. Cameras were everywhere; the goddamned UCC brass was monitoring them something fierce.

From the moment Stemmons first stepped foot into Pod J16 at the new jail, the inmates sensed the C.O.'s rage. How could they not? The swarthy C.O. scrutinized inmates through smoldering slate-gray eyes and a chip bigger than the ponderous tool that filled his pants. Stemmons' attitude – attitude with a capital A – proved to be a magnet for confrontation. Today, things were even worse than usual. Stemmons had learned he'd been passed over for the Special Operations Response Unit – again. The privileges of SORT membership included not only higher pay but also the authority to kick butt when the situation called for it. The veteran C.O. mulled joining a class-action lawsuit filed by former deputies claiming UCC's employment practices were discriminatory. According to the suit, UCC favored new hires for SORT.

The 150 inmates of Pod J16 seemed particularly pleased that morning to oblige Stemmons his attitude. A cacophony of curse words and derisive laughter echoed throughout the dreary steel confines as inmates, dressed in orange jumpsuits, milled about the floor of the unit. By mid-afternoon, the acrid din had frazzled the nerves of C.O. Stemmons. Eyeing the clock above his control station, he counted the minutes until 3:30 lockdown. To keep the inmates in the dark about procedure, each day he commenced inspections at a different cell. Today, he would start with C-3, halfway down the right side of the pod.

"You got any contraband in here?" Stemmons demanded as he entered the cell.

The inmate stepped aside. "Nothin', sir," Lupe Guerrero, answered.

"Yeah? We'll see about that."

Normally, the 8'x 8' cells housed two inmates, but Guerrero's "cellie" had been released the day before. Each cell consisted of a bunk bed on one wall, a lavatory, and a toilet. Stemmons rifled through the inmate's belongings as Guerrero waited outside the cell, rocking nervously from one foot to the other. A tuft of black chest hair peaked through the v-neck of his jumpsuit.

Lifting the mattress off the upper bunk, Stemmons suddenly spotted contraband. He snatched the object off the steel bed: "What the fuck's this, Guerrero?"

"What, sir? I don't know nothin' about it."

"You ever hear of a goddamned shank?" Stemmons tossed the object onto the bed.

"I don't know nothin' about it."

"Yeah, sure." Stemmons grimaced. At the old jail he could have kicked ass right then, when it counted. Immediate response: That's what these thugs needed to keep their fucking priorities straight. But UCC's goddamned regulations required him to alert Security. Reluctantly, he plucked a radio off his belt loop and punched in the extension.

"Security." Stemmons recognized the voice of Dan Wakefield, Chief of Security. Wakefield, a 10-year UCC veteran, had transferred to the new jail from another facility.

To prevent inmates from hearing, Stemmons cupped the mouthpiece. "Code 312 on J16."

Both men understood that "312" indicated a shank, a non-lethal object converted into a weapon. "What type?"

"A toothbrush."

"Damn," Wakefield thought. Toothbrush shanks were as common as body lice at correctional facilities. Any inmate could easily sharpen a toothbrush into a knife. Nevertheless, used correctly, a toothbrush shank could prove deadly. As decreed by Jail Policy 195.A-2, Wakefield immediately activated the SORT unit for a shakedown,

The 15-member SORT unit assembled hastily and advanced down a long corridor toward the security desk, where Wakefield waited to brief them. As the team approached, the Security Chief blew a whistle and the men stopped.

Squaring his shoulders, the security chief inspected the men. Because of his own rigorous daily physical routine -- 10-mile runs and two-hour workouts – the chief had no qualms about demanding a similar level of fitness for SORT members. He felt particularly pleased by the unit's uniform – beret, shirt, pants, shiny work boots – all black. The monochrome outfit looked intimidating, an effect that served the SORT purposes well.

Suddenly, Wakefield's gaze fell on Tim Harding, and his big cock pulsed. Goddamn, the young fucker was a pleasure to look at – and even more fun to fuck. This wasn't the first time he had violated UCC policy by fraternizing with a subordinate. And, most likely, it wouldn't be the last. Wakefield had few vices, but young cock and butt he found irresistible. Potentially, he could lose his job if Harding squealed. But if there was one thing he'd learned in twenty-odd years of corrections it was how to control his subordinates. It had become a game with him. A challenge.

Obviously, the blond C.O. had taken to heart Wakefield's admonition that SORT members remain fit. Initially, Wakefield worried that Harding was too much of a looker for a career in corrections. Good looks, after all, particularly extreme good looks, could potentially undermine a C.O.'s authority. But, much as he hated to admit it, Wakefield knew there was more to it. A fainter voice, a voice in the back of his mind, warned that in today's image-conscious corporate world Harding's good looks eventually could threaten Wakefield's own job. At 45, Wakefield still had time left until retirement – but considerably less than Harding. That harsh reality left Wakefield wanting to grind his boot into Harding's pretty face and then to order him to eat the Chief of Security's ass. Wakefield laughed to himself. If he had his way, all SORT members would be required to eat the Security Chief's ass. Well, the good looking ones, anyhow.

Harding had garnered Wakefield's attention his first day on the job. C.O Jake Stemmons reported Harding created a stir among inmates as the tall C.O. first entered Pod J16 and flashed his cerulean eyes. Despite Wakefield's initial concerns, however, in six months Harding's job performance had been nothing short of exemplary. Several months after his hire date Harding earned a spot on the SORT unit.

As Wakefield prepared to brief the men for the shakedown, Tim Harding, nervously eyed the wall clock above the chief's head. This would be his first shakedown, and he worried about his performance. The six-week SORT training had been rigorous. What if he fucked up? Beads of sweat dampened his forehead, and suddenly he felt woozy. His ears buzzed and his mind reeled. This was not just ANY shakedown. This was a Code 3 – a body cavity search. One wrong move and he could be out on his ass. That was the way it was in corrections. Even worse was the fact that before his promotion to SORT, Harding had worked on J16, where the shakedown was to occur. He hoped the inmates he worked with on the pod had either pulled chains or been released.

As Harding's gaze returned to the Chief, his half-hard cock stirred and his balls tingled. The square-jawed chief always gave Harding a raging hard-on, usually at the most inopportune moments. Damn, Wakefield was hot. To Harding, young pretty men were a dime a dozen. He craved seasoned men like Wakefield. Men who could tame his wild young ass. Wakefield was all man. Masculine with a capital M. A man's man. No one knew about his relationship with Wakefield, of course. If his coworkers found out, his balls would be in a wringer.

Powerful as it was, Harding recognized his connection to Wakefield transcended physical attraction. Why was Wakefield's approval so important? Damn if he understood why the Chief compelled him to ever-higher levels of achievement. A part of him resented Wakefield for worming his way into his life. But at this point there wasn't a damn thing he could do about it.

Suddenly, Wakefield's commanding voice jarred Harding from his introspective thoughts: "Harding: cite the policy on force."

Startled, the young C.O. grappled for an answer. Damn, why hadn't he kept his mind focused? Harding's heart hammered against his chest. It seemed like eons passed before his own voice unexpectedly rescued him: "The least amount necessary to complete the task, sir." Perhaps he was better prepared than he thought. As their gazes crossed, the C.O. detected a glint of approval in the Chief's eyes. Or had he?

At the conclusion of his briefing Wakefield cautioned: "Remember, men, in a shakedown, particularly a Code 3, surprise and intimidation remain your principle allies. Any questions before you go in?"

The SORT unit resumed its advance to J16. Wakefield telephoned ahead and ordered the pod officer to lock down the inmates in their cells: "Tell them to strip and lay prone on their bunks until further notice."

The steel door slid shut as the last SORT officer stepped into J16. Seven men fanned out toward the stairway to the upper floor of the pod while seven dispersed to cells on the bottom floor. One man stayed behind to guard the exit.

As he prepared to enter his first cell, Tim Harding tried to bolster his confidence by silently repeating Wakefield's two strip-search maxims: surprise and intimidation, surprise and intimidation, surprise and intimidation. Taking a deep breath, he tore open the door to Cell MM, stomped over to the inmate's bunk, and ordered, "Spread 'em, sir."

As Harding perused the inmate, he recognized the naked backside of Danny Jacobs. Jacobs had been housed in the pod when Harding worked it prior to his SORT assignment. To Harding's horror, his own cock pulsed as he scrutinized the inmate's beautiful moon-like buttocks. Damn. At a time like this, sex should be the last thing on his mind. Harding's mind reeled. Outside the cell, the clatter increased considerably as the SORT unit plundered its way through the inmates' cells. Harding's attempt to block sex thoughts ~~~~~ miserably. He yanked Jacobs' butt cheeks apart, clicked on the flashlight, and probed the inmate's rectum for contraband. Harding tried to ignore his own big tool, which had grown rock hard. "You got any shanks in here, Jacobs?"

The dark-haired inmate looked back at him, his green eyes blazing with desire. "It makes me goddamned hot when you take charge like that, Hard-on." Then he spread his legs further apart and lifted his torso slightly off the bed. "I'm all lubed up, man," he hissed, rolling his buttocks suggestively. "I need some cock in me bad, Hard-on. Plow my hole good. I know you got a big one, man. I know it. Give it to me - please. Do it now," he urged. "Before it's too late."

A flurry of opposing thoughts rampaged through Harding's mind. His hard, throbbing cock urged him to climb onto the bed and fuck the shit out of the inmate. Yet his sensible self resisted his animalistic urgings, imploring him to disregard the raging hormones fueling the inflated hose in his pants. What the fuck was he thinking? He was a goddamned professional, by God. Sex with an inmate would violate every rule in the book. Then, as his gaze fell again on Jacob's muscled butt cheeks, his resistance weakened and Harding's simmering meat gained control of him. As if in a dream, he watched his own hand unzip his fly and draw his dick out. Without hesitating, he scaled the bed, straddled the inmate, and plugged his throbbing cock inside his ass. The din grew louder outside the cell, and both men realized they had to finish quickly. Lubed and aroused, Jacobs gasped as Harding's massive hose entered him. The C.O. grasped the inmate's waist for leverage and slid his cock all the way in until his man-size balls slapped against the crack of Jacob's ass. "Do it," Jacobs urged breathlessly, digging his fingers into the side of the bed. "Oh, man, I love to feel your big balls slapping my ass. Do it!"

Harding fucked the inmate silly – in and out, out and in, faster, harder. Jacobs hissed and groaned and flopped his head against the bed. An instant later, Harding convulsed, arched his head toward the ceiling, and cried out "Mother fuck!" as he shot the inmate's quivering butt full of jism. An instant later, Jacobs cried out, "Oh, man!" as he jerked and fired his own load into the bed.

Back at his home later that evening, Harding tossed and turned in bed, besieged by guilt and confusion. What the fuck had he done? Six months ago during training class the warden cautioned the new C.O.s to "forget about this place when you go home." Good advice, but Harding was seldom able to heed the admonition, particularly after a stressful day. During the bizarre shakedown, he had managed to zip up and resume his duties, seemingly without detection. But he worried about repercussions. Had anyone seen? If confronted, Harding would lie, of course.

As he lay in bed staring at the ceiling, Harding recalled the three months he spent as a pod officer on J16. During that time, he came to know the husky, square-shouldered Jacobs all too well. Jacobs became a master at dishing out grief to Harding. It began the day a utility officer led the inmate into the pod. In vivid detail, Harding recalled how Jacobs' penetrating eyes had bore into him as the utility officer led the new inmate toward the check-in desk. As Harding fumbled for the paperwork to log in the new inmate, his own cock had pulsed with desire. Sensing Harding's discomfort, Jacobs thrust his head toward the ceiling and guffawed. Jacobs gained the upper hand that day and Harding never recovered from it. Each shift when Harding passed out supplies during lockdown, Jacobs would sit on the toilet and jack off his big tool when Harding entered the cell. "This cock could be yours, Hard-on," he taunted. "Anytime you want it." Most times Harding successfully averted his eyes. But on weak-willed days his gaze locked on Jacobs' throbbing meat.

The next weekend, back home, Harding was rolling the lawnmower into the garage when a pickup truck pulled into the driveway. Harding didn't recognize the vehicle, but when the driver got out he realized it was Jake Stemmons, the C.O. from Pod J16.

"Stemmons, what are you doin' out this way?"

The C.O. smiled as he walked up the driveway. "Looks like you about got your yard in shape."

Harding finished parking the lawnmower in a corner of the garage. "Damn grass gets thicker every year."

"I needed some supplies from Home Depot," Stemmons said, pointing to the load of materials in the back of his truck. "What you up to, now that the yard's done?"

"How about a beer?" Harding motioned for Stemmons to follow him inside.

"How'd you know where I live?" Harding asked. He popped open a beer and slid it across the kitchen counter to Stemmons.

"You told me when we worked together on J16. Don't you remember?"

"Oh, yeah," Harding lied, surprised that Stemmons would remember his address.

On the third beer, Stemmons dropped the bombshell. "I saw you fucking Jacobs that day."

Harding recoiled. His heart pounded crazily against his chest. Slowly, he met Stemmons' gaze. "What you gonna do about it?"

"That depends on you."

"How so?"

"When I watched you pounding Jacobs' ass that day, my first reaction, I admit, was to report you to the Chief. I'm sure it's no surprise, Harding, that I was pissed royally when you made SORT and I didn't."

Harding shrugged. "I guessed as much."

"But something kept my eyes glued on your butt, and suddenly I sprung a goddamned hard-on! Big as day!" He gulped down some more beer. "Me, with a goddamned wife and two kids."

"So?" Harding asked nervously. "What now?"

Stemmons drained the rest of his beer and slammed the empty can back on the counter. When he finally met Harding's gaze again, flames leapt in his eyes. "I got to have some of what that mother fucker Jacobs had." He crushed the beer can in his fist and gulped. "I got to."

By the time they got to the bedroom, Stemmons still seemed nervous, but Harding wasn't about to let that get in the way of a good time. Since Stemmons was a married man and appeared to have minimal experience with another man, Harding took charge. "Strip and get on the bed," he ordered.

When they were both naked, Harding pressed himself against Stemmons and French kissed him. One thing he couldn't stand it was a man who didn't like to kiss. To his surprise, Stemmons returned the deep kiss, his hungry tongue probing Harding's.

Harding led Stemmons to the bed. "I want you on your back," he said. "so I can watch the fire leap in your eyes when I fuck you." Harding pinned Stemmons against the bed as he reached into the nightstand for the lube. Harding decided Stemmons was as hot as Wakefield but in a different way. His 32 year-old body was lean and cut but not overbuilt. Broad shoulders capped his v-shaped upper. A smattering of dark brown hair was sprinkled across his u-shaped pecs.

His cock mirrored his body-perfectly shaped and just the right size, around 6 and a half inches of thick meat, Harding assessed.

Harding massaged lube into his throbbing cock. Then he squirted some more lube on his index finger and inserted it in Stemmons' hot hole. Stemmons closed his eyes and gasped. As Harding probed his hole, he began to roll his buttocks. "Stick your big hose in me," he finally managed, "not your damn finger."

Harding didn't have to be asked twice. Massaging more lube into his seven-inch dick, he lifted Stemmons' butt of the bed and guided his missile to the opening of Stemmons' fuck hole. Stemmons gasped again as Harding entered him. Stemmons pushed deeper, but slow enough for Stemmons to adjust to his tool. Finally, the tip of Harding's tool tickled Stemmons' prostrate, and the married man wailed with pleasure. "Don't stop now," he managed breathlessly.

Harding continued fucking Stemmons, slowly gaining speed. Then, grasping Stemmons' buttocks, he fucked faster, harder. Stemmons moaned and thrashed his head against the bed. "God damn, fuck me good."

Finally, Harding convulsed and pumped Stemmons' quivering asshole full of hot jism. An instant later, without ever touching his dick, Stemmons shot a load of cum against Harding's stomach.

As Harding climbed off him, Stemmons marveled. "I've never done that before. Come without touching myself, I mean. Except in a wet dream."

Stemmons left around five, just in time for Harding to get another load up before Wakefield arrived.

Meanwhile, former inmate Danny Jacobs, who had been released from jail that morning, prowled the streets for cock. He would never be satisfied again. Not until he had more dick from that goddamned blond, C.O. Hard-on.

# THE TAKING OF A BOY
## from "Orpheus to the Men of Thrace"

No reason for a poet to be coy.
I recommend the taking of a boy
To lunch, to heart and, somewhere in between
To bed. The ideal age is any teen.
No matter how complete he seems his youth
Will not endure. Develop a sweet tooth:
A boy will give you no return but honey
And sticky inspiration. Take some money
For the reluctant are coercible.
Oh, and their bodies are reversible.
  – *Gregory Woods, "May I Say Nothing" (Carcanet Press)*

# PRETTY BOY
## Brother Grundy

This pretty boy is kept, and sells his body
To pay the rent – for rings, a car, free toddy,
His is a rough trade, adding new scars
To twisted feelings from rejected childhood,
Wherein no constant image earned his love,
And where no step-relations understood.
Free rent, free rings, free liquor-
Poor substitutes, alas, for mother's paps!
He needs a girl so bad to prove his manhood,
The IDEAL GIRL, if he could only rape her
Once a night, he'd prove his point perhaps.

Opulent aunties breed such inner guilt
He picks the scapegoat queen and cracks his skull,
To fortify his feeling of himself as He;
A drink, a gun, and other manly gear
Prove then in public he is no damn queer.
Our sissy boy grows anti-social, tough,
Hooligan aggression leads to jail and bail,
Until the analyst at last will call his bluff.
He merely wanted money, but that was not enough;
Eros escaped him. Love is not for sale.

# IRRESISTIBLE
## Antler

If all that existed of boys
was the smell of their crotches
and armpits and healthy breath
It would be enough
to found a religion on,
It would be enough
to have a visionary experience over
that could alter the future of the world.
If only boys' cocks and balls existed
and the rest of their bodies not
and the boycocks grew from the earth
like mushrooms
or from trees
like fruit,
They'd still be great
and worthy
of getting excited about,
About wanting to play with them
and make them stiffen
and spurt.
Or if boys didn't have cocks and balls
but only buttocks
they'd still be
irresistibly desirable:
A beautiful pair of boy buttocks
isolated from the rest of a boy's body
and imaged in the minds of poets
since poetry began
Makes even dead prophets jealous.
Obsession? Perversion? Hardly.
A boy spends more time
thinking about sex in a day
than I do in a week.

# OH, THAT PLACE
## Carl Miller Daniels

down in the ruins,
naked boys collide like smooth boats with big masts.
fluids appear on shiny copper skin.
there is the aroma of the sea.
small talk evaporates like tufts of heated candy.
plaintive mouse-like cries bounce off the sides
of old buildings, covered in dust.
whimpers.
gurgling.
small birds sing from rotting roof-tops.
flashes of sunlight on
scraped elbows, dinged-up shins.
lips are dry, but licked with shiny spit.
when evening falls,
the same --
but dark.

# SPECIAL SECTION:
# COWPOKE TALES

Cowboys have always had a special place in the hearts of gays. These images from the past are courtesy of our long-time STARbooks contributor William Cozad.

# MUSTANG AND SADDLEBRED
## Lewis Frederick

Addison Lee had what my dear old drunken dad used to call 'fuck you money.' That meant he had enough to tell everyone to go to hell and never have to worry about being sorry for it.

The Lee estate out on Campground Road stretched as far as the eye could see, way over to the county line where the old army training base used to be. The Federal government still owned the Army base, but Addison Lee swore he'd have that acreage too one day and no one doubted for a minute he'd get his way eventually. That's what Addison did better than anybody – get his way. Sometimes it took him a while and sometimes someone had a real bad accident along the way. But Addison always won out in the end – most of the time anyway.

My family were shanty Irish who lived in the backwoods near the one-man sawmill my dad ran for a living, when he was sober anyway. We mainly lived on whatever my mom made taking care of rich people's houses, plus whatever she made at home, lying on her back, taking care of soldiers from the camp before it closed.

One summer, mom got a job working for the Lees during one of their big garden parties. It was one of those times when they took on extra help to impress all their rich friends even more. Mom dragged me along to help her lift the heavy garbage cans she was supposed to empty.

All that night, I hung about the kitchen of the Lee estate, helping out mom and snitching all kinds of crazy-looking little sandwiches off discarded food trays. I worked real hard too, carrying out trash and making sure my mom didn't tire herself out too bad. I had just turned eighteen and was big as a house, but all muscle and bone, skinny as a tall tree, with little ripples popping up all over my stomach, thighs and forearms. I don't think we even had a mirror at our place in those days so I had no idea what I looked like at the time. But every now and then, some woman I'd pass on the street in town would drop her jaw staring at me, or more to the point, at my crotch. So I figure I didn't look too bad in my own way.

Along about dusk, mom was elbow-deep in dishes and said it looked like she'd be there for hours, so why didn't I make myself scarce and go out and enjoy the evening air. Since it was hot and sticky in that kitchen, I jumped at the chance to get out of there. I wandered through the back regions of the estate, munching on more of those strange little sandwich things, and listened to the party cranking up real good over in the rose garden.

Over the sounds of the band, I heard another, more interesting sound. A horse whinnied from somewhere far off and I turned to see where the noise came from. That's when I noticed for the first time there was a huge stable, far from the house, but lit up like a Christmas tree, just like every other building on the place, and clearly visible now that it was dark. I had always had a fondness for horses, so I finished up my sandwiches and hurried on over there.

Coming up on that big barn at last, I felt like I was coming home. Inside, the place struck me just like a church. Its big boarded ceiling stretched up to a peak, the huge loft up there stuffed with fat bales of hay. Behind the stall doors, sleek, sleepy-eyed giants rustled their noses among their hay flakes, snorting gently to themselves and each other.

Those horses and that barn made my folks and my home look like wild things in a cage – they sure lived better and cleaner than my people ever did. I didn't mind, though, because I figured any animal as beautiful as these creatures must have been pretty special and deserved anything good they got out of life!

It never occurred to me not to do what I did next and that was walk right into each of their stalls and say hi. Some of the horses shied away a bit at first, but I soon got their confidence by talking real soft to them, until pretty soon we were all good friends. I couldn't get enough of them, put my face right into their necks and took long deep smells, hugging on them like they were long-lost buddies.

There's just something about a horse's coat that smells and feels so damned good to me. It's kind of like a nice clean man. You know the way they smell, down there that is, when they're getting worked up, kind of salty and sweet and musky all at once – I'm talking about men here now, not horses, for the moment anyway. Well, it's hard to describe, but that's one of the best things about horses. They smell just like a man who's ready for sex, only the horses smell like that all of the time, whether they're ready for sex or not.

I was thinking about this matter and figuring it all out for the first time, when I heard voices coming down the corridor. Two guys approached, looking like they were checking the horses before turning out lights for the night. When they got to the stall I was in, one of them punched the other on the arm and pointed at me.

"I'll be damned," his buddy said, his jaw dropping. "That crazy boy's in Satan's stall and he's still alive."

Later I would learn I had been making nice with a stallion that had been known to trample anyone who came into his space. At the time, I just thought he was a big old baby.

"You better come with us," the first guy said. The two ushered me into the tack-room and told me to sit down. That tack room was nicer than most living rooms I had been in, leather sofas and chairs all over the place, a wet bar, and saddle racks and bridle hooks all along the walls, dripping with polished leather riding gear. The room was empty when I got there but soon afterward the door opened and I saw Addison Lee for the first time.

He was an older man, but fit and young-looking under his silver mane of hair. He had a big frame with wide shoulders and burly arms, a barrel chest tapering down to muscled thighs that strained against the tux he was wearing at the time. I mainly remember seeing cool gray eyes against a pink, weathered face. It wasn't the kind of face I was expecting to find on the richest man in six states. I would have said he looked cruel except for something about his mouth, something kind of tender or pouty-looking there.

He didn't introduce himself or shake my hand or anything. He just stood there, looking me up and down, real cool and calculating, for a long, long while. I don't know what he intended with that look but if he meant to rattle me, it worked. I felt my stomach knotting up and sweat breaking out on my brow. And as usual when I get anxious, I started getting a hard-on. Addison didn't miss that detail either, but let his eyes linger down there a while before he finally spoke.

"I hear you have a way with horses," he said

"Well I don't know about that, sir," I stuttered. "I just know I love 'em."

He grunted and allowed himself a short smile that revealed perfect white teeth. "You looking for work?"

I jumped at the chance. "If you mean here, sir, sure."

He nodded and smiled a small smile again, then turned to go. "We'll start you under the head groom and see what you can do," he said. "I presume tonight will be convenient?" But he didn't wait to hear my reply. He was already out the door.

- - -

Well, I started under the head groom alright, and it wasn't long before the head groom was under me, so to speak. I never saw such a randy bunch of guys as the crew that worked in the Lee family's stables. We all shared a dormitory room up in the loft and it was fixed up real nice, considering it was just a flop house for a bunch of wandering wranglers.

There were nights in that dorm room that you couldn't tell who was doing who, but you knew from all the heavy breathing and cussing that some pretty heavy action was going on. I know I saw a lot of it on my own sagging cot. Me and the boys damn near broke the bed frame a time or two banging balls after lights were out.

Under the circumstances, it's amazing I ever learned anything about horses. But I did, and soon rose among the ranks of stable hands to a position of trust and importance. That meant the head groom let me shovel out of the stalls of only the most expensive and cantankerous of Addison Lee's babies. I don't mind admitting I was pretty scared of what that cold-hearted son-of-a-bitch. might do to me if any harm ever came to one of his animals. They were the only living things I ever saw him soften up to, and somehow his favorite ones were always the ones most likely to take a big bite out of your butt when your back was turned.

Even so, I loved those crazy animals and they loved me back. There wasn't a one I couldn't get close to eventually, and after a while, folks really did take notice that I had a way with horseflesh. That's when the good stuff started happening. The stable master put me in line to become an actual trainer myself, and I started learning the ropes from the bottom up.

I started with tending pregnant mares and birthing foals, then worked my way up to halter-breaking colts and gentling skittish yearlings. Before long, I was riding big five-gaited saddlebreds, mainly for their daily exercise or to warm them up for a big competition. Finally, I got to ride in an amateur class now and then in some of the smaller horse shows when the winnings were no big deal and the media weren't videotaping.

Finally we found ourselves at the World Champion Five-Gaited Saddlebred Show at the Kentucky State Fair. It was the first time Addison had traveled that far to a show and he had sunk a lot of money just getting there. The whole lot of us were nervous as hell just being there at all, everyone but Addison, that is. Like usual, he was cold as ice. Camera crews from all over the world were covering this event and he rode in almost every class himself. He was one hell of a horseman, probably the best I've ever seen.

Then just before his biggest class, the horse he was riding, Dominator, shied real bad when a couple of kids lit off some fireworks near the workout ring. Addison took a bad fall and wrenched an old game knee. Medical people were there right away, poking and prodding at him and trying to calm him down but he was cussing and waving them away.

"Put the kid on Dominator and follow through with the class!" he shouted as they helped him up. "The kid" was his name for me and that meant he wanted me to ride his best horse for him. I didn't have time to get nervous but just suited up real quick, mounted Dominator and went on out into the show ring.

That night it felt like I could do no wrong. Even though Dominator was a big, surly brute, he was one fine bunch of muscle and we had always gotten along just fine. He burst into that coliseum like a rocket and tore through the routine full of fire and glitter. I was just along for the ride and it was some kind of a ride all right.

When the judges announced their decision, sure enough, Dominator took first prize in the class. I rode him in a victory pass round the ring, holding the silver champagne bucket he had won high over my head. The crowd loved us and I made an extra pass, feeling special eyes on me somewhere.

Somehow in that crazy, cheering mob, I found Addison, leaning against a crutch and watching me with those cold gray eyes of his, drilling a hole in me with them. I didn't know what he was thinking, but I got a strange feeling in my gut. The feeling got worse when I left the stadium and got back to the stalls, where someone told me the boss wanted to see me right away in his room.

I don't know what I expected from Addison that night, maybe thanks or congratulations. But he had a way of doing the unexpected.

"Pull off these boots," he barked at me when I walked into his suite at the posh hotel by the fairgrounds. Some EMS people were still hovering over him, trying to talk him into going to the hospital, and they looked a little surprised at his harsh tone with me.

"Go on, get out of here!" he hollered at them then and they did, fast.

I did what I was told. This was The Man, after all, and I wasn't going to blow the best job I'd ever had. Tugging on his boots, I saw Addison wince a little bit and I have to admit I enjoyed seeing his discomfort after he had been so rude to me. I also noticed how thick and muscled his legs were as I made contact with him physically for the first time. He wasn't a tall man, but he sure was a big one.

"Now the socks," he said, once the boots were off. I peeled off his socks, noticing how soft and fine they felt. Addison never took his eyes off my face the whole time.

"Guess you feel pretty good right now," he grunted.

I couldn't help but smile. "It's been a pretty good day, sir, I must admit."

He just grunted again and this time I noticed a little smile playing about the corners of his mouth. "Help me into the Jacuzzi," was all he said.

I got him up with his arm around my shoulders and we started hobbling toward the bathroom. I was a lot taller than he was so it was a bit of a reach for him and he slipped his arm down around my waist after a few steps. Walking this way, his big, meaty hand was holding onto my hip, just inches from my groin. By the time we reached the Jacuzzi I had a major hard-on showing through my pants.

"Fill the tub," he said. "Then help me off with my clothes."

I did what I was told, noticing when I turned back from the tub that he was watching my every move. I still thought he was just in a mood, though, and began helping him pull his shirt tail out. Once the shirt was off I had to remark to myself what a massive frame he had. In spite of his age, his flesh was firm and gently muscled, the pink flesh glowing with health and dusted lightly with crisp black hair. Only his nipples were plump and soft-looking, a little darker than the skin around them, and I wanted suddenly to kiss one of them.

Sometimes Addison had the unsettling ability to make you think he could read your mind. I had no sooner formed the thought that I wanted to taste his nipples than he upped the ante on me considerably and changed my life for good in the process.

"Now the pants," he said in a soft, steely tone. I bent to unbuckle his fly and begin working his pants down around his legs when he stopped me. "No – on your knees," he said. I shot him a questioning look. "You heard me right," he said.

I still didn't know for sure what was going on but I figured I wasn't in a position to argue, so I knelt down on my knees and continued the business of getting his pants off. His legs, like the rest of his body, were pillars of muscle and dusted with short black hair. At the top of his thighs, that hair thickened and formed into little swirls. Beside those hair swirls, the already considerable bulge of his basket seemed to grow larger as I watched.

Just inches from his body at this point, I began to notice something remarkable, and that was the scent that rose from his flesh. I can't describe it exactly, but it was like when you walk into a really expensive clothing store, the type where you know there's all kinds of good stuff there and none of it you can afford. You smell leather, and wool and fancy colognes and soaps, all mixed together. Just about the time you're thinking you could really get used to a place like this, some uppity salesman comes up to you and says "Deliveries go to the rear!"

Well, that's how Addison Lee smelled to me just then. Hunkered down on my knees in front of him, staring at his crotch, I couldn't look him in the eyes just then because I was afraid he would see the kid in the store in me, the kid who just wanted to hang around awhile where the good stuff was but who always got kicked out for being white trash. I felt all funny and tender inside, almost like I wanted to cry. I don't know what was going on with me, but whatever it was, Addison burst the bubble pretty quick.

"Do you like your work?" he asked. When I didn't answer right away, he grabbed my chin in one of his powerful hands and squeezed a little bit, pulling my face up to look at his. His eyes were a mile deep and telling some story I couldn't read right now. "Answer me when I ask you a question."

"Yessir," I said. "I like it just fine."

"You want to keep your job?" he asked, almost a whisper now.

I just nodded my head, the jaw still clutched painfully in his tight grip.

"Then I think you know what to do, don't you?" he said.

All I really knew for sure then was that I was clearly out of my league here. Life on the Lee estate had been just fine with me. I liked my duties and I enjoyed my buddies in the dorm. I'd always kind of admired Addison and would have done just about anything he wanted on my own. But somehow he'd decided he had to make things tough on me. Rich people! There was no figuring them out.

Hell, why not, I finally decided, and pulled the elastic of his briefs down with a big yank. All of a sudden, I wished I'd just said 'no thanks' and quit. Addison Lee had the fattest dick I'd ever seen. Like pretty much everything else on his body, it was short but thick and full of life. It bobbed in my face right now, the broad, puckered head oozing pre-cum. Raised blue veins along its shaft pulsed so hard you could almost count his heartbeats in them. I was trying to figure out what to do with the damn thing when Addison got impatient and answered the question for me.

Shifting his hand on my chin to the back of my neck he grabbed my hair and pulled hard. When I opened my mouth to shout in pain he plunged his cock into it with one giant thrust. Taking my head now in both hands, he worked my mouth down around his meat all the way to the base, where my lips brushed against the coarse pubic hair.

I had always loved this moment with another guy, the time you first go down on him and drink in the sweet, salty smells and tastes. But even though I would have gladly done that with Addison, he seemed determined to choke me to death instead. He rammed that fat head all the way down my throat till I gagged.

On and on he went, fucking my face with his strong hands holding both my ears. Just about the time I'd begin to get the hang of how to work my throat and tongue around it good enough to get a breath, he'd push it in hard again and plug up my airway.

"More!" he'd shout now and then. All the while, his plump ball sac slapped against my chin, dripping wet now with my own spit and his pre-cum foaming from the corners of my mouth.

I was beginning to see little black spots when I felt his hands tighten and my lips detected a quick spasm coursing through the huge slab of meat stuck in my gullet. He shot off in three huge spurts that filled my mouth to overflowing.

"Swallow it!" he directed. Then after he was done with me, he slipped his big body into the tub and stretched his arms out along the rim, watching me with a small, unreadable smile on his face. I started to get up to go but he stopped me.

"Hold on there," he said. "Only I say when we're done here."

He told me to get my own clothes off and join him in the tub. The hot, bubbling water felt good and I was beginning to relax a little bit, when he told me to massage his feet. One at a time, I worked his feet over real good, till he looked like he was beginning to mellow out.

In spite of the nasty tone he kept taking with me, I enjoyed watching his face as the pleasure from different parts of his body connected with his brain. He was a handsome man, or had been once anyway. Most people would call him 'distinguished' now probably. I had never been into older men much, but the combination of silver hair, crow's feet and a giant dick was new to me. I figured I could get used to it if he would just slow down a bit on the bossy stuff.

I hadn't seen anything in the way of bossiness yet, though. About the time I thought he ought to be tiring out, Addison said, "I need some entertainment. Stand up and turn around."

I did what I was told. Like I said before, I don't figure I was any kind of movie star or anything, but one thing I've always known was that my body could turn some eyes. I was smooth and solid as a rock everywhere, my abs were like a twelve-pack and my butt was the round bubble kind with big dimples in the cheeks on both sides.

Standing and turning before Addison now, I enjoyed giving him a bit of a show, reaching down into the foaming water between my legs and throwing a couple of handfuls over my broad shoulders. But he couldn't be satisfied.

"No," he said in his abrupt way. "I mean show me what you've got. Bend over and spread 'em."

Sighing a bit, I leaned over the edge of the pool, grabbed an ass cheek in each hand and spread them apart, feeling the long shaft of my soft dick dipping into the hot water below. Suddenly, Addison was on me, all signs of his knee injury gone now. He came up from behind me and took each of my arms in his broad hands, pinning them down on the floor tiles. His barrel chest was up against my back, pressing my own nipples against the tub rim. The hard thrust of his meat was poking against my crack, looking for the hole but missing the mark so far, mercifully. I couldn't help but fight at the thought of that fat thing going up my ass. But he outweighed me by a good fifty pounds of pure muscle.

113

Somehow he got his hands on the silk tie he had worn earlier in the day that I'd thrown on the floor by the tub. He managed to work it around my face and into my mouth, almost like a bridle bit, then pulled on it until my back arched underneath him.

"This will be a lot easier for you if you just take the bit and go along for the ride," he hissed in my left ear, then shoved his cock up my ass with one merciless stab.

Before, I had almost passed out from lack of air when he made me suck him off. Now I almost passed out from pain. I had always been a top, but Addison lost no time in changing all that, shoving his rod into me hard and deep. He kept the silk tie in my mouth the whole time, pulling it tighter occasionally just to remind me I was totally at his whim. Now and then, he would put his hot mouth against my ear and whisper, "Buck harder."

Soon I felt Addison's hips shoving harder against my ass and his ball sac slapping faster against my own. In spite of my pain, I reached my own hand under my body and felt below the water for my wet dick, a huge boner still throbbing there.

Addison was making low murmuring noises now, no more barking orders and pulling my hair. I heard his breath beginning to come in short gasps in my ear, and I pulled on the end of my cock real hard a couple of times. With no more encouragement than that, out shot the biggest load of my life, stream after stream of thick, hot cum spraying all over the surface of the water and mixing in with the foam of the whirlpool.

With the coming of my own climax, my ass tightened like a vise around Addison's dick. That drew the cum out of him like a vacuum. He cried out loud, himself the one in pain now. Still I held onto his cock with my ass, squeezing the muscles inside of me as tight as I could around it, pulling myself forward and away from him at the same time, so that I had him held prisoner by his cock.

He had spent most of his load earlier in my mouth, so there wasn't much oozing around inside my hole to cause slippage on his dick. I kept coming myself for a long while, until there was nothing left inside of me to shoot. Finally spent, I jerked my tight ass off Addison's softening cock and turned on my side. He made a little moaning sound as I did and rolled over into the water.

Lying there next to each other for a minute soaking up the good feeling guys have after a good fuck, I could imagine a small shift occurring in the way things were between us. We didn't seem like boss man and stable hand anymore – just two men who had just gotten each other's rocks off real good. Looking at him resting there, totally at peace for once, I could even forgive the nastiness in him earlier. He had a kind of soft, almost tender look about him now, with his clothes off and his big, muscled body totally relaxed. Then he opened up those cool gray eyes, looked at me real hard, and ruined it all.

"You can go now," was all he said and nodded his head toward the door.

"Motherfucker!" I thought to myself, but I had the sense not to say it. This man was a cold number alright but he was still the boss, after all. I got up and gathered my scattered clothes up in a hurry. Heading for the door, I felt him jab one last hook in me.

"Oh, and another thing," he said. "My daughter Beverly has something of a crush on you. Show her a little attention, will you? Just don't do anything stupid."

I stood there naked in the doorway, my back turned to him so he wouldn't see the look in my eyes, thinking about how I had looked up to this man, thinking about how I'd just taken his dick up my ass and even begun to like it a little bit. I almost turned back around and dunked his sterling silver head under the water.

Then I got a better idea. "I'll see what I can do about that, sir," I said and went on out the door, calm and cool as you please.

Later that night, any doubts I might have had about following through on my plan were laid to rest. When I undressed, there in the crease of my briefs was the seal on my fate – a bright red streak of blood mixed with Addison's cum.

- - -

Well, starting the next morning I showed Beverly a little attention all right. She came down to the stable to ride every day, not a bad-looking young woman if I do say so myself. I showed her enough attention in fact that pretty soon she was trailing along behind me like a little dog. From there it was just a matter of time before I was drilling her daily in that fancy tack room of her dad's. At first I wasn't sure I could even do it with a woman, but I found I could manage it just fine if I thought about her dad's dick while I screwed her. I don't guess there are too many guys in the world who can lay claim to that one.

115

It wasn't long before Beverly came to me in tears one day saying she was late for her period. We eloped and got married by a justice of the peace. I talked her into keeping her pregnancy and our marriage secret until it was too late for anyone to do anything about it. Then she sprang it on her parents. Afterward, she told me Addison was furious. But there was nothing he could do about it; she was too far along with the baby.

Like a lot of rich folks, the Lees knew how to make lemonade out of lemons. They decided to make the daughter's surprise marriage the social event of the season. They bought off all the local newspapers, which ran a string of sappy articles about our romantic elopement and how it was to be followed by a big church wedding. Almost before we knew it, the big day had arrived.

On our wedding day, looking out from the dressing room behind the altar, I saw a church packed with all kinds of distinguished guests, some television and movie stars included. I guess there was more of the little boy in me than I liked to admit, because all of a sudden, I began to get kind of excited about the big show that was about to take place. Then I saw Addison coming down the aisle with a dark look on his face and I wondered what he had up his sleeve now.

He joined me in the dressing room and closed the door firmly behind him. "There's been a slight delay," he said. "The limousine's stuck in traffic and will be a while getting here."

I wondered what kind of an accident Addison had arranged to capture this extra bit of time. He pulled an envelope out of his pocket and handed it to me. "I believe you might find this interesting," he said.

I opened the thick white stationery and removed the contents, first a letter from a Swiss bank. The letter noted transfer of a huge sum of money into an account recently opened in my name. It also noted the conditions necessary for me to begin drawing on the account. All I had to do was to prove that I was a single male, living outside of the United States. There was one other item in the envelope – a one-way, non-stop plane ticket to Geneva.

I looked up at Addison, who was watching me with that bone-chilling look on his face again. "You can just disappear," he said with a small smile. "My attorneys will dissolve the marriage immediately."

I let him think I was considering it for a minute. Then I enjoyed the pissed look on his face when I tore the papers in two. "You just don't get it, do you?" I said.

I pulled out my own set of papers and handed them over to him. If looks could kill I would have been dead on the spot. He opened it and read, then looked up me, confused. "A lab report?" he asked.

"Yes," I said. "DNA test results, to be exact. They're from a stain on the briefs I wore home one night a while back. Maybe you remember that night?"

He was dead in the water and he knew it. Still the richest man in six states, still the most powerful guy I had ever met, Addison Lee shrank a little bit right before my eyes. His shoulders took on a little slump probably nobody else would even have noticed. But I saw it happening as I watched. Funny thing – he still struck me as the most attractive and desirable man I had ever known. Something about him had gotten under my skin and no matter how hard I tried to hate him, I couldn't bring myself to it. That didn't mean I couldn't enjoy this moment of triumph though.

He turned and headed for the door. Just when his hands reached for the knob, I stopped him.

"Hold on there," I said. "Only I say when we're done here, and believe me, we're not done yet."

His back stiffened and that new little slump went out of his shoulders a bit. He didn't turn around, though, just froze at the door with his hand reaching for the knob.

I walked up behind him, real slow and deliberate like. In the deafening silence that filled the room, I made sure Addison could hear the clicking noise my zipper made as I pulled it down as slowly as possible.

Coming up behind him, I opened my fly and reached deep into my pants. My dick wasn't near as fat as his but it was at least twice as long. It was going to hurt him like hell, I felt sure.

Out in the church, the organ started playing the first of a collection of love songs. The limousine must be back on its way to the church again. Addison and I would have just enough time to get to know each other a little bit better as loving father and son-in-law.

Humming a little tune with the organ, I pulled off my silk tie and threw it around his neck, guiding the fabric between his teeth with one hand. With the other hand, I reached down and unbuttoned his pants.

"This will go a lot easier for you if you just take the bit and go along for the ride," I whispered in his ear. Shoving his pants down around his knees, I rammed the entire length of my shaft up his virgin ass, enjoying the little whimper he made.

"Oh, and another thing," I said as I started to ride him hard. "My buddies in the barn have something of a crush on you. I'm gonna want you to show 'em a little attention...."

# SIDESHOW
## Corbin Chezner

Several thousand residents showed up at the fairgrounds for the carnival and rodeo that capped off Watermelon Thump, the town of Luling's annual tribute to its main cash crop. The carnival goers spent the afternoon on the midway sampling carnival delights such as cotton candy, scary rides, con games, and, of course, the biggest treat of all – sexy, wild-eyed carnies. Beer flowed freely, and by 6 p.m., when opening ceremonies began for the rodeo, a good portion of the South Central Texans was already drunk.

"Man, these yahoos like to party," Dan Jensen said, collapsing on a stool beneath the order window of a concession trailer. With the rodeo under way, finally, the midway crowd had thinned out and Dan took in a deep breath, content to rest his weary bones for a few minutes. At last, they would be able to shut their hotdog concession down for the day. Behind him, on the opposite side of the trailer, Mike Davenport, Dan's partner, stood at a stainless steel sink washing one of the big pans they used to mix the meal for the corndogs. Because the partners had been on the carnie route nearly three months that summer, they were weary and looking forward to the end of the season. As the sun began to set, a breeze surfaced, taking the edge off the oppressive summer heat.

Suddenly, the sounds of boots grating against pavement caught Dan's attention. Looking up, he saw two cowboys approaching the pavilion, some 20 feet away from the trailer. The cowboys were dressed similarly: Levis, snug-fitting Western shirts, sharp-toed boots, and black Stetsons. The way the two jostled against each other, Dan knew right off they were drunk. Laughing and flailing wildly, the cowboys staggered under the shade of the Midway Pavilion and stood looking toward the trailer.

Dan wondered if the cowboys realized the rest of the crowd had abandoned the pavilion booths and midway rides for the rodeo.

Hell, they've probably been behind the cow pens boozing and jacking off, Dan thought. One was tall and lean with black hair and a moustache. The other was short, blond, hunky, and clean shaven. They had something in common, though: both filled out their jeans where it counted.

"Fresh meat," Dan called back to Mike.

Mike stopped washing a pan and looked back at Dan. "Huh?"

Dan nodded toward the men. "Check out the cowpokes!"

"No shit!" Mike looked toward the cowboys and pursed his lips for a mock wolf whistle. "What'd they lose their way or somethin'? The rodeo started ten minutes ago."

"Looks like the rodeo ain't what they're lookin' for."

On a lark, Dan leaned into the order window and called out to the cowboys, "Got some beer left over. Won't be worth shit left overnight in these damn barrels. You two dudes want to sit a spell and share a brew or two with me and my partner here?" Dan pointed toward Mike. "On the house."

The cowboys looked at each other and shrugged. Sauntering up to the order window, the black-haired cowboy smiled. "Right neighborly of you. Had a few already, but one more can't hurt."

"No shit," the blond agreed. "One more sure can't hurt."

In a couple of minutes Dan and Mike had the concession closed down and they invited the cowboys inside. The tall, dark-haired cowboy introduced himself as Rick; the blond went by Barry.

When they'd converted the travel trailer into a food concession, Dan and Mike had tossed out an old couch, and they'd moved the two wingback chairs into the bedroom at the rear of the trailer. They left the dining room table in the front of the trailer between the service window and the utility sink. That way, the table served double duty: for food prep during working hours, for eating and socializing after.

"Looks like two guys good lookin' as you would have some pussy lined up by now," Dan said, slamming down the second round of beer on the table. Mike knew, of course, that Dan was testing the waters.

"Had us two but they got pissed royally. " Barry leaned back in his chair and scratched his balls. "Wouldn'a been worth a shit no-how."

In slurred speech, Rick explained that the women had stomped off when they'd learned he and Barry were not going to compete in the rodeo. "Hell, all those bitches wanted was to be damned queens of the rodeo!"

"Yeah," the smaller cowboy chimed in, "and to get their claws on some prize money!"

"How come you guys decided not to enter?" Dan asked.

"Hell, we was. But them bitches went and got us drunk. Next thing we knew, the damn rodeo was announcin' the start of bull ridin' events. And there we was, drunker'n skunks out behind the cow pens!"

Suddenly, the thought struck MIke that the four of them looked alike. Not identical, of course, but they did look enough alike to be ... well, brothers, maybe. Or cousins. The thought made Mike laugh out loud.

Sitting across from him, Rick looked up from his beer. "Whas sa matter?"

"It just hit me. We four guys. We..." – he chuckled again – "we look alike...."

Barry, sitting across from Dan, looked at Mike like he was crazy. "Hell, you and me don't look nothin' alike."

"Not you and me," Mike shot back, laughing again. He nodded toward Dan. "You and Dan. Me and Rick."

The four men traded glances. No one appeared sure enough to agree with Mike's assessment. But no one disagreed either. Mike didn't know if it was worth adding that he was talking merely about types. He and Rick were both dark haired and tall, Dan and Barry short and blond.

"Bet you guys' cocks ain't as big as ours," Barry suddenly blurted out, laughing.

Mike and Dan looked at each other. What a lead in. Mike searched for the perfect comeback, but his quick-tongued lover beat him to the punch. "Me and Mike done noticed you two had a hell of a package – both of you," Dan tossed in, laughing. "Meat and potatoes both!"

Rick took another swig of beer. "Hell, you ain't seen nothin', dude."

"Don't doubt it," Dan admitted. "Yes, sir, it'd be tough wager to outswing you guys' cocks. No doubt about that. But I'd bet ... I'd wager me and Mike could give you two a run."

"Oh, yeah?" Barry began rubbing his crotch. "What's the bet?"

Mike gulped. He and Dan had healthy packages, for sure, but he had doubts about how they'd stack up against these guys' ample endowments. Dan's wagering talk made him nervous.

Dan tossed down the remainder of his beer and slammed the cup down on the table. He wiped his mouth on the sleeve of his T-shirt. Then he looked from Barry to Rick and to Barry again. "Losers ... losers have to suck off the winners."

Mike had to get a grip on himself so he wouldn't laugh. Clever. Clever, indeed! He and Dan couldn't lose. No, siree! They would enjoy paying off this wager. Mike was hoping, in fact, that he and Dan would lose. And if he was remembering correctly how the cowpokes filled out their Levis, they probably would.

Dan suddenly pushed away from the table. He stood and reached to unbuckle his belt. "Ready, guys? Let's see who's got the biggest fuckpole!"

Barry started to get up, too, but stopped short. He looked at Dan. "We talkin' hard – or soft?"

"Pardon?" Dan asked, ripping open his button fly.

"Our cocks. We comparin' hard or so?"

Reaching for his cock and balls then, Dan declared, "I say, let's give it our all. How about you guys? Game?"

Rick pushed his chair away from the table then. Joining Dan on his feet, he said, "Might not be able to stop, though. Hell, damn meat of mine takes on a mind of its own when it gets hard. Might have to jack it until it squirts."

Dan had already started pumpin' his own cock. "Know what you mean, man. I got the same problem. Ain't no limits here. I say, pump it til you shoot, if you're so inclined." Jacking his growing cock with his right hand, Dan was using his left to massage his balls. "Yes, sir, men," – his voice now raspy and breathless – "whack it all the way!"

The four stood naked, facing each other from opposite sides of the table. Cocks were erect. Dan looked from Barry to Rick to Mike. "You guys ready for the showdown?"

"Better do it quick," Barry urged, rocking on his heels like a kid needing to pee. "Otherwise, I could be too far gone." The little cowboy's big hard-on had robbed the color from his face and the strength from his voice.

"Gotcha," Dan said. He padded over to the kitchen and retrieved a tape measure from a drawer. Slamming the door shut, he came back and stood next to Rick. "Give it all you got, guy. I'll measure."

"And I'll record," Mike offered, scooping up a pad and pencil from the shelf beneath the order window.

Moments later, the calculations complete, Dan stood wide-legged before them. Slinging one hip lower than the other, he cleared his throat. "Okay, guys, here goes."

Mike sucked and licked and wheedled Barry's cock and balls until, finally, the little cowboy tightened his grip on Mike's shoulders and pulsed his hot load into Mike's mouth. Moments later, as he fought to swallow the cum, Mike gave his own cock one final jerk and – wham! – he shot his load on the floor between the cowboy's feet.

An instant later, the bigger cowboy moaned and slammed his load into Dan's mouth just as Dan jerked himself to climax.

As the four stood shaking cum off the end of their dicks, Dan suggested that they have another round of beer. Everybody was in agreement, so the four sat back down and shot the shit for a while. Before they finished the round, it became clear that Barry and Rick both were on the verge of passing out. "Hey, you guys look like you're about done in, " Mike said. "We got a sleeper sofa in the back room. Welcome to stay over."

"Hate to put you out," Barry said, "but I am beat."

"Me too," Rick agreed. "I've had it."

"Ain't no trouble," Dan said, waving them toward he bedroom. "I'll set the sleeper up for you."

Dan and Mike helped Barry and Rick out of their clothes and the two passed out on the sleeper sofa. It was still early, so Dan and Mike went back into the front room for more beer.

"I'm still horny," Mike admitted. "The cocks were good but I could use some fuckin'."

"Me too," Dan said. "Hell, I'm game."

"Want to fuck their butts while they're asleep?"

"Nah. They wouldn't be no damn good that way. We'll poke 'em in the morning while their heads are still dazed."

"Good idea. But I don't want to wait 'til then."

"Who says we got to? Hell, we don't need them two dudes to fuck."

"True. Wanna do it out here?"

"I'd prefer the bed."

"Think they'll wake up?"

"Who cares?" Dan said. "They're welcome to join in."

Dan and Mike were versatile. Each liked fucking and being fucked. Sometimes they traded fucks. Other times one of them would fuck and the other would take it. Then the next time they were having sex they might change roles. And then again, they might not. There was no rhyme or reason to their love making. No system. They did what came natural at the time.

This evening Dan felt like fucking and that was fine with Mike. Mike wanted it doggie style, so he got up on all fours on the bed while Dan lubricated Mike's hole. At the same time each played with his own pole until it was rock hard.

When Mike's hole was ready, Dan pushed his fat cock inside the larger man. He went slowly at first, until his lover was ready to accommodate him.

Mike stopped jacking himself when he felt Dan enter him. Otherwise, he'd come too quickly, and he didn't want that. He preferred feeling the hunky blond ramming his butt good. He liked the feel of Dan's heavy ballsac slapping against his own balls. With Dan fucking him like that Mike could come without touching himself.

Dan pushed deeper and when Mike's sphincter relaxed the blond pushed all the way inside. The base of Dan's cock was nestled now against Mike's hole. Dan hesitated for a moment so Mike could feel the full benefit of Dan's fat cock. "That feel good, baby?"

"Oh, yeah! I like your cock in me. All of it!"

Dan retreated and then, slowly, he pushed back in again. His rhythm was slow but deliberate at first: all the way in, all the way out, in, out, in, out. Squeezing Mike's waist, then, Dan increased the speed of his thrusts: In, out, in, out, faster and faster. Finally, Dan sighed, "Damn!" and Mike felt Dan's hot juice squirting deep within Mike's bowels.

"Ahhh!" Mike gasped, and then his own cock let loose, squirting cum against the bed. Thankfully, he'd had the forethought to place a towel beneath himself, and he managed to hit most of it.

The alarm clock sounded at eight the next morning. Mike struggled naked out of bed to put the coffee on and Dan lay silently eyeing their two guests. The room was crammed with barely enough space for Mike and Dan's double bed and the sleeper sofa both. Neither cowpoke stirred at first. Finally, Mike came back to bed and soon the smell of coffee filled the trailer. The tall, dark-haired dude named Rick, the one who vaguely resembled Mike, squinted open one eye. "What the fuck?" His hand went to his head.

The little blond named Barry rolled over on his side and started snoring.

"You remember what happened?" Dan called out to Rick.

Rick lifted his shoulders off the pillow and squinted over at Dan. "Coffee?" he muttered.

Mike brought him some black coffee then and Mike sat up in bed and sipped it. Slowly, he came to life. All the while, Barry remained asleep.

As Rick sipped the coffee Dan could see the dude had sprung a big hard on. Dan had to say something. "That a pee hard-on? Or you just glad to be here?"

Rick laughed and cupped the fat pole in his hand. "Hell, I wake up with it like this most mornin's."

"Yeah?" Mike chimed in. "Looks to me like a big piece of meat like that deserves to be taken care of."

Rick looked down at his big cock. Then he met Mike's gaze and smiled. "Fine with me." He shrugged and flailed open his legs.

Mike got out of bed and padded over to the sleeper. He went down on Rick's cock while Dan looked on, pumping his own cock into hardness. After he'd sucked Rick's cock for a while, Mike whirled himself around on the bed so they could sixty-nine. Mike aimed his cock at Rick's mouth, and the two dark-haired men slurped on each other's cock.

Dan got so hot looking on he had to find a way of joining in. Finally, he said, "Hey, why don't you two come over to the bed. More room over here."

Mike and Rick fell onto the bed as Dan fumbled in the nightstand for the lubricant. Mike and Rick started sixty-nining again while Dan greased his cock. Then, when Mike and Rick rolled on their sides, Dan squeezed out some more of the lubricant and poked it into Rick's butthole. Rick moaned and squirmed a bit, but he kept on sucking Mike's cock. Dan probed the cowboy's hole with his finger, and the cowboy moaned some more. Finally, Dan poked his hard cock toward Rick's hole, and the cowboy moaned and squirmed again. Dan kept on, though, until he managed to enter the cowboy. When Dan was all the way inside, the cowboy turned wild, sucking and slurping Mike's dick like there was no tomorrow, all the while giving Dan all his hole – and then some.

Mike and Rick came in each other's mouth before Dan had a chance to get his rocks off. Dan considered pulling out of the cowboy's butt, but he decided to keep on until Rick stopped him.

He didn't. Dan keep fucking, all the way in, all the way out now. Deep, hard thrusts that soon had the cowboy panting again. "Oh, man, that feels good."

"You like my dick up your butt?"

"Fuck me good, dude," he said breathlessly. He started pumping his own cock again, like maybe he could rustle up another load.

"I'm gonna pump your butt full," Dan announced, finally, slamming his load inside the cowboy's ass.

An instant later, the cowboy moaned again, louder this time, "Mother-fuck!" as a second load shot out the end of his dick.

Mike and Dan gave Rick dibs on the bathroom, and, while they were alone, the other cowboy stirred to life.

Dan, especially, would get a second wind sometimes, and he'd taught Mike he could do the same. He also knew from experience that the second cowboy would come more likely to doing something with his buddy out of the room. The time to act was now – while Rick was in the shower.

Dan flew off of the bed and pounced on Barry's cock before the blond knew what was happening. "Hey...." came his tentative protest, but, by then, of course, Dan had already slurped down the cowboy's fat cock.

The cowboy raised off the pillow and flailed open his legs so Dan could get to the base of his cock. "Ah, man, suck it!" he hissed, arching his head toward the ceiling.

After a few moments, Dan did like Mike had done with Rick. Dan whirled his legs around and thrust his cock toward Barry's mouth while he continued sucking Barry's huge cock. Barry took Dan's cock in his mouth then, just as Rick had taken Mike's cock.

Mike gave the two time enough to enjoy their 69 before he joined in. He found the lubricant and greased his own cock as he looked on. When his pole was ready, he joined the two on the bed, backing up to Barry's blond-haired butt.

Rick walked naked into the room just as Mike was pumping another load this time into Barry's hole. "Hey, dudes," he broke in, cheerily kneading his half-hard cock. "Ya'll game for a four- way?"

Wide-eyed, Mike and Dan looked at each other and gulped.

John Patrick

# ANY COWBOY CAN
## Jack Ricardo

He was a small boy, sitting on the wooden rail, gawking, elbows on his knees, legs flopped open. His eyes were shining, his mouth was half open. You'd think he never saw a bunch of raunchy cowpokes preparing for the rodeo tomorrow, roping calves and sweating up a storm. But I would have guessed he'd ridden a bronc or two in his day. He looked the type. Dusty Wrangler jeans, warped cowboy hat rimmed with stains, scuffed boots. But he didn't look the type either. A star-struck cowboy wannabe, probably. Jail bait, but mighty tempting just the same.

I lost track of him by the time the long day ended. I was ready to trek down to the motel for a shower before heading out for eats, but decided on a cold beer first. The Corral was near empty. Two ladies were sitting at the bar. They eyed me like I was meat and they was starving. I sat at the other end and ordered a Lone Star.

I ignored the ladies the best I could before I spied him in the mirror facing me, settled in a booth behind, his lips wrapped around the neck of his Lone Star. I waved a finger at the barkeep and asked, "You serving kids nowadays?" I nodded behind me.

"He's twenty-two, checked his license, credit card, library card, and damn near took his blood. He's legit. You a fed?" I shook my head. The night was looking bright.

I ordered a couple more longnecks, scooped up both bottles with one hand and ambled over to the booth. He looked up. I set one beer in front of him, and my ass in the seat across. "Name's Randy," I said, and held out a callused hand.

"Wink," he said, and shook mine, matching callus for callus. He was grinning. His voice was thin and on the verge of a manhood he hadn't quite reached yet.

"Saw ya watchin' at the arena this morning," I said.

"Saw you too," he gushed, then flushed. "I wanna be a calf-roping cowboy, but not sure I got the right stuff." His dreams were glowing in his eyes. I didn't know they made them that innocent anymore.

"Takes a lotta hard work, and I mean hard. Training too," I told him, leaning into the table between us, sipping my brew, locking my knees between his. He didn't seem to mind. "Even I ain't won no championships yet and I been cowboying some twenty years now, since I was sixteen. But I keep plugging."

"Oh, you will, you will," Wink said, his knees knocking against mine in youthful excitement. "Man, I wish I could rope like you."

"Shit, any boy can be a cowboy," I told him, "If he wants it bad enough. I could give you a few pointers." The cock wrapped inside my jeans was rising to the challenge.

"Would ya?" he exclaimed, landing his beer on the table so hard foam splashed from the head.

You might think I was making a play for the kid, and I was. But he was so damn plucky and so damn anxious, I did want to help, maybe like a big brother showing the ropes to a little bro. "Where ya staying?" I asked.

He shrugged. "Hell, it took almost every dime I had just to get here! Figured I'd see if they got a YMCA...."

"Oh, they don't. Not here. But I got me a room at a motel round the corner. You can stay with me if you don't mind sharing a bed that's seen better days. And nights," I added with a grin. "You wanna?"

"Okay. Sure, dude."

I bought us some of the colonel's finest chicken before we headed to my room. We sat on the grungy floor chomping and sucking the bones clean. When Wink came back after dropping the remnants in the slag heap outside, I had stripped down to my jockstrap, but I still had my boots and hat on and my blue neckerchief tied round my neck

His mouth plopped open when he saw me standing there casually swinging a lasso. Maybe it was the jockstrap, maybe it was the hairy chest, maybe it was the honed body, maybe it was the rope. Maybe it was all. He ogled me like I was a god. "Lesson number one," I said and swung the lasso. It fell over his shoulders; I gave it a yank; it looped round his waist.

"He...he...hey," he sputtered and laughed. "That was such great roping." He pulled the rope over his head.

"Gets better," I said, looping up the rope. "Shuck off your clothes; let's see how strong you are?"

Wink didn't hesitate. He unsnapped his shirt and tossed it on the chair, lugged off his boots, tore off his socks, pulled down his jeans, and set them on the floor. I dropped the lasso and tugged my cock. A hard-on was hammering against the pouch of my jock.

The shaggy blond hair on the kid's head was unmatched by a tiny and surprising thicket of dark hair that centered a chest eager to sprout into manhood. His manhood was packed behind the white cotton of dank briefs. I could almost see through it through the sweaty shorts. I tackled him.

"Lesson number one," I said, panting, not from exertion but from lust, "Be prepared for anything."

He was on his back. My body was lying on his, the hair on my chest was mashed into the hair of his chest and my crotch was planted on his. His arms were over his head and linked by my wrists. My cock throbbed against the pouch of his shorts. He felt it. For one second his eyes held a hint of alarm. But it quickly disappeared when he replied, "I'm new at this, you know. Never did it. But I'll be ready next time. For anything."

Then I was taken aback when he bucked me off in one strong bound. He was standing over me, grinning like a kid who won his first fight. I was leaning on my elbows, my hat knocked off and behind me, staring up at one sweaty package of balls that overflowed the legs of his briefs with hairs climbing up inside and the beginnings of a hard-on outlined outside. The acrid aroma of his shorts gave off a heady smell, or maybe the odor was coming from my jock. Both. He grabbed his balls and grinned. I reached for the lasso and leaped to my feet.

Wink was up for it, circling me, his arms outstretched and trying to grab me before I roped him. I circled wide, ringing the lasso in the air over my head, slowly, with a practiced rhythm. When the kid dove down at my feet to knock me off balance, I let him, then flopped him on his back. My face landed smack dab in the crack of an ass covered with cotton and spiked with a potent aroma that rushed through me like a train through a tunnel. My legs straddled his head, the pouch of my jock was scratching his neck.

I swiftly spun around. He tried the same and didn't make it. I plucked up the lasso and had his hands bound together before he knew what hit him. I hopped up and raised my arms, the winner in the calf roping competition.

Wink wriggled around until he was on his side, the loose ends of the lasso dangling from his tied wrists. "That was damn good," he said, elated, his face flush with my victory.

131

"Get's better," I said. I lifted him up with one hand, and propped his chest on the edge of the bed, then swung one leg over his head and sat on the bed. His face was close to the pouch of my jock. He was staring it; he had no choice really. I wired my fingers through the straw of his hair. He was breathing hard; so was I. His eyes looked up into mine with a craving that was endearing if not downright hungry. I pressed his face to my jockpouch. He inhaled deeply and loudly and opened his mouth to suck up the grime and the sweat and the cock inside. I dang near busted a nut as I threaded my fingers through his hair and pressed his face hard onto my crotch. The kid grunted, groaned and gorged himself on the meat inside. I sloped forward over his head and gave his cotton-covered ass a hard whack with the flat of my hand. The kid groaned loader and suckled my meshed cock with a vengeance. I slapped him again. He groaned again and suckled again. I whacked, he groaned, he suckled.

When I stepped over his head and knelt behind him, the kid was panting like a young bull ready to ram his first cowboy. "The other way round, little cowboy," I mumbled to myself. Wink muttered, "Hhuh." I pushed his legs apart with my knees, my boots scratching into the threads of the rug. I shoved his shorts just under the cheeks of his ass. His cheeks were welted red. Two pert cherry tomatoes ripening. I kissed each one. Wink purred his, "Thank you," his words a gasping plea.

The same dark hairs from his chest were leaking into the crack of his ass. His ass stank of sweat and funk. I trailed the hairs with my tongue until I reached the rim of a miniature canyon craggy with wrinkles. I pinched the fingers of each hand into the hard flesh of each cheek until the pucker of his hairy little asshole was winking at me, breathing in, out. With eyes wide open, I licked it clean, inside and out. It flared open. I gorged myself with mouth open wide, tongue deep inside. I ate that naive little fucker's nasty little asshole out while he was shoving his ass so hard into my face, I dang near lost my head. Had to back up for air.

I sat on the heels of my boots and stroked the palms of one hand down both cheeks while yanking on the pouch of my cock. Not a more beautiful sight exists in all the universe than that of a young cowboy-to-be about to be dicked in one fine-looking ass.

I leaned over his back. His fingers were smashed between us and plucking the hairs atop my jewels. The pouch of my jock was scratching the red cheeks of his bare ass, my chest was scratching his bare back, my tongue was in his ear, the neckerchief round ɪ was sopping up his sweat. "You want it, young cowpoke?" I asked. It was a question that wanted an answer. "You want it," I demanded.

"I don't ... don't know," Wink said, his voice hushed and rushed. "I don't know ... if I can."

"A cowboy can," I told him. "Any cowboy can. If you wanna be a cowboy, you can," I told him, my voice as rushed and as hushed as his, my cock throbbing against mesh and humping the crack of the kid's lively little ass.

"I can?" he asked, breathlessly. I was humping with a rough rhythm that was bellowing my chest out. I reached under him with both hands. His cock was rock hard and leaking like a cow's teat. His balls were big and solid with wiry strands of hair. I fisted them and tugged them. "I can," Wink yelped. "I will," he gasped. "I want to," he shouted.

"How bad?" I whispered into his car, straining my ass from side to side until the hidden head of my cock was scraping his asshole and trying to plow inside.

"Bad...I want ya bad, Randy, so bad...bad...bad...!"

"How bad, Wink? How bad do you want me to plug my cock up inside ya, huh, kid? How bad you want it, huh?" Each word was prompted by a throb from my cock. It was aching against a hole that was widening and longing to suck it inside.

"Oh, please, Randy, I want ya, I want ya, I want ya...!" He emphasized each word with fingers clutching my short hairs and pulling frantically.

I flinched in pain, in pleasure, and grit my teeth. "You want it, little cowboy, you got it," I muttered.

My movements were disjointed with lust as I pulled myself from his back, tore my cock and balls from the pouch of my jock, drooled spit onto the shaft and lubed that fucking pole until it was red and shining. The head was dribbling with ooze. I swiped a finger over it and tasted before I pressed that cockhead against Wink's asshole. He started to say something but was shut up when my cockhead plopped inside. I could hear him gulp, just like his asshole was gulping up my cockhead. Fire spread through my veins; my body shook. I gave each cheek of his ass a good swat with both hands. Wink groaned, first in pain, then in pleasure. My cock started to ride up inside him.

He took it, felt it, my cock widened his asshole until the entire shaft was stuffed inside and my cockhairs were brushed across red skin while his fingers twined through those cockhairs. I grabbed his hips. My cock was pulsating inside him. I asked, "You like it, little bull?" gasping for air. "You like having my entire cock up your ass, little bull cowboy?" My cock leaped and touched the pure heaven of that young cowboy's asshole.

"Ye...yea...yeah, yeah, yeah," he was sputtering, louder, louder, shoving his ass deep onto my cock, pronging himself, spearing himself, stabbing himself with as much cock as I could give him.

I stayed put and let my cock have a leaping ball inside the kid's ass. I licked the sweat from his back. I slobbered over his neck. He flopped his head back to let me get drunk on the smooth, perspiring nape of his neck, on the sweat streaming between us. I hunched my ass back, my cock pulled out to the rim. My cockhead stayed inside. It was too warm, too wonderful, too magnificent.

I pushed my torso back to see this masterful sight – my cockhead clutched inside his asshole, my shaft shining outside. I watched as it again inched itself inside. I shivered as sensations zoomed over my skin. He was muttering and moaning and groaning and I was holding on for dear life. I couldn't stop now. Neither could he. My fingers held solidly to his hips until they were aching. I started fucking, pulling my cock out then watching it again plow inside, feeling, seeing that cock screw this little cowboy fucker, my balls tangled in the elastic of his briefs, watching this little bronc rider take it like a fucking man and ask for more, beg for more. "Yeah, Randy, yeah, Randy, yeah, make me you, Randy, make me you, Randy."

I was making him and fucking the shit out of that enthusiastic little fucker until we were both splashing sweat and moaning and roaring and soaring. I plunged deep and stayed deep because my cock was expanding, growing larger, digging deeper and spouting cum so far up Wink's ass it felt like I was spitting right into his throat.

Wink was riding me, riding my cock. I went fucking ferocious and slammed my hands under him and fisted his cock and squeezed until he yelled, "YEAAAHhhhhhhhhhhh." His cock shot off like a cannon, expanding, the cockhead spewing over and splattering his cum all over my fist. The muscles of his asshole were expanding, contracting, squeezing and strangling and holding onto my cock like it was that asshole's last link to earth.

When he broke apart, the air was rancid with sweat and cum. I was on the floor on my back licking Wink's cum from my fist. Wink's ass was still straddling the bed and shining with perspiration, his shorts a tangled mess on his knees. My cum was leaking from his asshole. I leaned up with sapped energy and slid my hand through my cum, flopping back down, tasting and mingling his cum with mine. I lay back, closed my eyes, and savored.

We showered, then hit the sack. Wink was in my arms. He told me, "I wanna learn it all, Randy. Teach me."

"I will, Wink. If any boy can be a cowboy, you can. You got what it takes, and you can take it."

"Yeah, I do," he said, a winning smile in his voice. "And I can take it, can't I."

"Yeah, you can, little cowboy."

# BILLY THE KID
## (West Hollywood Cowboy)
## Peter Eros

In my skin-tight jeans and cowboy shirt, boots and hat, I was the sexiest cowboy on the range, although in my case, the "range" was the streets and by-ways of West Hollywood, California. Yeah, I was cute as hell back then in the '70s, a fortunate inheritance from my slim and pretty Mom and the handsome buckaroo who fathered me, then fled from our life even before I was born.

Mom was a pretty one all right, and she had a string of lovers. The man who stayed with her the longest was Josh, a man I had learned to love very much and even called "Daddy." Then, one day, he too disappeared. Mom never talked about him but I knew he occasionally sent her money for "the kid." Mom took up with a hot Hispanic dude so I spent most of my life in south-central L.A., where a white kid like me was a curiosity, constantly in peril. But being dark-haired and deeply suntanned year round, by the time I was old enough to know my whiteness could be a danger, I was savvy enough to pass for a Hispanic a lot of the time.

I guess I began jerking off when I was eleven and by thirteen I was shooting huge wads of jiz, but I don't remember the first time it happened. I must have been about fourteen when my schoolmate Pedro Ramirez and I began masturbating together. Soon we were petting and fondling and even kissing, but we didn't know about fucking ass, except in the abstract. By fifteen we'd learnt about sucking dick and 69'd together regularly, even swallowing each other's cum. But we kept our activities secret from the rest of the gang, who were aggressively hetero.

After the Hispanic ditched her, Mom several more occasional lovers, but none of 'em ever seemed to stick around too long. When I became a teen, a couple of them showed more interest in me as they did Mom. She worked long hours in those days and I guess when you've got the itch you just need somebody to get you off, and I was pleased to oblige. My mouth was by now pretty talented, and the guys' attention was both flattering and satisfying. My ass was opened first by a huge, blond, German oil rig worker named Dirk.

We had already fooled around a couple of times, sucking and masturbating, when Mom was working. But one afternoon, when I got home from school, Dirk was already naked and waiting for me. He was smoking a joint, which he shared with me as he undressed me real slow, kissing my throat and sucking my nipples before laying me on Mom's bed and straddling me to 69. But after a little his mouth slid from my cock and his hands went under my thighs to pull me up. His tongue caressed the sensitive skin beneath my scrotum and began to probe my virgin shit chute. The euphoric feelings that engulfed me were beyond anything I'd ever experienced before. I groaned my appreciation and murmured, "Oh yeah ... oh do it more ... oh fuck, yes...."

After a while, he sat up and squeezed out some KY, poking it into my twitching hole. His hands were large, his fingers thick and gnarled. He gently pushed in one digit and massaged and stretched, then a second, and finally a third. It seemed impossible to me that those three fat fingers could fit in there, but he'd been slow and gentle and it felt terrific as they eased in and out, tenderly flexing, loosening and making more malleable my spasming rectum. I gleefully responded with gasps of ecstasy.

When he thought I was ready, Dirk withdrew his fingers and lay on his back and lit another joint, taking a hit before handing it to me.

"Inhale deep, Billy, it will relax you." He positioned me astride his muscular midriff as he liberally lubricated his, to my eyes, massive dick. I guess it was about nine uncut, very thick inches. Then he gently but firmly grasped my waist in those huge callused palms.

"Sit on it, Billy," he urged. "Take your time liebling. It will probably hurt a bit at first, so go slow. Just relax down onto it."

I grasped it at the base to guide it. At first the head seemed impossibly large, but the foreskin eased its passage. It was inside that it hit the obstacle. The pain was excruciating and I gasped and cried out, "No, ooogh! No, I can't do it! You're too damn big."

"Shhhh! Just wait a minute, Billy. Slowly...."

The chunky hands caressed and soothed me as my colon gradually adjusted to the enormous intruder. Something popped inside, the agony eased and I gradually lowered my unexplored rectum till I felt Dirk's scratchy pubes tickling my butt. As I raised myself a little and began to ride the rigid prick, feeling it tugging at my insides, I whimpered with pleasure, my asshole squeezing as I rode up and down, the thrill of it all climbing with every down stroke.

Dirk didn't warn me of his orgasm, but my own began when I felt his prick jerk and swell. My anus tightened and I gasped his name again and again as my cum gushed out, drenching him from chin to belly button. With his right hand Dirk scooped my cum from his chiseled abs and swallowed some with a satisfied smacking of lips before feeding some to me, the first time I'd tasted my own.

Dirk lit another joint as we cuddled and kissed. I was flying. I'd never felt so blissful and relaxed. We lay about half an hour, fondling and giggling with contentment. Then my German bear grinned broadly and tweaked my nose.

"Would you like to fuck me, Billy? Haf you ever done that?"

"Mmmm! Yes and no. I would like to, and no I haven't." I mumbled.

"Then let's complete your education."

Dirk lay back and handed me the blue tube as he spread and raised his legs, exposing his puffy anal ridge. I squeezed some on his pucker and slowly spread it and pushed it in with my fingers, as Dirk caressed and lubed my rampant prick. He pulled me down onto him as I inserted and pushed into his velvety warmth, his feet coming to rest on my back, pulling me against him.

"Oh ya, das is goot. Fuck me, Billy."

Initially I felt the tight pressure of his sphincter biting on the head of my cock, then slowly engulfing my entire shaft. I felt myself expand and stretch in the slick, moist chute, feeling the clinging tissues ripple and churn as his anal muscles contracted and relaxed. My nuts went taut, drawing up into me as I felt them churning, ready to shoot another load of milky liquid. I felt light-headed as euphoria spread from my groin to my extremities.

My hips began to buck, thrusting my dick deep into Dirk's tight, warm ass, as he drew a long, shuddering breath and murmured, "Ooooh, ya! ya!"

Dirk pulled my face down to his and his mouth devoured me, his need fueled by the slapping of my hips plowing his spread buttocks as his own cock rubbed vigorously against my belly, pumping his shaft. I worked my prick in and out, frictioning and filling him again and again, my balls crushing against his ass crack with each thrust.

"Mein Gott!" Dirk cried out as he shot his load simply from the pleasure of having my cock rammed in and out of his ass. I pumped harder and faster as I headed for orgasm heaven. I felt Dirk's rectal muscles grip as his hungry tail spasmed about my cock, chewing and sucking as I reamed him. His asshole squeezed me tightly as my cum spurted deep within him.

Our "matinees" became a regular event whenever he was ashore, for almost a year, but eventually the relationship with my mother soured and he never came back. I guess I probably drained him so much and so regularly that he couldn't satisfy my mother any longer. But I don't think she ever suspected our involvement.

When Mom got a waitressing job in West Hollywood and shifted us to a cheap apartment building closer to her work, I was suddenly the stranger at a new school where I knew no one and Pedro was no longer available to assuage my sexual needs. West Hollywood wasn't exclusively gay in those days, but it was getting that way. I picked up some gay papers and found out about gay clubs and movie theaters and bookstores. It wasn't difficult in those days to get a phony identification. Then a trick took me to see "The Boys in the Band," which was being revived at a small theater in WeHo. He said that I reminded him of the hustler known as "Cowboy" in the movie. I wasn't blond, of course, the way he was, but otherwise I was a dead ringer for him. The john bought me my first cowboy boots, plus a shirt and hat to go with it. We acted out a fantasy based on the scene in the movie when the hustler shows up as the birthday present for Harold. I adopted the garb as a uniform and quickly became known as Billy the Kid. It really seemed to do the trick, in more ways than one. I began to constantly cruise: the streets, the back alleys, the adult theaters, the bookstores – sucking and being sucked, even fucking and being fucked, in blissful anonymity. I had started charging twenty bucks for oral sex, but with my new persona I could easily get fifty. I took the bus into West Hollywood and sold my services on Selma, sharing the steps of the white-steepled church near Crossroads of the World with an army of hungry hustlers. I was the only cowboy, however, and my reputation grew.

Despite my success as a hustler, or maybe because of it, since I applied myself as never before so I would have time for my moonlighting, I managed to finish high school with decent grades.

Josh, the man I always thought of as Dad put in an unexpected appearance at my high school graduation. I hadn't seen him since I was a tiny tot and didn't recognize him and he seemed embarrassed and uncomfortable at first. I don't know whether Mom had been in touch with him. Either way, I was pleased to see him after all these years and more than a little turned on by his rugged good looks.

His tight 501s emphasized his muscular thighs and buttocks and the ample sausage squashed against his left thigh. It was a hot day and his sport jacket seemed tight and he kept fingering his collar where his necktie constricted his bull neck, till with an exasperated grunt he shrugged off the jacket and pulled the tie loose, undoing the collar button and the two below it, exposing a matted bush of chest hair. The shirt was short-sleeved, the exposed arms massive and tattooed with abstract tribal patterns, which are pretty common now but which were unusual then. They served to draw attention to the chiseled musculature.

Mom had to rush off to work after the ceremony and left us together, both of us a little shy, embarrassed and tongue-tied. As I slipped off the cap and gown, "Daddy" looked me up and down, then asked if I'd like to go eat with him somewhere. I shrugged and said,

"Sure, why not? I'd like that."

"Any preferences?"

"No. McDonald's is okay."

"McDonald's shit. We're goin' to the Brown Derby?"

"Wow ... I mean, yeah, that's okay too."

"You can take your tie and jacket off too, you know, if you'd like. It ain't that swank anymore. You've never known me as a dad really, so why don't you just call me Josh."

We drove in his Mercedes to the restaurant where he greeted the hunky parking valet by name. He'd ordered a booth at the rear and I was surprised that the obsequious waiters seemed to know him, the head waiter raising an eyebrow when I was introduced as his son. When we'd ordered and the salad had been served he turned to me. "I'm real sorry, Billy, that I haven't been there for you, y'know. I guess I owe you twelve years of explanation. I've thought about it a lot, but I still don't know where to start. I guess your mom hasn't told you too much about me. Do you know what I do for a living?"

"No."

"I'm a stunt man, Billy...."

"Really?"

"Yeah, started in movies but now I mostly work for the television studios. Actually, I don't do really so much myself anymore, but I organize a whole team of stunt specialists and plan the stunts."

"It must be nice," I said, interested now, but he changed the subject again, looking grave.

"Look, I don't know whether your mother ever told you why I left, but the fact is she caught me in bed with somebody else...." He hesitated. "Well, I think I can tell you now. You're grown, you understand these things."

"What things?"

"Sex stuff."

I nodded.

"See," he went on, not looking at me directly, "that somebody else was another guy."

I gasped at this revelation. He reached out and held my wrist, "I hope you don't hate me too much, Billy. I guess I always was attracted to guys, but I thought it was just a phase. I tried workin' it out. I met your mom and she was such a nice lady ... a real lady, you know. She had you, the cutest little kid I ever saw, an, well, I wanted it to work out. I really did."

It was sad, really, he was trying so hard to explain what was so obvious to me.

Hearing all this in just a few minutes brought tears to my eyes. Josh noticed my emotion and he moved closer and put his arm around my shoulder, pulling me close to him, trying to brush away my tears.

I hugged him and admitted, " Look, Dad, I like guys, too. "What?"

"Yeah, but I don't think Mom has no idea."

He sighed and grasped me by the shoulders, gazing into my face as I turned to him with a rueful grin. Then he laughed outright. "Well, I'll be damned."

The rest of the meal was a blur. We chatted, finding all about each other, discreetly fingering each other beneath the table cloth. Finally he asked, already knowing the answer, whether I'd like to see where he lived.

Josh's apartment was, incredibly, in a big building only a couple of blocks from where Mom and I lived. It was amazing we had never run into each other. The living room was tastefully and discreetly decorated, the only hint of sexuality a headless male torso emerging from a lush planter. But the master bedroom was a revelation. The walls were a deep purple and the vast bed was covered in some sort of fur. It was mirror-backed, with another large mirror on the ceiling. Indirect lighting emitted a softly glamorous glow. The only direct light fell on the breathtaking paintings on the walls.

"You like?"

"Oh, yeah."

He crushed me in his arms and engulfed my mouth with his own. I sucked on his tongue and absorbed his breath as though my life depended on it.

Then he held me at arm's length, my face clutched in his hands and looked at me steadily.

"I know this is probably not right...."

"I'm used to it."

"What?"

"Yeah, a couple of my mother's friends took an interest in me, too."

He looked shocked at this, but then grinned. "Your Mom can sure pick 'em , eh?"

"Yeah, she sure can!"

"Oh, God, Billy, I want you and I think you want me too."

"You know I do."

We undressed each other in a fever of anticipation.

Then he lay me on the bed and nestled beside me, appraising my face and body with eyes and lips and fingertips, until I couldn't contain myself any more.

I pulled him down on top of me, spreading my legs and cinching him to me with my feet on his buttocks.

"Fuck me, Josh! Fuck me!"

"Not so fast, Billy."

He slid down my body, sucking and nibbling then swung his body around so he straddled me, with his own massive uncut dick, glistening with precum, and huge, low-hanging balls dangling over my salivating mouth. His precum had a sweet, musky taste. Gradually I took his whole throbbing member into my mouth as he gently tongued the head of mine, exploring the folds of skin, before sucking the emerging knob into his mouth. We feasted on each other for several minutes, as Josh simultaneously explored my twitching asshole with lubed fingers.

Then he slid off me and nestled between my legs, forcing them up in the air. He placed the exposed head of his dick on my palpitating pucker and carefully started to penetrate me. His dickhead caressed my sphincter, stretching and then relaxing. With each small thrust more of his dick would enter me and then it would retreat, only to be thrust again a little deeper. It was exquisite, but it wasn't enough. I wanted it all – and I wanted it fast. He responded without a word being exchanged between us. He knew I was ready and slammed into me, his swollen, fleshy piston rod plowing my depths, sliding back and forth across my prostate with rapturous precision, inflaming and subjugating me entirely to his will.

He was ecstatic, thrusting hard for a while and then backing off, just putting the head of his cock in me, gyrating his hips, moving his cock in a circle inside of me. His face was wet with sweat, his mouth gasping, his nose flaring and eyes closed as he buried his cock deeply into me. Without even touching myself, just watching and feeling him, I was close to the orgasm of my life. With a loud cry Josh erupted in my depths and then cum shot from my dick, drenching us both. "Oh, Daddy," I cried as he collapsed on top of me. We fell asleep in each other's arms.

- - -

In less than a month, I'd moved in with Josh. Mom was upset for a few days, but she came around. Besides, she had met some new guy at work and was in love again.

It was there, with Josh, in that spectacular bedroom, that my real education began. Josh was a master cocksman and taught me things I'd never dreamed of. I didn't have to sell my butt any more, but Josh made sure I got some variety. "Part of your education," he'd say. He introduced me to all kinds of men, but one was special. In fact, Josh was part of it. He introduced me to a buddy of his, one of the actors on one of the TV series that he worked on, handsome Rick Morita. Very few people would guess from his macho persona on screen that he was gay. He was about five foot ten, with an incredible gym-toned body and an amazing cock: a thick eight inches when limp and swelling to a huge eleven inches when fully hard.

We'd all worked out together at the gym, and Josh invited Rick back for coffee. But it was soon obvious that coffee was not what either of them had in mind. Rick, after a wink from Josh, drew me into a tentative embrace. I opened my lips, gently kissing him on the mouth, probing with my tongue. He groaned and closed his eyes, as I let my hands slip down his body, sliding his tank top up his body and letting it fall to the floor, revealing his compact and delectable torso. I took his hands, guiding him towards me. Taking the hint he began to undress me as I played with his prominent nipples, feeling my cock bulge in my shorts. Soon we both stood topless, hornily grinding our crotches together.

I glanced at Josh and he cupped a crotch in each hand, massaging, squeezing, making us both frantic to satisfy our lust. He stood behind me, pressing his crotch into my ass as I kissed Rick's deep, wet mouth. Our mingled saliva dribbled down our chins. Josh's cock lengthened against my tight butt as his hands pulled down my fly, opening my zipper, slowly pushing my shorts down my muscled thighs. He cupped my ass, running his thumb down the crack, making me groan in anticipation.

He moved round to Rick, running his fingers down the guys thighs, rubbing his ass, then slowly peeling off his shorts as he had with me, leaving us both naked and horny, eating each other's mouth and rubbing our straining cocks together. Josh took us by the shoulders and propelled us into the inner sanctum. Rick embraced Josh, then running his hands over the muscled, toned chest, feeling the firm flesh under his thin tee-shirt began kissing him, real hot, wet and slow. His hands pulled the shirt up from Josh's waist, peeling it up. They broke briefly to let Josh pull it off, revealing his glorious muscular pecs, his abs begging to be licked, his nipples firm and inviting in their hairy nest, red and aching for attention.

They embraced once more, Rick tonguing Josh's neck, as he cupped his hard, tight buns, kneading the flesh. I stood watching them kiss and fondle, my erection iron hard in my hand as I stroked it and rubbed my nipples, getting more and more excited as I watched them enjoy the feel of each others' body.

I moaned encouragement as Rick undid Josh' waistband and slipped his hand into his crotch. Grinning at the hard dick he found there, he undid the zipper and slowly the shorts fell to the floor, leaving Josh's thick cock thrusting straight out, erect and threatening, promising ecstasy.

As Josh groaned in pleasure, Rick knelt and took the huge, angry red cockhead in his hot mouth, sucking it in as it stretched his lips taut, forcing his jaw open. Josh slowly started rocking his hips backwards and forwards, rhythmically pulling and pushing his flared thickness in and out of Rick's suctioning mouth. I was getting hot as hell watching them, eager to join the action. I could hear Rick gagging slightly each time Josh thrust his thick fucker deep into his tightly stretched throat. I decided it was time I had some action. I caught Josh's eye and he drew Rick up and we all moved onto the bed.

Rick returned to his sucking while Josh began to suck on him and I moved in behind Rick, liberally lubing his tight butthole, finger-fucking him before placing the head of my dick at the entrance to his asshole and carefully penetrated him. His sphincter felt like a warm mouth massaging as it caressed my cock, stretching and then relaxing, squeezing and then releasing. I tensed my asscheeks as I pushed home, forcing all of my cock into him, savoring the clenching of his buns around my dick. I pinched his nipples, toying with his firm pecs, feeling his beautiful hard body beneath my lustful touch, my fingers plying the ridges of his abs, feeling the soft, fuzzy hair on his hard, muscular torso and belly.

Josh grabbed the lube and spread a glob on my hole. He finger fucked me in rhythm with my thrusting before straddling and plugging my hungry ass with his huge, precum dripping boner. As we built momentum Rick, his face wet with sweat, eyes closed and nose flaring, was on the verge of orgasm, straining to hold back till his partners were ready to shoot their loads.

As Josh pounded into me Rick finally gasped, "I can't hold it any more, Billy. Ay Dios! I'm gonna come all over you. Shit, I love you up my ass! Ooooh, fuuuck!"

His cum erupted, peppering my heaving torso and lacing his own with sticky globs and streamers, gumming us together as I shot my own load with a final thrust that felt like my dick was deep in his stomach. Josh seemed to have expanded beyond anything I'd experienced, forcing my ass ring wide and wider. My cock was still hard and still plugging Rick as I pushed and pulled myself from one sensation to another, trying to drive into Rick's ass and make Josh drive into mine together, making violent, powerful thrusts between the two hunky bodies, gasping and groaning as I fucked and was fucked. Sweat flew off of me as my hips jerked between them, totally lost in lust.

Re-aroused, Rick groaned, bucked and twisted beneath me as Josh gasped above me, his hips slamming into mine. We came almost together, Josh collapsing on top of me, wedging his entire cock within me, forcing me into Rick with all my might. A few moments of thrusting, and I was getting off as never before, jerking my hips against them, as I screamed and came and came. My sperm spurted again deep inside Rick, my cock spasming and jerking, as I felt the huge cock wedged within me thicken and swell further as Josh came in my ass, his man-seed flooding my straining colon, overflowing and running down my inner thigh.

Completely spent, we all lay huddled together, exhausted. I awoke a couple of hours later, snuggled contentedly between my three-way initiators. I watched them sleeping, and realized, with their connections, Billy the Kid had really just begun his career in Tinsel town.

# ALWAYS ON THE PROWL
## Jason Carpenter

"Three darts for fifty cents! Break two balloons and take your pick of prizes!" I cried to the passing crowd with no response. The year of nineteen-seventy-five meant bad business on the midway, thanks to the ever-increasing cost of the games and a shit economy. Still, as a carny, it was my duty to suck money out of nearly empty wallets faster than I could suck cum out of my many male friends.

On the plus side, I got to watch all the young guys walk by wearing tight jeans, tooled boots, flamboyant western shirts and ten-gallon hats. That most of these cowboy wannabes had never been close to a horse didn't seem to dampen their enthusiasm.

As I called out again, a red-haired, green-eyed lad stopped to listen. "Try your luck, cowboy! Impress the girl in your life with one of these huge stuffed bears," I said, pointing at a five-foot tall blue bear that would cost a customer over $150 before he racked up enough points to earn the slightly moth-eaten animal.

He spoke so softly I barely heard him. "Wouldn't give it to no girl."

Hmm. Had Lady Luck sent me a new playmate? I waved him closer. "Got a fella, red?"

He moved up to my stand. His eyes seemed terribly sad.

"Got nobody," he said mournfully.

Shit fire and save the matches! A lonely soul I could take advantage of. "Want a fella?" I asked, giving him my best smile and a practiced wink.

His stony expression brightened a bit; and one corner of his mouth attempted to form a smile. He shrugged. "Never been with a guy, but I have these feeling sometimes...."

I stuck out my callused hand. "Jake Cates."

He put his hand in mine and offered a loose, damp handshake. "Larry. Larry Conroy."

"I'd like to help you with those feelings, Larry. We'll have some fun, okay? I can ride all the rides for free and I'd love to have you as my guest," I told him, my fucktube growing rigid as I examined him more closely.

His jeans were so tight I could see the outline of his cock through the denim. He was slim and his cock appeared to be abnormally large for the rest of him. My cock thumped in rhythm with my heart. He finally smiled. "Okay. When can you take off work?" he asked.

I leaped over the front counter, reached up and drew down the heavy wooden shutter, and slammed shut the combination locks at either side. "How about now?"

His eyes traveled to my bulge. The tip of his pink tongue darted out and licked his lips. "Want to ride the tilt-a-whirl, Jake?" Larry asked.

"I'd rather ride the Ferris wheel," I said, giddy with anticipation.

"No one can see inside the gondola. I could, uh, blow you at the very top," I ventured.

His smile brought me to an incredible nine-inch erection. Our hands brushed as we walked toward the Ferris wheel.

Joe, the attendant, recognized me and welcomed us aboard. He locked the safety bar across our laps and closed the door. We slowly inched our way to the top as other people boarded.

Acres of rides and games stretched to the gates of the Coliseum where the rodeo was in progress. The air smelled of stale grease from the thousands of corn dogs, French fries, onion rings and turkey legs being sold to the strong-stomached throngs.

The Ferris wheel began to move. I put my palm at the back of Larry's neck and drew him closer until our lips met, first softly, then in a heated hunger. He wasn't completely uninitiated, I noticed, when his tongue slipped into my mouth. Pre-cum seeped from my dick-slit.

I whimpered.

Fumbling in the close confines of the cage, I found Larry's zipper and tugged it down. His swollen meat jumped free. I encircled his cock with my hand, unable to reach completely around the big sonovabitch! His own slippery oozings provided adequate lubrication as I fisted him from tip to base in an easy, leisurely motion. If he wasn't eleven inches, he was close enough!

Our tongues continued to wrestle as I stroked his meaty muscle. He braced himself against the seat and fucked my hand, now licking my neck and darting his wet tongue maddeningly into my ear. His hot breath made me squirm like a worm on a hot-plate.

Tiny whines of pleasure echoing from his throat told me he was ready to pop. This boy was long overdue for having his pipes flushed. His cum boiled upward from his reddened slit explosively, spurting a creamy fountain as his balls contracted and emptied. I swiftly ducked my head and engulfed his flaming lance with my eager lips. I sucked hard, drawing his steaming jizz into my mouth while manipulating his heavilyveined shaft, squeezing firmly, milking every pungent, salty drop onto my tongue before luxuriating in one long, delicious swallow.

His fingers played lovingly in my hair as I licked him clean. "Great, Jake. That was fantastic," Larry breathed.

"Only the beginning ... if you're game," I said, already imagining how tight his sweet ass would be around my cock.

"My turn," he said. He wriggled his way beneath the safety bar and knelt between my legs. He unzipped me, exposing my purple-headed club to the cooling air, then took me in his mouth. I fed him my cock by degrees. His jaw popped as he took every inch. He licked and sucked amateurishly, but it didn't matter. I was so excited I couldn't hold back. I thrust in and out of his mouth with long, quick strokes. "I'm face-fucking you, Larry! Eat my cum! Swallow my cock, you bastard!" He relaxed the muscles in his throat and got most of my turgid prick down the back of his gullet. Faster and faster I pounded into his mouth until I felt molten jism spew out of me, splashing his throat with my salty sex-juice. He gagged briefly, but managed to swallow my load.

"You are the best damn cocksucker I've ever met," I lied.

"Bull. I bet you say that to all the boys."

I smiled down at him. "Yeah. Matter of fact...."

He gave my shriveling dick a firm tug.

"I'm kiddin'! You're the very best, I swear to God!"

"Okay. That's better," he said, as the ride came to an end and we adjusted our clothing.

Brought closer by trading blowjobs, we continued our stroll around the midway. "Oh, look, a fun house," Larry said excitedly. He gave my ass a surreptitious pinch. "Can we go?"

"Sure. Let's go," I said, playfully bumping my shoulder against his.

The fun house was a building containing dark corridors, a maze of mirrors, moving floors, and other delights, such as monsters leaping at us from the blackness. Larry clung protectively to my shoulder. I could hear other people somewhere ahead, screaming. Then I felt Larry's hand on my dick-bulge. He pressed me against the wall and fumbled in the darkness to free my cock and balls from my pants. I heard his own zipper, and a second later felt his cock rubbing against mine in the blackness. I took my meat in my hand like Larry held his and we played dueling dicks while kissing hard and hot. I trading my handful of sex for Larry's, and felt him do the same. We stood like that, fondling and caressing for several minutes until we heard other people coming up behind us. We moved on reluctantly.

Outside once again, I asked Larry if he wanted to see the Rodeo currently in progress in the large coliseum adjacent to the midway.

"Naw. The smell of horseshit doesn't get me off," he answered. "What I'd really like to do is be alone with you. Is there some place...?"

"Yeah, my trailer's nearby," I volunteered.

"Okay. Take me there," Larry said, is green eyes filled with adventure.

I led him to my thirty-foot-long trailer and ushered him inside. I wanted to ream him out more than I wanted to draw my next breath. The thought was transmitted downward from my brain. Fire spread through my stomach, rushed to my balls, and made my dickmeat solidify into a shaft of steel. Figuring I might as well not beat around the tush, I came right out and told him, "Larry, I want to butt-fuck you."

His pretty mouth twisted into a picture of doubt. "I don't know ... I never liked enemas."

"It ain't the same. You'll like it. I'll make sure you like it," I said, hearing the pleading tone in my voice.

"Shit, if it means that much to you...."

"Oh, it does! It sure as hell does," I said, unsnapping the buttons on his western shirt. Larry's chest was boyish. Hairless. Smooth. His ribs showed through his pale flesh. I fell to my knees and unfastened his jeans, tugging them to the floor. He was fully erect. And I mean fully. I've seen movies where vampires were dispatched with wooden stakes smaller than Larry's cock.

Hurriedly undressing, I took his hand and led him to my unmade bed. I crawled to the middle of the bed and patted the space beside me. Larry snuggled up to me. We kissed. I wrapped my hand around his throbbing rod and felt it pulse with his desire. He watched my cock fill with blood and stiffen, prodding his belly.

I rolled him to his side, with his back to me, his pale ass jutting out. Holding my poker in my hand, I ran the cum-dripping crown up and down his blonde-fuzzed asscrack. His ass-eye was a wrinkled, pink nub. I poked it, virtually screwing my cock into him, stretching his virgin ass-ring to new dimensions. "Ouch!" I heard him say as, with a final grunt, I stuffed my whole shaft up his tight, hot ass and began buttfucking him. I clasped his stomach to pull him closer.

"I can feel you all the way up here," he said, his voice trembling, as he placed my hand high on his abdomen.

"You okay?" I asked, slowly humping him.

He nodded. "That's nice. Really nice."

"I bet you say that to all the guys...."

"No, no. I don't usually...." He laughed.

The smell of his ass was strong in the air as I took my time with him, ramming my rigid member ever more deeply up his hot guts.

I fisted his monster cock, jerking him off to my own rhythm. Wet sounds filled my ears as his pre-cum squeaked between my fingers. I hunched and probed his assmeat for what seemed like hours before I felt my cum spurt up from my ball-sac, rushing hot and strong like water through a burst spillway.

Quickly rolling Larry to his stomach, I spread his legs, climbed between them, and pounded against his asscheeks, faster and faster, deep into the sweet-meat where we'd all live if we could, until my hot fuckcream shot out of me, bathing his guts with the slippery splash of my dick-honey. "Aaahhhhggg! I ... Man, oh man!" I cried out, filling his dark cavity to overflowing, grunting like a wounded beast. His gush of cum spewed and bubbled into my palm.

The scent of hot sex was intoxicating, but, exhausted, we slept.

I awoke with my meat still plugged up Larry's asshole and moved off him until it slipped out with a deep sucking sound.

Larry was also awake. He rolled over to face me and fingered a stray wisp of my dirty blond hair off my forehead. "Was I any good?" he asked.

I kissed him. "Cherry's always good. Nothing like it. You'll see ... if you decide those feelings you've had lean this way."

In answer, he got on his hands and knees and wiggled his ass. "Fuck me again, please?"

"Okay." Kneeling behind him, I parted his asscheeks and bent to lick delicious circles around his now ruptured ass-bud. Then I fed my cum-slick prick to him, stabbing away until I had all of it in. The his pubic hair tickled my testicles. I spanked him with my pelvis.

"Fuck me hard ... really hard ... please," he begged. Over and over, going crazy with me in him.

I gave him the fuck of his life. I thrust as hard as I could, over and over. Shortly, my stomach muscles cramped and I spurted ribbons of cum up Larry's very willing ass. Judging by Larry's grunts, he had shot his load, too, as my stiff cock hammered his sensitive prostate.

Later, showered and dressed, I led him back to the midway. As we parted, I said, "I'll be in town another week. Come back and I'll show you some tricks."

"You showed me plenty today," he sighed happily.

I shrugged. "Still, I'll let you fuck my ass if you want."

"No. Can't!" He flashed his white teeth. "There's this guy I know from school – I want him to be my first."

"Think he's cherry?"

"Almost positive."

"Hmm. Well, bring 'im back with you sometime," I suggested, always on the prowl.

Friendship is one thing, but new meat is another.

# RAMBLING WITH CALIFORNIA SWEETWATER
## Joe Sexton

When I was six I fell in love with California Sweetwater, the hired man on my grandfather's West Texas farm. Perhaps it wasn't love in the usual sense, but whatever it was, it must have impressed me deeply, as most of my lovers over the intervening forty years have resembled him.

"Cal," I once asked him, "is California Sweetwater your real name?"

"Depends on what you mean by real. I give it to myself, so it suits me better than what I was born with."

"It doesn't sound like any name I ever heard. What made you think of it?"

"Well, I was born in Sweetwater, Texas, see, and later when I was rambling, California was the place I liked best."

"What's rambling?"

"Oh, just wandering wherever the notion takes you, looking for excitement, working for your keep or a little money when you need it, raising hell when you feel like it, moving on when you're tired of a place."

It sounded then like a great way to live, and I could hardly wait to start rambling myself.

Last night, driving home late after a movie, I passed the "It" Club, one of those bars on San Pablo Avenue that feature Country entertainment, so popular among the exiled Texans and Okies who have settled in the blue-collar suburban communities across the Bay from San Francisco. The miniature theater marquee over the door announced:

THIS WEEK ONLY: LIVE!
JOHN EARL BOBBITT – RICHMOND RAMBLERS
LADIES WELCOME – DANCING

My Texas roots suddenly gave a sharp tug and on impulse I pulled over, parked, and walked to the entrance. I seldom go to straight bars, but the prospect of seeing and hearing a live hillbilly show, as we used to call it, drew me in. The small room was crowded and smoky and smelled strongly of beer and sweat. The dance floor was packed with couples dancing closely together in variations of the fox trot or just shuffling slowly in time to the music.

I shoved my way to the bar, ordered a drink, and looked around. Through a hidden speaker Crystal Gayle was wailing the lyric "Don't it make my brown eyes blue?" at an almost unbearable volume. Most of the men were in jeans, some wore boots, Stetsons, cowboy shirts. The women were heavily made-up versions of Dolly Parton and Loretta Lynn.

There was a small platform in the corner, crowded with microphones, musical instruments, and amplifying equipment. As I watched, a short, fat man walked to the nearest microphone; a spotlight speared the darkness, illuminating his bald head, the recorded music ended abruptly, and he announced in the expectant hush, "Ladies and gents, we've got a treat for you tonight. All the way from a week's engagement at the Pioneer Club in Fresno, let's give him a big welcome, folks, along with our own Richmond Ramblers, ladies and gentlemen – JOHN EARL BOBBITT!"

A young man sprinted from a door in the rear and jumped on to the platform, amid sparse applause and a few whistles. He was followed by three bored-looking middle-aged men dressed in pieces of Western garb mixed with ordinary street clothes. John Earl wore a spectacular suit-of-lights, the kind of costume that used to be obligatory for the successful Country-Western singer. The crimson suit hugged his tall thin body, and the jacket, pieced with sky-blue sections set off with black scrollwork, displayed a line of silver fringe across the chest. Down the outside of each leg ran a stripe of flashing sequins. Hair like shredded wheat fell over his forehead, and long sideburns licked at the corners of his mouth. I almost fell off the stool when I looked at his face. There stood California Sweetwater! Cleft chin, slightly crooked nose, and wide clear blue eyes that seemed made for gazing across prairies.

Bowing deeply from the waist, he acknowledged the few handclaps as if they were an ovation, picked up his guitar, and stood there for a moment, sparkling and glowing as if with an inner light, rays shooting out in all directions.

"Thank you," he said, strumming and tuning his guitar. "I want to thank you folks for coming here tonight. It's great to be here in--uh--Richmond, and I want you all to have a great time." His voice was smooth and confident, with no trace of accent that I could detect;

he was a farm boy, perhaps, from the Central Valley, who grew up listening to WSM Nashville and Buck Owens out of Bakersfield.

"I'd like to start off with a great old song by one of Country Music's great songwriters, Floyd Tillman, recorded way back in 1939 by Gene Autry, 'It Makes No Difference Now'. Hope you like it ... one of the all-time ... uh ... great songs."

After a brief instrumental introduction, he began to sing in a rich baritone, accompanying himself on his guitar, while in the background the band provided discreet harmony and rhythm. He sang with head thrown slightly back, gazing down at us earnestly through half-lowered eyelids, patting time with the toe of one black-and-red-booted foot, and moving his entire body in a slow, sensual roll.

I gazed back at him, not wanting the song to end. (It was one of California Sweetwater's favorites.) After a moment I shut my eyes, a curtain was pulled abruptly aside, and there, on the bright stage of memory, I saw enacted in minute detail scenes so many years ago....

"Go to bed, Joe," Mom said, for the third time in five minutes, sounding as if she really meant it this time.

"But I can't sleep with the light on and everybody talking," I countered, with my usual argument that never convinced her.

"Nobody's talking and you know the lamp doesn't bother you. Now move!" She handed me my pajamas and pushed me toward the middle room to change.

I walked reluctantly toward the unlighted middle room to change into my pajamas. I passed Grandpa Wood sitting in the corner in his swivel chair, Bible open on his knees, bifocals half-way down his nose, eyes closed, as if pondering a passage he meant to expound on in church on Sunday, but a gentle snore betrayed him. Next to him, sharing the light from the room's single kerosene lamp, sat Grandma Wood, in her favorite ladder-back hide-bottom chair, crocheting squares for a bedspread. On the front steps outside the open door Cal sat picking out a tune on his guitar, and singing along in a voice so sad and beautiful I wanted to cry. His sun-bleached hair glowed gold in the lamplight and his hard, weather-beaten face (he was only twenty-five) looked soft and blurred through the mesh of the screen.

I changed quickly into my pajamas, raced back to the front room, hopped into bed, and within minutes was asleep.

Cal and I shared a double bed in the "front parlor" of the three room shotgun house Grandpa Wood had built himself – the rooms were strung together in a row with connecting doors, so that if you stood at the front door and fired a gun toward the open back door, you'd hit nothing at all – the shot would simply speed unimpeded toward the distant horizon.

Cal had been orphaned as a baby and had matured early, roaming the Great Plains, the West, and the Dust Bowl, working at odd jobs here and there, and coming to rest finally on my grandparents' farm. Grandpa Wood needed an extra hand, and Cal had tired of his homeless hand-to-mouth existence.

I used to try very hard to stay awake until Cal's bedtime so that I could explore in the dark intimacy of bed the strong attraction I felt for him. But I managed to do that only once.

At this time my mother and I lived with my grandparents; my father was in Houston, working as a milkman for Borden's and learning the electrician's trade in night school. He said he didn't want to spend his life as a tenant farmer working somebody else's land. He used to send packages occasionally, and it was almost better than Christmas to tear off the battered brown wrapping paper and find inside a celluloid wind-up car, or a Charlie McCarthy doll, or Kandy Korn.

"Mona Fay," Grandma Wood would say disapprovingly, "you ought to write G.W. and tell him to send something useful. Joe needs clothes." I almost hated her then. As far as I was concerned, my father could do no wrong, but he wasn't very real to me. It was Cal who occupied my thoughts. During the day when he was busy at his chores around the house and before he left for the field, I followed him everywhere, and sometimes he let me help him slop the hogs or carry water from the well to the house. In the evenings he and Grandpa Wood sat smoking and talking politics on the back steps while the women prepared supper.

During this time, Cal taught me how to roll a cigarette with the Bull Durham tobacco and thin white paper he carried in his shirt pocket. I got so good at it, learning to lick the paper just enough to stick but not enough to get soggy, that when he felt like having a cigarette, he'd just pull out the makings, toss them to me and say, "How about a smoke, pardner?"

Cal was tall and deeply sunburned except for his forehead, kept white and smooth as a girl's by the big Stetson he wore. He radiated a powerful masculine appeal that I recognized and appreciated even then. I do not know if he was handsome in the usual sense. It didn't matter – there were no other men in my life his age, no one to compare him with, except a few faded portraits from an earlier generation in Mama Wood's photograph album.

I would awake in the mornings aware of his warm scent in the depression next to me – he would be up and already at his chores by then. I would lie there, listening to the faint clatter of breakfast dishes being washed in the kitchen, and promise myself once again to use every stratagem to postpone my bedtime to coincide with his.

When Cal wasn't around and my mother had time, she read to me. I loved sitting in her lap, looking at the pictures in Holland's Farm Journal while she read aloud the children's column, about an elf who wore a paint box slung over his shoulder by a shoe string. Every week he solved a different problem with that box of paints. I think it was then I decided to become a painter myself. Other times she read from the Bible, and I liked that too, especially the exciting stories like Daniel in the Lion's Den or Moses Leading the Children of Israel out of Egypt. Her voice was musical though somewhat husky, and to me she seemed more beautiful than any of the models in the Sears Roebuck catalogue.

When she whipped me, as she occasionally did, using Papa Wood's razor strap, she cried along with me, and hugged me afterwards and begged my forgiveness. She always explained very carefully why she had to punish me, and though I can't say I didn't resent the discipline momentarily, I forgave her and was ready almost immediately to climb into her lap again for another story.

That was the year I started school. I looked forward to it eagerly; it was a chance to meet and play with other children, to learn to read, and to have books of my own. The school bus, a faded yellow relic patched with scraps of wood and baling wire, stopped at our gate about 7:00 every morning, and I found myself having to get up almost as early as Cal.

School was exciting, even more than I'd hoped, but I found myself missing Cal's companionship; I missed helping him with the chores and rolling his smokes and planning for bedtime. Getting up so early made it even more difficult for me to stay awake evenings.

Gradually I began to notice how Cal and Mother looked at each other at the supper table, and how she laughed, flushing an attractive pink, at everything he said, whether it was funny or not. I suppose I was jealous. I wanted him all to myself, and I wanted her all to myself; it was all right for them to like each other, but not that much, and only when I was around to keep an eye on them. I wondered why my grandparents didn't seem to notice it.

One Friday morning in the second or third week of school, I stood next to the castor bean bush in the front yard, waiting for the school bus to appear through the heat waves already shimmering in the distance where I imagined the Pacific Ocean to be. It occurred to me that I would like to stay home that day and help Cal with the chores. Why not? I was doing well in school and I was sure no one would notice or care. On impulse, without thinking about it further, I turned and ran around the house toward the dugout in the back yard.

The dugout was a cellar situated halfway between the house and the barn. Its exterior resembled a miniature mountain, and on one side was a wooden door lying slanted to the angle of the slope. Inside the door a short, narrow flight of steps led down into an opening no larger than six by ten feet, with a ceiling just high enough to allow an adult to stand comfortably. It was used for storing the fruits and vegetables Mother and Mama Wood had put up during canning season, for hanging hams and sides of bacon, and for protection when a tornado was approaching.

I lifted the door, crept down the stairs, and crawled under the cot that stood against the far wall. A ragged patchwork quilt lay over the cot and hung down almost to the floor--it was a perfect hiding place. I didn't mind the dark; I had fallen asleep there many times before, in tornado season or during severe sand storms. I loved the familiar smells of chalky earth, pumpkin seeds hanging in mesh bags to dry, and the worn-out leather harnesses and saddle parts put there for future repairs. I was in the habit of going there frequently just to breathe the cool pungent air and daydream. A little daylight filtered down through the air vent in the ceiling; there were also a kerosene lamp, candles, and matches on the table next to the cot, but I preferred the darkness, and knew the precise location of each object and piece of furniture.

For a few moments I lay there quietly, listening for the sound of the school bus approaching from Causey, near the New Mexico border, over the corrugated, pot-hole-riddled dirt road that ran straight as the edge of a ruler past our house and, I used to think, on to infinity. The motor chugged and wheezed, almost stopped, then labored past. I was safe. Mr. Milsap, who drove the bus, and who seemed ancient to me, although he was probably only my grandfather's age, never stopped or honked if his passengers were not out in the designated spot waiting for him. He considered it no business of his to round them up. (I'd heard this lecture several times already.) If they were sick, too bad; if they were late, it served them right to be left behind, and they'd sure as hell be on time the next day.

I had discovered he meant what he said one morning when I'd been a few seconds late. I was actually at the gate, and waved – I'm sure he saw me – but, as I wasn't already outside on the edge of the road, he drove on, ignoring my frantic calls and gestures. I'd been made to walk the three long dusty miles to school.

Lying motionless I soon grew tired and began to realize I was not so safe after all. How could I come out of hiding and join Cal in his chores without being seen by Mother? And even if she didn't see me, would Cal feel it was his duty to turn me over to her? As I grappled with these thoughts and the dawning knowledge that I had acted unwisely, the door was suddenly flung open, and I recoiled, backing further into my dark corner. It was all over, I had been seen, my hiding place discovered. Voices flooded the small room--Mother and Cal were coming down the steps. Just as I was about to slide out and surrender, rather than allow myself to be dragged in an undignified struggle from beneath the cot, I noticed that the voices were low, whispered, secret, voices not meant for my ears. It was clear that my presence was undetected.

"Come on, Mona Fay," Cal said, in a low urgent whisper. "Give me a little sugar." This was followed by a few moments of silence.

"No, Cal, that's enough," Mother whispered back. They hadn't closed the door and I could see their feet standing in a bright patch of light spilling in through the opening, as I peered cautiously through the narrow crack between floor and quilt. They were facing each other, standing very close together at the foot of the stairs. "I've got to get back--Mother wants me to bring a ham. No! Now stop that!"

Her words sounded mad but the tone was curiously pleased, almost teasing.

"Just a few minutes, honey," Cal begged, his voice sounding hoarse and strange. "We're wasting time."

There was a creaking of springs as Cal sat on the edge of the cot. I moved farther back, away from the ominous bulge. I felt cornered; my favorite hideout had become a prison. There were more creaks and another bulge as Mother joined him on the cot, and then began a series of sounds I couldn't identify, a scuffling, a rustling of clothes, noises like my lungs made when I had an asthma attack, thrashings about. What could they be doing? Whatever it was, I wished it was me there with Cal in the half-light, with him wanting something from me so badly it made his voice sound gravelly with excitement and his breath come in gasping grunts.

After a few minutes of this there was a long pause, when all motion and sound ceased. I held my breath, fearing it might be heard in the sudden silence.

Then both rose at once and Mother said, "That better be the last time. G.W.'s coming back in a few weeks. I'd die if he found out." Her voice sounded flat and sad. Cal didn't answer but I heard him strike a match and I smelled the familiar odor of Bull Durham tobacco as he began to smoke.

"You hear?" she persisted.

"Yeah, I hear," he said after a moment.

I heard her running up the stairs and then Cal sat down again on the cot as he finished his cigarette. I could see the heels of his scuffed boots with the pointed toes and the fancy scroll-work on the sides. They were so close I could reach right out and touch them, grab them just as I did when he came in from the field and let me pull them off for him. It was a kind of game: I would turn my back to him, take one of his legs between mine, grasp the heel with both hands and pull, while he pushed gently on my rear with the other foot; then, just as the boot came loose, he would kick harder, sending me flying – I would fall sprawling, rolling over and over, exaggerating the force of the kick, repeating it again with the other boot.

Finally he heaved a great sigh and I heard his steps fading as he slowly climbed the stairs. Darkness enclosed me again as he shut the door behind him, and I lay for what seemed a very long time, pondering what I had just seen and heard. Somehow the episode seemed related to my night-time yearning for Cal, but I wasn't at all sure how or why.

One thing was certain: there was an element of betrayal here. Hadn't Mother said she'd die if Daddy "found out"? There were too many conflicting emotions at work inside me – jealousy, envy, love, curiosity. I finally gave it up and concentrated on extricating myself from my present predicament. There was only one thing to do, it seemed – walk to school and try to slip in without being noticed.

The next day was Saturday and I enjoyed following Cal around as he worked at his chores – there were no holidays on a farm, as Papa Wood was fond of saying. Cal seemed friendlier than usual, more relaxed, more willing to talk and notice my presence. We spent several hours wandering around the pasture, dropping heads of poisoned maize down the prairie dog holes.

"Didn't you ever have a home of your own, Cal?" I asked him.

"Naw – nothing that deserved the name," he replied. I could never get much more than that out of him about his previous life. "Miz Wood's the only mother I've ever had, and they ain't a better man living than Mr. Wood. Reckon I'll just stay on here for quite a while. They'll need me, especially after you and your mama go to Houston to live with your daddy."

"Thought you liked California best," I reminded him.

"Well," he said, grinning, "a fella can change his mind, can't he? Besides I never said nothing about girls. They ain't nothing can beat a Texas girl."

This didn't make much sense to me. There weren't many girls around that I could see – not Cal's age, anyway. Somehow I never thought of my mother as a "Texas girl."

That afternoon I watched while he made a slingshot for me, carving the handle from part of an old board, and using a scrap of rubber inner tube for the business end. He showed me how to aim and shoot it, and how to hold the handle so I wouldn't hit my own hand when I released the pouch. I practiced shooting at the prairie dogs that kept popping up from their burrows to scent the air and to bark at each other across the fields, but I never got good enough to hit one of them.

As usual on Saturdays, supper was early. I watched as Cal helped himself to the last biscuit on the plate, broke it open, and used the pieces to mop up the last traces of beans and sorghum syrup. Although I had already finished, watching him made me hungry again. Cal rarely spoke during a meal, keeping his eyes on his plate or staring blankly into space, savoring each bite, a connoisseur of intricate subtle flavors. The muscles in his hard, lean face moved slowly and deliberately as he chewed the mounds of food shoveled into his mouth at regular intervals. He erected small pyramids of food on the back of his fork, using his knife as a trowel, with moist crumbs of bread or mashed potatoes as cement. After each pyramid had been carefully constructed, he would sprinkle his creation with hot red pepper, move his head close to his plate, and with never a drop spilled, engulf the mess.

When Cal's plate was white and glistening, he tipped his chair back and sighed, hooking his thumbs into the side pockets of his jeans. He waited until Mama Wood gave him permission to smoke, pulled his tobacco pouch from the pocket of his faded blue shirt, and threw it over to me. I rolled him a cigarette in record time – I was an expert now. Papa Wood filled his pipe and they both sat smoking quietly as the women cleared the table and washed the dishes.

"What say you and me go to the picture show over in Morton tonight, partner," Cal said to me, looking past me to Mother. "They got a new picture show just opened – don't have to drive all the way to Littlefield now."

I had been to a movie only once before, so long ago I could hardly remember it.

"Yes!" I shouted, raced around the table, jumped up and down, and generally created havoc in the kitchen.

"Think we ought to ask your mother to go along, just to make sure we don't get into any mischief?" he asked, again looking at Mother and winking. "I'd be glad to take y'all too," he said to my grandparents, "if Mr. Wood will let me borrow the pickup. I've got a little money saved up."

"Well, I don't know," Mother said hesitantly, looking at Mama Wood. "Joe's not used to staying up so late."

"Oh, y'all go on," Mama Wood said. "It won't hurt him for once, and tomorrow's Sunday. He can sleep late. Do you good to get out. And with the boy along, can't nobody talk." She lowered her voice. "You know how people are."

"Don't you and Mr. Wood want to come too?" Cal persisted, but I could see he was saying it just for politeness. I was surprised he included me in the invitation, after what I'd seen the day before, but I supposed it was because he really liked my company, and maybe he knew it would please my mother. It never occurred to me that my role was that of chaperone, but even if I had known, it wouldn't have bothered me, as long as I got to go.

"Now I don't want to hear another word about it," Mama Wood said firmly. "Go on before it gets too late – and be careful."

After the movie, I dozed most of the way home, sitting between Mother and Cal, resting my head first against one, then the other. The evening had been exciting and exhausting, full of new experiences: the line of people stretching halfway down the block, the theater lobby smelling of hot buttered popcorn and new carpet, the dim interior softly illuminated by regularly spaced pairs of glowing orange and green light fixtures, like giant frosted Popsicles. Dreaming of seven dwarfs who whistled while they worked, a handsome prince who looked exactly like Cal, and a Snow White with no face at all, I was vaguely and lazily aware of the whispered conversation between Mother and Cal.

We arrived home late, but I woke up quickly, refreshed by my nap, suddenly excited by the prospect of joining Cal in bed while both of us were awake. I changed into my pajamas, jumped into bed, and pulled the covers up to my chin. Cal turned down the lamp wick, blew out the flickering flame, and joined me almost immediately. I was surprised that he was naked, although I caught only a glimpse of pale angular torso and darkly sunburned arms and face.

He lay on his back and within moments was snoring. I moved close, fitting myself into the depression along his side and throwing one arm over his chest. My heart pounded, and there was something the matter with my breathing; his sweat-and-tobacco smell enveloped me; I wanted the moment to last forever. Fearing that sleep would overtake me at any moment, I decided to delay no longer, and I moved my hand slowly over the hard ridges of his rib cage, down the flat abdomen and through a nest of tightly curled hair, to that warm appendage of flesh that seemed to me so beautiful and mysterious. Just as I grasped it and felt its smoothness in my hand, and began with intense excitement to explore its weight, its size and shape, he started violently, giving a sort of gasp, and flung my arm back roughly.

"Goddam! What the hell are you doing?" he whispered in an ugly tone I'd never heard him use before. "Don't you never do that again, you hear? Unless you want to get beat half to death. It ain't natural." He turned away from me and moved to the far side of the bed. Humiliated and frightened, I lay for what seemed hours, not daring to move, at last drifting into a troubled sleep.

The following morning my mother called me several times before I reluctantly allowed consciousness to return, aware even in half-sleep that all was not well. Cal had been up for hours and I had to dress hurriedly without breakfast to be ready to leave for Sunday services on time. This was a baptizing Sunday – the late summer revival meeting had been unusually effective – and instead of driving over to the Baptist Church in Goodland, we had only to walk half a mile down the road to the Ponder place, where baptisms were usually performed. The southwest corner of Bailey County boasted several larger cattle tanks, but this one had the advantage of being owned by a deacon of the Church who didn't mind having his water muddied occasionally if it meant a few more souls being washed in the Blood of the Lamb.

I was glad of the excuse to get away from Cal--he never attended church services. I was still smarting from his rough words and I dreaded having to face him. I decided I would pretend that I remembered nothing or that I had been dreaming.

Dressed in clean white cotton robes that flashed with a blinding intensity in the brilliant sunlight, the new converts stood in a semi-circle around the inside perimeter of Mr. Ponder's wooden cattle tank. Circled by wide metal bands and standing some three or four feet high, it looked like the truncated end of an enormous wine cask.

The small congregation huddled like sheep in the scant shade of the windmill and sang "O Happy Day" while Brother Self immersed each of the newly saved in the cold clear water recently pumped from the nearby "eternally flowing" artesian well, intoning repeatedly, "I baptize you in the name of the Father, the Son, and the Holy Ghost."

The windmill creaked and groaned a mournful accompaniment, the blades whirring erratically, slowing almost to a stop, then picking up speed as the wind renewed itself.

I observed the ceremony with a certain anxiety, wondering when, if ever, I would be "saved", what it felt like, and whether I would know when it happened. Then I closed my eyes tightly and asked God to forgive me if what I had done with Cal, what I felt for him was a sin.

When we arrived back home Cal was sitting on the front steps waiting for us.

"You want me to kill and dress a fryer for dinner, Miz Wood?" he asked.

"Why yes, Cal, would you?" Mama Wood said. "That White Leghorn with the limp will do – she looks like a good layer, but her leg's not getting any better. I suspect someone's been at her with a slingshot," she went on, casting a significant look in my direction.

"Come on, pardner, you want to give me a hand?" Cal said to me, and I stood gazing at him, amazed and grateful that he had forgotten or intended to ignore last night's incident, but still deeply hurt and puzzled, and I shook my head.

"Sure you do," he said. "How am I going to catch her if you don't help?" He took me by the hand and I allowed myself to be led into the back yard where a dozen or so hens, pullets, and a rooster named Scrap ambled about, pecking in a desultory manner at invisible seeds on the hard cracked ground. Most were Rhode Island Reds, who seemed to thrive best, live longest, and lay the most eggs, but a few White Leghorns strutted among them, aristocratic and arrogant, bred not to work for their dinner, but to be dinner.

"There she is," Cal said, pointing to the limping pullet I accidentally had lamed with a stone from my slingshot. It wasn't really an accident – I had aimed at her, but I was as surprised as she was when I actually hit her.

"You get behind her and drive her over this way," he suggested, "and I'll catch her just as she heads for the gate."

After some deliberately ineffectual movements on my part, he nevertheless managed to grab her, tucked her head under her left wing, which immediately quieted her, and handed her to me.

"Hold on to her a minute, will you, while I get the axe."

I stood irresolutely, unwilling to be an accomplice in the death of a creature that had already suffered enough at my hands, and reluctant to seem to forgive Cal so quickly; yet I didn't want to cut off all chance of a reconciliation. Before I could make up my mind, Cal returned with the short-handled hatchet reserved for this purpose, the beheading of chickens.

Killing a chicken for dinner was common – it happened at least once a week – and I always watched with a certain equanimity and curiosity, but usually from a distance and never as a participant. Somehow that seemed to make a difference.

"Now hold her steady," Cal instructed me as he helped position the tranquilized bird on the scarred chopping block that was black with years, blood and grease. Then he pulled her head from beneath her wing, stretching the neck taut, and she began to squawk and struggle with a surprising amount of noise and commotion. But this was cut short with one quick stroke of the hatchet. I released my hold and jumped back, but not quickly enough to avoid a crimson splatter of blood across my white Sunday shirt. The carcass flopped and tossed itself about with great agility for a few moments, and I watched as blood spurted from the neck and left dark irregular patterns on the thirsty ground.

The chicken's head still lay upon the block, one eye staring out at the world it seemed reluctant to leave. Then, slowly and deliberately, the inner eyelid began to close, winking at me as if we shared some slightly humorous secret.

Cal stood watching me with a strange smile. He grabbed the twitching body, its sleek white feathers now covered with blood and dirt, and flung it into the pot of scalding water my grandmother had prepared. After a few minutes he retrieved the bird, and plucked it quickly and efficiently, reducing it to naked blue-white flesh and yellow scaled claws. Hating him, and vowing never to eat chicken again, I turned and ran into the house, wanting suddenly to get as far from the scene as possible.

At the dinner table, I sat silent, sullen and queasy, for once not enjoying the spectacle of Cal's gastronomic technique. He and Mother seemed entirely too pleased with themselves. I felt definitely out of sorts and angry, not knowing exactly why, and that seemed to make it worse.

"Eat your chicken, Joe," Mother said, noticing my lack of appetite. "Why you haven't touched a thing! Are you sick?"

"No Ma'am."

"What is the matter with you? You've got the drumstick-- that's your favorite piece, isn't it?"

"Yes ma'am."

"I believe you're pouting about something. You stick that lip out any farther, someone's going to step on it!"

"I'm not hungry. May I be excused?"

Mother stopped eating and looked at me searchingly, her eyes all at once serious and stern. "Yes, you may be excused, but first I want to know why you were late to school on Friday. I saw Mrs. Chambers at the service this morning, and she told me you didn't come in until mid-morning. She said she wanted to check with me before doing anything about it. I was so embarrassed! I had to confess I knew nothing about it. Where were you?"

Caught off guard, I stammered something about being there, and that Mrs. Chambers must have just overlooked me.

"But Mr. Milsap said you didn't catch the bus that morning, either. And your little friend – what's his name? Carl? – said you didn't get there until recess. Now I want the truth!"

All eyes were on me. I was trapped. There was no way out but to resort to tears, which I did, but Mother was not impressed.

"Get the razor strap and go to the parlor. I'll be in after dinner," she said, her voice sounding more puzzled than angry.

As I neared the door I heard Mama Wood say, "Now don't be too hard on him, Mona Fay. All boys play hooky once in a while."

"It's not his playing hooky I mind so much, Mother, it's the lying. I hate to do it, but I'll have to whip him."

I walked slowly to the alcove where Papa Wood's razor strap hung, removed it from its nail on the wall, and headed on into the front room. Staring out the door past the barbed wire fence that followed the road in each direction as far as I could see, I watched a tumbleweed roll slowly across from Ponder's pasture. It came to rest at the barrier created by other tumbleweeds piled up to a height of two or three feet all along the fence. From the west a whirlwind of dust and sand moved erratically down the road, disintegrating as it reached the gate. Why was waiting for a whipping almost worse than the whipping itself?

When Mother arrived at last, she looked almost as worried as I felt.

"Come here, Joe," she said, sitting on the edge of the bed and pulling me to her. I refused to meet her eyes and stared steadfastly at a point between her shiny black Sunday pumps. "I don't want to whip you. If you tell me the truth now, and promise not to lie again, I'll let you off this time." I remained silent. "Look at me," she said, still gently, taking my face between her cool soft hands. I looked into her clear hazel eyes that gazed back with such concern, and noticed a new little wrinkle that had appeared between her eyebrows. Her dark bobbed auburn hair curled jauntily around her smooth oval face, and her lips trembled slightly at the corners, as if she were the one waiting to be whipped. I suddenly was filled with love for her, but at the same time I perversely wished to hurt her.

"Where were you Friday when you should have been in school?" she asked again, as if for the last time.

"The dugout," I muttered.

"What?"

"I was in the dugout," I repeated. "You know, where you and Cal go to have fun." My voice was loaded with as much venom as I could muster. "I was hiding under the cot when y'all came in."

She stared at me for a moment, her face slowly drained of color, and her eyes grew wide and dark.

"I'm going to tell, Daddy," I added, immediately regretting my words.

She continued to stare, and into her eyes came that veiled and almost hostile expression I had sometimes seen when she dealt with strangers or someone she distrusted. It struck me like a blow, and I knew I would give anything to have her look at me again as she used to do.

She gave a little laugh – I think it was a laugh – and said, "Oh, Joe, my poor baby! How did we get ourselves into this mess? We'll just have to give him up." Then she hugged me so hard I couldn't breathe and we fell back on the bed together; the little laugh turned into sobs, my tears joined hers, and we clung to each other until we'd cried ourselves out and lay exhausted. I may have slept a little.

Some time later we sat up and she handed me her handkerchief with the blue forget-me-nots embroidered in one corner. I wiped my eyes and nose on it, inhaling the scent of her face powder and lavender cologne.

"Your daddy's coming home soon," she said, looking straight into my eyes. "You won't say anything to him about this, I know. It would hurt him so terribly. It would hurt all of us."

I nodded and put my head in her lap.

"Don't blame, Cal," she said, running her fingers through my hair. "It wasn't his fault. It wasn't anyone's fault. It just happened. No, go wash your face."

At the door I turned and looked back to where she sat, small and crumpled, reddened eyes staring out the window.

"I'm sorry, Mother," I said, and when she smiled back at me I knew we had patched it up.

The remainder of that Sunday I spent wandering around the fields, shooting at prairie dogs with my slingshot. I didn't try very hard to hit them, and was glad to hear the taunting bark that each one gave as it disappeared into its burrow.

The wind blew and whistled and sent tumbleweeds racing across the barren ground, piling them up against an occasional mesquite tree, or hurling them westward across the miles on a long, rambling journey to California, like California Sweetwater in his rambling days.

Supper that night was quiet and meager. Cal's chair was empty and I dared not ask questions. Mother seemed bemused; she smiled vaguely at me at times while I toyed with my "crumble-in," a soggy concoction of cold cornbread broken into small pieces and covered with sweetmilk. It was Cal's favorite Sunday night meal, and to this day I cannot imagine why.

When I returned from school on Monday, I noticed that Cal's guitar was missing from its accustomed place in the corner. With a growing alarm I peered under the bed, and my suspicion was confirmed--it was gone: the black leather suitcase that had been with him through all his travels, patched and scuffed, covered with dozens of colorful decals depicting places he'd been: Salt Lake City, The Black Hills, Chinatown, The Golden Gate.

"Where's Cal?" I asked Mother, who stood chopping onions in the kitchen.

"He's gone, son," she said softly, pausing to look at me and drying her hands on her apron. "It's best this way."

"But he didn't even say goodbye. Where's he going? I wanted...." I didn't know what I wanted. An explanation perhaps, a chance to put things right, a reassurance of his friendship. A sense of loss and disappointment swept through me and remained; I was filled with the ache of frustration, and I gradually became aware of something worse, something I would come to know very well even before I could give it a name: guilt. I was responsible for sending Cal away from the only home he'd ever known. I should have kept my mouth shut about what I'd seen. Or maybe God was punishing me for what I'd done in bed with Cal, for the way I still felt about him. Hadn't Cal himself said it was "unnatural"?

"It's best this way," Mother repeated, looking at me with an expression that pleaded for my concurrence. "Your daddy's coming home in a few weeks. Aren't you looking forward to seeing him?"

"Yes'm", I mumbled, and flounced out the back door, allowing it to slam, and sat on the steps. It was my first experience with the knowledge that some things can never be changed, that there are situations left permanently unfinished, and that people can go out of your life suddenly and forever.

My father returned and took Mother and me back to Houston. I grew up there, went off to Austin to the University, spent four years in the Air Force, and settled at last in California, teaching art in a large East Bay community college.

Mother never spoke of California Sweetwater again. I was often tempted to break the silence, especially after my father died, but a distance had grown between us that I hesitated to bridge, fearful that too much honesty on her part would obligate me to reveal more of myself than I wished.

At times I wondered about the possibility of finding him. If I could see him again, I would explain everything, assure him that it was never my intention to send him back to that aimless rambling, that whatever I had done was done with the jealous love and ignorance of a child.

But I never made a real effort to find him. Even a private detective could not be expected to locate an itinerant farm laborer who hadn't been heard from in forty years, and who went by the ridiculous name of California Sweetwater.

At the "It" Club John Earl and The Ramblers finished their last set, the recorded music blasted forth again, and a few couples returned to the dance floor. For several hours I had sat drinking, listening to the new California Sweetwater, basking in his beauty, picking like a scavenger for bright scraps in a landscape of tangled memories. Reluctantly and somewhat unsteadily I pushed through the crowd and went outside.

A thick fog had moved in during the evening and the street lights up and down San Pablo Avenue were glowing islands, a double string of blue pearls decorating the darkness. On the corner in one of these islands stood John Earl Bobbitt, smoking a cigarette. In that light he looked almost ordinary – just a tired man dressed in a cheap flashy outfit. He still resembled Cal, but not so vividly as I had imagined. I could see dark smudges under his eyes; he looked closer to thirty than twenty, but nevertheless he was peculiarly attractive in a beat up sort of way.

"How about a smoke, pardner?" I said.

He offered me a Marlboro and lighted it for me with a fancy gold lighter.

"Not Bull Durham?" I murmured.

"Pardon me?"

"Never mind. You know, I'm the one who requested that old Floyd Tillman song three times – and sent over the twenty."

"Oh yeah?" he said, smiling and taking in my neatly trimmed graying beard, white turtleneck and blue suede jacket, the polished Bally boots. "What's so special about that song?"

"Someone I knew a long time ago sang it frequently."

He nodded. "Yeah, it's one of my favorites. Always has been." He turned to leave.

"Wait," I said. "Would you like to come home with me for a drink?" I had said it before thinking. I never picked up strangers; it was the first rule of a gay boy's survival.

"What?"

"Well, I like you, I want to know you better."

"I dunno...."

"I've got some whiskey, gin, whatever you like. We could have some drinks, listen to some records – Buck Owens, Dolly Parton, Emmylou Harris – talk. I don't live far." I ended in a rush, wanting to get it all out before he could refuse.

Now he looked at me more closely, and gradually a slow smile started. "Well...." He fondled the bulge at his crotch. "I think I know what you want, kid. You wanna suck my cock? Is that what this is about?"

I was a little taken aback – he really got to the point, no beating around the bush. I could feel myself blushing – I wasn't used to picking up straight guys.

"Well, yes," I whispered – it was too late to back out now. "I wouldn't mind sucking your cock, if that's what you'd like."

"How much you willing to pay?" he asked, in a more businesslike tone.

"Pay?" I wasn't ready for that either. I knew this kind of transaction took place all the time, but I had never paid for it myself in my entire life.

"Yeah, pay! You think I'm going to do that for free? I ain't no faggot!"

"Well, how much do you want?" I countered.

"Let's see, this gig tonight didn't pay shit. I got to recoup some of my losses. Tell you what, I'll let you have it for five – if it don't take too long."

"Five dollars?" I asked, incredulous.

"No, asshole – you kidding me? Five big ones – five hundred!"

Holy shit! That would really put a dent in my cash reserves that I kept at home in a drawer for emergencies. But wasn't this an emergency? I'd been looking for this guy all my life, or someone very much like him. Was I going to quibble over a few dollars for having a lifelong fantasy come true? "Okay, it's a deal," I gave in at once. "Here's my card – it's got my address on it. I live just a few blocks from here." I pointed down the street. "Just go three blocks that way, turn left at the light, and it's the second house on the right."

"I got one more set to do. Should be finished in about an hour or so. You have the money ready for me!" He turned back to enter the bar and went in without looking back.

Back at my house, I got everything ready, turned the lights low, put on some Dolly Parton, and waited nervously. I put the $500 in my pocket. That left me with $500 more which I hid carefully in the closet of my bedroom. I began to think again about the real California Sweetwater. He had been tough, but tender and gentle most of the time. But of course I was just a boy then. Now I was grown with even a little gray in my beard, and waiting for a man who was the spitting image of Cal to give me the thrill of my life. I had been waiting for this since I was six years old! My cock began to swell and throb as I imagined what was about to happen. I had never been so excited, and I didn't dare even touch myself for fear I might come prematurely.

After about an hour and a half there was a heavy tread on the porch and the doorbell rang. I opened the door and there he was – dressed in tight faded jeans and a close fitting cowboy shirt unbuttoned halfway to his waist, revealing a well-sculpted chest sprinkled with golden hair.

Without the red "suit of lights" a little of the magic was gone, but he still wore the fancy cowboy boots and still looked amazingly like Cal, with his blonde shock of hair and sideburns and those blue eyes now looking searchingly at me.

He walked in and just stood there. "Well, where's the money?" I pulled the $500 from my pocket and handed it over. He counted it and stuffed it into his back pocket. I hesitated--neither of us seemed to know quite how to get started. I was going to lead him back to my bedroom, but before I could move, he unzipped himself and pulled out his cock. It was already growing quickly and began to throb and buck like a wild horse. As I watched, fascinated, it grew to enormous size, at least nine inches. "Get on it," he ordered, and don't waste any time. I got to drive back to Fresno tonight."

I longed for a more romantic approach, but I couldn't resist putting that great pulsing organ into my mouth immediately. Falling onto my knees in front of him I kissed it and licked the long shaft up one side and down the other, then carefully extracted the balls and caressed them as they swung low and heavy in the hairy sack of his scrotum, savoring the odor of sweat and cigarette smoke that clung to his crotch. Then I began the kind of sucking I had been practicing for all my life. I was going to give him a blowjob he'd never forget! But he stopped me almost at once.

"Wait a minute, I got a better idea. Why don't I charge you by the inch? You can suck as little or as much as you want, it'll be up to you. If you want to suck just the head, that'll be two hundred, then every inch after that will be another hundred. Okay?" Now so mesmerized by the beautiful monster and so eager to have it back in my mouth, I nodded. Quickly I reached up and unbuttoned the top button of his jeans and pulled them down. He wore no shorts. I cupped his lean tight buttocks in my hands and pulled him to me.

I began to suck his cock again, concentrating mostly on the engorged reddish-purple head, itself a good two inches long and almost as wide. Suddenly he forced it deeper into my throat. "Uh-oh," he whispered. "Now you've gone and taken six inches, that's six hundred bucks worth, might as well take it all now," and he shoved again, forcing my mouth all the way to his pubic hair. "Now you've got all nine and a half inches – -you've got a nine hundred and fifty dollar cock in your mouth! You like it?" Impaled on the still-throbbing cock, I could only nod. "Let's call it an even thousand bucks. And I'll let you take my cum – all of it, kid. That okay?"

I nodded again.

Now we went into the cadenza-like Home Stretch, with me still on my knees, mouth distended to its widest to accommodate the incredibly long and thick, fleshy ramrod, and him standing with legs wide apart, humping my mouth so vigorously that I was now pushed back against the opposite wall.

I knew he was manipulating me, had probably planned all along to keep raising his price, after he had me hooked. But I was hooked. The fact that it was all so businesslike seemed to add spice for both of us and soon we both came, me in my pants without even touching myself, and "Cal" deep in my throat, the shaft of his cock pumping spurts of his hot juice deep inside me, as if he were never going to stop. A glorious finale! I felt it was worth every penny of the $1,000 I was going to have to pay him. My savings had been wiped out in a single night, but I felt almost carefree, exhilarated, as if I'd just paid off the mortgage or settled a long-standing debt.

After we put ourselves back together, more or less, I went back into my bedroom to get the extra cash. When I came back into the living room, he was gone, but the front door was hanging open. I sat down on the couch and noticed that his box of Marlboros had been crushed flat. Suddenly he appeared in the doorway and I blinked when I saw he was carrying rolling papers and a pouch of Bull Durham tobacco!

"I ran outta smokes," he said. "Guess I'll roll some here before I hit the road."

As he sat down on the couch beside me, I smiled at him and said, "Here, let me do it for you...."

# PROWLING FOR A LONGHORN
## Lance Rush

"...I was so famished for cowboy dick,
my restless tongue rattled at the shaft's base...."

Cowboys have always fascinated me. Prowling the bars of
The Big Star, with so many hunky, tight-jeans, crotch-hugging
buckaroos, I felt like a gay kid at his first rodeo. Hell, maybe I was.
But not one seemed remotely interested in what this boy had to offer.
I left the 4th bar and drove. Somehow, me and my battered Mustang
came to rest outside some whorehouse, itching to get laid. Then, this
man, swaggered out the door, part pissed-off cowboy poet, part
trouble in a Stetson. He seemed a tad drunk, fired up. Somebody'd
dun him wrong, and he was talking junk.

"Fuckin' house of syphilitic cunts! Free liquor, and all the
pussy you can eat! Bullshit! Fuck ya! Fuck ya, all! Dick's gone limp
as a damn dead rattler, anyway! Who needs ya muhfuckas!"

I wondered, Who the Hell is that!? He was like some outlaw
from a Wild West show. Decked out in cathouse finery; his
mosey-into-town-and-get-your-wang-wet duds: Open cowboy shirt,
bleached doeskin chaps and dusty Nocona boots. Big ones. Still
pissed off, he spat on the ground, and lumbered away in a huff. Then
turning, he discharged four shots into the air with his pearl-handled
.45 . Suddenly, night sat alive, active! He jumped into his pickup and
stormed away....

Up for adventure, I revved up the Mustang and followed his
zig-zagging trail to some dive down the road. Inside, Garth twanged
on the box. I sat nearby as he engaged the barkeep. Yep. He was a
real cowboy. His name was Hoss Brady, and most everyone seemed
to know him. His thick Texas tongue began drawling tall tales of
barroom fisticuffs, sleeping beneath the stars outside a bunkhouse,
and all those lonesome prairie nights. As the old polecat bragged of
his "beer can sweating", I couldn't help but be intrigued. As he
waddled into the john to "drain his snake", my biological need kicked
in, and I followed a minute later.

Joint was small and funky with the hot smells of piss, cum
and asshole. Stepping to the filthy urinal, I didn't see him anywhere

around. I unleashed my stream of rented Red Dog. I'd polished off five cans of a six pack. As I shook the last drops from my pipe, that hot horny sound of slapping meat ripped from the last stall. Ah, yes!

THWACK! THWACK, THWACK, THUUUG! THWACK! THWACK! THWACK! THUGG! I bent and saw two sets of feet. One pair clad in dirty sweat socks, the other in dusty Noconas. Hot damn! I flushed, washed up, opened and closed the door, pretending to leave. The john was silent a few moments. But then, I heard a man's voice. Hoss's. Deep, gritty, and hotly southern:

"Fucker's gone. Now get back on my rod and suck it hard! Polish that fuckin head! Oh! Ya like big dick, don't you? Careful with it. Aw! No teeth, just lips and tongue! Mmm! I'm goin' deep!"

I heard choking. Violent choking! Instantly, my dick lifted, hardened into a rigid eight-inch bat! "It's too fucking thick, man! Take it easy!" the second voice begged. The kid sounded even younger than me. Like he'd bitten off more than he could chew. Me? I'm very experienced for my age.

"Shudup! Didn't hear ya complain when you drooled over it at the urinal, hungry little fag!"

Wild slurping continued. I hauled out my raging cock, beat along to the sounds, as all that toilet talk got raw. He laid it on thick, bragging, as he continued.

"Yeah! Now you got it hard! This fucker's the size of a Buick! And I'm gonna drive it hard through that faggot ass, ram it, full throttle! Oh! I'm gonna dip this fat pole through that flaming-pink manpussy, and make ya call me, Daddy! Yeah! Suck! Suck this big hard buck meat!" Jism was boiling down my pisser! I quietly tipped into the next stall, and slowly closed the door. Yes! Hello-oo Glory Hole! I peered through, and the vision was hot enough to make me bust a hardy nut! A blond kid, no more than 18, was struggling with youthful gusto, trying to ingest a fierce, thick slab of rutting manmeat. Wasn't the size of a "Buick", but it might scare a few horses from the barn! Hefty fucker! Long fingers gripped the partition to my right. Dirty nails to match his dirty mouth. One hand held the kid's mouth wide open making way for that great pistoning cock. The kid was no slouch in the rod department either. He was violently flogging a stiff seven-incher, which jutted vertically from his fuzzy blond lap.

Suddenly, my Johnson was spitting juice randomly down my shaft.

I tipped over, glanced through the hole, eyes scaling up to see Hoss' hot, middle-aged mug. Dark, goggy with fatigue, his eyes looked glazed. Despite his dubious name, Hoss Brady was an original with a dark, weathered face so stern, almost ridiculous in its masculinity. Wasn't a huge dude, about five-ten, 180 pounds – but more man than most. Still, I'd a feeling he'd go off half-cocked at any moment. The Stetson was gone. His head's thrown back, that bristled face fixed in a lusty grimace. Moving down, his open western shirt revealed a furry black and iron pelted chest. No sign of his .45. Must've left it in the pickup. A big belt buckle clanked as he fiercely humped blond face. Suede chaps were yanked past his beefy haunches as they kept storming forth. His frame was compact, but built like a brick shithouse. Man, he was so fuckin' hot, uninhibited and real, I wanted him for myself! But then that horny pile-driving fucker pushed the poor kid to the filthy floor. He stood on the crapper and commenced to torpedo his hard, fat, daunting dong down the kid's throat. Damn! He's merciless with that big dick! The blonde's gasping for air. He's trying to stop him from ramming that choke-thick piece down his gullet, but to no avail. A part of me wanted to bust in, and pull that sadistic fucker off his slobbering young prey! But I was too busy watching, and jacking my now combustible meat. Then all at once, the kid's eyes shot open wide! I think he saw me. The burly cowpoke barked, "I'm gonna brand that asshole with his big hot motherfucka! Ya want me to buck it up that flaming manpussy, don't ya boy! Oh yeah. Ah! Mmmm! Aw! Arrrgh!"

But seeing my prying eye must've spooked the kid. Suddenly, he yanked the fuck slab from his mouth like a big ole bitter horse tablet. He grabbed his clothes and bolted, half-naked from the stall! I heard the men's room door slam shut before ole Hoss could even ask, "What the fuck...?"

There he was, hard dick shooting out like a fucking silo before him, thinking his little wild time was over. But the sight of him was so hot, the cock prowler in me hissed through the suckhole, "Slide that hot motherfucker through, pardner. I'll suck it off real good for you..."

That was all the motivation he needed on a horny Saturday night!

I watched him amble up to the gaping grotto, holding that fat, vibrating dong like a goddamn Texas tuning fork. Slowly, the bulbous head bobbed through, followed by a long, thick shaft! I clutched his hard angling cock. Oh, shit! Beyond Big! This buckaroo had a real-life longhorn!

Grabbing the fuck tool's root, I licked the wet throbbing mushroom where it flared and pulsated on my tongue. With one mighty thrust, the fucker torqued up, and a gush white gold petered out! It rose in big stubborn jerks! It was a dick made for sucking slow and wet, by a deep throat that appreciated it!

"Damn big rod you got there, Buddy!" I panted. "Fuckin' horsemeat must be fuckin' ten inches long!"

"Try eleven, pardner," he bragged. "But you like 'em big and hard, don't you? Suck it nice and slow! Yeah. You love it. Suck it. Eat that big horny dick up! I know you like big cock! Tell me!" "Yes, sir. I like em, BIG!" I panted, slurping slowly down the thick, protracted shaft. A thick and willful dong, it flexed, bent and slithered down my gullet in a cocksure lunge. I gagged! Yep, Hoss was a hot one, but a tad too cocky for my taste. Just then, I remembered there was a chilled Red Dog left in my chest pocket, cooling my left tit. I opened it, before the wrangler could ask, "What's that?" I took a big swig, then spat out a sudsy stream along the jutting shaft. "OOH! SHEEEIT! What's that? Shit! You some kinda freak, boy?" he asked, cock shuddering.

I gobbled the prickhead, swallowed most of the shaft, and tingled to the taste of beer-drenched dick! Mmmm! A smooth glide. Man! What a prick! Not a vein or knot marred its beauty; just cool throbbing cock skin. With one willful lunge, it slid to the pit of my slick throat. I gagged, took a breath, and slid down for more beef. Its thick rubbery glans spilled a hot tangy fluid. He bucked. Wet lips, slippery dick worked as one, sucking, mad thrusting. He hoisted those bull nuts through the suck hole. Prying my lips from his pulsing cock, and I lapped his hairy low hangers.

"Yeah! Lick them sweaty nuts, boy! Show Big Daddy what he's been missing at home!" he grunted. "Yeeeeeah. You know how I like it!"

I was so famished for cowboy dick, my restless tongue rattled at the shaft's base, and along his balls, licking, swabbing those tightening fuck stones. I plopped one fuzzy orb in my jaw. He bristled, but I went to town slurping it. Then, he wagged that rod and I went back to his fat, throbbing prick. I suctioned that juicy overgrown head, lassoed his burly shaft. Damn! Dude was a real grower! As I lapped, the more his freaky fat longhorn unfurled. Inches increased, drumming urgent beats on my sloshing tongue. Suddenly, he spun around, and aimed his furry asscrack to the suckhole. He winked its anal eye and with a voice full of smoke and bluster, he bellowed a command, "Get your fuckin' tongue up my goddamn asshole! Lick that stinking asshole out for me!"

Tongue it? Lick it? No, I ravished it. That funky sweaty crack was tight and gritty, and my tongue went crazy in it. As I lunged inside, his earthy smell zoomed up my nostrils. This was an ass that had ridden and broken in its share of braying bucks, and it showed. Deeply muscled, hairy, taunt and still sitting high in the saddle. He humped back and forth as I lapped it, like a prairie dog slurping its water! Man! I wanted to crawl up that hole like a snake in its burrow. Shit! I was a madman up his ass, whipping through, tonguing it so deep, my fucking chin's in it!

Then his gruff voice drawled the horny question, "So. Wanna fuck Hoss' hot heinie hole, boy?"

"Yes! Shit, yes!" I managed to pant. Though I couldn't believe he wanted to get fucked, there!

That luscious cowboy's bum disappeared, and in seconds he was knocking on my stall's door. I opened it. He stood, Stetson in hand, rock-hard, iron man, hair and hard-on everywhere I looked. He's a rough dream. Maybe 45. Shorter than me, but Brawny! Smells like cigar smoke. Looks like the Marlboro Man, in heat. Can't beat a macho stud who ain't afraid to take it up the ass!

I stood. He turned, flashing his fur-laden man-butt. I groped mounds of taunt, hairy ass-hide.

"Stick it in me," he groaned, swirling it slowly around. "Big Hoss is built to take it."

He parted those globes apart and showed me his world! A pinched brown spiral winces for my dick. I jabbed two fingers in it. His whole body jumped.

He laid his head against the wall, spread his hefty legs wide. He was ready. My fingers left the warm tension of his chute, as he demanded, "Fuck it good! None of that bullshit push and slide, either! Plow it! Ride it, boy!"

I aimed my stiff cock through his beckoning asshole. Oh, shit! The rubbery puckered knot broke. His bushy guts clamped a tighter-than-tight hold of me, pulling me further, deeper through a moist flexing tunnel. Yes! It swallowed my lunging cock up with a swoosh of intense suction.

"Fuck it! Fuck that nasty ass! Give Daddy that young hot stud cock! Plow me, damn it!"

I pulled back and rammed him! His big donkey dick slammed the wall. "Fuck me!" he insisted. He wanted it, bad! Inner man-muscles gripped tight to every fuckin fraction of my burning prick! I pumped him hard, steady, increasing speed with each shuddering thrust. My nuts slapped his cheeks. I grunted as I humped. That slick asshole opened wider to me. His tart scent filled the stall.

"Fuck me!" he demanded. My dick jolted him, deep! In deeper, out farther. He braced the wall shaking, yet taking it as my cock drilled for oil. He swirled that bum, meeting my strokes and I plodded, punched through that latching grip tensed, flexed, and released me. My fuckin nuts were humming! With each stroke and plunge inside it, I'm building, building up to a monumental cum! "Fuck me!" he grunted, pushing that anxious ass into me. I gripped his waist in one hand, and tugged his Texas Titan in the other. I'm jolting him deep, jacking that prick swiftly, roughly, bullying the hefty motherfucker to shoot in a hurry before someone walked in, and busted us! "Yes! Aw! Fuck it!" he cried out as his tube oozed and surged a wild pulse in my pumping fist.

I boar down harder, faster, hips pounding his pumping hips. We achieved a quick and nasty rhythm. Suddenly, he clutched my dick in his intense vise. Those moist walls grip, and spasm.

"Fuck! Shit! Big Daddy's gonna blow his gasket, kid! Hmm! Mmm! Arrrgh!" He yelped a coyote's howl as a rush of cum thundered through his shaft! I felt it quaking! Then, with sudden climatic quickness, great chunks of jism fired in rapid charges from his Stallion-like prick. Damn! It smashed the partition in loud, heavy vaults! Aww! Shoot it Big Daddy! I pulled from the depths of his pucker with a sound, POP! Whipping my tool a few swift strokes, I splattered his writhing back in a flood of white seed that dripped to his gaping asshole and crawled to his hairy nut sac. "Aw! Damn! You came! Too bad, 'cuz you ain't really lived till ole Hoss Brady sucks you off! Guess, I won't go back to the homestead with a belly full of cum, tonight. Oh well. You sure put a hurting on my ass, kid!" he sighs, brushing my fevered cheek. "Well, dude, there's always next time," I said, my eyes staring at his wilting cum-gooey dick.

As he pulled up his jism-soaked chaps, and tucked that heroic Cowboy's bone away, he said, "Fuck next time, kid! I'm bout to take ya back to the ranch, and have at the sweet boy-cunt of yours!" I jumped in the Mustang and he followed him in his pickup, and we ended up on his spread. And once arriving, I was promptly spread! He popped three fingers up my ass. Hoss had magic digits. I could feel myself knees weakening to his thorough probe. he held me close, staring into my eyes, and pushed his hardness against my own. With one thrust, he seemed to say,

I'm not just gonna fuck you... No! I'm gonna wail the tar out of that ass, kid!

Hoss wanted to fuck outside in the Great Outdoors, in front of the cows, the bulls, all of nature, and anyone else who cared to watch. He hauled that big, fat Texas titan free on the front porch. I fell down before it, and give his economy-sized rod another good and thorough tongue lashing. It really turned me on, sucking on that cock of his, under the blue-glow of the moon, my spittle making it so hard and glossy, as all his raised dick veins caught the light.

Then, and took me, right there on his lazy hammock. As I lay on my belly, swinging to and fro, he licked my nervous bud free of sweat, and then he aimed that dick through it. Oh! Hoss Brady buggered me but good! His obscenely thick, overgrown measure had this boy howling at the moon and stars like a prairie dog baying at the heavens! Then, he went in deep, so deep, he and that dick almost wrecked me. I could not believe how quick he fucked. I swear, I thought that hammock would break, and collapse under protest! As I lay there, swinging, pitching, moaning, groaning beneath his wind, I'd never felt a bigger, more willing sensation burrowing through my little brown ring. But Hoss Brady not only fucked with his dick. He used his cock, his hips and ass, with a determined bang-bang-bang! OH! He banged, like a man who had no age, and I'd defy any boy he's ever laid to contest that fact.

When he lessened his stroke, my breath's became labored, ragged gasps for air. Finally, he stiffened, and pulled out, and sprayed me with gush after sticky gush of cock cream. I came soon after, beating my raging prick, beating it until it spit a geyser to the hot, moonlit sight of him.

So what if he turned out to be a supposedly straight, and married, with a family. I didn't care. Straight, gay or bi, Hoss Brady had no trouble adjusting to the notion of fucking, and yes, even getting fucked by a boy, on a lonely night. And that night, the man in the Stetson proceeded to ride his new pony, hard, rough and sore!

But that's what this pony-boy gets for prowling those Lone Star State bars, only to find that, yes, things really do grow Bigger in Texas.

# A COWPOKE DOWN UNDER
## QM3 Rick Jackson, USN

I lay there wishing the creature would hurry the fuck up. My ankles didn't hurt, but the fishing line had started biting into my wrists as I twisted about to get comfortable. More to the point, I felt more goofy than sexy all staked out on the bed. My position did bring to mind an image I hadn't thought of in years even though it had teased ceaselessly at my nasty adolescent little mind the whole time I was growing to studhood. The clip ran relentlessly through my teenage fantasies as I shanked my crank. I'd seen it in some bad western movie where the Indians had staked a lone cowpoke out to die of exposure in the cruel Arizona sun. I remember nothing about the movie except the Technicolor image of the guy – his blond shock of hair cast carelessly down over a heroic brow, a boyish dimple or two, and a lantern jaw.

I'd always started my workout sessions with his face and then slid down across his powerful tanned pecs as they broiled under a sexy dapple of glistening sweat in that harsh heathen heat. His belly was flat and hard, but for reasons past understanding, the idiot Indians had neglected to pry my hero from his trou. If I'd been the Indian chief, I always told myself, things would have been done right. The camera would travel across his gorgeous torso, down along his hard flanks, and end showing his toes wriggling, bootless, in the harsh glare of relentless doom.

As I lay there staked out in the bedroom of the small apartment in suburban Perth, I returned for the first time in years to that central fantasy of my youth – and remembered what the B-movie had left out: how I would happen across the poor cowpoke. I'd save his ass from the ants or scorpions or whatever, and he would show me how grateful a good western buddy could be. After I lost my cherry to a girl in high school, I decided I'd just been going through a phase and stopped dreaming of reaming out sun-fried cowstud. Pussy was more immediate than the lost glories of the Old West and, besides, by then I knew what was socially acceptable and what wasn't. In the years since, I'd often compared my body with those around me. You don't spend four years on a `gator in the US Navy without seeing hard, naked manhood in its prime; but I was always able to banish the occasional quirky idea about my shipmates as a relic of that unfulfilled phase of my youth.

Lying there, staked out and helpless that day in Perth, I knew one thing for sure: the tart I'd picked up was taking for fucking ever to come out of the crapper. Maybe because it had taken me so long to get to women, I'd never been as interested in sex as most of the guys on my ship. Still, after five months floating around the Indian Ocean with nothing but the usual strained faggot jokes and my hand to keep me company, I needed relief bad enough to try Claire.

A pack of us had gone to a bar our first day in Fremantle. The babes were all over us, fighting to buy us drinks and get us home to bed. I can't think why. God knows the place was crawling with men that would set Hollywood on its ass. I guess maybe we were just exotic or something. I'd held out for something a little fresher, a little more stimulating, but finally, when just she and I were left, I decided it didn't really matter what I blew my load into. I let Claire drag me home. My plan was to pop a nut and run, but she wanted to play cowboy and pioneer wife. At first, I couldn't be bothered with her bondage crap; but it was soon clear I'd tap a gusher a lot faster if I played along. Sweetie had no sooner gotten me staked out, than she had to pee. They always do, for some reason, and never think of it until they start. It's either that or needing a drink of water.

I lay there, my mind drifting back again to the sweaty cowpoke meat hidden inside those dusty pants, and came back to reality to find my dick harder than a rustler's heart. After what must have been five minutes, I yelled at my date to get her ass into gear. At the time, of course, I had no way of knowing the crapper had two doors or that she was long gone.

I nearly shit when the dude ambled out of the john. First a quick thrill surged through me: he was fucking gorgeous. Then my wrists and boner reminded me of my position and made me hope the guy wasn't the husband wronged – though I couldn't imagine what else he could be. Something about the leer on his face didn't seem to fit, but I was past noticing subtleties. I started to babble an explanation of sorts when I noticed his dick. Then I really got confused. He'd shambled about half way between the door and me and just stood there watching, feet apart, hands by his sides, dick belly-up and beautiful. I felt my own meat pounding against my gut like a Morse key in an lightening storm. Like a fool, I stopped babbling only to ask him where Claire had gone. His grin grew as he pried his dick down away from his flat, hairless belly and let it slap back up with a meaty thwack. I needn't worry about her. She was gone. We were alone. I asked him what the fuck he was up to – and silently felt sure of the answer, deeper within me than I'd known I could feel anything. Something about his stance and manner and, especially, the hungry look on his face as he took inventory of what I had told me the whole story. I never did learn the details – who Claire was, what their relationship was, and or where she fit in. Just then, I was too busy learning the shape of his studly body Down Under to bother about trivialities and later – well, never mind later for now.

I showed him my pissed-off defender-of-freedom persona, explaining what I was going to do to the bastard if he didn't get me up off the bed on the double, The more I ranted and threatened, the wider his grin got, the more his eyes sparkled, and the quicker his dick did a tom-tom imitation against his tanned belly.

When he finally spoke up again in his foxy Aussie accent, he ignored my tirade as irrelevant to our present circumstances and sounded almost as though he were making idle conversation on a bus: "What's your name, Yank?" I tried not to think about his swollen dick – or about my own. I'd never been harder. Despite my cocky talk, I was afraid of what was going to happen; yet every part of my body except my brain yearned for whatever he had in store. Here, at last, I was out of control. Whatever delicious perversion he had in mind was his karma's problem. I was off the hook. At last, those adolescent fantasies seemed close to reality. My dick was so swollen it seemed ready to split down the middle like a frank left forgotten to simmer to bits in a picnic pot.

I growled my name and repeated what I was going to do to him when I got loose, but the gorgeous bastard only grinned harder and told me his name was Alec. He didn't look much like an Alec; he looked more like a fucking Apollo. Looming over me, he was about six-one, 200 pounds of pure surfer-stud muscle. His hair obviously started out a dark blond, but was bleached golden above the neck.

Like my dream cowpoke, he had a shock of hair hanging low across his forehead, setting off thick blond brows that seemed almost to merge above his classic nose. He, too, had dimples and a strong jaw filled with sparkling teeth; but he had more hard muscle than my cowpoke had ever seen. A thick neck lead down from his cute little ears to spread into shoulders wide enough to throw an ox. The bastard obviously lifted weights as much as he surfed; his massive chest and bulging arms set off a belly that would have almost disappeared from sight except for the meaty signal pulsing in front. Before long, I was to see his world-class butt, hard and firm, hanging off his hips like some futuristic anti-gravity fuck-machine. I'd see his strong legs and feel the hard muscle of his back. Just then, though, my universe was filled with the biggest, hardest, meanest-looking dick I'd ever seen.

I don't know whether Aussies are uncut more often than Americans, but Alec made me hope so. Oz is supposed to be an enchanted land, after all. At first I could see much of his dick except the bottom, but that was enough. Impossibly hard as he was, a great ruffle of soft, wrinkled skin peeked out from between his dick and belly, making my mouth water as though I were one of the "cocksuckers" squids always joke about underway. His huge balls hung low and heavy between his legs, swaying slightly as he stood silently before me -waiting, looking, savoring the moment. When he spoke again, almost drooling with every syllable, my last doubts about what lay in store for me vanished: "She said you were the best bit of meat about, she did."

The more I growled about his slut of a bitch and about how he was a faggot, cocksucking, ass-wipe, the harder we both got. He didn't say dick as he eased his way the last few feet to the bed and looked down at me twisting about. I writhed and thrashed, struggling with the physical bonds that held me, yet snapping free the last vestiges of my priggish inhibitions as I inwardly yielded absolutely to the demands of the moment.

His right hand reached out slowly, as though relishing a slight delay to intensify his ultimate pleasure. Deep brown eyes that seemed at odds with his bright, golden hair glowed with a primal hunger. When his fingertips ultimately made contact with my thigh, he might as well have been hooked straight to a nuclear reactor. A spark of lust and excitement and deliciously forbidden pleasure jolted up through my leg to disorient me. Flat on my back, I felt myself swept away by a maelstrom of fears and joys past my understanding. One part of my brain heard a low, bestial groan of exquisite pleasure escape my lips and I knew for certain that I was lost.

His hand on my thigh slid slowly upwards, sending shivers and gooseflesh before it. He stopped inches from my balls and started back down again, murmuring something to himself about softness. His left hand reached out next to glide across the very top of the rust-colored thatch that grows thick on my chest. I've always found it wiry and harsh, but Alec's palm was obviously fascinated by the texture. His own hairless, brazen chest was dappled with sweat and stippled by gooseflesh of his own. Those spaniel-brown eyes slipped shut as his hands continued to take the measure of my body as though every hair and bulge were a religious relic to be venerated.

The smile was gone from his face now; he was beyond boyish smiles. Short, shallow grunts jolted a jerky melody from the very depths of his soul. As his palms eased across my flesh, as his fingers pried away my past prejudices and inhibitions, as my flesh surrendered to him, I stopped resisting the inevitable and lay still beneath his touch. I gave myself up to an enjoyment that far surpassed any spit-palmed adolescent fantasy. His touch glided across my flesh, slowly, reverently, deliciously. His grunts of appreciation grew louder, teaching me to meet his touch with my body, pressing my muscle against his hands, giving him my body as I had yielded up my soul to the wicked, wonderful world he represented.

My own groans of pleasure soon rivaled Alec's and seemed to seduce him from his trance. Those brown eyes opened again and he said something about my knowing what I wanted after all. Like an idiot, I strained at the bonds that held me down; but now I was struggling to reach his massive dick. Escape was the last thing on my mind. I had become a slut.

Right then, I was willing to give Alec anything he wanted, but he wasn't about to accept any gifts. Unless he could take it, he didn't want it. I twisted and torqued my way toward his hands and he pulled backward to take stock of the possibilities. I wasn't sure what to expect. I'd heard about faggots being done up the butt, but he'd have to untie my ass from the bed first. If I was thinking at all, I probably expected his monster dick shoved down my throat. When he really got going, I discovered how sick a bastard young Alec really was.

He started off on my right tit – with his tongue. Alec slid his face over my chest. His breath came in short, hot spurts that chilled the sweat oozing out of my pores. My chest hair rippled like Iowa corn as his panting grew more frantic. When his wet tongue tip slashed down through the forest of rust-colored hair to snipe down at my nubbin of passion-pumped flesh. I'd never thought of my tits as sexy, but Alec's bumpy tongue slid across raw nerves I'd never known I had until I was sure I would come from pure shock.

Somehow I stood up to the tit-torture, even after his tongue slid back between his lips and they went into action. His nose snuffled through my chest pelt while his lips, as slick with his spit and as they were experienced in what young American seamen need, locked around my nipples like a vampire dervish in a blood bank, twisted and tugging, determined to suck up every possible particle of pleasure. His furrowed lips tightened hard with every up-stroke along my blood-gorged stocks and then released their grip to glide down on a hot layer of spit as his bumpy tongue darted deep down my shaft to torment me.

At first, only his nose and lips and tongue touched me, but I was able to smear my chest against his face, begging for more like the slut he had made me. My overpowering urge to grab his blond locks and shove him hard against my chest kept me jerking at the nylon line despite common sense. The bastard had me where he wanted me and was in no hurry at all.

His tongue and lips alternated between teasing my tits and rougher play. Now and again, he'd let a dangerous edge of tooth glide down my stock; but just the raspy, cat-like torment of his tongue was enough to set my every nerve alight. Alec kept using my right tit and then my left until they both numb with delight. Then the sick slut slipped his face into my armpit and began lapping up the sweaty musk that lived there. Now his tongue slid across my flesh in great canine swaths of wet love that taught me yet another lesson about how a man's body can be used. Too soon for either of us, he'd lapped me clean and moved up across my shoulder to my neck and, ultimately, across to my left ear lobe.

His face pinned my head to the pillow while he went to work. Lips and tongue alternated again, sucking, pulling, scraping, urging my flesh into him as though he were a hyper-attractive man-magnet. The feral snorts of breath that escaped his nose roared into my ear just ahead of his tongue, drilling deeper into my head than any human should have been able to reach. Like a starving ant-eater, he flicked his tongue deep and curled it upwards as he sucked at my lobe with one lip and I cried out every filthy thing I knew. I was past knowing what I wanted. His tongue-fucking was so perfect, so brutal, that I knew I would go mad if he didn't stop; yet, once I'd felt what he could do, I knew I'd never be able to get enough. Almost as though I were watching from outside, I felt my body shiver and thrash, my hips convulsing upwards as they fucked the air and wished it were him. The louder I screamed, the faster his tongue snaked in and out of my ear and the more self-satisfied his porcine grunts of pleasure grew.

Whether to take my mind off my ear or maybe just to be a dick, he slid his fingers down to my left tit and started twisting – hard. The delicious brutality of the moment transformed what should have been agony into something even worse. I'd been close to a breakdown before; now I slipped over the edge. Sensation blurred into surreal sensation; I was helpless to do anything but clench my eyes shut and wait for the universe to steady itself. I heard myself screaming again but as though at a great distance. One convulsion followed another, each fiercer, more sadistic and pure than the last. Then my brain just fucking shut down.

I remember drifting back to consciousness and thinking how wet I felt. My ear and neck were cold and clammy now; Alec had moved south. I lifted my head and saw him lapping a gigantic and very messy load of my best work from my chest and belly. I'd apparently lost it entirely and blown a huge cargo of Yank seaman semen up into the dense thicket of fur that covers my torso. Alec wasn't letting it go to waste. His lips had surrounded the nacreous globs of cum and was busy sucking them out of my hair. Then he went back, using his tongue to round up any strays that had escaped from the herd.

Turned on as I was, I couldn't do much at that point but breathe. I'll never know how long Alec had been up my ear, but it took me five or six minutes before I could gulp down enough air to live. By then, my captor had finished harvesting my sperm-farm and was ready to get serious – but he wanted an audience. When he saw I would live, he went after the last thick threads of jism left – dangling from my cum-slit and down across my dickhead onto my belly. He started low near my navel and slurped upward. His terrible tongue-tip tore into my jism-hole, drilling out the last of my load before his lips slid slowly upward to encircle my throbbing meat.

If his lips had seemed possessed as they sucked my tits; once he proved what a cocksucker he was, I was ready to nominate him for a Nobel fucking Prize. He used the same basic method: letting his lips sneak up on my nerve endings on a layer of hot spit and then ripping into my weakened defenses with his bumpy tongue. Now, though, his suction went into overdrive as well – all while he was working his face steadily downward along my nine thick inches. My dick was so stiff and lying so tightly against my belly that he had trouble bending me high enough to handle – but by now he'd moved between my wide-spread legs and was taking his time. I'd just shot the finest load of my young life, but every throb of my naval weapon brought me closer to doing it all over again. Through the fuzzy cloud of pleasure that obscured reality from fantasy, I remember his snuffling slurps and the shit I was talking. I'm sure I sounded like the worst-written fuck flick of creation, but the torment his face was giving my dick was too serious a rush for me to consider coming up with anything creative.

He worked my swollen dickhead deep down into his throat and locked me in place, scraping the tender pink tissues of his craw across my head, pulsing his suction like an organic milking machine stuck on overdrive. I saw his head bob up and down along my shank and felt his lips at work but my head stayed locked tight and deep inside this throat until I knew I was about to shoot off again. For the first time ever, I felt my load being sucked up from my nuts and knew I was going to hump Alec until he bled.

But I was wrong. He did fine until my balls tightened against his chin. Then, just as I was ready to have one seriously fine time, he eased his face off my dick and knelt between my legs, grinning down at me, hoping I'd beg for his service. I did, too – but the bastard wasn't about to swallow my load again – yet.

He watched me squirm for a few minutes and then sank back down to my crotch. Now that my weapon was loaded and ready to fire, he concentrated on it, sucking first one nut and then the other into his mouth for some rough ball-handling action. They were already slightly sore, first from long, underway weeks of relative inaction, then from the strain of spewing my personal-best load of spunk. His lips locked around my nut-sack and his suction started up, pulling blood down into my nuts and making them swell and throb and ache with the unbearable weight of their next load. I started moaning again and kept it up as he switched back and forth between balls for the next twenty minutes or so.

Now and again, he'd stop and lap at my ballsac as though he were some cur dog going at his own 'nads on a dusty country road. He took time out to slurp along my thighs but the absolute limit in kink came when he used his nose to lift my nuts aside so he could snake his tongue back underneath me. The farther back he got towards my butthole, the better we both felt. I'd have given a nut to give the ass-lick what he wanted, but my legs were tied too tightly for me to arch my hips up enough off the mattress to manage.

When he'd sucked my second load of the day back down where it had started, Alec moved back up to my dick and swallowed me again. He was an old friend and my dick knew what to do. I slid straight down past his tongue and let his throat lock around the head of my joint like a family dog slipping into a collar. This time around, though, he had less chance of escaping my spray. My hips were loose enough to fuck his face, slashing upwards, driving my dick home where we both knew it belonged. His head met my meat on the up-stroke and tried to hang in there on the down-stroke, but now instinct took control of my dick – and his face.

I reamed and twisted and slammed dick deep down his throat until I felt my load being sucked up again. This time it happened faster and with a violence and frenzied ecstasy bred of Alec's need as much as my own. Once again, though, he jerked his head up off my joint; but now he was too late. My plume of cum shot out, spraying my belly and chest with more thick threads of cum than I'd ever seen in my life. Alec knew when he was beaten.

He wasn't going to slurp his load of seed up, but his lips puckered tight and pressed my dickhead down into my belly fur as I shot spasm after glorious spasm up onto myself. As soon as I was pinned and knew it, his tongue flicked out through his lips, fluttering along the super-sensitive V beneath my dickhead, at once forcing me even harder against my belly and raking a whole other set of nerve-endings that were already exploding. His lips and tongue worked harder, feathering frenzy against the bottom of my dick as one jolt of jism after another spewed out the top. Pressed hard against my belly, my dick pumped the last volleys of cum into a pearly pond that formed right at the end of my dick.

If anything, the second load took me longer to lose and was more fun. At least, I suppose it was; since I remember dick about most of the first gusher, I can't be sure. When, at long last, I humped out my last few threads of jism, I was ready to lie back content while Alec licked me clean again. He had other plans. The moment he saw I was dry, he hopped to his feet, straddled my waist and started to shit on my crotch – at least that's what I thought he was doing. Instead, he slipped his asscrack along the underside of my dick, just grazing the surface and keeping it from going limp. Within seconds, he was gliding along my meat, dipping low enough to drag his ass through the pool of jism that lay just north of my dick. Then on the back stroke, he dragged his butthole harder along my dork – scratching his ass like a dog scooting across a new white shag carpet. Each trip got his butt slicker than the last and made my bone the more ready to see what he had in store.

Now, of course, I'd know what to expect; but when he reached down with his hand to pry my joint away from my belly and eased his asshole around it, I figured my life was just about perfect. In the fear and discovery and mind-numbing ecstasy that had come before, I'd forgotten about my cowpoke fantasy; but the moment Alec slipped his tight asshole past my trigger-ridge and I felt the thrill of reality after so many years of fist-fucking fantasy, that Technicolor cowpoke popped into my head one last time.

Looking up at Alec wobbling back and forth as he worked himself down my shank, I knew I'd never have to conjure cowpoke again.

From now on this bizarre afternoon would be the yardstick against which all my future fantasies and realities would be measured. As his shithole stretched its way along, I also knew I'd never bother with the Claires of the world again, either. Some assholes might not like the idea of guys doing guys, but now that I'd felt what a hard young body like Alec's had to offer, there was no fucking way in hell I'd put up with the nasty slackness of slatterns. In fact, watching one expression after another slide across Alec's face as my pole disappeared up his hole, I was even ready to see what his impossible dick felt like stretching my guts apart. It was at least ten inches long – and probably more. His head was swollen enough now that I could see his cum-slit oozing a steady flow of pre-cum. Soon the crater formed by his foreskin overflowed dicklube and a thin trickle rippled down his joint to drip onto his balls and then onto my belly. Almost at the same time, Alec's asshole seated itself around the broad base of my dick, grinding this way and that across my Brillo-like pubes, and his soulful brown eyes rolled back in his head. I made up my mind to find out what it felt like to have a man up your ass.

I lay silent for a moment or two but some ancient instinct set my hips back to work. My ass arched upward, driving my dick even deeper into Alec's butt. His eyes eased open for a moment so he could look at my Navy-issue body one last time before he slipped from into a world of his own. His lips parted slightly and the moment was passed. He was on autopilot now, stroking up and down my joint, scratching the itch that lay buried deep within him like a bear an even thicker log. My dick drilled upwards as his ass matched my rhythm, twisting slightly to screw himself along the throbbing blue vein that guided me up into his guts. Every movement stretched my shaft tighter, pulling the twin lobes of my head tighter and bringing me closer to launching an impossible third load up into the secret depths of his guts where it belonged.

Suddenly I felt something hard bounce off my dick as I slipped into him; Alec shivered in a spasm of shattering sensuality so severe that for a moment I was jealous. I didn't know about prostates at the time, but I knew what made him feel good and was determined to deliver. My ramrod changed its angle of entry just enough to slam hard into his explosive buttnut on nearly every stroke – sending one ripple after another of gooseflesh across his body and ripping one animal moan after another from the very depths of his being. Alec was still grinding his ass along my crotch, but now that I knew what to aim at, I went to work pounding his prostate for all it was worth.

My dick loved the firm, slick texture up his ass, but Alec went ape-shit. His head flew back and he opened his mouth for a soundless scream fierce enough to deafen mankind. His gasping breaths stopped dead and, while I slammed harder and faster with every butt-lashing, gut-wrenching stroke, my captor proved he had more than pre-cum down his dick. I'd never seen another man shoot off before. Alec was an impressive place to begin. At first he seemed to be having a seizure, but as his lungs clawed at the suborn air for breath, his massive manmeat exploded, shooting globs of iridescent white shrapnel up onto his body and out onto mine. Some of the larger globs splattered against his hard, hairless flesh and began the slow, easy drip down. Many arced through the air to land on me or on the bed beside me. Once his gusher had come in, Alec reached down to get a grip on himself and pumped his well dry, sending his Australian cream up like an explosion in a fireworks factory.

My rod was ready to keep reaming his butt, but once his body seized up, that tight Australian bunghole clamped down tight enough to break my joint off at the nub. The sight of his jism arcing through the sky, the strangle-hold he had on my meat, the noise he was making, the fierce friction of tender flesh against hard bone, and, especially, the perverse thrill of having my dick up a man's tight ass while he shoot off, all conspired to send me over the edge again as well.

I couldn't see my watch, but this had to be my third cum-crop inside as many hours. Alec had taken his time; neither of us seemed in any hurry other than the one built into a man's nature. Now, at least, I was putting what I had where it would do some good – up his ass to lube it out. My first jolt did just that. I couldn't feel my cum splash off the inside of his guts, but his butthole magically started slip-sliding along my shank so I picked up my speed and really let the Australian asshole have it.

Alec must have crested first, because when I opened my eyes, he was all doe-eyed and grinning. He was also seriously dripping jism, but at least none of it was mine this time. I knew where mine was. He fucked with my dick for a few more strokes and then leaned forward, smearing his chest and belly against mine. The remains of my second load and his fresh first melded together in milky satisfaction as he eased off my joint so we could get in some quality belly-fucking time. Over the next eight or ten hours, we kept each other from getting bored. By the time I finally fell asleep with Alec lying atop me, I'd learned a lifetime's worth about lust and love – and where a man fits in.

Probably the major disappointment in my life was that I never felt Alec's gorgeous uncut dick up my ass. At one point he did tease me with it, sitting on my belly so I could suck on his `skin and the very tip end of his crank. Why he wouldn't let me treat him the way he deserved, I'll never know. I'm sure he had good reasons – in any case I was bound to do as he wished. I only know that when I awoke the next morning, he was gone with nothing but dried jism on my belly and a lifetime's worth of memories to prove he'd ever been there. I found a knife by my hand and cut myself free. Every muscle I had was cramped and stiff, but at least now I knew how to uncramp the muscle that matters most.

I took a long, hot shower and decided to wait until Alec came back. He never did. I should have wondered why Claire brought me through a door that led directly from the to the back bedroom. I discovered why easily enough: the rest of the apartment was vacant. Whether it was a model apartment or one Alec just kept rented so he could screw Yank sailors or what I never figured out. I obviously wasn't meant to. Alec had shown me what I wanted out of life and how to get it; if he wanted to be a tad kinky with bondage or shy about the rest of his life, I guess that was all right with me. I left the apartment on his terms – knowing nothing about him other than that he and the single, glorious night we spent together, slavish master and devoted bondsman, would remain with me bright and alive until my final hour.

# A HUSTLER'S CONFESSIONS
## In a Series of Erotic Tales by
## Frank Gardner

## *I. EARLY SIN*

As a kid, I was taught that confession was good for the soul, but I quickly learned that it was great for getting off, too. The priests were more helpful in assisting me to come to terms with my sexuality than they will ever realize.

It all started with one confession. I began with the usual, "Bless me, Father, for I have sinned." Then, I started my list of sins. "I stole some beer," I said rapidly, "got drunk, and...."

An impatient "Yes?" resounded from the grill. The priests were usually in a hurry and couldn't be bothered with a reluctant penitent.

"...And did two sins of impurity," I stammered in a whisper. I bet that would slow him down. The priests liked talking about sins of impurity.

"Where did you do these sins?" Suddenly, the priest was no longer in a hurry.

I had noticed how often I felt like I just had to do it after my confessions. Maybe this was because of all the questions the priests ended up asking about my sex life. I decided to give this one what he wanted.

"I was sleeping late, Father, and the bed was warm and I was half asleep."

I remembered how good it had felt, and my cock became stiff and warm.

"You know how wrong that was, don't you?"

"Well ... I was half-asleep."

"That's no excuse." Then he wanted the sexy details. "Exactly what did you do?"

"I took off my pajamas and put a pillow under my back."

I was getting turned-on.

"Yes, and then?"

"I spread my legs out so my balls would bounce, and pumped it."

I squeezed and fondled my crotch. It was dark. I knew the priest couldn't see me through the grill.

"Did you entertain lascivious thoughts?"

"Lascivious?" I asked.

"Did you think about a girl's breasts, for example?"

I had actually thought about how my cute, hunky roommate's hand would feel on my cock while he slowly jacked me off.

"Yeah," I said, thinking about my roommate.

"You should not allow occasions for sin to arise like this," the priest said. "You should get up immediately upon awakening to make sure it doesn't happen again."

"I'll try, Father."

By now, my cock was stiff and thrusting down the leg of my pants.

"You'll just have to try harder," the priest replied. "You said you had two sins of impurity. Did you indulge in this impurity again?"

"Well, uh..."

"Yes, my son, please continue," the priest's tone was syrupy. "I'm listening,"

"Yes," I thought, "I'll bet you are – avidly."

I stroked my tool through my pants. It was getting ready to shoot.

"I was taking a shower in the dorm," I continued eagerly, "and the water was so warm. I got my hand all soapy, and slicked it up and down."

My voice was husky and I had to swallow. My pant leg was bulging. I cupped the bulge with my palm and pressed down hard as I rubbed it.

"My thing got really stiff," I continued, "and I got so excited that I stuck a finger up my butt. I worked it way up!"

I squeezed my cock bulge and stroked it more rapidly. My cock was getting ready to shoot. I couldn't hold back anymore.

I burst out, "But I know now how wrong it was, and I'll never do it again!"

With that, I shot off in my pants.

I held my breath so the priest couldn't hear me grunt. I kept rubbing and shooting.

I said, "It was so awful what I did."

"Another occasion of sin, my son. You must guard against these occasions and maintain a pure mind in a pure body. Have you tried prayer?"

"Yes, Father."

I wondered if any cum had soaked through my pants.

"And cold showers?"

"Yes," I replied, looking down to check my pants.

I didn't see any cum stains, but I would keep it covered when I walked out.

"You must simply try harder!" said the priest sternly.

At long last, came the promise of being "heartily sorry," forgiveness, and a penance.


Earlier, I had noticed that the priests always seemed very interested in my sins of impurity. I had squirmed with embarrassment when I answered questions about how I jacked off. It was as if some of them enjoyed making me feel awkward and ashamed.

One of them asked me, "Where were you when you did this?"

"Up in the attic."

"What exactly did you do?"

"I took it out of my pants and pulled on it until it squirted."

"You know that was a sin, don't you?"

"Yes, but it was so hard I couldn't help myself."

"That is no excuse. You must avoid these occasions of sin, my son."

"I know, Father. I won't do it again."

These confessions had invariably left me with a red face and feeling ashamed. However, they also gave me eight inches of stiff, throbbing meat. When I was alone, I would pull out my cock and jack off. I just had to do it!

Usually I would picture myself masturbating frantically while I confessed. Why not? When I confessed to a priest I could make my confession so incredible that he too was pumping his cock and panting so hard he couldn't hear – or even care about – what I was doing or saying.

"That would be really something!" I thought while I shot off.

Maybe my confessions made the priests as turned-on as they always made me. I believed that was why the priests asked all those questions about my sins of impurity. Maybe I could make my sins of impurity exciting enough to give the priest a hard-on and get him to masturbate.

I could confess about how a football player did it to me.

And that's just what I did. I confessed this wild scene to one young, inexperienced priest.

"I don't know if this was a sin of impurity, or not," I told him.

My cock immediately began to harden and swell under my pants.

"Why is that, my son?"

"Because it was something another guy did to me, Father," I replied, squeezing the bulge in my pants. "I was in the shower, and this football player came in. When he went by, he brushed his hand on my crotch."

"Perhaps this was an accident."

"I don't think so, Father," I pulled down my zipper while kneeling at the grill. I pulled my cock out and worked my balls up through the opening of my fly. I admired the way my cock stood up stiff and straight while I stroked it. I continued my confession. "Not with the hungry way he looked at my cock."

"You must avoid this kind of temptation, my son," the priest said. "You should have taken a cold shower."

"I know I should have, Father," I agreed, "but..."

My voice had taken on a note of urgency as I spread my legs and squeezed my balls. I fondled my erect cock and pulled the foreskin back tightly.

"But you were too excited by what this husky football player had done?"

"Yeah!"

Now I was on the right track. The priest was getting into it.

"He was so big and husky, that it was like I had to go along with whatever he wanted."

I kept my foreskin pulled all the way back. I jiggled it rapidly, stretching and loosening the smooth satin skin of my glans. Nice! I could hear a rustling behind the grill. I figured the priest was pulling his cock out.

"So you went along with this?"

"Yeah. My prick got hard and stuck out because of the way this guy looked at it." I was feeding the priest's husky football player image. "Then he came right up close to me and touched it ... and rubbed it up and down. My cock got all...."

"You couldn't resist?" the priest asked.

His voice was tight and strained. I could hear him panting. There were muffled thumps on the other side of the grill. "No, I couldn't resist him." I continued my sexy story. "I liked it too much – the way he made my cock hard! Oh, it was great!"

By now, my bag had tightened up. My cock was glowing. I jiggled the end of it harder and tighter.

"His hand felt s-o-o-o good moving up and down on my cock, Father." I kept on. I knew I had him now. "Then the guy's face got all red," I continued, "and he looked like he was hungry and licked his lips. Then you know what he did?"

The thumping noises were louder now, and the priest was breathing heavily. "He sucked on it?"

"Yes, Father, he got down on his knees and put it in his mouth."

"He actually put it in his mouth and sucked on it, my son?" From the grill came more rapid thumps.

"Yeah, he sucked on it real good!" I began to grunt out loudly, as I rapidly unbuckled my belt and pulled my pants down. "He was good! Real good, Father!"

I thrust my hips back and forth so I could rub my bare ass back against the cold wooden wall behind me. I squeezed my balls and frantically pumped on my cock.

I burst out, "He was a great cocksucker!"

"He took it in his mouth?" asked the panting priest. "All...the...way?" He began to grunt, "He sucked it! All the way? Uh!"

The priest was coming!

"All the way! And hard!" I gasped. "He sucked on it real hard, Father!" I shot. "Yeah! He sucked it! He sucked it good! Oh so good! uh!"

I didn't care now whether the priest could hear me or not. My cum shot all over the place. I could see shiny gobs of it on my pants as I pulled them up.

I had finally gotten a priest to masturbate during confession. The young priest was also aware that I knew he had jacked off. Because later, when I saw him again, the priest's face got red. He gave me an embarrassed grin.

I kept working hard to make my sex confessions even hotter. After I had confessed to another priest about using a pinball arcade near Farnsworth College as a base for my street hustling, I told him about a well-dressed man who approached me.

"Father, he came right up to me, and gave me some quarters, and said, 'I think you're a very sexy young man.' Then he asked me if I had ever played with myself. I told him that I did but that it was a sin of impurity. He said, 'Well, does it make you feel good?' I said, 'Yeah it makes me feel good – feel real good.' Finally, the guy wanted to know if I'd go for a ride in his car. Naturally, I went. When we started to drive, he reached over and put his hand on my leg, then on my fly. He said 'I'd like to see you get horny as hell and beg me to pull it out of your pants and jerk it off for you."

I rubbed my crotch. This sexy story was giving me a nice hard-on.

I continued. "The guy rubbed my crotch and kept saying he wanted to see my cock get all big and hard, Father. He just kept rubbing it and rubbing it. It got hard like he wanted."

I unzipped my pants and pulled my cock and balls free. I kept pulling up on them while continuing with my story.

"My cock got so hard and felt so good that I finally begged the guy to take it out of my pants and pull on it. He unzipped my fly and took it out and played with it. All at once, my cock got really hard."

In the confessional, I gripped my genitals tightly, and continued to pull up on them, over and over. Nice.

"This guy said he had a really big beautiful cock. He wanted me to pull it out and play with it."

"And did you?" asked the priest. There was a strangled sound in his voice.

"Yes, Father, I did. I pulled out his cock and put my hand on it. I rubbed it up and down like he was rubbing mine. He had a big one, and I could hardly get my hand around it."

I heard a thumping noise, and then some heavy breathing. Meanwhile, my cock grew harder. I scooted down, spread my legs out, and kept pulling up on my cock.

"And the man said, 'That feels awfully good, please keep doing it to me.' And he kept rubbing my cock."

I could hear more thumping and heavy breathing from the grill. I had done it. I had gotten the priest to jack off with me. There wouldn't be any big lecture this time – not with all those cum stains splattered everywhere.

"This guy was grunting a lot ... He was going, 'Uh! Uh!'"

I grasped my balls and pulled up hard on them. "Uh!" Then I pulled on my cock. "Uh!"

"The guy kept going 'Uh! Over and over,'" I said, "so I could tell he liked the way I was pulling on his dick."

From the grill, a question that sounded almost like a series of grunts tumbled from the priest's mouth. "Did you like what he wanted you to do to him?"

"That part of it was okay, I guess," I said, "but that wasn't all. This guy looked at my cock. He was still jerking it while I jerked his. He asked me if he could take it in his mouth. I then asked him why he would want to do that."

I heard more panting and grunts from the grill. There were no questions now. The priest was too busy.

"The guy didn't say anything, Father. He just took my dick in his mouth and sucked. He kept sucking on it while I rubbed his cock until he squirted."

I got out my handkerchief and wrapped it around my cock. I pulled up on it with little jerks.

"He sucked on it so hard, Father, that I shot off in his mouth!"

Just then, my cock spurted, and I caught my cream in my handkerchief.

"The guy just kept sucking ... uh!" I grunted while I jerked up on my cock and balls until I finished coming. "He just kept sucking and sucking!"

There were louder and more rapid thumps from the other side. I wiped the cum from my cock.

"Then the guy told me I had a nice soft hand, and he gave me twenty dollars to thank me for making him feel so good."

A gasp and a heavy sigh came from the other side. I put my cock back in my pants.

Then from the grill came a whispered, "Is that all?"

"Yes, Father."

## II. THE PREPPY STUD

I had decided to play the role of a young preppy stud, so I was dressed neatly – you know – with a tie and a soft wooly sweater.

My hair was blow-dried and my pants pressed, and I was practicing the bright-eyed look of an eager student searching for just the right teacher. A teacher who could teach me all kinds of new ways to make love.

I was cruising the park near the university when I spotted him. He was well-dressed and looked like a young professor in his late twenties. I could tell he was attracted to my young preppie look by the way he kept giving me the eye. I finally walked up to him, smiled and said, "Hello."

He relaxed and smiled back. "Are you still in school?" he asked.

"Yeah."

"How are you doing in English?" he asked.

"Not too good."

"I'm a graduate assistant in the English department at the University," he told me as he checked out my basket. It was obvious what he was really interested in, and my cock was stiffening in anticipation.

He continued to stare at the lump in my pants. "English isn't hard," he said.

"It is for me," I replied. My crotch was swelling.

He cruised my growing basket again, then looked at me. He was blushing. "Not if you go at it the right way," he replied as he slowly licked his lips. I knew then what he wanted.

"Hal's my name. What's your name?" I asked, deliberately thrusting my hips forward.

"Hi, Hal."

He gave my crotch another hungry look.

"Brad," he replied. "My...my name is Brad."

It was easy to see where this good-looking, young and obviously gay teacher was coming from. I could even predict his sex fantasy.

The university had a lot of rich jocks, particularly wild, rich jocks, who if they had been poor could have ended up in jail. But these jocks weren't poor. They were well-nourished and well-built, with muscular butts and thighs and horny swelling crotches. Crotches that one of them could thrust out and scratch in front of Brad while saying, "Gee, this is awfully swollen. It's really sore. I wonder if there is something you could do to help me?"

And at the same time he could give Brad a seductive smile that said, "You look like the kind of a guy who'd really like to suck my big hard dick. How about it?" Then as he watched Brad's embarrassed response, give a sly smirk that said, "I know you want my cock in your mouth, but you're too scared, huh?"

Sexy, rich and arrogant, these were students who could harass a new and inexperienced young instructor like Brad. They could brush against his prominent rear accidentally and whisper, "Oh ... nice!" Or write "IT'S STIFF! WANT TO SUCK IT?" on the blackboard before Brad came into the classroom, then snicker at his blushes.

No matter how deep he tried to stay in the closet, Brad was going to have a tough time concealing his gay fantasies about getting it on with one of these boneheaded muscular students in his Freshman English class. Some luscious hunky who could give Brad a piece of that stiff meat he was so hungry for, and then demand arrogantly, "Give me a good grade or I'll tell."

That is where I could play the role of that attractive but potentially dangerous student, and do it safely.

I knew it wouldn't be long before I had this closeted young professor on his knees and eating me. I started to lay the groundwork for an erotic scenario, a sexy drama that would give Brad a big, stiff cock to suck. A cock that was already swelling in my pants.

"I have one teacher who's kinda funny, if you know what I mean," I said.

Brad looked hopeful, "You do? How is he funny?"

"He likes to stare at my crotch." Brad looked down at mine as I said this and I added, "Just like you."

Brad blushed and gave me an embarrassed smile.

I continued with my sexy story, "I sit in the front row with my legs spread and he's always checking out the big bulge between my legs."

Brad smiled and licked his lips. "Really?"

"Yeahhh! So I decided to give him what he wanted so badly."

"What do you suppose he wanted?" Brad asked.

"I think he wanted something nice and hard," I cupped my heated crotch and stroked it. "He wanted something big and thick."

"So did you give him what he wanted? Did you give him something nice and big and thick?" Brad asked nervously.

"Yeah!" I nodded in reply as I looked at Brad's mouth. He had full moist lips and he was licking them. His lips were pouty, sensuous and self-indulgent.

Brad's lips were also trembling. I knew what they wanted sliding between them: My hard, pre-cum dripping cock.

"This teacher had thick, juicy lips, a lot like yours, and I thought about how good it would feel to have them kissing and nibbling on my aching cock."

I looked at Brad and wondered how long it would be before I had him on his knees. Brad's face was flushed, and his pants were bulging and throbbing. It wouldn't be long.

"When I caught him watching me, I thought of what it would be like to tell him, 'Kiss it! C'mon, smooch it good!'"

Brad was squirming and sweating profusely. "You wouldn't have minded him doing ... that?"

"No. I figured that sooner or later this teacher would invite me to his office for a private tutoring session and that's finally just what he did. I told him about my biggest problem and how it was interfering with my studies.

"'I think we can handle that,' he said, 'Sit up on the edge of my desk.' He pulled my pants down and that's when I told him, 'Kiss it! C'mon, smooch it good!' His big thick lips kissed, nibbled and slobbered all over the head of my cock. It felt really great!

"He made me so hot and bothered that I shoved his head all the way down my drooling prick, sliding the full length of it into his warm, sucking throat. After I slid in deep a few times, he slowly sucked up on it. U-m-m-m! All that talented suctioning was making my balls tingle!"

I checked out Brad's crotch. He was stroking his meat through the silky material of his pants.

"He gave me something nice: his warm wet mouth; and I gave him something nice: my hard cock. He really liked big cocks, you see."

Brad's mouth was open and his eyes were glazing over. I was getting closer to his secret fantasy, probably some cute dewy-eyed blond in the front row he wanted for a teacher's pet. I could take care of that.

"Well, Brad ... eh ... how about giving me some private tutoring?" I suggested as I caressed my throbbing meat. Brad's face turned crimson with embarrassment, but he had a sly smirk that told me how much he wanted my meat in his mouth.

"Do you have a classroom we could go to?" I asked.

"Not nearby, but there's an empty one over there," Brad pointed out, "in that building." He seemed to have trouble breathing. "Would you like to see it?"

"Sure." I grinned at him. "I'm looking forward to it."

As we walked over, Brad asked me, "What happened then?"

"Oh, after he enjoyed swallowing what I had to give him, and getting it all slippery, I gave it to him up the ass. He really liked that!"

"You did it on his office desk?" Brad asked in disbelief. He licked his lips. He was hungry for more. "Did he...?"

I wasn't sure what Brad was after and since I wanted to know what he found exciting, I just replied, "We did a lot of different stuff, and he was pretty good at it."

"Did he...did he want you to sit in the front row of the classroom, while he took out your cock?" Brad asked.

Now I had a clear picture of Brad's fantasy. A big hunk, maybe a football player, in the front row with his legs spread arrogantly and with a bulging crotch between his husky thighs. Brad wanted to suck his favorite hunk's big chunk right there in class!

We reached the building, and Brad led the way into an empty classroom. He pulled the shades and turned on the lights. "You can sit over there in the front row," he instructed.

I was right. This was going to be a classroom sex drama. I sat down and spread my legs. I had a massive hard-on bulging against my zipper, and I slid forward so it was prominent.

Brad stood at the blackboard. "Actually," he said, "I'm interested in phonetics. It's going to be my thesis topic."

This could be interesting. It was something I had never heard of. My cock was so swollen now that my pants were damp with my dripping pre-cum. I pulled at my crotch. "What's this phonetics stuff?" I asked.

"Phonetics is the systematic study of human speech-sounds," Brad replied.

"Huh?" I gave him a blank look.

"It's about how sounds are formed as the mouth muscles shape the air flow. Would you like me to demonstrate?"

I became his ideal eager student. "I certainly would, sir!" I said. I grinned and spread my legs open wider. At last I was going to get my cock sucked!

Brad moved up between my legs and fondled my basket. "This looks like it might be just what I need." He knelt and eagerly unbuckled my belt and unzipped my fly. I lifted my ass up so he could pull my pants down, and my stiff cock sprang up as I gave a sigh of relief.

I spread my legs and thrust my stiff tool forward into Brad's soft caressing hands. He fondled my tender balls and stroked my quivering shaft. "Beautiful!" he murmured. "Just what I need." He ran his fingers lightly up and down my throbbing cock. "Um-m-m! Nice and hard."

Brad pulled my foreskin back and pressed his lips against the swollen head of my cock. Then he puckered up his lips, giving it little sucking kisses with sounds like "pa!" and "ta!" all over the tip. He finally went all the way down on me with blowing "f-f-f-f" sounds, followed by wet slurping "s-sp-sss-spp" sounds as he sucked wetly back up.

All those sexy and slippery vibrations were getting to me! "Uhhhhhh!" I groaned as I thrashed around, ramming my cock into his warm, wet, vibrating mouth. All those slippery muscle movements of his mouth and tongue and the air whistling in and out! This went way beyond any vibrating vacuum pump I had ever tried!

He finally went all the way down on me and hummed a series of juicy "U-m-m-m's" around the base of my thick cock. I yelled one "Ahh...Uhh!" after another. I plunged in deeper and faster, filling his throat full of my swollen cock.

"Oh!" It felt so good! "O-o-o-o-h! More.....uuhhhhhh!"

I had never felt anything like it before. I pushed and pulled my throbbing cock frantically in and out of his sucking, vibrating mouth. I was finally reduced to a blob of deliciously quivering, spurting meat.

"A-h-h-h fuck!" I began shooting, dumping load after load deep into his vibrating mouth. "O-o-o-o-h yeahhh, swallow it, professor," I yelled as he sucked me harder.

He worked his lips and tongue rapidly up and down my squirting cock. Then I plunged my cock deeply into his throat as he made gurgling "Guh-guh-guh!" sounds on its swollen tip and tried to swallow all of my spraying cum. "Uhhh! Uhhh! Ahhh!" I yelled.

Brad continued to suck and nibble on my spasming shaft until he drained my preppie balls dry.

After my orgasmic convulsions had finally subsided somewhat, Brad asked, "Interesting subject, isn't it?"

"Yeahhhh!" I replied eagerly, "Do you think we could do that again sometime? I'd like to learn more about this phonetics stuff."

"Certainly. Would you like to sit in on my Freshman English class?"

"In the front row, maybe?" I suggested.

"Definitely in the front row."

"With my legs spread?" I teased.

"With your legs spread and your crotch bulging."

"I guess I could do that."

"And if I need more help with my phonetics thesis, could you stay after class?" Brad asked.

"I guess I could do that, too." I hadn't pulled my pants up and my cock was still sticking up, teasing him. "How 'bout helping you some more right now?" I asked.

I groaned as Brad pulled my foreskin back and pressed his lips against the swollen head of my cock with those little slurping kisses! "A-h-h-h!"

I reached out and pulled on the soft warm cheeks of his prominent ass. He was making my dick all wet and slippery. Would he like it sliding up his ass as much as he liked it in his mouth?

Probably. "U-m-m-m!"

# III. NATURAL BORN COCKSUCKERS
# (A Study in Scientific Sex)

One very warm night in May I met Brad, a young English teacher, in the park. He took me into an empty classroom and turned me into a quivering blob of spurting meat with his delicious blowjob. I liked it so much that the next day I sat in on his freshman class! As we had arranged, I sat in the front row with my legs spread and my crotch bulging. Then, after my sex display during class got Brad all worked up, and the class was finally over, it was understood he would suck my cock.

Of course, his excuse was his phonetics graduate thesis. He kept telling me how much he needed to see just how the movements of his mouth muscles shaped the air flow into sounds: "U-m-m-m! Ah-h-h! Guh-guh-guh!"

Brad was a natural-born cocksucker – and we both knew it. He loved sucking my cock and I loved his talented mouth working on it. But we just didn't call it that. Instead, it was all for science.

I had also told Brad about how proud I was of my ability to uncover suppressed sexual fantasies in my johns and how I was looking for better ways to uncover them.

I think that was why Brad told me about Cy, another graduate student in psychology. Cy had some equipment he was using to investigate the sex fantasies of horny young college students.

I asked Brad to introduce me to Cy. Maybe he could help me find ways to unleash even more explosive orgasms for me and my johns.

Cy was an attractive guy. He was about twenty-two, blond, and well-built. His ass, especially. While he showed me around his laboratory, he caught me looking at it. He smiled as he picked up an inflatable rubber cuff five inches wide with Velcro on it. "This equipment," he said, "will help me find out what really arouses you sexually."

I figured that he already knew what aroused me from the way I was admiring his ass. I could hardly keep my hands off it.

"How can you do that?" I asked innocently. I was pretty sure now that this guy was just as gay as Brad, and it looked like he had his own scientific way of getting into my pants.

"I can show you by wrapping this cuff around your penis and inflating it."

"Go ahead," I said.

"Take off your clothes and climb up on that table."

I looked at the table as I stripped. It had stirrups at the foot of it. "What are those stirrups for?" I asked.

"To fully expose your genitals and make it easier for me to work on them," Cy replied.

I could feel my cock beginning to swell in anticipation.

Work on them, huh? I've always enjoyed another guy's experienced hands working over my cock and balls.

I could already picture him fingering my balls while he pulled my foreskin back and forth slowly and lasciviously. "Um-m-m." Obviously, I like a good hand job.

Cy looked down at the swelling cock between my husky thighs. I could tell he was already anxious to get his hands on it. But he just said, "Get up on the table and put your feet in the stirrups."

I was getting aroused by wondering just what Cy planned to do with my genitals. I climbed up on the table and placed my feet in the stirrups.

I wondered if all this scientific stuff was just another way to seduce college students like me.

It was a good set-up. Cy's lab was private. He could lock the door, and get the student to spread his legs and then seduce him.

With my cock and ass completely exposed, Cy could get me excited and he could do whatever he wanted to me. He could jack me off, suck my cock or fuck me. I wondered which it would be.

But I've always liked having a guy's hands on my cock. They all handle it differently.

I even had one roommate who was timid and would only play with my cock when he thought I was asleep.

His teasing touches up and down my cock really made me hot. I wondered how Cy's hands were going to feel.

"Now it will be easier for you to wrap that cuff around my cock," I remarked casually to cover up my growing excitement. And that wasn't all that was growing.

Cy ran his fingers lightly up the inside of my thigh and fondled my balls. "Most subjects are very shy about exposing their sex organs like this. But Brad told me that you have done some hustling."

"Yeah, a little. I was helping him with his phonetics thesis."

"Yes, I know." Cy grasped my exposed cock. "Did you enjoy all the sounds he made when he sucked your cock?"

"Yeah!" I thrust my cock up into his warm hand.

"So did I," Cy said. He stroked my cock lightly. It felt good. I liked his hands on my cock. My cock twitched and began to get hard. I hoped he was going to try some new way of jacking me off.

"A slight swelling when the cuff is applied is not unusual." Cy said as he pulled on my cock and wrapped the cuff around it. "You'll soon get used to it."

Cy inflated the cuff and turned on the graph recorder. "Now I'm going to ask you to tell me about your favorite sex fantasies.

"If your penis swells, this puts pressure on the cuff, and moves the pen on the graph. Once I discover your sexual desires, we'll work on ways to make them more satisfying. Now, what will give you a good hard-on?"

I thought of the stories I used to get my johns excited.

"There's one story I use when I'm playing a farm boy new to the city," I said. "I wear an old pair of overalls with holes in it, so the john can see that I'm naked underneath. This gets him hot. To get him even hotter I tell him about what happened to me on the farm.

"Tell me about it," Cy asked eagerly.

"It's about me and our young hired man up in the haymow. I can tell he really likes me a lot by the way he keeps looking at my crotch. When I catch him, his face gets red and he looks away."

"Please continue; your penis is swelling."

"Like one day we're up in the haymow and he pulls his cock out and says, 'I'll bet you've got a big one. Why don't you take it out so we can see if its bigger than mine?'

"I pull my cock out, and he says, 'I can make it even bigger.' He puts his hand around my cock and rubs it, and it gets bigger and feels real good."

"Good, the cuff pressure is still increasing."

"Then he wants me to rub his cock like he's rubbing mine, and I do.

"I'm telling this story to the guy I'm having sex with. I vary it depending on what kind of sex he likes. If he likes hand jobs, I describe how we jack each other off. You know, using a slow two-fingered teasing, fisting it fast with the balls bouncing, or kissing at the same time, different stuff. Whatever gets him hot.

"And maybe like how I get the hired man to play with my cock, and how good it feels. I really like a nice, smooth hand job, especially if I can feel up the guy's bare ass while he's doing it to me."

"We're getting an increase here."

I noticed that Cy's pants were also getting an increase.

"You like getting hand jobs?" he asked eagerly.

"Sure! Always have."

"And you like feeling up his ass while he jacks you off?"

"Yeah! I like the way a guy's bare ass feels, all smooth and round, but with muscles underneath. I like just looking at them, too. Makes me so horny. That's why I like watching football games. All those hunky asses!"

"Good! You're aware of how much these thoughts excite you. Let's find something you've suppressed."

"If he's sucking my cock I tell him how the hired man got down on his knees and sucked it just like he's doing. Then he really goes to work on my cock – gets me hotter, too. There's some kind of name for this, isn't there?"

"It's called 'technical augmentation,'" Cy explained. "Like stroke books and sex movies. Please continue."

"Anyway, I try to relate my stories to what the john is doing, and get him even more excited."

"That's what we're doing here," Cy said, "looking for what turns you on. What other things could you do with the hired man?"

"I could suck his cock."

Cy was watching the graph. "Umm-hm."

"I could stick my cock up his ass."

"Ummh, that's somewhat stimulating."

"He could fuck me."

"Uh-huh!" Now Cy was getting interested! "So tell me about how the hired man could fuck you."

"Well, I take off my pants and get down on my hands and knees. Then I spread my legs and put my head down in the hay to make my ass stick up. He reaches between my legs and pulls on my bag and plays with my cock...." I paused. This drove Cy nuts.

"Ah-h-h!" Cy screamed. "Continue!"

"Well, then he spits on his cock and my hole, and sticks his cock up into me. I grunt. He grabs my cock and pulls back on it hard as he rams his dick into me. I shove back to keep my cock from hurting, and this drives his cock all the way up my ass.

"Then he pulls my cock away from him as he pulls out of my ass. It hurts, so I jerk forward. He's making me give him my ass just the way he wants it! Me too! I'm fucking him as much as he's fucking me! His cock feels so good when I push back to drive it in deeper!"

"Very good! This is what I had hoped would happen. The pen is practically off the graph! Now I can try another experiment I've been wanting to do."

"What's that?" I asked.

"You'll see." Cy was smearing KY jelly on another implement of rubber, shaped like a dildo.

"Now relax. I'm going to insert this dildo into your ass," he said and slowly pushed it into me.

"This will be a different set-up," Cy told me. "Now I'm connecting the cuff and dildo air-lines to a pump. But first, let's make sure the anal balloon is at the right pressure."

Cy began to squeeze a rubber bulb, and I could feel the balloon swell. "Let me know when it feels uncomfortable," Cy said.

I didn't say anything and Cy continued to pump air into the dildo.

"You can tolerate a big one!" Cy was surprised. "Now I'll ease the pressure back, and set the differential pressure, so the balloon's size will swing from very small to very large."

After adjusting this, Cy turned his attention to the penile cuff. Since my cock had swollen, he reduced the pressure in the cuff.

"With this set-up you should feel like you're being fucked up the ass. Just lie back and enjoy it." Cy put a pillow under my head and started the pump.

I could feel the balloon-dildo slowly swell and then relax in my rectum.

As the dildo relaxed, the cuff squeezed my cock.

Then, as the cuff relaxed, the dildo slowly grew larger.

"Uh!" That rhythmic swelling and squeezing! My cock was hard and pulsing inside the cuff.

"Let me know the speed and pressure you like. Return to the haymow scene. You're getting fucked."

"Oh-h-h yeah! I'm bent over, and he's pulling my cock back and forth and ramming into me."

"I'm going to increase the pressure and speed little by little." Cy was now stroking the bulge in his pants. "Let me know when it's just right."

"Oh! Y-e-a-h! That's great!"

I had never felt anything like this before. First, the slow swelling in my rectum. Like an explosion of incredible energy filling my guts! "O-o-o-o-h! It feels s-o-o-o good! He's shoving his big cock up my ass!"

Then the cuff squeezed my throbbing cock! "Ah-h-h!" My cock was glowing! "Oh-h-h!" I groaned. "His hand feels so good!"

Cy increased the pressure.

"O-o-o-o-h! I want him deeper, all the way up in me! Uh! Uh!"

Cy increased the speed of the pulses. Now he was rubbing his crotch against the table. "Uh..uh..uh!" I was grunting. "He's shooting up my ass!"

I thrashed my pelvis violently. The dildo throbbing in my guts was too much! I spurted creamy white jets of cum all over my belly.

"Uh! Uh! Uh! A-h-h-h! O-h-h-h! It feels s-o-o-o good! Um-m-m!"

After I was breathing easily again, Cy pulled the dildo from my ass, and unwrapped the cuff.

"What do you think of that for an invention?"

"Pretty neat!"

Cy saw me looking at the big wet spot on his pants. "I'm glad you liked it as much as I did!" he said. He gave me a big grin. "Oh by the way, would you like to come over to my place tonight? We could work on your smooth hand job fantasies."

"That would be great!"

"And I have some classic football tapes we can play."

"We can do both together?"

"Sure!"

I grinned back at him. "Wow!" I said. I was already getting another hard-on.

- - -

Yes, Cy was right. His football tape was a classic – all of that ass action! He leaned over me as I watched the game, pumping on my throbbing cock and caressing my balls.

"Could I take down your pants?" I asked.

"Want to feel my ass?"

"Yeah!"

I unbuckled his belt and pulled down his pants and undershorts. I reached around him and stroked his buttocks with both hands. They were so smooth ... and warm!

He was caressing my balls with one hand as he pulled lightly on them. I groaned as I thrust my big throbbing cock up into his other hand.

Cy had moved up towards my head to make it easier for me to cup and fondle his firm, round ass cheeks. Now his cock was waving right in front of my face. It was so hard that his foreskin was partly pulled back, and the head of his cock looked delicious.

I just had to put my mouth on it! I brought one hand around to pull his foreskin back. Then I lapped and kissed his glans like Brad with little nips, "Pah!" and sucks, "S-s-sp!

Cy yelled, "O-h-h-h yeah! Do that some more!" He pulled my foreskin back and forth, as he worked up some spit and took my cock into his mouth. He slathered his lips and tongue rapidly in and out under my foreskin and around my swollen glans, making incredibly exciting sucking sounds.

"Uh! Uh!" I grunted and went all the way down on his cock, pulling on his ass, so I could suck his cock all the way into my mouth. I tightened my lips around the root, sucking hard and humming "M-m-m-m!" just like Brad.

Cy's hands were working all over my cock and balls, as he grunted and moaned and sucked harder and harder.

"U-m-m-m!" I yelled. I ran my mouth up and down his cock, rolling my tongue lasciviously around it as I came back up to the head and kissed and fluttered my tongue over it. I could feel his cock swell and knew he was about ready to come, so I caressed his ass, and tickled his asshole.

Cy thrust deep into my throat. I was grunting, "Guh! Guh!" as his cum shot into my spasming throat and I greedily milked the cream out of his balls.

His cock was deep and throbbing in my throat and felt so good! So good, that I just had to ram my cock deep into the back of his throat!

I came, intensely! "Uh! Uh! Ah-h-h!"

We lay there for a moment, savoring each other's cum-covered cocks.

Then we pulled out and swung around to hug and kiss one another. "Great, huh?" I asked.

"Yeah!" Cy replied. "We'll have to get Brad to give us some more of his cocksucking lessons."

I grinned at Cy. "Do you suppose we're just as much natural born cocksuckers, as Brad is?"

Cy smiled. "Looks like it."

# IV. THE REAL THING

It all began when I was having coffee with Cy, a grad student in psychology who said he was collecting statistics on the sex fantasies of students for a paper. "Horny males always lie about their sex lives," he said, so he wanted to prove his point and had the practice of wrapping a cuff around their cocks and showed them sex pictures. When their cocks swelled, it showed up on a recording graph he had. Then he knew what kind of sex they really wanted.

Of course, Cy showed them straight scenes; but since he was gay he included pictures of guys having sex, so he could find out who was gay and what they liked.

How did I know all this? I was one of those students. And after Cy found out I liked getting hand jobs, he actually gave me a few.

He also discovered that I liked tight muscular asses and watching football games. Looking back on it, that's probably why he told me about Roddy and his problem. Roddy was a quarterback.

"Now I'm experimenting with a new project," He told me. "I'm working on a cure for masturbation."

"Huh?"

"I claim that masturbation is caused by excessive anal tightness," Cy continued. "I've modified my equipment by adding an expandable dildo that I can stick up the guy's ass and pump it up. This way, I can train these students to relax their asshole muscles."

"You think guys jack-off just because they've got tight assholes?"

"Could be. I've got one quarterback who wants to overcome his 'shameful habit.' I've been sticking my special dildo up his ass for a couple of weeks now. He's learning how to relax and he's even beginning to have anal orgasms. The only thing is, if I succeed in curing Roddy of masturbating, he'll probably end up with a terrific desire to take it up the ass."

I could picture that tight quarterback ass swivel as he fell back for a pass. My cock warmed and I fondled it. "I'll be happy to help, if Roddy feels the need."

Cy looked at my swelling crotch and smiled. Like I said, he knew why I liked watching football games.

A bit later, I saw Roddy reading a textbook in the University Union dining room. I walked over with my coffee, and sat down.

"Tough subject?" I asked.

"So-so," Roddy replied, "But there's a lot of crap in this course."

He showed me the book he was reading, Sex and Health.

"What crap is that?"

"All this crap about how masturbation isn't harmful." Roddy leaned closer. "I'm getting help, you should too, if it's a problem – is it?" he asked me eagerly.

"Occasionally." I didn't add that it was only a problem when I couldn't get a nice smooth hand job from my roommate. "You said you were getting help?"

"Yes, from a graduate student who's exploring new ways to cure young men of this shameful habit. He has a whole new approach." Roddy rubbed his buttocks against the seat of his chair. His face flushed with embarrassed pleasure.

"What's this whole new approach?"

"I can't go into that." Roddy whispered. He squirmed his ass against the chair seat. Roddy's shy pleasuring of his ass was giving me a hard-on. Now he had me hunching my own ass.

Roddy's voice became low and sexy, "My therapist told me it's best not to say anything until his research is complete."

I swallowed a grunt. "That's probably wise," I said. My God, this big hunk was like putty in Cy's hands.

Roddy looked at his watch with a frown. "I've got to beat it. Nice talking with you."

Cy was getting results. I watched the flexing of Roddy's ass muscles as he left. Now if I could just get into that seductive butt. "A-h-h-h...uh!"

But Cy had beat me to it. Two or three times a week, he had those firm round buttcheeks spread out before him.

I could picture Cy manipulating Roddy's asshole, delicately spreading it open while he slowly inserted his dildo. Then inflating it while watching Roddy's squirming ass and pleasure-flushed face. "Let's try for a little more pressure this time, shall we?"

Lucky bastard!

- - -

I thought about how I might help Roddy. The opportunity came when Cy was away from the University for a month.

I saw Roddy in the dining hall. I picked up a cup of black coffee and a donut, and joined him. He seemed anxious, which I could understand; since he wasn't getting his "treatments." He was squirming again and rubbing his buttocks against the chair.

"What seems to be the trouble?" I asked, as if I didn't already know.

"My therapist is away for a month."

"You really need help?"

"Yeah, I'm desperate. I can't keep my hands off it."

"Well, I've also worked with Cy some. Of course, his equipment is locked up while he's gone." And it would stay locked up. I figured this guy needed the real thing – which was already stiffening in my crotch, warm and eager for Roddy's tight butt.

"Maybe you can help me," Roddy said.

"I might be able to. Do you have a place?"

"I have a room in the dorm."

"Fine," I said, "Let's go, but I want to stop by my room for a minute."

In Roddy's bedroom, I ordered him to strip. He hesitated. I pushed him, my voice more demanding. He relented, finally, and when he was completely naked, I got a good look at his ass. Oh, man, it was nice.

"Where Cy's machine isn't available," I said, "we'll simply have to do the best we can."

I had picked up some latex gloves, a condom, some K-Y jelly and a butt-plug in my room. I slipped on the gloves, and smeared the K-Y on them.

"Now just lie back and put your legs up on my shoulders," I told him. "I'm going to try to duplicate the treatments Cy gave you, so breathe deeply and relax. The first thing we'll do is check for anal tension." I pushed my middle finger up into Roddy's ass-pucker.

He flinched. "O-o-o-h...."

"Yes, I can see that there is still some tightness there. Am I hurting you?"

"No, it's just that it feels so funny."

"Didn't Cy do this as part of your treatment?"

"No, he just pushed that dildo up into me."

"Well, I want to relax your anal muscles before I go deeper."

I worked my fingers around Roddy's tight hole, pulling it open and flicking my fingers over his exposed anus to get him really horny before I gave him his deep massage. Roddy's prick was sticking up now, ready to go.

"How does that feel?"

Roddy gave a deep sigh. "U-m-m-m...."

"All right, close your eyes, and relax. I'm going to give you a short break."

I took off my pants, then rolled on a condom and greased it. "Now, keep your eyes closed, and relax your ass muscles. I'm going to give you a deep massage."

I spread Roddy's hole with my thumbs, and pushed my cockhead up into it. "This might be a bit uncomfortable at first, but I'm sure you'll like it."

"There!" I pushed deeper. "Can you feel your muscles relaxing?"

"Yeah, you're really stretching them."

"Now for some deep massage." I slowly worked my cock all the way up his ass. "Feel that?"

"O-o-o-h!"

"Nice, isn't it?"

"U-m-m-m! Oh, y-e-s-s-s!"

"There!" I thrust deep and levered my cock against his asshole. "Doesn't that feel more relaxed?"

"O-h-h-h...y-e-s-s." Roddy moaned softly, his face reddening. He realized now that I was fucking him and his secret shames about getting a cock up his ass were coming to the surface.

"This is going to be a more personal treatment, designed just for your own special personal needs."

"Just for me?" Roddy whispered.

"Just for you," I said softly.

Roddy opened his eyes wide. It was like he was surprised at how good I was making him feel. I locked my eyes with his, projecting a flow of love and concern. "We're going to lick this problem of yours."

I rammed into him, deep. Roddy's anal ring spasmed tightly around the root of my cock. It felt so good squeezing my cockroot! I kept thrusting with little rabbit jabs. His ass was s-o-o-o nice and tight!

Roddy threw his head back and from side to side, hunching his hole against my stiff tool. He was squirming and writhing against me now.

Roddy's dick was sticking up, hot and hard. It began to twitch and he came. He yelled and spurted jets of cum all over his chest. "Uh! Uh! Ooooo..! Gee! U-m-m-m."

As he came, his asshole muscles spasmed tightly around my cock, convulsively gripping my cockroot like a tight throbbing glove.

"Uh! Uh!" I came. "A-h-h-h!"

I lay on top of him for a few minutes, then pulled out and rolled off the condom. I put on my pants.

"There is something else I want to show you, Roddy." I showed him the butt-plug. "Do you see this?"

"What is it?"

"It's a butt-plug to help you relax your ass even more. I want you to insert this in the morning just before you come down to breakfast."

I showed him how to insert it. "Feels good, doesn't it? Now you can take it out and put it in just before breakfast. Then I can check on how well it loosens you up. Okay?"

"Okay ... sir!"

The next day, I was having breakfast in the Union when Roddy joined me. "I'd like to thank you for your help," he said.

"Was there something special about what I did for you?"

"Yeah, that deep massage." Roddy's eyes glistened with admiration.

Roddy wouldn't come right out and say that I had fucked him. But he knew it. And he had liked having my big cock shoved up his ass. Liked it? It was more than like – Roddy had loved it!

"And I...." I couldn't help reflecting the unabashed love flowing from Roddy's eyes, "I loved ... helping you." I had almost said, "...fucking you."

I looked steadily into Roddy's eyes. They were wide and glistening with – admiration? – adoration? – awe?

I had never had anyone look at me like that before. My cock throbbed. I was afraid I was going to come in my pants!

As he looked at me, Roddy shifted on his chair, pulling at one of his buttcheeks. Then he pulled on his other cheek.

Roddy moved his behind rhythmically back and forth and smiled at me with embarrassed pleasure. He was working the butt-plug up his ass!

On occasion, he would look around to see if anyone was watching him, then continued rubbing his ass against the chair.

"Well, how's it working?"

"Pretty good," Roddy looked up, blushing.

I looked into Roddy's eyes as he squirmed his ass without missing a beat. Being watched seemed to embarrass him and turn him on at the same time.

Now I could see his eyes fill with a submissive yielding.

My cock swelled and throbbed, poking further down my pant leg. I could feel the pressure build up in my groin. I was going to come any minute now!

Roddy squirmed more frantically, his lips parted. His breathing became harsh, raspy.

Suddenly, he gasped, then looked down.

Cum stains were evident.

I yielded to the admiration in his eyes. My cock throbbed. Our eyes locked as I came in my pants! Then I grinned, "Well, it seems this treatment is working."

"Ohhhhhh, y-e-a-h!" Roddy replied. "I didn't even have to touch it. I guess this means I'm cured." He looked anxiously at me. "But you'll keep working with me, won't you?"

"Sure!"

I knew what he wanted. He wanted more of my big cock up his ass.

And my big cock up his ass is exactly what Roddy got! And it seemed that he just couldn't seem to get enough!

Eventually, he became very inventive. He wanted it on his back, on his belly, on his side, on his knees, even lying on the edge of the bed, where he wanted me to spank him and pull his warmed-up buns apart, so I could stick my cock up his ass.

It seemed that Roddy was finally cured of his "shameful habit," but I knew better, and it wasn't long before he learned to enjoy my mouth on his cock, and how to give me a nice, very smooth hand job.

"O-h-h! Y-e-a-h!" Roddy would yell, "Do that to me again!" Then, always, "Let's try it this way!"

And my reply? "U-m-m-m-m! Nice!"

# V. FARM BOY IN OVERALLS

I had one role I used when hustling that was very popular with businessmen and the professors: that of a luscious, dewy-eyed, young farm boy. Over time, I played this role to the hilt, feigning being unsophisticated and awkward. They couldn't resist this fresh-faced but gawky hick new to the city and awed by it all.

I had bought a pair of blue denim overalls, bleached them, and ripped holes in the thigh and ass areas, revealing patches of my creamy tanned flesh.

I was naked under the overalls and the rough denim rubbing against my genitals helped keep me semi-hard, while the shoulder straps constantly scraped against my nipples, making them red and swollen. By the time I got to the client's place, I was horny as hell.

The clients swooned when they saw this farm boy with tousled, straw-colored hair and a freckled face, who was obviously going to be submissive to them, with a nice, very ripe bottom swelling out my overalls.

And swelling out my crotch, was my "coming attraction." Like in the movies, there was always a special attraction. My special attraction was my fully eight-inch long, very tasty prick that filled my crotch to bursting, as this bashful farm boy awkwardly scuffed his feet and reluctantly made his offer. I really turned them on with: "I've never done this before, Mister. But I need the money real bad – awful bad."

I was bashful farm boy meat, real cheap. Now on special! Tonight only! And it drove the johns crazy....

"Are you new to the city?" the man asked. He glanced furtively at the bulging crotch in my tight, well-worn overalls.

"Yeah, I've never been in any place this big before," I replied. "It's quite a place."

I pretended not to notice those furtive glances at my crotch, even as I thrust it forward and looked the man over. The guy looked like a typical businessman, clean and respectable. "What's your name?" I asked.

"John," was the reply.

I smiled and thought, "Yeah, I'll bet."

"You having a good time?" John asked, now openly checking out my crotch and chunky buttocks.

"So-so. I've had better days, let me tell ya/"

"Hmmm. You're quite a big boy, aren't you?" John gave my bulging crotch a bolder look.

"Well, yeah!" I pulled at the tightness around my crotch. "I'm pretty big. I seem to be still growing..." I pulled at my crotch again, with an expression of discomfort. "Some guys say that maybe I'm too big."

"You do seem very uncomfortable down there." John put his hand over mine, then slid it down over my bulging overalls.

"Yeah," I replied bashfully. "I guess you could say that."

The john took his time fondling my crotch. "Do you want me to help you with it?" He was beginning to breathe hard and his face was red.

"Yeah, I could use some help. But it's not just this...." I pressed the man's hand on my bulge. "Like I said, I've seen better days. I'm down on my luck right now, man. I need to get a place to stay. I need some money awful bad."

"Well, I can help you with that...." the john said. He reached in his pocket and pulled out a twenty. "Will this help?"

"Hey, it sure will!" I stuffed the twenty into my pocket. "That's real swell of you to help me out like this."

I pressed John's hand on my bulging crotch. "Do you think you can help me out with this, too?" I moved the john's hand up and down. "Feel it. It's so stiff!"

The john was starting to sweat, "Well, I'm pretty sure I can help you with it."

"How could you do that?" I asked, all wide-eyed and innocent.

"Well, let me take a look at it. Perhaps I can tell what's wrong. I've had some experience with first-aid." John reached over and unbuttoned my bulging fly. "Your sex seems to be badly swollen," he said, as he reached in and pulled out my eight inches of throbbing prick.

"My God, how on earth did it get so swollen?"

"Gosh, I don't know," I replied. "But it gets that way a lot. Must be going through a phase. I'm always so fuckin' hard! It gets so hard that it hurts!"

"Hmmm. Have you shown it to a doctor?"

"Pa don't believe in doctors. 'Sides, we don't have no money hardly. Paw says it's the devil gettin' in it, and you got to drive him out by stickin' it in some crushed ice."

"I'll bet that hurts!" John licked his lips and smiled. "There ought to be a better way to drive the devil out than that. Do you ever massage it? Sometimes that can ease the swelling."

"Nope!" I said righteously, "Not supposed to. Paw, he's a preacher, you know, he says touchin' it is a sin, 'cause a what it says in the Bible."

I was warming up. I went on with my rant: "Cain't do nothin' that the Bible says is a sin."

John fingered my erect and swollen hard-on. "I know what you mean, son. That's too bad. What can you do for relief?"

"Gotta wait til I marry Susie; she lives next door. But we gotta do it just right, or we'll git inta' some awful sinnin'...."

"What are you, about twenty?"

"No sir. I'm jist eighteen."

"Well, perhaps I can show you something that will help," John said.

"It's not touchin' it, is it? Cain't do that." I said.

"No, no, it's not touching it. Not that way. I took a first aid course for emergencies like this. It's more like the standard snake-bite treatment. If a snake bites you, you have to suck the poison out."

"Yeah," I said, "I heard'a that. I guess the devil gettin' in it is like a snake bite - but that crushed ice hurt awful!"

"This won't hurt a bit," John smiled, flicking his tongue over his lips, "It's not at all like crushed ice. I think you'll like it."

"I sure am glad ta hear that," I said. "Where d'ya go for this treatment?

"Oh, right here. It's perfectly safe here in the park. Hasn't been a soul up here since we met."

"Yeah," I replied. "I noticed that...."

"Now, it will make the snake-bite treatment easier, if you drop your overalls."

I unfastened the shoulder straps and pulled my overalls down over my thighs. I was naked, and my cock stuck out.

John knelt before me, admiring and fondling my cock and my naked thighs and buttocks. Then he skinned my swollen cock, and slobbered his mouth over it, rapidly lapping and kissing it.

"Are you real sure you ain't jerkin' it?"

"Yes, I am, very sure. This is right out of the snake-bite manual, page twenty, 'How to Begin Treatment.'"

Now John was telling me some big lies. But then I had no preacher Paw, and I was damned sure John had never seen a snake-bite manual. A lively lying contest – very creative, with a sex-scene right from scratch. To my way of thinking, that was always fun.

John continued to stroke my buttocks and thighs as he kissed and licked my cock. "The next step is on page twenty-five, 'Poison Extraction.'"

John slid my foreskin back. Then he puckered up his lips and thrust them out, kissing the end of my dick. Big drooly suction kisses, right on my hole, with quick, hard, smacking sucks.

Each kiss made me grunt and thrust, "Uh-h-h!" I was trying to get deeper into John's mouth.

Finally, John took all of my exposed glans into his mouth, tightened his lips around the ridge, and gave a big sucking kiss.

I yelled, "Ouch! You said it wouldn't hurt!"

"Sorry," John said, "That's why I lapped it, so it wouldn't hurt. Guess it needs more lapping." John ran his lips and tongue over my cockhead, coating it with his thick drool, and giving it quick light sucks.

"Oh yeah, that's nice," I said, "it feels better already."

"Good," John said, "now to page 30, and 'The Full Treatment.'"

John bobbed his head on my boner, opening his mouth and twirling his tongue around it, going down, then sucking smoothly as he pulled up.

Now I figured it was time for my Hayloft Story, the one that encouraged johns to give me a really good blowjob. "Gee!" I began, "this reminds me of a hired man we had once."

"I knew he liked me a lot," I told John, who was now busily sucking the devil's snake-bite out of my cock, "because he kept giving me funny looks. One day we were working in the hayloft and the hired man says, 'I'll bet you've got a big one, it's pro'bly bigger'n mine. Why don't'cha you show it to me? We can see who's got the biggest one.'"

John kept sucking avidly as he listened. Then he took his cock out and pumped on it, sucking faster and harder. He had good suction.

I groaned, "Uh-h! Nice!" and continued my story, "I showed it to him. He put his hand around it and rubbed it, and said I'll bet I can make it even bigger than that, and it did get bigger and felt good. I said this don't count as touchin' it, does it?' An' he said, 'No, this is just to get it hard so we can see who's bigger.'

"Then the hired man pulled his cock out and put my hand on it so I could rub it and make it hard. We put them side by side, and sure 'nuf, mine was bigger."

John was now gobbling up my cock like a hungry wolf gnawing on a piece of raw meat. He looked up, "I'll bet yours is bigger than anybody's! Big and beautiful!" Then he went back to his voracious sucking.

"The hired man wanted me to rub his cock while he rubbed mine, his hand felt so good I started to rub his. But I figured, 'Oh No! That'd be touchin' it,' and I told him that was prohibited in the Bible, so he stopped touchin' me. Then you know what he did?"

"Ummph! Argh!"

"He got down on his knees, and did just what you're doin'. He must have read that same First Aid Snake-Bite Book, 'cause he took it in his mouth and sucked on it just like you're doing to me."

The panting and sucking businessman was still eating up my imaginary haymow story, along with my luscious cock and balls. He looked up at me, red-faced and panting, "Am I better than him?"

"You sure are." I replied. I knew cocksuckers need a lot of praise. It helps them suck better.

John went back to work, slobbering and slurping. I fucked his mouth. "Uh! Uh!" I grunted. "Suck! Suck it! Suck that bad old devil out! Ah-h-h...oh-h-h...uh-h-h! The devil's coming out!" I yelled.

I shot off, and convulsively shoved my throbbing cock deep into John's throat. "The devil's a-comin' out! Glory! Glory!" I yelled, twitching and jerking all over and ramming my cock in and out of John's mouth.

"Ar-r-r-gh...ugh...ugh!" John gurgled. He almost choked on my creaming cock, struggling to swallow all of my spurts of thick come.

"This is just like when the hired man sucked the devil out of me!" I told him. "And I jerked and hollered and twitched, just like I'm doin' now, and the devil shot right out of me.

"Take 'im, take all of him, suck him all outa me!" I pulled my cock half-way out and rammed in and out, as my come oozed and dripped from John's lips.

"Oh, I see him now! He's comin', he's a-comin'." My semen coated and lubricated my slick cock as I finished coming.

Then I tried to pull out of John's frantically sucking mouth. John didn't want to let go of my cock. He wasn't done jerking off yet. He smacked his lips over my dick, taking it deep and sucking hard to keep it in his mouth, until his own cock finally spurted.

"Ummph...Argh!" John gave a final smacking suck as he came.

I pulled my cock out, patting John on the head, "You really know your first aid, John. You got the devil right out of me! See how soft and relaxed it is?"

I placed John's hand on my limp cock. "You've done just what the hired man did, John, you made the hardness go away. It's all nice and relaxed again, for today, anyway."

"Glory, glory, you did it, John. The devil's all gone out a' me! Thank you, thank you, John! And I didn't touch it, not one bit, did I?"

"No, not at all. You did not touch yourself. Not one bit," John replied, wiping the come from his lips with a grin.

Well, that was another one under my belt: Another busy businessman who just had to rut feverishly with a sexy farm boy for a few uninhibited ecstatic moments, before going home to his humdrum TV and wife and kiddies. "Yeah," I said to myself as I pulled up my overalls, "There's definitely something special about a farm boy."

## VI. PLAYING THE SKINFLUTE

I was on the bus returning for my sophomore year at Farnsworth when I met Jared. It was late at night and I was in the back of the bus in the smoking section – you could still smoke on the bus then – when Jared came back and sat beside me.

He was about my age, nineteen, and looked like a hunky farm boy. He had freckles on his face and arms and was well-muscled. I especially noticed his husky thighs and his prominent ass as he swung in beside me. He was wearing shorts with an elastic band to hold them up. They were tight and really showed off the muscles of his tanned thighs, the ripe, swelling globes of his ass and his well-packed crotch.

My own crotch stirred and I could feel it already getting excited at the thought of what might happen between me and this attractive young male. Fleeting images flashed through my mind, of me pumping on his tantalizing boner while I avidly sucked it into my mouth, then spreading his asscheeks and shoving my cock between them.

I could feel my cock swell and stretch down the leg of my shorts. I looked down to make sure its shaft wasn't sticking out the bottom of my shorts.

He asked me for a light. I gave him one, and asked him, "Are you going to Farnsworth University?"

"Yeah," he replied, taking a drag. "I'm going to be studying soil science so I can go back and help my parents on the farm. They're into organic farming. We don't believe in all this pesticide and artificial fertilizer stuff."

I could go along with that. "Just encouraging nature, huh?" I asked. That's just what I wanted to do with Jared. Encourage his nature, his natural sexuality. And mine as well, which was already stiff and throbbing.

"Yeah!" He replied. "Keep the soil healthy. That's all you need to do." I could see him looking at the swelling in my shorts. "Is Farnsworth University where you're going?"

I began to see the future sex possibilities if I could get it on with this good-looking and sexy young student.

"Yes, I'm just beginning my sophomore year." I told him. "My name is Hal. What's yours?"

"Jared. What are you studying?"

"Well, I'm not sure just yet," I replied. "I'm somewhere between pre-med and English Literature, mostly Shakespeare. And I'm also taking a Sociology course this year. That sounds like it might be interesting."

"Shakespeare, huh?" Jared looked at me and smiled. I figured he was thinking the same thought I was, that Shakespeare was just another way to say "jacking off." "Shakespeare," he murmured thoughtfully. "What do you like about him?"

Now I wanted to describe my interest in a way that would give Jared a hint of my desire to have sex with him, and see how he responded. How we could shake our stiff throbbing spears together. So I began telling him about the recorder scene in Hamlet.

"Well," I said, "he has some interesting ways of describing things, like in the recorder scene."

"What's a recorder."

"It's like a wooden flute. Hamlet has been playing it. Then he realizes that these two guys sent by the king are just trying to manipulate him. So he compares himself to the flute by saying, "You would play upon me ... do you think I am easier to be played on than this flute?""

Jared laughed, "Do you think he was comparing himself to a skinflute that these guys wanted to get their mouths on and blow?"

I smiled. He was getting the idea. "I've never seen that interpretation played out on the stage, but it sounds like a good one."

"Thanks," Jared replied. "I'm going to move up to the next seat and stretch out."

As Jared moved up to the seat ahead, I wondered if I had turned him off. But he didn't seem upset by the idea of guys giving each other blowjobs. Probably on the farm, sex was just another part of organic nature.

Then I did something I didn't really understand at the time. I began to hum a tune directed towards him which I had developed while studying the play, based on the soliloquy beginning with the line, "Tis now the very witching time of night...." I had interpreted this as a moment when Hamlet could express his suppressed tenderness.

I had been humming this only a couple of minutes, when Jared jumped up, came back and sat beside me. He placed his left hand only about an inch from my right hand, and I wanted very much to reach over and touch it. It was only an inch away!

But it seemed to take a tremendous effort. I finally did move my hand over to touch his, but it was a very hard thing to do. I guess you could say I've been in the habit of repressing my sexual affections.

He surprised me. He responded quickly by taking my hand and pressing it down on his crotch, where I could feel his hard-on pressing up. I ran my hand up and down over his bulging crotch.

Then he grasped my hand again and pushed it down under his elastic belt. He didn't have anything on under his shorts, and his naked cock pressed against my palm. I caressed the tip of his uncut cock, skinning the foreskin back and forth, then ran my hand down over its stiffness, and cupped his small, tight balls carefully, since I knew how sensitive my own balls were.

Jared sighed and I continued to slide my hand up and down over his stiff cock shaft. At the tip, I played with his foreskin for a while, and then went back down to his balls. He started thrusting his cock into my hand, and then gasped and took hold of my wrist, holding it still and finally pulling it out of his shorts.

"What's the matter?" I asked.

"I'm almost ready to come." He said. "I'd better go finish off in the bathroom, so I don't get my cum all over everything."

"You don't have to do that!" I licked my lips.

Jared grinned. "You mean you want to play on my skinflute?"

"Y-e-a-h!" I pulled his shorts down. His cock, a beautiful eight-incher, sprang up.

Jared looked up the row of bus seats. "What if someone has to use the bathroom?"

He had a point. We were right next to the bathroom.

"It's dark here, and you can see if anyone is coming."

"Besides me, you mean?"

"Uh-huh." I leaned over his crotch, and wrapped my fingers around his cock, bringing it up to my mouth. I put my lips around his foreskin and pushed it back and forth, masturbating him with my lips, while I fluttered my tongue over his satin- smooth and swollen glans.

"O-h-h-h!" he moaned, as I gradually sucked my way wetly down on his throbbing cock.

I took it deep into my throat, swallowing spasmodically on the tip of it. I knew that felt good. Then I simultaneously cupped his balls, squeezing and rolling them around.

"Golly! Gee! Oh-oh-oh-o-o!" he moaned softly as he shot directly into my moist, clutching throat.

I swallowed all he had to give me as I continued to suck lightly up and down on his big tool. Then I pulled off and looked directly at him. "Like that?" I asked.

"Sure did! Hey, you really do know how to play on a skinflute, don't you?"

"Yeah," I said, "but I can always use more practice."

I was looking forward to a very interesting sophomore year.

# VII. THE KAREZZA STUDY METHOD

Jared and I had had so much fun in the back of the bus that we decided to continue our sexual explorations while studying in the library. We would sit closely together while we caressed and excited one another's cock. This definitely encouraged our study habits.

But it was awkward, shoving a hand down under the elastic belt of the shorts. So, after a while, we made this mutual stimulation easier by cutting off the pockets of our shorts. Then we could slip our hands into the other guy's crotch and feel him up a lot more easily. I could slide my left hand in and run it up and down Jared's naked cock and balls, stroking and cuddling them, while he did the same with his right hand to my own blood-engorged organs.

We had to be very careful, of course, and fondle each other's stiff hard-on and tight balls very lightly, in order not to reveal by our grunts and groans what we were doing. Even so, every once in a while, I would let out a muffled gasp and so would Jared.

When the library staff seemed to be getting suspicious about what our hands were doing so frequently under the table, we looked around and found a study carrel that was in an isolated spot. Now, we could more easily tell if anyone was approaching.

You might not believe it, but we did actually manage to get some studying done, even if our major concern was to keep one another in a constant state of sexual arousal.

We used just enough teasing and tickling and fondling to maintain our thobbing hard-ons, but not enough to make us shoot. Besides, if we shot off, our cum would get all over our shorts and the carrel where we were studying. It would also be a dead giveaway of our surreptitious practice of friendly male sex.

I later found in a sociological study of an ideal utopian community, that they practiced something similar to what we were doing, that they called "karezza."

This was a sexual practice that controlled the number of pregnancies in the community. Older women would teach the young boys how to reach a state of sexual arousal just below the involuntary need to ejaculate. When trained in this way, hours of sexual pleasure could be continued without a final orgasm. Then, it was only with the consent of the whole community, that a male would be allowed to impregnate a female.

It occurred to me that this could also be done by older men teaching the boys this "karezza" technique of keeping a hard-on, while continuing and intensifying their sexual pleasure. In this case, it would be done for the natural pleasure resulting from the practice and not to avoid a pregnancy. Of course what the men and boys had learned together, could be applied later, if they then fucked a woman.

I might be imagining this practice of "karezza," by the men and boys, because it hasn't been reported in the literature. But it gives me a hard-on just thinking about a whole community doing what Jared and I had found to be so enjoyable.

The men and boys could learn how to skillfully fuck their partners up the ass, in order to maintain the maximum sexual pleasure without an orgasm, and in this way, continue fucking one another for hours.

The boy could learn to get his cock sucked or stroked by the men for as long as he liked, learning how to poise himself right on the edge of an orgasm, and then reducing the level of stimulation, over and over again. After the boy had found a way of preventing an orgasm by reducing his excitement, he could then let himself get worked up again to new and even more exciting sexual sensations.

The men and boys could even teach one another how to masturbate in this way. Stretching out the pleasure by arousing their genitals almost to a sexual peak and then shifting this pleasure to another part of the body, by moving their attentions to the mouth, the nipples, or the anus.

That's what Jared and I were doing, while we were slowly pleasuring one another in the library.

But sooner or later, Jared or I would groan, "I've got to get off. I don't think I can hold back any longer! Let's go out in the park – there was one nearby – and finish this."

So we would pack up our books, concealing our bursting crotches with them, and go to the park.

There we had enough privacy so we could lie down together, hugging and kissing passionately. Then we would slowly take off each other's shirt and shorts, while running our hands all over each other's warm, naked skin.

But we still wanted to continue to hover at the edge of the final bliss, taking our time and savoring our slowly mounting excitement.

If I was getting close, I'd tell Jared, "That's enough pulling on my cock. Now squeeze my nipples! Pull on them, harder!"

This would take my attention away from my cock and keep it from squirting.

Or one of us would say, "Oh yeah! Kiss me!" And we would tongue fuck each other, sucking tongues while we mashed our swollen lips together.

Then, "Okay. You can play with my cock some more." Then it was slowly, teasingly, skinning the foreskin back. Shifting to the balls and tickling beneath them. Back and forth. Right up to the edge again.

"That's enough! Feel up my ass now. Um-m-m-m! Stick your finger up it! O-o-o-o!"

And while we were doing all this, at the same time we were gradually getting naked. When we were nearly naked, we would let ourselves go. Each time was different.

I could be sitting on his chest with my cock in his mouth with him voraciously slavering over it with lots of grunts, "Ohhh! Guh! Guh! U-m-m-m!"

"Suck my cock, harder!" I would yell while I reached back and squeezed his balls and pulled rapidly on his tool "Uh! Uh!"

Or I could be on my knees while he rammed his cock in and out of my ass, "Oh-h-h yeah! Fuck m-e-e-e! F-u-c-k!"

Then he would be pulling at the same time on my swollen red cock. That would make me grunt, "Uhhh!"

Or, we could be side by side, sucking vigorously on each other's cock, "Um-m-m-m! Uh-h-h!" while ramming two or three fingers up the other guy's ass. "Oh-h-h! Deeper! Wiggle your fingers around! Y-e-a-h!"

We always shot buckets of cum over or into each other. Cum up an ass, down a throat or spraying all over our bodies.

Yelling, "I'm comin'! Y-e-a-h!"

Or, "Here it goes! Take it!"

Then we'd lie there relaxing for a while before we put our clothes back on.

"Pretty good, huh?" I'd ask.

"Oh yeah!" Jared would reply. "Isn't this a great way to study?"

- - -

It certainly was. Maybe someday I'll set up a special course in advanced study techniques, and call it "The Karezza Study Method."

I could advertise this method by claiming that it had a new and more powerful way of motivating students, and that these methods were superior to both the carrot and the stick.

Then when the guy asked, "What's that?"

I could just reach down and show him.

"Oooooooooooooooh," he would moan. "I see what you mean!"

## VIII. SWEET SUBMISSIVE MEAT

I ran into Cy in the dining hall. "How's it going, Hal?"

"So-so."

"Would you like to take on another little project as a sex therapist?"

I fondled my crotch. This was a habit I had acquired while hustling. "Could be."

"I've had one really cute freshman who doesn't know how much he wants to suck a stiff cock or get it shoved up his ass. The recorder practically went off the graph when I showed him pictures of guys sucking and fucking."

"So? That's really what you're looking for, isn't it, with all your 'scientific' investigations of young college student sex fantasies?"

"Yes," Cy said. "But the funny thing about Luke, was that he denied having any homosexual interests at all. He just got all sweetly shy and embarrassed about it and claimed that he 'was just like everyone else.' But he had no signs of arousal on any of the heterosexual pictures. Just on guys masturbating and having sex with each other."

"So how did you handle that?"

Cy grinned. "I told him about a good-looking young guy named Hal, who was studying to be a sex therapist. and might be able to give him just what he needs."

"And his response?" I asked.

"He brightened up when I said, 'a good-looking young guy.' And so then I made an appointment."

"Oh? And without consulting me. For when and where?"

"Tomorrow, in my apartment. For ten in the morning. You don't have any classes then."

"Well, what the hell. Might be interesting."

Cy smiled, "I think you'll find Luke very interesting."

- - -

"My name is Hal, and I'm here to help you understand your sexuality better," I told him. "Now, take off your clothes, Luke, while I watch."

Luke looked up; his eyes were pleading with me for something. Something he wasn't ready to admit. Then he hung his head and blushed as he bashfully began to unbutton his shirt.

I helped him unbutton it. I reached in under his shirt and slid my hand back and forth over his firm little nipples, and flicked them lightly.

He gasped, "Oh!" I knew it felt good, because plenty of guys had done it to me. Luke's nipples were just as sensitive as mine. I pinched them. He squirmed with pleasure. So now I knew one way to make him horny.

"Come on, you know you want it," I said, "You not only want it, you need it. Hurry up and strip down."

He pulled back. "I'm not sure we should do this...."

I reached down and felt his cock bulging down his pants leg. I stroked it up and down, and could feel it harden even more. He definitely wanted it.

"Take your shirt off," I growled.

This was what he needed. He looked up at me with admiration in his eyes. I sensed his submission.

He pulled his shirt up over his shoulders, and my cock swelled as I watched him strip it off. I was fascinated by his smooth, heaving chest and firm nipples.

He saw me looking at his nipples hungrily and his eyes widened. He was embarrassed, but I knew that in back of Luke's red-faced squirming were his suppressed sexual fantasies – and his need for throbbing cocks in his mouth and up his ass.

I wanted to hear him blurt out how much he wanted me to do some kinky things to him. Wild voluptuous things that would make him wriggle lasciviously and forget all that Sunday School talk his head had been filled with. Stuff that his crotch didn't know anything about.

His cock and his balls had their own sensuous needs, and I was going to get him acquainted with them.

He held his head down as he unbuckled the belt of his pants. "You want to see me naked?" he asked in a low, shy voice.

I knew he wasn't ready to tell me what he really wanted, but it would come out sooner or later. If I had my way it would come out soon. Very soon. Right now, it was like he was doing me a favor, giving me just what I wanted. He was going to find out, though, that there was something he wanted, and wanted very much.

"Yeah...." My voice was husky and my face was getting red. And not just my face. I was getting hot all over! "Yeah!" I repeated with a sexy voice, "I want to see you bare-assed, so drop your pants."

He was so bashful it made him slow and I was getting hotter by the minute. I reached over and fumbled with his fly, helping him zip it down. Our hands touched and I saw him look at me with an awkward smile.

As I pulled the flaps away from his crotch I could see that his little pecker was beginning to harden beneath his Jockey shorts and I brushed my hand over the neat swelling mound that it made.

He took a deep breath and flinched a little, so I put one arm around his shoulders and hugged him while I ran my other hand down inside his briefs and cuddled his cock and balls, wriggling my hand around and getting him worked up so that his cock swelled and stiffened. He twisted his crotch convulsively against my hand and put his arm around me.

A look of anxiety came over his blushing face. "Ohh, gee, I don't know...."

I didn't wait for the rest. He was having second thoughts, but I would take care of those.

I quickly stripped his briefs down and they dropped at his feet. I pulled on his cock with one hand, while I squeezed and cuddled his balls with the other.

I could tell just by looking at him how much he liked it. He liked it more than he wanted anybody ever to know. That was okay, I could keep a secret.

I ran my hands all over him, and finally cupped and squeezed his firm round buttocks. Beautiful!

I gave him a big smile. "You have a beautiful ass."

"I do?"

"Uh-huh," I fondled his asscheeks. "Nice ... a nice, smooth, very warm ass."

I slapped his ass. "Okay, now turn around and walk up and down a few times."

I wanted to see his naked ass move. I'd admired it when he had his tight pants on, but now I could see him bare-assed, and blushing at his nakedness. God! He was beautiful.

"I like watching your ass move."

"You want me to wiggle it?" He was getting bolder, but his attention was still on what I wanted.

"Just walk the way you usually do." He walked away from me, and it was a beautiful sight. "I like the way your buttocks move as you walk. And I can see how much they need some special attention."

I said, "Good! Now come here." He walked back with his cock sticking up, ready to do business. I put my hands on his shoulders. "Kiss me while you play with my cock."

I wrapped one arm around him and pressed my lips to his while moving his hand down onto my cock.

I told him between kisses on his full warm lips, "Go ahead...." I pressed my lips passionately against his smooth full lips. "Feel it!"

My hands were all over him.

"Play with it."

His hands fumbled in my crotch.

"Mmake it big and hard!"

"Gee, it's big!" he blurted as he closed his fingers around it timidly. His eyes widened as he looked down at it. I could tell he really liked the feel of my warm thick cock in his hand!

"Oh, yeah, that's it!" I said. I loved what he was doing to me! "Feel it ... make it big ... so when I stick it up your ass, you'll really squirm." I clutched his buttocks tightly and spread them, "You like doing this, don't you?"

He stroked my cock slowly up and down. "Yeah," he said wonderingly, "Yeah, I guess I really do."

"You're going to like my cock up your ass even more."

His hands were so tender and warm, I couldn't help myself and my hips ground back and forth convulsively against his hands.

"Ahhh, that's so good ... you have nice hands. Just peel it back ... s-l-o-w-l-y."

He did it; he pulled my foreskin back very slowly, just the way I liked it.

"Ohhh! Nice!" I moaned. "Feel it all over."

I kissed him as he felt up my cock, and ran my fingers tenderly over his smooth firm ass.

"Run your hands all over me, while I kiss you and make your behind feel good."

I pulled his ass butts apart, and tickled his asshole. Then I wet my finger and worked it around his tight sphincter as he groaned and pressed against me.

"Ohhh," he moaned. "I like that."

I knew he wanted me to stick it in, but I just kept playing around his asshole. I wanted him to say what he really wanted.

Then he did, "I like your finger playing with my asshole. Stick it in! Please!"

I worked it gently into his rectum. He pressed his ass back.

"Deeper, ohhh!...Stick it in deeper!"

I wiggled my finger around and he kissed me again, and pushed his tongue into my mouth. I stirred my finger around in his twitching asshole.

He pressed his cheek against mine and whispered in my ear, "I need your big cock up my ass." Now he was beginning to admit what he really wanted. "You do?"

"Yeah!" He was pressing his cock against me, hard. His hands were all over me.

"I need your cock up my ass." He pulled on my cock. "Feel good?" he asked.

"Yeah!"

Luke cupped and caressed my balls, then ran his hand up over them and slowly up the length of my throbbing cock. "It will feel even better when you stick it up my ass, he said. "Way up ..." He squeezed my cock and moaned. "Way up ... ohhh ... way up my tight ass!"

"You really want it?"

"Yeah!" He blurted. "I really, really want it. I really want it ... I never wanted anything as much!"

"Oh, kiss me, Luke!" He wriggled against me and we kissed and kissed. "I want it too."

"Will you fuck me now?" I could feel his warm breath in my ear. "Please! I want it. Will you fuck me?"

"Okay, okay. Lie back on the edge of the bed and spread your legs. Yeah, wider ... oh, yeah that's it."

"What are you going to do to me?"

"I'm going to do what you've wanted someone to do for a long time. C'mon, Luke, tell me what you want ... straight out."

"I want..." This wasn't easy for him, but he tried. "I want...."

"Yeah?" I asked and worked my tongue into his mouth.

He wrapped his lips around my tongue and sucked on it, then pulled back and looked directly into my eyes. He said very slowly and seriously, "I want to suck your cock!"

"Really? You do?"

"Yes. I want to suck it and suck it and kiss it all over and get it all wet and slippery, and then...."

This I wanted to hear. "Uh-huh, and then...." I breathed into his ear.

He squirmed against me. He was panting. "And then I want you to stick your cock in me. I want you to stick it all the way up inside me, way in deep. It's like I need to feel your cock way up inside me."

He pressed his naked body against mine, rubbing his genitals against my thigh.

Luke rolled onto his back. "I need to be fucked! I really do!" He wrapped his legs around me and rubbed his beautiful ass frantically against the bed. "I really want you to fuck me!" He was panting wildly. "Fuck me!" His body was writhing against me. "Please!" he yelled. "Fuck me!"

"Okay. But first you're gonna suck my cock and get it all hard and slippery, so it will slide right up your sweet young ass and not hurt a bit."

I climbed up over his chest, straddling it. I put a pillow under his head to lift it up. I rubbed my cock over his face, pulled back my foreskin, and then teasingly rubbed my red swollen glans back and forth across his lips.

"Gee, I don't know...!" he mumbled.

"Oh, sure you do!" He had opened his mouth enough so I could press my cock between his sweet full lips.

"Uhhh!" he groaned

.

I pushed my cock in. "C'mon, open up and suck it!"

It didn't really surprise me when he finally yielded to his inner hunger, wrapped his lips around my cock, and sucked it all the way in with a sigh of contentment. I watched his beautiful lips sucking eagerly, like a baby at his mother's breast. Just as Cy had told me, here was another natural-born cocksucker.

He did pretty well for someone whose mouth was a virgin to cocks, and it wasn't long before he had my cock well covered with spit.

I pulled out. "Okay, now you're getting what you've wanted for a long time. A cock up your ass! Spread your legs out, and pull them up to your chest. I want your asshole spread wide open for me."

Luke did what I asked, and I spread his hole even more with my spit-covered thumbs, working them around to make his hole even hotter for my cock.

Then I shoved my spit-slicked cock all the way up into him in one smooth motion. His face was crimson and his eyes wide as I went into him.

"Oooooooo, uh!" he moaned, yielding his body completely to me and surrendering his sweet ass to all those voluptuous sensations my thrusting cock was giving to his convulsing creamy rectum.

I leaned over him, kissing him full on the mouth, as I fucked him slowly and smoothly in his ass. I thrust my tongue into his mouth, fucking him now on both ends. He sucked on my tongue, as he thrust his beautiful butt back eagerly over my cock. It felt like his tightly clutching anal sphincter was sucking my cock up into the sweet undulating massage of his rectum, pulling it in deeper. Even Luke's ass was a natural born cocksucker!

I rammed into him hard and deep and gave him a really great fuck. I could feel his throbbing prick shoot cum all over my belly as he gasped, "Oh! Oh! O-h-h-h!"

I shoved my tongue deep into his mouth, "Um! Umm! Uuh!" as I shot a fairly substantial load of cum up into his rectum.

I pulled out and gave him an appreciative kiss. "Ummmm! Okay?"

"Ohhh yeah!" Luke's eyes were wide with submissive admiration, and he cuddled up closer to me. "I've been needing that for a long time."

Luke pressed his warm body, yielding and soft, up against me. "And you gave it to me ... God, did you ever!" He squirmed, then added, "You can do anything to me. Anytime!"

"Like right now?" I asked.

"Y-e-a-h!"

And that was when I relished for the first time, the first of many times, the total and voluptuous surrender to me of Luke's magnificent body.

- - -

The next day, I went over to Cy's lab. "You were right," I said. "Luke is another natural born cocksucker. He was really suppressing his need to suck a cock, and then take it up his ass. He could actually suck my cock with his ass."

"Glad to hear it," Cy said. "I think he might be ready for another session in the lab."

"What are you planning?"

Cy blushed and looked away. "More on what turns him on."

I could tell that Cy wasn't telling me all of his plans.

I looked at the table with the stirrups on it. I could imagine Luke stretched out naked on it, with his feet in the stirrups and his legs spread open wide, offering up his cute cock and balls and his rosebud asshole, ready and willing and eager for anything Cy wanted to do to him.

Just thinking about Luke spread out like that, all creamy, naked and vulnerable, made me hot. Maybe I could get Cy to let me give Luke a special sex session.

I could also picture Cy spread out on the table, totally naked, with a big hard-on, smiling and writhing in ecstasy as he thrust into Luke's tender warm mouth and watched him eagerly suck on his cock.

And then Cy getting Luke stretched out on the table, with his head down between Luke's widely spread legs, lapping and sucking on his delicious balls, and finally taking his little pecker into his slavering mouth, while he stuck a finger up Luke's tight rosebud.

Cy asking, "Want my cock up your ass?"

And Luke squirming and thrusting his ass up. Groaning, "Ooooooh y-e-a-h!" as Cy pulled the lips of his asshole open and tickled and probed it with the tip of his cock and felt Luke's eager hole squirming tightly around the head of his cock and trying to suck it deeper into his bowels.

Cy ramming all the way in as he leaned over and kissed Luke, clenching and hunching his creamy muscled buttocks as he shot up Luke's ass and moaned, "Ohh! Ahhhhh! Uh! Uh! Uh!"

While Luke voluptuously surrendered his body up to him completely, shooting off and yelling, "Ooooooooo! Uh! Ooooooooo!"

My cock was almost ready to shoot off in my pants just thinking about it! But I didn't want to enter my next class with cum spattered all over my crotch, so I left hurriedly.

I didn't think Cy was going to need any scientific assistance with this particular freshman. I could tell Cy was planning something new, perhaps an experiment with all-natural sex, now that he had someone as sweet and submissive as Luke for a subject.

Why did I think that?

It was the look I saw in Cy's eyes as I left, his lascivious smile, and the swelling in his bulging crotch that he was rubbing so salaciously against the table.

Yeah, Cy was another natural-born cocksucker and buttfucker, just like Luke and me.

# SPECIAL PREVIEW

*We present a special excerpt from John Patrick's new novella, Brother Love, which will be teamed with its sequel, Beyond Imagining, in the forthcoming anthology, Taboo!*

That fateful summer in Paris, Tony was reunited with his older brother Tommy, who was living with their father in Paris while Tony lived with his mom in the U.S. Tony found that his brother started to take notice of Tony's cock: "You're gettin' as big as me, you fairy."

"Nobody's as big as you," Tony said.

"Like it, eh?"

"I don't know. I've never had another one."

"But you've seen plenty, like at school, right? And dreamed about 'em?"

"No. I've never seen anybody else hard." Tony ignored the question about his dreams. He didn't want to admit that he only dreamt of his brother. He spent hours and hours playing with himself, remembering, and dreaming of the next time. This trip, Tommy had developed an interest in Tony's ass as well as his cock.

"How does that feel?" Tommy asked, moving his finger into Tony's virgin ass.

"Okay." Tony was embarrassed that he had a hard-on despite the pain. Or maybe it was because of it, he didn't know.

They lay together, Tommy's crotch in Tony's face, his finger working Tony's ass, for a long time before Tommy decided he wanted to get off again. He came quickly the first time, and then he was ready to play for a while. It wasn't always like that, of course. In the very beginning Tommy would just have Tony suck it and then he would hurry away, leaving Tony wondering what he had done wrong. Tony knew he had learned the techniques well; Tommy had taught him. "Teeth," Tommy would cry, "watch the teeth." Tommy would hold Tony's head, guide him. A couple of times, he came so quickly Tony swallowed some of his load. Although Tony thought it was wonderful, Tommy apologized, said he would never do it again, but after awhile he knew Tony liked it and let him have it all the time.

For a long time, their sex was always the same: A quick blowjob, with Tommy mounting Tony and slipping his erection in

247

Tony's eager mouth. Tommy propped himself up over Tony and fucked his face. But he could only do this for short while. Tony knew he would want to watch it going in and out of my mouth, so he pushed Tony against the headboard. After Tommy came, Tony began to lick it, kiss his balls, and made a fool of himself over Tommy's beautiful cock before Tommy was hard and ready to come again.

And then Tony could come himself – and begin dreaming of the next time.

After three weeks of bliss, during which Tony literally lost count of the number of blowjobs he gave his brother, Tony had to return to the States. "Au revoir" was a nice word, and he said it to Tommy.

"Let it be soon," Tommy said, taking Tony's head in his hands and guiding it to his crotch.

Later, after Tony had taken Tommy's load again, Tony began to weep.

Tommy comforted him. "Don't cry, little brother. Hell, we'll always have Paris." Tommy, Tony found, had picked up their mother's way with a classic movie line, although he insisted she had stolen it from him. Tommy, Tony had become aware, had his own strange way of seeing things, and Tommy's way had little to do with the truth.

...It was night in Singapore, a little more than one degree north of the equator. It was hot and damp, and the night was filled with smells: curried turn-overs frying in the open-air food stalls; jasmine; sandalwood smoke curling through a hedge. A Malay in a white shirt walked by, smoking a clove cigarette. The moon was full, and I was desperately horny.

In Chinatown, the buildings were pastel green, lit with dim fluorescent strips, giving everything the same sort of cool green glow. The tables were piled with spiny green fruit, durian, the size of pumpkins or fresh coconuts. The fruit gave off a sweet and frightening stench. It grew there on the Malay Peninsula and all over South East Asia. Chinese and Malay men pick over the green fruits, lifted them to their ears and shook them to listen to something, God only knows what. They wore leather gloves to protect them from the spines.

"Only men shop for durian," said Max. "They think it's too important to let women do it."

"Why do they shake them?" Tony asked.

"Listening for air pockets; when you can hear the seeds shake, they're ripe." At the end of the rows of durian was a single table with a fruit Tony had never seen before, like eggplant, but apple-sized, brownish-purple. "Mangosteen," Max said. "I won't tell you what it tastes like, except that it's amazing. You're supposed to follow durian with it, it clears your mouth, your brain."

They bought a small durian and a dozen mangosteen to go with it, putting them in a backpack which Max had lined with folded newspaper.

In Max's grand suite at the Hilton, where he said he always stayed, Tony started to tell him about the last time he had eaten durian, with Tommy in Paris.

"Sounds very romantic," Max said.

Tony shuddered. Tony was relaxed with Max; Max was, Tony thought, somehow, a kindred spirit. He reminded Tony of another one of his father's pals from his Hollywood days, Clifton Webb. Yet Max was younger, less prissy. Tony really liked Max. Tony loved listening to his stories of his days in Hollywood. Max was a long-time aide to Tony's father, Zachary, head of Monarch Studios. Among his duties for the elder Taylor was looking after the mogul's sons. This summer, Max had taken on responsibility for Tony while the lad was on his holiday

Now that the subject of Tommy had come up, Tony decided it was time to shock Max, if that were possible. "And one night we were alone," Tony told him, "and we ate the fruit together. To get the smell of the fruit off, we showered, then things turned crazy. We got this crazy desire for each other. We were mad at everybody for keeping us apart for so long, so we decided to make up for it. At least that's how I look at it. God knows what Tommy thinks."

"Oh, dear," Max said, appearing flustered. He changed the subject and began talking about Zachary again. Max called Tony's father "the last mogul," as in "movie mogul," and he expressed deep regret that his father was, it seemed to him, no longer actually making movies, just making deals.

Earlier in the week, Zachary finished making his deals and went off to meet Genevieve somewhere. He left Tony in Max's care. Tony told Max the last time a son of Zachary Taylor was left in someone else's care, he ended up in a brothel. Max laughed out loud at that, saying he already knew that. Zachary told him the story a hundred times. "Your brother, I hear, got a girl pregnant."

"Yes. I know that for a fact."

"Quite a cocksman," he said.

"Yes, he is. That's what happens when you get taken to a brothel."

Max promised he would not take Tony to a brothel. But he did say that here in Singapore it was school vacation, and, with a wink, said that this was the best time for someone looking for a bit of action. But Tony knew the kind of action he was thinking of wouldn't involve going out and looking for it.

They finished the durian and, with a sharp knife, Max cut around each mangosteen and lifted the cap off, revealing the pale translucent segments inside. He showed Tony how to spoon them out, and the taste was of strawberry, peach, pineapple. Tony was glad they bought so many, because Tony couldn't get enough of this taste. He licked the inside of the rind. It was tart, and perhaps that's why it was useful after the custardy richness of durian. Watching Tony's greedy progress through the mangosteen, Max asked, "How long did it last with your brother? How did it end?"

"It has never ended."

"What?"

A half an hour later, Tony thought the moment that he'd hoped would come was at hand. Max told him he had to go back to his own room, that he was tired, but Tony sensed he was afraid, afraid of what might happen between them if Tony stayed. After all, talking about Tommy had given Tony a hard-on and Max saw it.

Tony obeyed Max, and went to the bathroom and took a long shower and went to bed. But he couldn't sleep; he was like a little kid on Christmas morning. Bundled in his new bathrobe, he went to Max's room. Max yawned and told him to go back to bed but Tony just kept banging on the door. Finally he let Tony in.

"I can't sleep," Tony whined.

"I'll fix you a little something," Max said.

Tony made himself comfortable on the bed while Max puttered in the kitchen. He came into the bedroom with a steamy brew. "Here, this will help you relax."

Tony sipped the tea. It was bitter and Tony asked what the hell it was. That started Max talking about teas, and Tony set the cup down and sprawled out on the pillows.

Max reclined on the bed in his robe. That he was well-endowed was clearly evident through the folds of his robe. Tony was as excited now as he had been earlier. Max extended a long, elegant hand as he talked on about teas and, for a moment, the absurd notion flitted through Tony's mind that Max might expect him to suck him the way he did Tommy. That might come, but what Tony wanted was to have someone do to him what he had done to Tommy. Tony held his eyes with his own and studied him with an intensity that caused Max to blush. Then, as Max covered himself to hide his excitement, he began looking Tony up and down. Apparently satisfied with what he saw, Max nodded his approval, dryly declaring Tony "a beauty."

Tony began to move smoothly, casually, allowing his robe to fall away. The fabric slid down either side in two draping folds, revealing that Tony too had become aroused. This salacious view of Tony's youthful groin Tony could see caused Max considerable discomfort. Max tried to keep his eye on Tony's face as he chatted away but Max found them inevitably drawn back to Tony's erection.

Tony listened attentively, his eyes studying Max's face. Max stammered, coughed to hide his embarrassment, and he ducked down to quickly take a sip of the tea he had made for himself.

"So, did the tea relax you?" he asked.

"Do I look like I'm relaxed?" Tony asked, lifting himself up so that his cock was just inches from his leg.

"Goodness, that's a lovely cock," Max said.

"You know what to do with it, don't you, Max, to make it relax?"

"Yes," Max smiled. "I know just what to do."

Tony's heart was beating faster with the excited prospect of Max's mouth about to go to work on his engorged cock. But Max would first tease him and build the desire within, until Tony could take no more playing. Max softly blew his warm breath up and down the length of Tony's throbbing shaft. First he circled, then he went up and down, then he moved from right to left. Tony could even feel Max's breath blowing through what little pubic hair he had. When Max had teased him enough with his breath he prolonged Tony's agony further by starting to lick his smooth skin, from near his knees to the tops of Tony's legs his wet, hot tongue slowly worked its way up, then down again. Max's tongue came closer and closer to the cock. He licked around the cock. Then, suddenly, Tony felt the tip of his tongue dart across his cockhead.

"Yes!" Tony cried out in relief when he finally felt his cock slip into Max's practiced mouth. Tony could feel the firmness of Max's hands as they held his inner thighs. Shivers of tingling pleasure shot through Tony's body as Max went to work on Tony's cock. Tony moaned, loving the way Max's tongue massaged the length of his cock, the way his hands stroked it. Tony's ever-seeping pre-cum saturated Max's eager, experienced mouth and throat. Tony could feel his lush, cock-worshiping mouth frantically devouring his erection like a hungry stray dog.

Tony yelled at Max like Tommy yelled at him sometimes, "Suck on that cock! Suck on that cock like it was the last cock you'll ever get! Suck on it! Suck on it! Suck! Oooohh!" Max found this very amusing. He pulled off the cock and smiled up at Tony. Tony kept on urging him on.

Max deep-throated Tony and Tony began grunting at Max on the edge of his climax. With another thrust, Tony realized that he was past the point of no return, and although he tried holding it back, it was no use. With one last hard thrust, Tony crammed his tender teenaged prick all the way down Max's eager throat, forcing his lips to hug around the cock at the base. His nose was nuzzled into Tony's little patch of crotch hair. Max stopped Tony's demanding thrusting and Tony held the back of his head to keep his throat wrapped around his cock, as if Tony was holding on for dear life, absolutely still. Tony felt his cock swell as it remained lodged deep in Max's throat. Soon Max was milking out a slow stream of Tony's sperm even before he began his full pumping orgasm." Ohh, ohh yeah, ohh – "

Max gripped Tony's thighs to steady him, and Tony moaned as his entire body began tingling and his temples were pounding. Suddenly Tony began to tremble uncontrollably. The whole room began spinning, his panting echoing through the room as his sex-swollen and sweaty balls exploded.

Max gagged at the force and volume.

"Oh, yeah, go ahead, swallow it all!" Tony pleaded.

Max's mouth frantically sucked on Tony's spunk-squirting cock.

Finally, Tony was through and he sighed and laid back as he licked Tony clean – cock, balls and even his asshole. Tony knew what he wanted there, but he pushed his head away. He was saving that for Tommy. Max noticed that there were still a few drops of the boy's cum that slowly dribbled from his now half-hard cock. Max leaned forward and lapped them up, then lay his head beside the spent cock. "God, Tony, I love your cock. It's the most beautiful cock I've seen in a long time." He took it gently in his mouth again. It was milked dry from his service, but he tried to arouse Tony again.

Tony pushed him off, to give it a chance to rest. Max propped himself up next to Tony and stroked his arm. Tony was finally silent after all the filthy talk and moans and groans, but he was still struggling to catch his breath. He had never had a more intense orgasm. Max looked up at Tony and said, with unusual softness, "I knew it would be wonderful."

"Why?"

"I knew you were experienced."

Tony didn't know how to react to this. He was hardly experienced, but he was pleased Max was pleased. Max continued to kiss it and fondle Tony's balls. "I'm sorry I'm not responding."

"But you are responding. You're giving me something very rare. You have quickly made me your friend, your co-conspirator. We now have our own little secrets."

Tony suddenly felt what a burden it must be for gay people to keep silent. Love wants to be mentioned, as though recognition of it makes it more real.

# THE CONTRIBUTORS

## *Antler*

The poet lives in Milwaukee when not traveling to perform his poems or wildernessing. His epic poem Factory was published by City Lights. His collection of poems Last Words was published by Ballantine. Winner of the Whitman Award from the Walt Whitman Society of Camden, New Jersey, and the Witter Bynner prize from the Academy and Institute of Arts & Letters in New York, his poetry has appeared in many periodicals (including Utne Reader, Whole Earth Review and American Poetry Review) and anthologies (including Gay Roots, Erotic by Nature, and Gay and Lesbian Poetry of Our Time).

## *Kevin Bantan*

The author now lives in Pennsylvania, where he is working on several new stories for STARbooks.

## *K.I. Bard*

The author's first story for STARbooks appeared in Juniors 2. Future stories are in the works. He lives and thrives in Minnesota.

## *H.A. Bender*

The author's first story for STARbooks appeared in Fresh 'N' Frisky. He is a major contributor to gay journals and has promised to give his stories featuring youths to us.

## *Jason Carpenter*

Texas-based Jason's last work for STARbooks appeared in Juniors 2.

## *Corbin Chezner*

The author is an experienced writer of erotica who lives in Tulsa, Oklahoma. His credentials include a master of arts degree with mass communications. His first story for STARbooks appeared in Sweet Temptations.

## Carl Miller Daniels

This new contributor of erotic poems lives in Virginia. Carl's first chapbook, Museum Quality Orgasm, is currently available from Future Tense Books, Portland, Oregon. His new chapbook, Shy Boys at Home, is available from Chiron Review.

## Peter Eros

The popular author's work also most recently appeared in Play Hard, Score Big and Sweet Temptations.

## Lewis Frederick

This is the author's first story for STARbooks. He lives in Kentucky. Future stories will appear in Taboo! And Huge 2.

## Frank Gardner

The author lives in Maine where he is working on many more hot stories for STARbooks.

## Rick Jackson

An all-time favorite writer of erotica, Rick recently saw another collection of his stories published by Prowler Press, London: Shipmates.

## Thomas C. Humphrey

The author, who resides in Florida, is working on his first novel, All the Difference, and has contributed stories to First Hand publications. A memoir appeared in the original Juniors.

## R. J. Masters

The author, who lives in Maine, is a frequent contributor to gay erotic magazines under various pseudonyms. His first novel, Foreign Power, an erotic tale of sexual awakening, a young man's introduction into the world of S/M, was published by Nocturnis Press.

## Thom Nickels

The famed Philadelphia-based columnist and writer had a much-talked book-length work, "Once A Hustler," in the best-selling Intimate Strangers. Thom has prepared a major work for the forthcoming Huge 2, and contributed a lengthy essay on famed gossip columnist Billy Masters for John Patrick's The Best of the Superstars 2000: The Year in Sex.

## Jack Ricardo

The author, who lives in Florida, is a novelist and frequent contributor to various gay magazines. His latest novel is Last Dance at Studio 54.

# ABOUT THE EDITOR

John Patrick was a prolific, prize-winning author of fiction and non-fiction. One of his short stories, "The Well," was honored by PEN American Center as one of the best of 1987. His novels and anthologies, as well as his non-fiction works, including Legends and The Best of the Superstars series, continue to gain him new fans every day. One of his most famous short stories appears in the Badboy collection Southern Comfort and another appears in the collection The Mammoth Book of Gay Short Stories.

A divorced father of two, the author was a longtime member of the American Booksellers Association, the Publishing Triangle, the Florida Publishers' Association, American Civil Liberties Union, and the Adult Video Association. He lived in Florida, where he passed away on October 31, 2001.

www.studio2000video.com
STUDIO 2000
The leader in Gay Erotic Entertainment
SEE WHAT YOU'VE BEEN MISSING
• Streaming Video
• Live Sex Shows
• Exclusive Models
www.studio2000video.com
Join today and Save $5
Use promo code
"starbooks"
You must enter your promo code for your savings